ROTAR
and
the
SILVER BOOK
of
KNOWLEDGE

May your dreams reach far into the Universe!

J. A. Bisson

I.A. BISSON

ROTAR
and
the
SILVER BOOK
of
KNOWLEDGE

TATE PUBLISHING
AND ENTERPRISES, LLC

Published by Tate Publishing & Enterprises, LLC
127 E. Trade Center Terrace | Mustang, Oklahoma 73064 USA
1.888.361.9473 | www.tatepublishing.com

Tate Publishing is committed to excellence in the publishing industry. The company reflects the philosophy established by the founders, based on Psalm 68:11,
"The Lord gave the word and great was the company of those who published it."

Book design copyright © 2014 by Tate Publishing, LLC. All rights reserved.
Cover design by Joseph Emnace
Interior design by Deborah Toling

Published in the United States of America

ISBN: 978-1-62902-448-6
1. Fiction / Science Fiction / Action & Adventure
2. Fiction / Mystery & Detective / General
14.02.12

ACKNOWLEDGEMENTS

An 'out of this world' special thanks to those invisible mentors with their telepathic voices who hounded me, flooding me with this story, never yielding or allowing me to let it go of its completion.

I dedicate this now to my family and friends who encouraged me along the way. Roy & Jane Aasen, Eric Aasen, Heidi Studt, Elaine Simpson, Elyse Kassis & Steve Sheppard.

And a sincere gratitude to my writing critique group, Karen Newcomb, Sally Rains, Anna Lee Braunstein and Caryne Anglin who persevered through this mysterious journey in the creation of Rotar and the Silver Book of Knowledge.

No pessimist ever discovered the secret of the stars, or sailed to an uncharted land, or opened a new heaven to the human spirit.

Helen Keller

PROLOGUE

Coppet, Near Geneva, Switzerland

Not since the blunder that sent him to planet Earth had Rotar made such a grave mistake. The *Silver Book of Knowledge* was missing and until its return he feared that the fierce Autumn storms would continue.

He shivered at a sudden blast of cold air that blew into the damp cave. He knew it was a warning, but he didn't quite know what to do about it. Before he could consider his options and calm his irritation, a swirling funnel the size of a mini tornado spun into the cavern churning up dirt and dust. A cat sprang from the debris and shrieked at him.

Irritation turned to alarm. "Where did you come from?" he asked the unexpected visitor.

An awkward silence. The cat squeezed together slanted eyes and swished its two tails.

Rotar broke the hush and said, "You remind me of a precocious Siamese cat I had many years ago except it was not so beautifully adorned. You must belong to someone very special."

He leaned over to pet the animal, inspecting its silver collar studded with amethyst stones. Brownish-lavender spots dotted its ivory fur. When he stroked its head, both tails fanned outward, each waving independent of the other. "You cannot be from this planet. Why are you here?"

"Mee-wee-cro-lif-ium," cried the cat in a high-pitched voice.

"Are you saying that you are a crolifium transmitter? Impossible!"

The cat rubbed against his boots in a figure eight pattern but said nothing more.

"Have you come to me for food? There are plenty of fish in the lake if you are in need of nourishment."

More silence.

He started to pick up the cat when his galactic radio crackled and bleeped in a repetitive high-alert signal. Rotar grunted at the metal box and slumped into a chair made from the same material. The chair melted into a gooey liquid and adjusted its contour around Rotar's chunky frame. The cat jumped into his lap as though it belonged there. The bleeping stopped.

"And now the world weather," a serious male voice announced in hollow sounds from the small box. "Storms continue to plague several global regions in what some are calling an apocalyptic sign from the heavens. More unseasonal weather warnings have been issued in the following locations: In the US tornadoes have destroyed countless homes in central Kansas, rescue teams hampered by treacherous winds. Abroad, a cyclone-level African mistral is ravaging the French Riviera. Hurricanes in the North Sea have necessitated cancellation of all ferry service between Denmark and Norway. Tourists in London were injured while riding the storm-stricken Millennium Wheel and all flights in and out of Paris have been delayed due to bad weather. In the Far East, Japan has just issued high-sea alerts to all vessels in the region. If you are planning to travel, check your local weather station for updates."

Rotar let out a grumpy snort and manually turned off the radio. Normally he used his magic wand for such tasks. Another irritation.

From outside, the loud roar of crashing waves against the Lake Geneva shoreline confirmed the storm's wrath. He picked up the cat and paced across the dirt floor, gazing down at the colorful rug that followed under his feet. Whenever he stopped and considered his dilemma, the rug also stopped and unwrinkled itself.

The cat wriggled and stretched its head toward the old leather-bound classics that filled Rotar's bookcase. Shifting the cat under one arm, he reached up to an empty slot where the missing book had once rested but felt no lingering trace of it. Tears pooled in his eyes.

He stood on tip-toe and stared into the mirror wedged between works by William Shakespeare and Edgar Allan Poe. The cat snarled into the reflective glass. Inside the mirror a purple door opened, the interior revealing a bright endless tunnel and a glittering purple rock. Rotar had never seen it before, and when he blinked, his own dull eyes stared back, the sparkle of light still missing. Had the planetary intelligence stored in him also been lost? He touched the silver starfish-shaped pendant hanging from his neck, rubbing the eye in its center. It felt cold. "Modified atoms, regressed souls, alien dimensions," he muttered, willing the information back, but it didn't work.

Emotions swelled inside him. He didn't like what he saw and turned away from the puffy face mirroring back at him. He wanted to be tall and slender like the humans he'd met, opposite of the dwarf-like form he had mutated into when he arrived on Earth. People thought he looked strange and treated him like an outcast.

He glanced at the surviving sections of his spacecraft stacked neatly against the cave's back wall and realized they were of little use to him without the information in the missing book. Allowing himself a small sigh, he padded over to his tree-stump table and put the cat down before warming his hands on the flame of a small candle. Its heavy lavender fragrance almost covered the putrid smell of mud and mildew. "At least my infinity candle continues to burn," he grumbled. "If I still had my powers I could intensify the candle's strength and heat up my cave."

A silent stare was all that the cat offered back.

"Where is my commander when I am in such dire need of help?" Rotar shouted at the angel ornament dangling from a tree root overhead. Without warning, an explosion of wind surged from nowhere and sent the left-over decoration flying straight toward him. He stumbled backward, hitting a small cabinet and knocking over a bowl of merry berries. The cat screamed in a deafening wail and leapt onto the bed shaped like a nose-cone of a rocket ship. Both of its tails waved in frantic rhythm.

The breeze circled the room and Rotar waited, unsure of what to do. The bookcase shook, a cup tipped over, papers flew upward and settled. His commander, Aeolius, controlled the wind and his anger could be devastating. Could it be that the commander was in the cave? The tunnel hummed louder until the noise faded away into the outdoors. Then nothing.

Rotar gathered his precious 'personality pills' scattered on the floor. They were all that remained of a large supply he'd brought from his planet.

"We have to go out and investigate," Rotar said, jamming his arms into an old leather jacket and grabbing the cat. While hurrying through the cold tunnel, wind whistled and water dripped from above. "If I can whip up some magic, I'll find you something to eat," he added.

The cat snuggled into Rotar's chest, wrapping its forearms around his chubby neck.

At entering the night air, a gust of frigid wind slapped Rotar in the face. He squinted and nodded his usual greeting to the jagged mountains across Lake Geneva. They rose like dark fortresses against the night sky, and a constant reminder of longevity. The massive peaks were forged long before the arrival of mankind and so Rotar believed they were his to claim, but he had never asked a human what they thought about that. Not since a local villager had called him a pudgy dwarf and a foreigner. Earth people were so primitive.

He skirted the large boulders and overgrowth shielding the cave and walked through a neighboring orchard toward the lake. Moonlight glimmered off the restless waves. Holding the cat firm, Rotar stepped on fallen apples, squishing them underfoot, but he ignored the sour odor of the rotten fruit.

"I am afraid that I am to blame for a most severe problem," he explained to the feline. "I fear that waiting four-hundred Earth years to locate the right scientist was not long enough. My former friend and partner betrayed me with his insatiable curiosity and now I must find a way to stop his research and retrieve my cosmic journal."

He shifted the cat under one arm and pulled out a knotted stick wedged in his belt, pointing it leftward of the Big Dipper. *"Ver-it-zi-gun-kum!"* he cried, using a command learned long ago from the ancient missing book.

Nothing happened.

"I am Rotar the Mighty," he shouted to the heavens. "I am here once again to confess my mistake. I beseech you, restore my powers!"

In a choked voice he added, "Grant me this wish so that I may find my book of knowledge for I am still its appointed guardian and wish to make amends…"

He waited. Moments seemed like eternity. Had they heard him? Did they care enough to return his powers?

The cat cried out in a symphony of high-pitched tones. The sing-song melody was totally foreign-sounding and unfamiliar to Rotar. Was this some sort of an undocumented space-cat language? One that had eluded him? His storehouse of languages encompassed hundreds of thousands.

And as though responding to the cat's concerto, a shooting star appeared and stopped mid-sky, aiming a faint beam of energy into Rotar's eyes. A flash of white light surrounded his gnarly stick with bright crystals. The eye in his starfish-pendant cast a slight glow. Elation filled him; his request had been answered. He pointed his stick and shouted, *"Trans-fer-ium Lak-u-mancia!"*

Both he and the cat were whisked to the water's edge a hundred yards from where they stood. A small bell on the tip of Rotar's hat tinkled. Overcome with excitement, he set the cat down and smiled up at the faint light twinkling between scudding clouds.

"I am exceedingly grateful. I vow to find my renegade partner and take back the silver book."

The distant star cast a light-beam, caressing his chest with a familiar surge of warm energy. He smiled as it faded from view.

Rotar looked around but the cat had disappeared. A crease of concern marked his face. "Where did you go? he asked. "We have something to celebrate."

A purple rock, smaller than a goose egg, lay in the grass. He picked it up and examined its fuzzy surface embedded with tiny glistening gems. It looked like the mysterious rock in the mirror.

Eyes tearing from the harsh wind he gazed skyward. "Did you leave this to help me?" But the star was no longer there.

The rock felt warm in his hand and began to vibrate. Its surface glowed and turned translucent, revealing a miniature image of the two-tailed cat. A cry of *"Ze-he-brak,"* came from within it.

Rotar's eyes enlarged; his hands shook. "What did you say?"

Silence.

"How did you get in there?"

Purple smoke swirled inside the rock and the cat disappeared.

A sound like exploding firecrackers drew Rotar's attention to a barn west of the orchard. Strange lights flashed and danced through its windows. The wooden structure had been converted into a research lab used by his former partner, Dr. Peter Tregnier, and Peter's retired associate, Dr. Vidollet. As far as he knew no one had worked inside for days.

He tightened his grip on the rock and aimed his stick at the barn. *"Trans-fer-ium Lab-or-un-cia,"* he commanded in an urgent voice.

He was at once transferred to the loft where he squatted out of view in what had become his secret hiding place. He scanned the great room for the missing book. Its cover gleaned like aluminum and was larger and thicker than a double box of jumbo cereal, yet it weighed less than a box of puffed rice. Disheartened, he saw no sign of it.

Below him Dr. Vidollet stood hunched over the worktable, his balding head revealing traces of wispy white hair. His work shirt looked like he'd slept in it. The doctor studied a stack of notes and inspected labels on a row of glass containers. The stench of rotten eggs filled the room from a percolating beaker filled with a green jello-like substance. The liquid formed a swirl of glittering crystals that bubbled over the sides. When drops hit the gas flames they popped and crackled.

Rotar drew back. Heavy steam from the liquid rose upward agitating a mobile that swirled and curled with several moons. Vidollet appeared unfazed by the noises. Was he experimenting with the secrets in the book?

Rotar gripped his stick in one hand and squeezed the rock with the other. He felt his body temperature rise from worry and was certain his chunky cheeks would soon match the color of his red hat.

Vidollet turned off the burner and shuffled to the kitchen cabinet, removing a bag of cookies. Under the desk a goose squawked and waddled out to greet him. He handed it a cookie. "A treat for my little Fanny," he said in a gloomy voice.

Rotar stood up and waved the purple rock. "Dr. Vidollet, it is me. I have brought you and Dr. Tregnier a gift from the stars."

Vidollet looked up with sad eyes. "You are too late. Peter is gone."

He caught the concern in his voice. "Gone where? I have come to retrieve the silver book…"

Vidollet shrugged and offered the goose another cookie.

"Do you know what Peter has done with it?"

With a stern expression the doctor said, "He does not consult me about anything. He carried out his experiment against my strenuous objections and left during the night without my knowledge. I tried to recreate his work but I cannot make out his notes."

Inside the rock, the cat snarled and glowed red-hot in Rotar's hand. It startled him and he dropped it.

The miniature two-tailed feline sprang out of its small container and ballooned to normal size. It instantly arched into attack mode and leapt down to the main floor, hissing at Dr. Vidollet.

The doctor backed away and waved his hand at it. "Shoo! Get that foreign thing away from me!"

Rotar watched, uncertain of what the cat would do. Why so aggressive? Was it angry about the missing book?

Fanny flapped her wings at the cat and honked.

The cat hunched its back, exposing sharp teeth. Purple smoke swirled around its body as it slithered toward the goose. *"Ze-he-brak!"* it shrieked at the frazzled-looking fowl.

Before Rotar could utter a command, Fanny spread her wings, nipped angrily at the cat and scrambled out the back door.

The cat chased after the goose. Dr. Vidollet chased after the cat.

Rotar zapped himself to the lower floor and followed after them in close pursuit.

CHAPTER ONE

Washington, DC

Amanda Tregnier could think of better things than being jolted from a much-needed nap, but awakened she was by a pounding noise of tree limbs lashing against the bedroom windows. The relentless storm that had plagued the Capitol for several days assaulted the two-story Brownstone, causing it to shudder and creak like an old ship. Tree limbs clawed and scraped the brick walls. Thunder clapped in the distance.

The annoying disturbance had also brought her out from a recurring nightmare. She sat up and sucked in her fear, spying the dark corners of her room. A dimming sky cast strange shadows across its pale-gray walls. She pulled the covers up around her neck, wary that the man chasing her in the dream was in the room. "Hello?" she managed to whisper, but all that answered back was the wailing sound of the wind, its noise drowning out her ridiculous call for him to show himself.

The same stranger always pursued her through the same alley. But this time he had come so close that she could feel his breath on the back of her neck and she had also picked up an odor of stale cigarettes. It had felt so real. Who was he? What did it mean? Why did she now detect a hint of smoke in the room? No one in her family smoked. Was her imagination on overload or was her brain hard-wired to some sort of premonition?

She thought of her husband's years of research, partly inspired by his dreams. But his sleep-time brought him knowledge and ideas whereas hers brought terror. Or at least more frequently than she'd like.

She'd often wondered if it was due to some unresolved issue in her life, but she'd never taken the time to explore it. The countless volumes of work accumulated by parapsychologists hadn't provided any suitable explanations for dreams, good, bad, or all mixed up. But neither had man found a cure for the common cold, and she'd been nursing a pesky bug for several days now.

Reminded that she hadn't heard from her husband in over a week, tension gripped the back of her neck like a twisting steel coil. She knew that Peter's work in science obsessed him, but she hadn't realized how much until the last few months.

She swept long dark hair to one side and checked her cell phone for messages.

Nothing.

Frustration escalated to anger as she considered what she would say to him when he called. She'd already let him know how fed up she was with his long work assignments abroad and the neglect of their two children. She worried that his prolonged absences would cause serious abandonment issues for them. The stress had made her sick, but he wasn't even aware of that.

The screeching sound of car brakes and the blast of a horn outside startled her. Through the window she saw a cat scamper across the street while a gray sedan drove away. The scene felt like an ominous forewarning. What if something had happened to Peter? At least both her children were safe indoors.

The phone rang.

About time—she knew it was him.

"Is that you Peter?" she blurted into the bedside phone as she fell backward onto the bed.

"Darling, you always know when it's me."

Darling? He never called her that and the voice echoing in her ear sounded garbled and croaky. In a huffy tone she said, "I can't explain why I know things ahead of time. You know that."

"Like I keep saying, that's my psychic wife. Sounds like you have a cold?"

"I'm just getting over it. Michelle brought it home from school. But your voice really sounds creepy. Is this a bad connection or are you sick too? I've been worried. We thought you'd be home days ago. When will you be here?"

"Soon sweetheart, soon."

More vague promises. "What does that mean exactly, when are you coming home?"

"Not sure. But I need you to do something for me. Listen carefully. You have to come to London right away and bring me my good luck piece."

She stiffened and rubbed the back of her neck. 'Good luck piece' was his code for the project he had worked on in the attic on his last trip home, but he hadn't shared the details. "Why? Have you discovered something?"

"You know my research is secret. Just come to the London lab. I'll meet you there."

She considered their finances. "Can we afford this?"

"Not an issue."

Her grip on the phone tightened and her mind raced. "But what about the kids?"

"Don't bring them," he blurted in a choking rasp. "Can't Hillary watch them for a few days?"

Her best friend traveled frequently as a journalist and had just returned from France after covering a story about a religious sect challenging the Catholic Church. "She's already taking time out of her busy schedule to go trick-or-treating with us. I really feel I'd be asking too much."

"Ask her anyway. If she knows you're meeting me…"

"Can't you come home and get it yourself? The kids are in the attic putting on their costumes and they miss you Peter. And you and I have a lot of things to discuss, starting with these long absences."

"You know I'd be there if I could but I'll be home soon. This is very important."

She'd heard that before. His wheezy breathing echoed in a loud gurgle that hurt her clogged ear. She stood up and switched the phone to the other side. "You sound like a bull frog at the bottom of a pit. Are you broadcasting from the ozone or something? Tell me what's going on!"

"Probably interference. You'll find my lucky piece with our honeymoon shells. The black one. But don't tell anyone, understand? Not even Hillary."

More infuriating drama. "What's there to tell? I live in total ignorance of your work."

"For God's sake Amanda, don't get spaced-out on me."

"You're the one who sounds like you're calling from outer space Peter! Can't I just send it Fed Ex?"

"Too risky."

"What risk?"

"Amanda, please just take some cold medicine and book a flight. My battery's almost dead. I'm counting on you."

"Wait…"

But he had already hung up.

She slammed down the phone, tired of the games, the secret projects, secret formulas, secret trips. Peter's voice sounded much worse than just satellite interference. And none of their shells were black so what was that reference about?

Thinking about the intricate shells they'd collected on the beach in St. Thomas reminded her of Peter's romantic honeymoon promises of their future together. Her mood dampened and loneliness crept into her heart. She slumped onto the bed and blew her nose, longing for some balmy tropical heat and a much needed vacation alone with her husband. She felt worn down from her cold and the howling storm outside exasperated her further.

She went into the bathroom and leaned into the mirror to pinch some color into her cheeks. Sorrowful eyes stared back.

What she needed was to heal and put her marriage back on track. The trip to London would at least provide a long over-due confrontation, one on one, face to face. The hope for an imminent resolution boosted her spirits.

Now she had to tell the kids. But how much of the mysterious conversation should she even share with them?

CHAPTER TWO

Outskirts of Geneva, Switzerland

Peter Tregnier sat on the cement floor hugging his spindly knees. The odor of rodent feces lingered in the damp warehouse and mice scurried across the room. A streetlamp in the alley outside shone dim light through the windows. He dropped his elongated head into boney hands and moaned. The sound reverberated off the walls. Why had he done this to himself?

While waiting for workers in the adjoining buildings to go home for the night his mind kept rerunning the events at the Coppet lab like a rat in a squirrel cage. Wild elation and jubilance. The discovery of a lifetime and the heady promise of fame and fortune. He had done something no one else had ever accomplished. The sheer wonder of beating the overwhelming odds.

Drunk on the ecstasy of the moment he had made a fatal error, dropping the usual routine of check and recheck, test and follow up. He had ignored the advice and warnings from his partner, Dr. Vidollet, and Rotar, his trusted mentor, and become his own guinea pig. He had taken a leap into the unknown. What happened next made him shudder.

Precisely at midnight, he tipped the vial into his mouth, anxious to step into his regressive adventure. The green sparkling mixture slid down his throat with an icy sting. Sudden pain, when pressure ballooned inside his body, hot and intense. He ran outside in panic. His thoughts accelerated, moving him through time at an unfathomable speed. His mind whirled through a white abyss until he entered a dark cylinder as if being squeezed through a pudding-like substance. Crystal lights flashed in the surrounding darkness. Another sharp pain spun him in frightening twists and turns until he collapsed and lost consciousness.

He woke up behind the shed next to his make-shift lab, a farm he'd inherited from his grandparents. According to his cell phone no time had passed, yet it seemed like he'd traveled a long time. A shimmering green glow surrounded an unfamiliar white garment that covered a longer and thinner body. The sight startled him and he gasped out of reflex, discovering his voice had also changed. It sounded like a croaking frog. An itch on his cheek caused him to scratch, accidentally breaking through delicate skin. Green blood oozed out over an elongated fingernail as miniscule sparks of light emanated from its tip. His thumb and little finger were gone, leaving him with three long extensions on his hand. That would be cumbersome. He also worried about what his face must have looked like but there was no reflective surface around to see.

Even though his lab was only a few yards away, he couldn't return there because Dr. Vidollet had threatened to report his research to the authorities. Instead he had wandered through the countryside searching for a hiding place. At the city outskirts he located a warehouse owned by his clandestine financial partner in Geneva. The facility stored a vast supply of pharmaceutical supplies for the company's operations.

When Peter perused the exterior he discovered he could see right through the walls to the building's interior like an x-ray machine. More revelations—his eyes could spew fire like a blow torch. He directed them at the locked door and burned off the deadbolt. The heightened blasts of sound in the surrounding area told him his hearing had also become more acute, another handy tool. And when his phone battery began to fade he re-charged it in seconds, using the electricity that emitted from the tip of his fingernail.

The discovery of these new special powers left him feeling overwhelmed. Not only had he mutated into something alien but he had also acquired powerful defensive capabilities. It wasn't what he'd set out to accomplish, but useful, nonetheless.

In spite of such powers, Peter anguished over his predicament. Rows and stacks of crates containing the drugs he'd used for his private experiment filled the room. The owner had offered him millions if and when it worked. Hah! He'd become proof that it worked, but now he couldn't come out of hiding to collect the payoff.

The initial lab work was done in a building in downtown Geneva that was staffed by foreigners. Even Dr. Vidollet, his closest confident, knew nothing about his association with them. Peter's research there had eventually led him to discover a regressive chemical he named 'phlenamium'. Peter had rejected Dr. Vidollet's warnings that regressing humans too far back was considered risky and unethical and so had used the secret location to test volunteers. The effectiveness of his drug had proven to be more powerful than hypnosis. Psychotic patients were taken back to traumatic incidents in what were thought to be previous lives. Their recollections and acceptance of painful, often horrific events had helped them to understand their irrational and addictive behavior.

The success of the project had excited Peter. For as long as he could remember he had always wanted to know where he came from. From recurring dreams of another planet, Peter believed he could develop a drug that would take him back to a former life. The dreams had always been the same: He floated, suspended in a milky sky of endless space. Seven moons surrounded a distant orb enclosed by a gigantic transparent dome. But whenever he tried to get a closer look, he always woke up. Now he was left with more questions than answers. Why was he still on Earth and not on another planet? Did it exist somewhere? Who was he in the dream? Could it be a past life?

The phlenamium drug was Peter's hope of exploring his past to a memory of life on the mystery planet. He had taken it back to his converted lab and enlisted Rotar's help. The new discovery was further enhanced by adding a variety of natural ingredients translated from the silver book. And then, without anyone's knowledge or consent, Peter tested the formula on himself. But instead of exploring past-life memory, he'd achieved an actual physical metamorphosis into an alien form.

Rotar's words haunted him: *All beings carry memory from their past lives, it is stored in your DNA.*

Those were the words that had convinced Peter to take his research to the next level, but as he continued his work, Rotar warned him of further possible consequences: *You are experimenting with the soul Peter, the core of your existence, you must be careful at every step.*

Now Peter was trapped in a freak's body, desperate and wondering who or what was at fault. Somehow he had to change back. He'd formulated an antidote that he hoped would neutralize his transformation, but it would only work if his calculations were correct. A big if…

Hunger gnawed at his belly—he hadn't eaten for a couple of days. The previous evening he had ventured out to a nearby farm in search of food but a farmer had discovered him hiding in the barn, forcing him to run away. The incident made him wary of being detected, so now he waited for the cover of darkness to go out again.

Afternoon crept into twilight and the room grew colder. Peter noticed that his breath was green. It drifted toward a black spider crawling across his three-toed foot. "I should have tested my formula on one of you first," he said in a throaty voice that echoed through the room. "My partner refused to let me experiment on one of his sheep, you see."

The spider scurried away.

"Oh my seven miserable moons he tried to stop me," Peter moaned aloud. He patted the bota bag at his waist that held what was left of the formula. Had he really discovered something monumental? Or had he sailed recklessly into uncharted space and ruined his life? He dared not believe the latter.

The loud backfire sound of a truck in the alley startled him. Through a broken window he saw workers going home. Dark clouds blanketed a dimming night sky. Soon he would be able to leave and return to his own lab a few miles away. He had to get something to eat and clothes that would hide his deformities.

A new worry entered his mind. What if Dr. Vidollet refused to let him in? There was nothing recognizable about him except what he knew of their work together. And even then the doctor might not want anything to do with him. He needed to show him where he'd hidden Rotar's book and convince him that he needed his help formulating an antidote.

Peter stood up and tested his mobility, floating across the room, bouncing and touching the floor. It would have been funny if he'd had a choice but gravity had little effect on his body. He stopped the exercise and settled on the bed he'd made from flattened cardboard boxes, wondering if Amanda would enjoy Halloween without him. If he hadn't rushed into this crazy experiment he could have gone trick-or-treating with his family. Even the children's arguments over sharing their candy wouldn't have bothered him. The thought of fresh popcorn soaked in melted butter and hot chocolate with gobs of whipped cream made him salivate. But longing for the comforts of home would do nothing to resolve his current dilemma. All he could do was exercise patience and wait for Amanda to deliver the good luck piece. He would arrange the next step with his foreign associate.

His breathing suddenly quickened and he sat up with a start. His heart began to race and small green lumps like warts covered his arms. Were they just goose bumps or something else? Was the cold damaging his body?

His stomach growled again. A piercing squeak of a mouse jolted him into alertness. The sound of dinner?

Even if he had the strength to catch it, did he have the guts to torch it with his eyes and eat the poor thing? He gagged at the thought and wished he could undo this whole mess. Tears began to leak from his lidless eyes. Where they green tears? He was too tired and distraught to find out.

CHAPTER THREE

Before Amanda could tell her children about the impending trip, she needed to freshen up. She splashed warm water on her face, but when she turned the antique faucet it nearly came off in her hand. Everything in her mother's old house seemed to be wearing out and Peter was never around to fix anything. Even her marriage seemed to be worn out. Agitated by her own frustration, she swallowed a large swig of cold medicine and blew her nose. She was ready to break the news to her kids.

A sudden sound of shattering glass raised goose bumps on the back of her neck. Her daughter shrieked from the attic. The dog started barking.

"Mom!" her son shouted.

Panicked, she rushed up the narrow stairs to the top floor. "What is it?" Amanda cried, bursting into the stuffy room. Instant relief when neither Michelle, nor Howard, looked injured or frightened.

Michelle stood on a wooden chair in her tutu, pointing at the floor. Sharp pieces of glass from a broken window surrounded a small purple rock. Howard shuffled forward in a knight costume, dragging his metal-braced leg. A series of operations for club foot had left him with a limp. He stabbed at the rock with his wooden sword. "Holy McBat wings, Mom," he said, using slang adopted from trips to McDonalds. "I thought it was a bat or somethin', but it's only a stupid rock."

She scowled at the damaged window and looked outside. "Who did this?"

"I don't know," Howard said. "Maybe a Halloween prank?"

"But why not break a larger window on the lower floors? It doesn't make sense."

"A lotta' pranks don't, Mom."

She picked up the rock, intrigued by the sparkles embedded in its fuzzy surface. It had a faint lavender scent. She shook it and let it fall into her other hand. It began to vibrate. She gasped and dropped it on the floor. It didn't move.

"What happened?" asked Howard.

"Nothing," she said, thinking fast while examining her hand. "I thought it cut me, but there's no blood."

Howard whacked the rock with his sword. "There, I killed it!" His coal-black eyes flashed with pride. She tried to sweep his dark bangs away from his sweaty forehead but he pushed her hand away. "I'm twelve, Mom. Don't baby me."

Embarrassed, she realized that he was too old for that kind of mothering. She also recognized some of her husband's more difficult characteristics in her son's face. He looked dogged, determined and assured. His gray tunic and navy leotard accented with a studded leather belt enhanced the effect.

"Leave it," she told him. "I want to check it out in better lighting." She scooped up the rock and pocketed it.

"I saw a kid outside a while ago," Howard said. "He coulda' done it."

At the window she looked across the street where daylight faded behind the trees swaying in the wind. Costumed children ran along the sidewalks with trick or treat bags, some clinging onto their hats. Brownstone houses, their porches and windows decorated with jack-o-lanterns, oversized spiders, witches, goblins and black cats flanked a small park. A gray sedan drove by at reduced speed. From its passenger seat a man in a dark jacket and tie stared up at her. Was that the car she'd seen earlier?

Alarm needled her already jittery nerves.

She knew from living in DC that most government cars were gray but why was someone looking up at her when the street was full of people? It felt like more than coincidence.

Something else caught her eye. From behind an oak tree across the street a pudgy boy stepped out in leather clothing and a pointed red hat. An elf costume. He might be the one Howard saw.

The boy stood under the street lamp and pointed a stick at her, then ducked behind the tree. First the government car, then the elf boy. Halloween was a night for elves and wizards, witches and warlocks, ghosts and vampires. All in fun, of course...or was it?

Howard said, "Good thing it didn't hit Dad's telescope. Boy would he be mad." He pointed his sword at Michelle. "You shoulda' been here Mom. It really scared ol' McSissypants." He laughed, teasing and jabbing his sword toward his sister.

Michelle raised her nose at him. "I wasn't scared." She took a ballet leap off the chair. It wobbled a little and Amanda caught her breath. But her tall-for-her-age, six-year-old landed beyond the glass shards and raised her arms, twirling like a graceful princess. Her taffy brown hair spun into a fan.

"Michelle please don't do things like that," Amanda said, letting out the breath she'd been holding. "You could have hurt yourself."

Amanda brushed sticky cobwebs off a small broom and then swept the glass to the wall. "Watch out for this, both of you...I'll cover the window later."

A walkie-talkie lying on the floor began to crackle. They all glanced at it. "Isn't that yours?" Amanda asked Howard.

He picked it up, pressed the button a few times and set it on the shelf. "Yeah, Dad has the other one. Maybe he's on his way home."

"Even if he was he'd still be out of range."

"But he took it to test the distance," Howard argued. "He said it had a really long range."

Amanda lifted a brow. "Not *that* long."

Howard knelt down to dress Pluto their Scottish terrier. Michelle joined in.

"Can he move in all that?" Amanda asked. The dog wore Michelle's pajama top patterned in moons and stars. The wiry tail wagged while Howard tied a hand towel printed with space ships around the wiggly neck.

Michelle beamed. "It's his flying cape."

"Cute," Amanda said, "but the flashing light on his tail and those sloppy tentacles on his head, won't that annoy him?"

Howard looked at her in irritation. "No Mom, he's a space dog."

Michelle put a red hat on her head. "Are we going now?"

"Where did you get that hat?" Amanda asked. It looked just like the boy's hat outside.

"Over there." Michelle pointed toward the workbench covered with stacks of papers and science publications and left-over pizza they'd eaten earlier. A hint of pepperoni and green peppers lingered in the room. She threw the hat at a trunk against the far wall.

A bell tinkled when it fell, hitting the wooden skis leaning against the wall. They tumbled over a pair of snow shoes and old tennis rackets before everything crashed to the floor. Michelle scrunched up her face and covered her ears.

Amanda's head ached and the noise pounded it.

Howard teased Pluto with his sword. The dog barked and barked.

"Stop that racket," Amanda wailed, her face contorted with pain. "I have a headache."

The children stopped, but Pluto kept barking.

Howard grabbed a slice of cold pizza and shoved it into the dog's mouth. Pluto gobbled it up and whined for more.

Amanda pinched the bridge of her nose. "This attic is full of ghosts and goblins and Halloween trickery. Let's go get our jackets. It's cold out there."

"But what if Daddy's on his way home?" moaned Michelle. "Or calls us?"

Amanda's heart sank. "He just called and can't get home just yet. He's working on something important and wants me to meet him in London."

Howard released Pluto, his tail flashing on and off as the wiry dog disappeared down the stairs. Howard stood up and sheathed his sword. "I'll go with you Mom and protect you."

She wrapped her arms around him. "Thank you. That would be wonderful. But what if Aunt Hillary stays with the two of you instead?"

Howard's dark eyebrows gathered together. "McBoring."

"That's not nice," Amanda said.

"She's not our real aunt and she's too old-fashioned. Plus I never get enough to eat."

She kissed his forehead. "She's your Godmother and she's British—it's their way. And it wouldn't hurt, my sweets, to lose a little weight."

He pulled away from her. "Yeah sure, then I can play soccer and run around like all the other guys in school…"

The sarcasm bruised her heart. He'd inherited his disability from an English ancestor of hers so she was extra attentive and understanding about his physical challenge. "Howard you know how much we love you. You're brilliant and advanced and brave and strong. Maybe someday you'll be able to do the things you want but regardless of that we'll always love you."

"Dad doesn't," he mumbled. "He doesn't want me around 'cause I'm a cripple. He said he'd fix my leg but he hasn't."

"Daddy's working very hard on that," she said, sounding vague even to herself. She held the rock up. A misty film whirled inside it. For an instant she thought she saw the tiny image of a cat waving two tails at her. Then it vanished. Were the meds making her goofy? Was the rock dangerous? She laid it on the work bench and backed away.

Michelle pointed a shaky finger at it. *"Ze-he-brak,"* she whispered.

Amanda stared at her. "What?"

Michelle shrugged.

"What does that mean, sweetie?"

"I doooooooon't knoooooooooowwwwwww..."

Howard sneered. "She's always talkin' to her invisible friends."

"They're not *imbisible*," Michelle insisted.

Amanda remembered how at her daughter's age she herself had talked to friendly ghosts late at night. But her son had a different make-believe world in vivid dreams of knighthood that he insisted were real. He had decorated his room with medieval castles and collected swords and always wore a knight costume on Halloween.

"Michelle knows what she sees Howard. Don't mock."

"Oh yeah? She talks to ghosts just like Dad." He rolled his eyes. "Dad comes up here at night and talks to the moon."

"What?" She tensed.

"I've heard him. When I can't sleep I watch him from my hiding place. It's like he's talking to people who aren't there."

She felt bad that the children had been exposed to Peter's eccentricities and wished he could be a normal father to them. She pressed her temples and aching sinuses. "Was he going over formulas?"

"No."

"Talking to himself?"

"No Mom, he wasn't."

Michelle interrupted. "Why can't we go to London Mommy? We all went there with Grandma before she died."

"I know and you'll go again. We'll talk about it later."

Pluto started barking downstairs.

"*Yoo hoo*, I have arrived and right on *schhhedual*," Hillary shouted in her Oxford accent. "Where the blazes is everybody? Your porch light is out and I nearly tripped over a pumpkin. And who left the front door open? Is anybody here? I thought we were going out?"

CHAPTER FOUR

Amanda slipped the rock back into her pocket and shouted to her friend on the way downstairs. "Coming, Hillary."

Howard limped past her in the second floor hall.

He must have left the front door open when he took the dog out earlier, though it wasn't like him. She held Michelle's hand and followed him downstairs on worn carpet that had withstood three generations of busy feet.

Hillary greeted her with a quick hug and doubtful eyes. Amanda resented the way her friend always assumed she couldn't manage on her own when Peter was away. But from their two-decade friendship she knew that Hillary needed to be needed. Amanda concealed her anxiety over Peter's phone call behind a genuine smile for her friend while Howard grabbed Pluto's collar.

"I almost didn't make it back," Hillary said. "Caught the last flight out of Paris before they shut down the airport due to nasty weather. It was a bumpy ride I might add." She smiled at Howard and Michelle. "Great costumes, kids. They look familiar. Didn't you have the same ones last year?"

Howard looked at her with stormy eyes.

"They like them," Amanda hurried to say as Pluto barked at Hillary. The dog tried to pull free from Howard's grip.

"Hush up, you irritating dog," Hillary snapped. "Are you trying to frighten me with that outlandish get-up?"

Howard scowled. "He's a space dog."

"You've made the poor fella' into a circus monster," Hillary said, "but let's stay focused on planet Earth, shall we? I brought pumpkin pie—hope you have plenty of hot chocolate. And where's Peter? Not back yet? You said he'd be home this week.

And that porch is so dark I nearly tripped over your pumpkins which weren't lit either. Can't see your handy-dandy carvings kids if you don't light the candles."

Amanda bristled at the string of criticisms. "It's too windy to light them right now and the porch light must have burned out. Peter just called. He's been delayed." She rubbed her nose and sniffled.

"You have a cold?" Hillary asked.

"Michelle got it first. I'm surviving on soup and chocolates."

"Stressing you out again, is he? And *still* in London?"

"Fill you in later Hil'." She was anxious to look for the boy she'd seen and would wait to break the news of her trip after the trick-or-treating.

Hillary opened her large carry bag. "I brought you more *divine un-stressors* from duty free at Charles de Gaulle. Godiva chocolates." She handed the lavishly-ribboned gold box to Amanda and pulled out more gifts. "And for you young man, a model of the Carcassonne Castle—it's double walled and Medieval."

Howard's face lit up. He studied the small model that almost fit in his hand. "Thanks. Is it in England?"

"No. France."

"Oh-h-h…" He stretched the word out in disappointment.

Hillary added, "I know you're dressed like an *English* knight, but this castle is special with extraordinary features from extensive renovations."

"I'm not *dressed* like an English knight," he interrupted, "I *am* an English knight…"

"Of course, dear."

She turned to Michelle. "My, my, your plaid coat is exceptionally smart, and for you, an angel. She sings a lullaby when you wind the key."

Michelle's eyes widened in awe. "McWow. Thanks Aunt Hillary. Another one for my collection."

Amanda hugged the box of chocolates and smiled.

"Can we leave now?" Michelle asked, tugging her mother's hand.

"Okay, go get your bags from the kitchen."

Michelle scooted off and Howard hurried after her.

"What did you want to tell me later?" Hillary asked.

Amanda put on her jacket. "No time."

"Come on, be a chum and share. I can't wait."

Amanda shook her head and popped a chocolate into her mouth.

Hillary frowned and leaned into the hall mirror, tucking a blonde ponytail under her tan beret. Her friend had the kind of fresh face and natural reserve that people trusted and a bright smile that gave an impression of understated intelligence. "You look great, Hil'. Wish I had your athletic figure."

Hillary turned with a twinkle in her eye. "But you're tall and willowy and I'm stuck with average height, so I want what you have and we're both dissatisfied."

"Not true—you were the gymnast and honor student in school…"

"And you were homecoming queen and the musical wonder child. And now you've got two great kids. But you're changing the subject. What were you going to tell me later?"

The children returned with their candy bags and Amanda put her arms around both of them. She took a deep breath. "Okay. I'll fill you in but then we really have to go. I need to join Peter in London for a few days. I considered bringing these two along— but if you're back in town?"

Hillary shook her head. "I'm on a turn-around myself headed the same way. I have an interview with the *esteemed* Archbishop of Canterbury in three days."

Her friend's excitement was obvious. "Congratulations, Hil'. Why don't you come with us tomorrow instead? We'd have a day together in London and after your interview you could take the kids home with you. Peter and I need to spend some time together."

Curiosity flashed in Hillary's eyes. "Has he finally gotten a raise? What's going on?"

Amanda longed to tell Peter's secrets but recalled his implied warning. "I'm not sure. He didn't say."

Michelle tugged at her mother's jacket. "Let's goooooooo before all the candy's gone."

"Okay princess, time to leave." Amanda looked at Hillary. "Well? Can you come with us tomorrow?"

Hillary smiled and nodded. "I haven't gone trick-or-treating in years and now a trip to London with all of you, what a delight."

Instant relief calmed Amanda. With Hillary along she'd be free to deal with Peter on her own. A big smile crossed her face. "Okay then let's go for it."

Outside, Howard escaped across the street. Pluto scampered after him. Amanda snatched the dog leash from the railing and sneezed. She reached for a tissue in her pocket and touched the purple rock. It felt warm. "Hil' would you go ahead with Michelle? I'll find Howard and catch up." She knelt and re-tied her faded red high-tops. Her lucky shoes.

"Right. He ran into the park. You'll miss all the fun if you don't hurry." Hillary winked and led Michelle away.

Amanda waited a moment before hurrying across the street. She couldn't see Howard anywhere. Heavy tree limbs swayed in the wind, dropping more leaves. Pluto barked at the overgrown bushes, his Halloween tail flashing bright red. She caught up and attached his leash. "What is it, Pluto?" She looked around shouting, "Howard where are you?" An empty path curved under the oaks but it was difficult to see in the dim light. Pluto stopped barking and growled, pulling on his leash.

Sudden fear gripped her as she held on to the dog. "Howard!"

The sharp smell of chimney smoke drifted past with a hint of lavender. Lavender in October? Was her cold clearing up or were the meds jumbling her senses again? She glanced at trick or treaters up and down the street. Michelle stood with Hillary at a neighbor's house, her candy bag open.

Pluto whined, his attention still fixed on the bushes. She shivered while the wind lashed dust and hair into her face.

A loud gurgling noise made Pluto yelp and strain at his collar. Amanda's throat tightened. She tried to pull the dog back but he refused to budge.

Howard charged out of the small woods just as the wizened face of a dwarf peeked out from behind a bush.

Pluto jumped.

Amanda almost screamed but saw the dwarf's elf costume and realized that he wasn't a boy at all. He was a small man.

The stranger stepped out and smiled, putting a finger against his mouth to quiet her. His plump face looked cute in an ageless way. Long earlobes dangled over a short neck and his cheeks matched his nose, round and puffy. But it was his warm eyes that captured her—wide-set, deep pools, sparkling with chips that flashed like diamonds. He wore a red hat just like the one in the attic. Wind tussled its tip and the bell tinkled.

Howard gawked at the man, then looked at his mother. "You found the little guy..." He held up the walkie-talkie. "This was goin' berserk again Mom. I tried to find a source or a connection or somethin', but there's nothin' out there..."

She handed Pluto's leash to Howard and turned to the dwarf. "Who are you?"

"Yeah, did you throw that rock?" asked Howard.

The little man held his smile and bowed his head. "How do you do. My name is Rotarious—Rotar for short, and I am very glad to meet you, Mrs. Tregnier. And you too, master Howard." He held out his hand to Amanda. She shook it but wished she hadn't. His stubby fingers were dirty and grimy. She wiped her hands on the back of her jeans while he talked. A faint scent of lavender hung in the air.

"I apologize for breaking your window," he continued. "I did not mean to frighten you. I was merely trying to get your attention."

"Why?"

"I am seeking to find Dr. Tregnier. He and I are partners."

Partners? How could this very odd stranger know their names and where they lived, while she knew nothing about him? Confused, she asked, "Why are you looking for him?"

"It is a very long story. Do you have the time to listen?"

"Can you give me a short version? We're on a heavy schedule." She glanced down the street but didn't see Hillary or Michelle among the roving children.

"I will try. Your husband…uh…used knowledge from a book that belongs to me and now he may be in danger… "

Her stomach clenched. More secrets. She should have guessed from Peter's odd behavior over the past year. "What kind of danger?"

"I do not know how bad the situation is but I must find my book."

"What book are you talking about?"

"That is a part of the long story. Is he here?"

"No."

"Then I must look elsewhere. It is exceedingly important."

He was evasive just like Peter, but she had to know more. "If you're his partner, where did you meet?"

"We worked together in Switzerland."

She felt crushed. Peter had promised to take her to Switzerland and show her his small family farm. But how long had he been working with Rotar? His research was in London. Or was Rotar talking about Peter's home project, the good luck piece? She sniffled and cleared her throat. "What work do you share with my husband?"

Rotar's eyes fell. In a sad voice he said, "I do not wish to disappoint you, but it is confidential."

Not what she wanted to hear. "I'm his wife—you can tell *me!*"

Rotar shook his head. "You do not have the time and you would not understand. Will you ask Peter to contact me? It is *extremier* urgent."

"*Tinkle, whirr, boiiiing,*" came a mechanical sound from Rotar's throat.

Howard gasped. Pluto barked and pulled on his leash.

Rotar covered his mouth, looking embarrassed. "Oh dear, my computer again. My apologies. Correction: It is *extremely* urgent."

"Mom?" Howard whined. "Is he a robot?"

"What did you mean about your computer?" Amanda asked.

He waved it away. "It is nothing. I have been traveling many miles and my head sometimes feels dizzy, that is all. I call the mind my computer. And I am most certainly not a robot." He looked amused.

Skeptical she said, "I'll let him know when I see him."

"When will that be?"

"Soon I hope, according to him."

Rotar perked up. "He has contacted you?"

"Yes, but he wouldn't tell me anything."

She saw Rotar's downcast look. "But I'm meeting him in London," she added, regretting the words as soon as they left her mouth.

He brightened. "Then I will see you there."

"You're flying over?"

"I have…" he hesitated, "private transportation." He pulled a knobby stick from under his belt.

She stepped back. Howard gripped Pluto's leash and moved in front of her, pulling out his sword.

Rotar raised a hand. "Do not be concerned. This is simply part of my ritual."

"Ritual?" she asked.

"What ritual?" Howard echoed.

"Think of it as exercise," said Rotar. He looked amused again.

Bewildered, Amanda pulled the rock from her pocket and held it up. It sparkled in the lamplight. "Is this yours?"

Rotar nodded. "Keep it and take it with you on your trip. It will protect you."

"How?" she asked.

Instead of answering Rotar pointed his gnarly stick at the sky. "Miles of smiles," he uttered.

The wind strengthened, swirling dust around. Howard raised an arm to shield his face and dropped the leash.

Amanda closed her eyes for a moment.

Pluto barked and ran off.

A bell tinkled.

When the wind calmed Rotar had vanished.

CHAPTER FIVE

Coppet, Switzerland

Leo Braun knew that others envied his position with US Intelligence in Geneva. After retiring from the Army with a questionable performance record he'd been given a second chance at a new career thanks to his late uncle's achievements in the Swiss financial world. And now he had a shot at global notoriety. Something alien had been witnessed at a farm near Coppet. This could be an opportunity for him and he was not going to let anyone interfere with his investigation. He was in full command and would soon get to the bottom of the sighting, whatever it was.

Braun's driver sped to the rural location, hurrying before the light faded. Joseph Reinholt, the farmer who had reported the mysterious intruder, knew Braun from a chance meeting at an invitation-only space exhibit sponsored by his uncle's bank. Through casual conversation they learned that they both banked at the same financial institution and both admired the bank's founder. Braun remembered his surprise when the farmer had taken an interest in his own US connections to paranormal investigations—a world away from farming. The man had expressed a personal interest in space exploration and in particular space agriculture. He believed mankind would grow ample food supplies inside future space stations and somehow equated that to world peace.

In his distress call Joseph insisted something alien had threatened his livestock. He had contacted Braun direct out of fear of ridicule by the local authorities. Unfortunately, he had chased whatever it was into the woods.

At the farm, Braun stepped out of the car and hoped his new friend wasn't some sort of wacko hoaxer. Joseph happened to be out for the evening with his son at a science fair and his wife had gone to a church meeting, leaving Braun free to investigate on his own.

Inside the barn he scanned his flashlight across the floor and walls. Other than a horse and two cows standing silent in their stalls he detected nothing but the unpleasant odor of manure. Agitated and cold he pulled his collar around numbed ears and returned outside where he prowled behind the barn for evidence of a mysterious visitor.

In the dim light there was nothing out of the ordinary. He pulled out a small recorder and spoke in a soft tone that even his driver Charles, wouldn't hear. "No evidence inside the barn," he whispered. "No footprints outside and no indentations of any kind, but the ground has hardened from the cold weather so that's not unusual. If Joseph…that's Joseph Reinholt of *Ferme de St. Vache en Coppet* is just hallucinating, I won't let him make me the laughing stock of Switzerland. Claims he saw an elongated wispy figure glowing lime green and insisted it's not from this planet. The *thing* was floating, landing occasionally on spindly feet. Sounds like a teenager or vagrant, or even a Halloween costume, except the Swiss don't have that event. If his claims are true this *thing* can't just disappear into thin air, but no evidence has turned up to corroborate his alleged sighting. Good thing he called me first on this one."

He stopped recording.

When he shifted his stance his right foot broke through a crusty surface and sank into something soft. His flashlight lit up a large patty of cow manure by his shoe. In the manure he also saw something else—the slight indentation of a footprint.

The flashlight quivered in his hand as he bent down for a closer look. The imprint was longer and narrower than a human foot and had three toes. He'd never seen anything like it and it fit no animal or bird he could think of. He fumbled for his camera and took a photograph, then several more. An empty weathered crate leaned against the barn. Braun put his camera away and placed the box upside down over the fresh cow dung, anchoring it with a rock.

"Charles, over here," he yelled, heading for the car. "I'm a smelly mess. My hands are filthy and my shoes are ruined. Bring my wet wipes and a towel…"

His driver got out of the silver Mercedes grumbling about the cold and pressed down his toupee to keep it from blowing off. "Sir?" He handed him the wet wipes and towel.

Braun barked orders like bullet points: "Get Washington on the line. I want to speak to Sam Henry." His eyes bulged with anticipation. "Could be a promotion in this Charles, even a reward."

Charles nodded.

Braun cleaned his hands while Charles jumped back into the car and dialed. Then he leaned into the sedan's side mirror and wiped the top of his balding head. From under an upside-down ring of dark short hair his small eager eyes beamed back at him. A short red-veined nose protruded over thin lips that curled into a calculating smile. He pulled away and saw himself as a powerful leader with a loud bark. The bark being far more important than good looks.

"I have Sam Henry on the line sir," Charles said.

He jerked the phone out of his driver's hand and suppressed his excitement under a cheerful tone. "Sam, how the heck are 'ya?" Not waiting for an answer he continued. "And how's the weather in DC? It's downright freezin' over here."

Braun listened to Sam complain of high winds and abnormal low temperatures. Then he took a long breath making his requests in a calm professional manner. Less than ten minutes later he had an added budget with additional manpower and special equipment for the investigation. He was delighted to still have control, yet keep his true purpose covered up. Sam Henry only knew that he was either chasing down a potential terrorist or investigating a hoax.

After hanging up, his mouth widened into a victorious smile. He bragged to Charles. "I'm good, I'm really good."

When settled into the back seat of the car he smirked, knowing the evidence pointed to something extremely odd and probably real. He had exposed more than one hoax in the past, but this one looked different.

And now he had the means to uncover it.

If everything went his way he'd soon be honored with fame and fortune, just like his uncle, Deiter Braun.

CHAPTER SIX

Uncertain fear consumed Amanda's thoughts. Her eyes darted in all directions, but she couldn't see Rotar. First Peter's inexplicable call and now this curious visitor.

Howard asked, "Where'd the little guy go? Into the woods?"

"He couldn't have vanished into thin air," she said. "What a strange little man."

"Mom, Pluto's scared."

She turned to see Pluto flying across the street, his legs a blur and tail flashing. Howard searched the bushes, stabbing them with his sword.

Pluto barked non-stop from their front porch. Leaves rustled in the darkness.

Amanda felt vulnerable. "Let's go back Howard. Now!"

He took another whack at the shrubbery. "I haven't checked the trees or the park."

"Never mind. I need a brave knight to rescue Hillary and Michelle. They didn't get very far, probably a block or two."

"But I haven't gotten any candy yet… Rotar isn't dangerous, is he?"

She considered the question. Of all the strange things going on lately Rotar seemed the least dangerous, yet the oddest. "I don't know, but I'll buy you all the candy you want when we get to London. Let's hurry."

She took his arm. "And remember, not a word of this to the others, understand? Just tell them we have to cut the candy collection short to get ready for our trip. Now bring those damsels back and be careful."

"Don't worry. I'll guard 'em and stay on the lookout. I'm ready for hot cocoa, anyway. It's freezin' out here." He half ran, dragging his leg down the street.

She hurried back to the house, its porch light glowing again. The bulb seemed much brighter than the one she'd inserted a few weeks earlier.

The rock in her pocket vibrated. She didn't dare touch it. Could the rock somehow affect the light? How did Rotar vanish so quickly? And what on earth could Peter have done?

Confused, she waited on the front porch for the others. Her part-time music career hadn't prepared her for something like this but she had to remain calm and strong for the children.

Howard, Michelle and Hillary returned in a rush of talk and excitement. She followed them inside and locked the front door behind her.

Seated at the kitchen table eating dessert, Michelle complained. "I don't want to share. Why can't Howard get his own candy?"

"There wasn't time," Amanda said. "He had to help me with something, and he'll share with you when he gets extra candy in London. We need to pack and get ready."

Hillary finished her pie and looked at Amanda. "You're not all here tonight. What else is wrong? 'Husband dearest' got your nerves?"

Amanda put down her cup of hot chocolate and flicked a warning glance at her friend, nodding toward the children. "There's so much to do, I just can't seem to relax." She took her dishes to the sink. Hillary joined her.

"You need to *dee-stressss*, Amanda."

They both turned when Michelle squealed and ran out of the kitchen, clutching her sack of candy. Howard followed with Pluto nipping at his heels. Hillary shouted after them. "Let's not get on a sugar high, kids, you might want some sleep tonight."

She turned back and whispered. "When I arrived this evening I saw two men in a gray sedan staring at your house. Is there cause to worry?"

"Of course not," Amanda whispered back with an irritated glance. "Just a coincidence." She twisted her paper napkin into a ball and threw it into the trash. Peter's warning nagged at her. She put away the whipped cream and slammed the fridge shut. "I don't mean to be rude, Hil', but I'm a little on edge with the beginning of a nasty headache." She heard the children arguing in the hall and shouted, "Kids, please get ready for bed and lay out the things you want to pack. I'll help you later." She turned to Hillary. "Sorry, I have to stay focused on our trip."

"Will it help if I spend the night and get them packed up?"

"Yes, and double yes," Amanda said with a grateful smile.

The children scooted upstairs and Hillary asked, "But I don't quite understand why you're rushing off to London at Peter's beck and call. The weather's abominable over there, and he should be here instead. You're always alone. Why continue this ridiculous farce?"

Amanda's face darkened. "I don't want my kids to grow up without a father like I did."

Hillary shook her head. "But they're growing up without him anyway…"

"Temporarily. And I think that's about to change. Something has happened, and perhaps…"

"Is he actually delving into something you can deposit at the bank? Enough to fix up this old house of yours? Take you on vacations? Has he found that cure for Howard's leg he's always boasting about?"

"I can only hope, but let's drop the Peter questions and stay focused on the trip. Would you book our flights on United? Peter has accumulated more than enough points for all of us."

"Of course."

"Thanks." Amanda got their passports out of the living room desk and laid them on the entry credenza. "I've boarded Pluto a couple of times at Happy Farms. If you could drop him off tomorrow on your way home to pack it would really help. I'll call the school and my music students in the morning, and then…"

"Slow down Amanda. Let's make a list."

"Good idea. You're a true friend, Hil'. I have to go cover a broken window upstairs."

She left her friend with the children and went upstairs where the moon cast sinister shadows into the dark attic. When she turned on the dim over-head bulb, sinister changed to shabby. In her mother's old free-standing mirror a cat stared out of it waving two tails. The same cat she thought she saw in the rock. Panic froze her and she squeezed her eyes shut in horror. When she opened them, the cat faded away through a pale reflection of her own image. She searched the mirror.

Nothing.

The rock in her pocket felt warm.

"What's happening?" she whispered, jerking her hand from her pocket. "Good grief, I'm talking to a rock."

The wind howled through the broken window, agitating her husband's mobile of swirling planets. Gusts fluttered his outer space posters and stirred dust off his shelves of books on magic and the occult, chemistry, molecular biology, mathematics, herbal medicine, astrology, and astronomy. The large conch shells holding down stacks of his old science fiction comic books hummed in the breeze. Could she duplicate these sounds on her flute?

Maybe the hum.

From the family trunk she pulled out crumpled Halloween costumes, a wooden flute her grandfather had made for her and a marathon trophy with its missing handle. She'd thrown it against the wall and broken it the day her father left their family and moved back to France where he was born. Peter's old school sweater lay near the bottom. Under it she found the small wooden box they'd used to contain their honeymoon shells.

She lifted its lid and found the shells still intact. Touching their delicate curves, her hands trembled. Peter had drilled small holes in each one for a necklace, but never finished it. She decided to string them herself and wear them on the trip.

Thoughts drifted back to the beach in St. Thomas when Peter had talked about the shells as if they were alive. To him they were like empty bodies waiting for a new soul to be washed up by the tide. He believed they were proof that nothing ever died. She couldn't remember the last time they'd had a discussion about the meaning of life or anything else important. On his brief home-comings the children always came first.

Beneath the shells lay a thin pocket notebook, its black leather cover embossed with a conch shell. Peter's good luck piece… She took it out and flipped through the pages. Her husband had scribbled on the first page: *Moonchild, Vidollet, Rotar.*

Was this the book Rotar was looking for? Moonchild was Peter's pet name for himself, but who or what was Vidollet?

Full of chemical and mathematical formulas, the book had to be his home project. On the last page he had written: *It is my destiny.* He'd told her she was his destiny when he asked her to marry him yet here it was again. She doubted this notation referred to her. But whatever it meant to Peter it was important enough to hide. Could this be the breakthrough for Howard?

A smile crept into her heart.

A blast of wind diverted her attention. Through the broken window she saw the tail lights of a light-colored sedan driving away down the street.

Was the house under surveillance? Were they in danger?

She found the old wooden shutters and jammed them back into the frame tight enough to hold until repairs could be made. Then she raced down to the first floor, making sure all the doors were locked. Not sure of what to do next, she popped another

Godiva chocolate into her mouth for a quick shot of euphoria. She'd gone over her two-chocolates-a-day limit, but today was an exception.

Hillary was right. Ever since Peter had started working in London their marriage had suffered. He even criticized her chocolate habit, calling it nothing but a pacifier for giving in too easily to stress. But for Amanda chocolate and ecstasy were synonymous.

She gulped down another and got the fire extinguisher from the kitchen, setting it under the hall coat rack for a handy weapon, adding a poker from the fireplace. Confident she could defend herself if necessary, she grabbed the box of chocolates and hurried to the second floor where Hillary and Michelle's giggles could be heard from her daughter's room. "You have everything you need, Hil'?" she called. "I'm going to take a bath and get some sleep."

"Everything's just ducky," Hillary shouted back. "Nighty night…"

More giggling.

Pluto barked in Howard's room. She tapped on his door. "Keep Pluto with you, Howard. G'night, everyone."

She escaped into her room and worried. The men in the car couldn't be watching her, could they? Admonishing herself into a calmer state, she ran a bath and relaxed in the steamy hot water. She imagined Peter greeting her with open arms at the London lab. For the first time she felt excited about the trip and dared to hope that the tight family budget and global separation of their marriage might soon end.

Soothed by lemon oil and wrapped in a fluffy white robe she glanced out the window. The trick or treaters had gone, but the wind still scattered leaves. No gray car or slow cruisers. The house was quiet.

She tucked the black book under her pillow and crawled into bed but had trouble getting to sleep. Heavy gusts of wind startled her by shaking the screens. Passing car headlights spooked her.

Tree limbs scratching the walls frightened her. She tossed and turned, her thoughts churning. Should she call Peter and let him know she'd found his good luck piece? The time was too early in Europe—he'd be sleeping. And besides, he'd been so rude.

She got up and took an extra dose of cold medicine. Her favorite music box sat on the nightstand. She wound it up and listened to it play <u>You Light Up My Life.</u> Hoping the purple rock would protect her, she clutched it to her chest until the music finally lulled her into an exhausted sleep.

CHAPTER SEVEN

Amanda woke up late feeling rested. She ignored the gloomy weather and finished packing for their evening flight. Howard and Michelle ran into the room, excited about the trip.

"We're going to see Daddy," Michelle squealed, skipping and jumping while Amanda tossed an extra six-pack of Tic Tacs into her suitcase, her backup to chocolate.

"Does Dad even know we're coming, Mom?" Howard asked.

She decided not to answer. "Did you both remember underwear? And socks?"

"Figures," he concluded. "He's not even expecting us."

He waved his sword, lunging at a spider in the corner. "And we got enough stuff. Hillary helped before she went home to pack, and I'm bringing my sword."

"Sorry, but it'll just be confiscated at the airport."

His face drooped. "But it's only made of wood. Can't you put it in your suitcase? Puuuleeze?"

He son rarely pleaded. Maybe she was being too rigid. "All right. Leave it with me. If it's checked through it might make it."

Howard beamed. "Thanks, Mom." He tossed it into her case.

"Make sure your school books are packed and tooth brushes."

Both children ignored the comment and scrambled out of the room. Michelle shouted, "If Howie gets a sword, I'm bringin' my angel."

Amanda called out, "The stuffed one without the wind up. No metal allowed…"

"Ooooo-kaaaaayyyy," she hollered back.

Amanda packed the opal pendant on a gold chain Peter had given her the previous Christmas. She could wear it on a night out in London. She'd misplaced the matching earrings but felt certain they'd show up again.

She had no time to look for the gray sedan as she checked off each item on the to-do list one by one. And just when she fastened the honeymoon shells around her neck the cab arrived. Everyone was ready. When they drove away, Amanda looked around on the block but noticed nothing unusual. She should have felt relieved, but had a nagging suspicion that someone or something was watching. But at least she was out of the house and her children sat safely beside her. On the way to the airport they picked Hillary up at her condominium complex. The chatter that ensued diverted Amanda's attention to the flight and to the horrid weather outside.

At the international terminal travelers hurried in all directions. Their foursome snaked through the crowds to the United check-in counter line. Howard whispered, "Did you bring the rock, Mom? To show Dad?"

She nodded and touched it in the pocket of her London Fog. It felt icy cold. Should she worry? Would it get through security? She moved it to her over-sized travel bag slung over her shoulder.

Michelle held her mother's free hand, clutching her angel with the other. "*Ze-he-brak,*" she whispered.

Amanda's brow furrowed. "What is it, Michelle?"

The girl shrugged and fidgeted with her angel. Amanda didn't want to press. Michelle was nervous about flying.

Amanda's arm concealed the slight bulge of Peter's small notebook under the band of her bra. She skirted through security and the book passed through undetected. When her purse rolled through x-ray and the rock didn't set off any alarms, she relaxed a little. But how could that be? The rock seemed to have powers that could disturb a walkie-talkie and restore a light bulb... How could it not set off sensitive surveillance equipment? If Rotar was for real, he'd better have some answers. But what if he never showed up again?

When they approached their aisle, she was delighted to see four seats together in the center section of economy class. Hillary had done well. Amanda took the aisle seat and Howard plopped down next to her. Michelle sat between Howard and Hillary, squirming and hugging her angel. She kicked at the seat in front of her. "No kicking, sweetie," Amanda said. "Listen to a story on the children's channel."

Howard helped Michelle with the earphones. Hillary leaned forward. "If no one sits next to me on the aisle, I'll move over and Michelle can lie down and sleep."

Amanda nodded.

"I don't wanna' sleep," Michelle protested, kicking again.

The man sitting in front of her turned and glared.

Michelle stopped kicking and chewed on her angel's wing.

They buckled up and waited for take-off. Amanda took a deep breath. Her cold had cleared and she could smell coffee brewing in the galley. While she helped Howard with his headset she caught a strong whiff of English after-shave nearby. A soothing aroma. She looked up and met the eyes of a man walking by. He was tall, with an imposing demeanor. She smiled at him and then closed her eyes, tapping her fingers on the armrest, pretending to play a happy tune on her imaginary flute.

Anthony Ramsey, known as Tony, was on assignment following Amanda Tregnier on her flight to London. An international attorney working mostly on US government projects, his profession made a good cover for clandestine operations like this one. He also consulted on military jobs and many of his missions were classified top secret. On the side, he had interests in space exploration and U.F.O. investigations and from time to time was called upon to assist with unexplainable phenomena.

He had requested the last row of business class divided by a bank of lavatories in front of economy class. Doubtful about the

value of the trip, he was even more skeptical about the anonymous tip that had alerted the C.I.A. to Dr. Tregnier. But it had
to be followed up.

The information he'd received claimed that the scientist's
research was aimed at tampering with the human mind in some
way and therefore of possible danger to the world. Tregnier's
former laboratory in the US would only divulge that he'd been let
go for exceeding the boundaries of their work parameters, whatever that meant. A mole at the London lab where the doctor currently worked had yet to discover anything out of the ordinary.
The surveillance of his home in DC had produced nothing useful
either. The tag seemed like a waste of time, spying on a crazy scientist and tailing his innocuous family. He was anxious to expose
the truth quickly and work on something more rewarding.

Dressed in a dark gray business suit and striped tie he blended
in with the professional working crowd. Moving down the aisle
to the coach section which was about two-thirds full, he spotted his target right away. A stunning woman, much better looking than her passport photo. Porcelain skin, large hazel eyes and
long lashes in a symmetrical face with dark eyebrows arched over
a sculptured nose. Glistening black hair cascaded to her shoulders. He envisioned a Greek goddess, but her profile said she
was English and French. She finished helping her son with his
headset and leaned back. Then she glanced his way and smiled.

When their eyes met he experienced a strange and unfamiliar
flashback. He saw her calling out for him in a tropical location
with odd colors. Beautiful colors, but wrong. The déjà vu moment
jolted him; he hadn't known anything like that before.

But his training kicked in. Instead of lingering, he kept moving and returned to his seat. Shaken by the surprise vision, he
calmed down and focused on the task at hand. Their initial contact had to appear natural. If luck was with him, he'd find a way
to befriend her during the flight. He had to gain her trust enough

to learn more about her husband, and once they were airborne he only had a few hours to accomplish that.

While he waited for takeoff, he slipped on his earphones and listened to Tchaikovsky's <u>1812 Overture.</u> The music relaxed him and he searched his memory. Where did that tropical forest scene come from? A dream? A book? A movie? A childhood trip? Or even more disturbing, had this disarmingly beautiful woman invaded his private thoughts?

He drummed his fingers on the armrest in rhythm with the music, baffled by the mysterious incident. He mulled over his strategy and wondered if she had some hidden powers? And if not, which made much more sense to his otherwise pragmatic mind, had she felt something too?

CHAPTER EIGHT

Before take-off, the Captain announced the air speed, altitude and estimated time of arrival for their flight, informing the passengers of possible turbulence over the Atlantic.

Amanda sat straight up. She hated turbulence and gripped the armrests. Howard touched her white-knuckled hand when the plane lifted into the sky. "It'll be okay, Mom."

Michelle started to kick the seat in front of her again but Hillary held down her legs. "We'll be just dandy," Hillary said, changing the channel on Michelle's head set. "Listen to this story dearest."

Michelle pulled the gear off. "I'm scared."

"No need to be, we're riding on the clouds now," said Hillary.

Michelle's face pinched into a frown. "I'm thirsty."

Hillary clasped her hand. "The attendant will be along soon with drinks."

The jet bumped and wobbled, shaking in the turbulent weather while continuing to climb.

Michelle started to cry and thrash. Hillary tried to calm her. Amanda reached across Howard to soothe her. "Are you hurting, Michelle?"

A female attendant scrambled toward them. The fresh-faced redhead with faint freckles hung onto the seatback and spoke with a Boston lilt. "Is something wrong?"

"She's flown before," Amanda said, "and it scared her but not like this."

The attendant looked perplexed and asked, "What's the matter little one?"

"My ears hurt, and the plane's gonna' crash."

"No it's not…"

"Howard said we're gonna' crash."

Amanda glared at him. He looked away and shrank down in his seat.

"He must have been teasing you," the attendant said and turned to Amanda. "Can I bring her anything?"

Amanda raised her hands and shoulders in an 'I don't know gesture'. "She just got over a cold. Do you have any gum? That might help."

The attendant pulled a stick out of her apron pocket and handed it to Michelle.

Her daughter chewed fast; the jet wiggled and shook. When the plane bumped, she spat out the gum and wailed.

About to change places with Howard, Amanda hesitated when the same man who made eye contact earlier approached. Tall and fit, the scent of his after shave reminded her of English leather. Chestnut brown hair combed to one side of his suntanned face emphasized the whiteness of straight teeth. His warm bright eyes had a calming effect and when he gripped the seatback in front of her she couldn't help noticing his manicured nails.

"Excuse me, but the young lady's distress caught my attention. May I help?"

Michelle sounded on the verge of a melt-down.

"Are you a doctor?" Amanda asked him.

"No, but I'm trained in first aid and emergency response."

"Me too," said the attendant, turning toward a man in a coughing fit near the rear. "I'll be back," she said.

The man nodded to the attendant and continued. "What seems to be wrong?" His voice purred like a radio announcer.

"She's flown before but doesn't like it and she's getting over a cold," Amanda said. "Her ears hurt and she thinks we're going to crash." She cast an annoyed glance at Howard, but he ignored her and pretended to read his comic book.

The man looked toward the rear of the plane. "I know a remedy," he said. "Give me a minute."

Amanda traded places with Howard. The man returned with a bottle of red liquid. "The attendant's a paramedic but busy with someone. She gave me this from the emergency medical kit." He handed her a bottle of children's cough syrup. "And this…" he pulled a pill enclosed in a plastic seal out of his pocket, "is for motion sickness. Half a pill with the cough syrup should calm her right down."

Amanda had used the syrup before but not with motion sickness medication. Safe enough for a six-year-old?

He must have read her thoughts. "It works. I have a teenage daughter and I used the same thing for her when she became agitated in flight. Now she loves flying."

He punched out the motion pill, breaking it in two. "Give her this with a cap of syrup."

"Thanks." Amanda took the bottle and pill. "Here Michelle, this will help."

Michelle shook her head.

"Come on sweetie, some for you and some for your angel. She's hurting too!"

Amanda persuaded Michelle to drink the liquid and swallow the pill. They pretended to give some to the angel. Michelle stroked its hair. "Will we be okay now, Mommy?"

"Yes. We'll all be safe now."

The annoyed passenger in front of them turned and grunted. "Sorry," Amanda said. "She isn't feeling well."

She turned to the English leather man. "I don't know how to thank you."

"No need. She'll be asleep soon."

His smile triggered hers and her mood lifted. "I'm Amanda, and this is my son, Howard, and my daughter Michelle. And at the end there my friend Hillary."

"I'm Tony," he said, nodding at everyone.

"Charmed," Hillary said, waving.

Michelle's eyelids drooped.

"Are you going to London, or farther on?" he asked.

Amanda flushed. "Just to London; it's family business. The kids got a short break from school, right Howard?"

Before Howard could reply Tony asked, "You have family in London?"

Amanda ignored the question. "We'll be busy and sightseeing."

Michelle's head slumped toward her chest and she fell asleep.

"Thank you, again," Amanda whispered, pointing at her daughter.

"Finally some peace," Howard said. "How come you can walk around with the seat belt sign on?" he asked Tony.

He lifted a soft smile. "No one stopped me. And should you find the time I'd like to extend an invitation to all of you for a guided tour."

Amanda shook her head at the suggestion.

"Cool," Howard said, getting up. "I have to go to the bathroom Mom."

Amanda looked up and saw that the seat belt sign had turned off. "Okay," she said.

"Mind if I sit down while he's gone?" Tony asked, his eyes sparkling.

Grateful for the man's rescue of Michelle, she nodded. "He won't be long though."

Tony sat down. "I hope you'll have time to enjoy yourself in London?"

"I'm sure we will. We're meeting my husband. What about you?"

"Business. My daughter was supposed to fly over with me, but my ex-wife shut down our plans. Now I'm left with two tickets for *The Phantom of the Opera*. Have you seen it?"

She remembered her disappointment a few years earlier. "No, I almost saw it once but had to give the tickets away when my kids came down with the flu."

"Well then, perhaps you can find some time to use my daughter's ticket?"

"I don't think so. I'll be busy with my family." She changed the subject. "What kind of work do you have in London?"

He hesitated. "I'm an international attorney. Some of my work's with the government, some with private business. I travel a lot and I miss my daughter. She's in boarding school and we were both looking forward to this trip…" He stared at the seatbacks in front of them.

His mention of government work raised her alarm antennas. Could he be a plant? She shook away her paranoia. "Maybe you'll have another chance to take her to the musical."

"I hope so. I've seen it twice, but she hasn't."

Amanda thought of her own music world. "At home Howard plays the guitar and my sleeping angel rattles the tambourine. I'm a part-time music teacher, so I guess I influenced my kids. I play the flute."

Tony said, "Sounds like you've got the beginnings of an ensemble. My father wanted me to become a symphony conductor, but I had other plans."

The music connection seemed too convenient. "From conducting to international law? That's quite a leap."

"Yes, my family's very involved in music. They established the Music and Heart Foundation for budding young musicians who can't afford tuition."

Surprised, she gawked at him.

"You've heard of it?" he asked.

She nodded, realizing Tony came from wealth and lived far above her middle-class lifestyle. "I applied for their scholarship to obtain my masters at Georgetown. The foundation offered me a substantial stipend, but I dropped out when I had Howard. Then Michelle came along. But a friend got her degree through your foundation."

"Who?" Tony asked.

"Wendy Weinberg."

Tony looked at her with surprise. "She teaches my daughter. What a small world. I knew we had something in common…"

"How could you know that?"

"When I came down the aisle earlier I had an odd experience. Sort of like déjà vu."

Déjà vu? A new come on? Was he making it up or trying to charm her?

He caught her disbelieving look. "I guess I shouldn't have mentioned that," he said. "Now I'm embarrassed."

She frowned.

"But if you can't come to the musical, will you at least have tea with me at the Connaught where I'm staying?"

She recalled high teas shared with her mother sampling sandwiches and cakes in elegant tea rooms around London. The Connaught Hotel was famous for catering to the elite. "Thanks," she said, "but I'll be tied up with the children."

Hillary leaned over. "I couldn't help overhearing. I could watch the kids for you," she offered.

Amanda scowled at her. "There won't be time, Hil'."

Hillary lifted her hands and shrugged.

Tony chuckled. "Even your friend thinks you should come. What does your husband do, may I ask?"

"He's a scientist, but I can't share his passion for it, the research is too complicated." She shifted, realizing she may have said too much.

Tony's eyes searched hers. "Surely if he's working you'll have an hour in the afternoon? I feel so strongly that we've met somewhere before. I'd like to tell you about my strange vision."

She shook her head. "Sorry."

"Where will you be staying?"

"With my husband." She was really becoming annoyed now. "And here comes Howard."

Tony stood and removed a business card from his wallet. He wrote something on the back. "Call me at the Connaught if you have a free moment. I wrote my mobile number on the back."

She took the card. "Thanks again for your help, Tony. I appreciate it, but don't expect a call."

His face fell. "I understand. Have a great time."

Flattered by his attention, she found his persistence annoying. He ambled back to his seat and Hillary frowned at her, one eyebrow raised.

Amanda grabbed her bag from the floor and scurried around to the other side of the aisle, plopping down next to her friend.

Hillary said, "You just turned down a gorgeous gentleman for no good reason. It's only a spot of tea for heaven's sake."

"He was too pushy."

"You're a beautiful woman Amanda, and you don't even know it."

"I'm married." She saw that Howard was listening to something on his headset and Michelle slept. "I don't know the man," she added. "His invitation was completely inappropriate."

"But how do you know Peter's not out having tea with someone in London?"

"Who'd have tea with him? He can't even match up his socks."

Hillary rolled her eyes up. "He's still good looking and a free bird in London. So tell me, what's he discovered?"

She longed to share but dared not. "He wouldn't tell me on the phone."

"Any guesses?"

"I hope it's a breakthrough for Howard, but I honestly don't know." She shifted her arm and felt the notebook against her skin.

"Well, if he wouldn't say and you're flying all the way to London, it must be something fabulous. Is he delving into some sort of psychotic abyss again? I used to think he was just another boor, but I confess his eccentricity fascinates me. I want the exclusive rights to the story, understand?" Her eyes sparkled with mischief.

Hillary's comments made her wary. She looked around, but no one seemed to be listening. The noise of the engines drowned out their conversation. "If you're looking for scientific intrigue, Hil', you'll be disappointed. And since you specialize in religious commentary, wouldn't that be a conflict for you?"

Hillary shook her head. "Not at all. It provides me with a different point of view, without which my research and opinions wouldn't be needed."

"I'll hold you to that the next time you criticize Peter, and on that note I need a chocolate break." Amanda opened her bag and took a quick bite off the end of a Hershey bar. She offered Hillary a taste, but she declined. The purple rock inside glowed in shades of lavender light. Had someone turned on some sort of energy? Frantic, she hurried back to her seat. Howard removed his headset.

"I'll be in the restroom," she said. "Order me an orange juice and a bottle of water for Michelle, okay?"

"Sure, and I'm sorry about scaring her, I was only teasing…"

She saw the remorse in his face. "Apology accepted. Just don't do it again."

Something moved inside her bag. She opened it a little. A Siamese cat with lavender eyes stared back at her waving two tails. It filled up her entire purse. She squelched a scream with a gasp and shut the bag so hard its noisy metal click blanketed the gasp. Purple feline nightmare…this is insane, she cried in her head.

Howard pointed. "Your purse is wiggling, Mom. What the McZanies is in there?"

Relief at seeing Hillary preoccupied with a book, she said, "Stay here and keep an eye on the others, Howard. I'm just going to the restroom."

CHAPTER NINE

Just ahead in Business class, Amanda spotted the back of Tony's head listening to something on his headset. She dashed out of sight between the lavatories. They all showed occupied. When the door to her left opened and a woman came out, Amanda clambered inside and locked the tiny compartment.

She opened her purse and a cat with two tails jumped out, landing on the toilet seat. It purred and squeezed its eyes shut, a lavender sheen shimmering from its body. She tried to touch it, but her hand went right through the creature like a ghost.

"Go away," she whispered through gritted teeth. "Is this a bad dream?"

The cat whined and jumped onto the wash-basin counter.

She closed her eyes and willed herself to call out even though she thought it was crazy. "Rotar… I need hellllpppppp…"

The cat stared at her with menacing eyes.

A bell tinkled and a puff of purple smoke filled the cubicle. She detected a hint of lavender. Rotar appeared wearing the same leather clothing as before and stood on top of the toilet seat.

She stared at him in shock. How could he materialize out of nothing?

The soft Basset hound layers of his face hung in folds. He grinned with a twinkle of amusement. The cat leapt into his arms.

She pointed a trembling finger at the creature. "How can you hold it when I can't?"

Rotar bowed. "Meet Dot Comet."

"What?"

"That is what she calls herself. She is a bit aloof so it took some time to learn her name, but now she trusts me. That is why I was able to leave the rock with you."

"But she's a ghost cat. How can she be in a rock?"

"It is a crolifium transmitter. Dot Comet somehow shrinks to size and hides inside it."

He stroked the cat and smiled. "Do not be frightened, Mrs. Tregnier. I can hold the cat with my outer-dimensional energy. Did you do something to arouse her anger?"

"Not that I know of."

"What exactly were you doing?"

"Eating chocolate."

"Ahhh… Dot Comet is hungry."

"The cat eats chocolate?"

"She will eat anything, but she is especially fond of chocolate. I will feed her proper food and send her back." Rotar locked grave eyes with hers. "I responded to your distress call, but I have not yet found your husband. Where is he?"

"I told you, I'm on my way to meet him."

Rotar's focus drifted, and his voice cracked. "I must reach him soon…"

"How did you get in here? We're up at forty thousand feet!"

Rotar ignored her and studied the cat for a moment. He waved his wand, *"Fish-ung-li-ton Tu-na-man-cia."*

A wooden dish filled with tuna fish manifested on the vanity. Amanda drew back.

A loud rap rattled the door. "Mom, you okay in there?" asked Howard.

The cat ate like it was famished and emptied the bowl.

"That's my son. Can't you make it disappear?" Amanda asked.

Rotar grinned, *"Re-trac-to-fron-tum."*

The cat vanished along with the bowl and the fish smell.

She felt the weight of the purple rock back in her bag and peeked to make sure.

"It is not so easy being responsible for the secrets of the universe," Rotar said in a disheartened tone. The pupils of his eyes whirled into dark pools revealing a massive silver book. It opened, flipping through page after page at high speed. He closed his eyes. When he re-opened them, the book was gone. "I have made a grave mistake and need your help."

"Mine?"

He nodded.

A triple pounding on the door again. "It's okay, Howard," she yelled. "I need a few more minutes."

She glared into Rotar's eyes. "But how can I help? And what on Earth is going on?"

Rotar smiled. "Not *what on Earth*, but *what in the universe...* I can track you with the rock. Keep it close."

"But if you can do that, why can't you just *zip* yourself to my husband and get your book back?" She was tempted to give him the black notebook but changed her mind. It didn't look anything like the one in his eyes.

"I cannot. He is protected by an outer-dimensional shield..."

Her eyes grew large. "Meaning?"

"The rock will not locate him. Even Dot Comet could not find him and came back to me."

Her face crunched into a knot. "Why not? And you just said *dimension?* You used the same term to explain your special energy. What do you mean?"

Another bang on the door. "Mom?"

Rotar placed an index finger to his lips for silence. "Patience," he said.

"No, tell me now!"

His stomach heaved with laughter. "You are full of curiosity. Fathoms of fantasies..." he whispered, disappearing in a puff of smoke. The bell on his cap tinkled.

She sputtered. "Wait..."

But he was gone.

She needed to meet her husband in *this* dimension—in London—on planet Earth. Perhaps she should have told Rotar about the little black book after all. She leaned on the sink to steady herself. What had Peter been up to? He never told her why he'd been fired from the American lab. And now he was connected to an alien midget and a two-tailed cat. She wanted to scream.

The door banged again. "I'll be right out," she shouted.

Her brain spun into a cramp. She ran water over her trembling hands and patted her forehead. The mirror reflected hollow eyes in a gaunt face. Dabbing a few drops of the airline's cologne on her neck, its lemony pine scent soothed her.

When she opened the door, Howard looked annoyed. "You sure you're okay, Mom?"

He must think I've seen a ghost, she thought, straightening up with a faint smile. "Just a little motion sickness. Do you need the bathroom?"

He shook his head.

Food carts came down the aisle. Meal service had started—time to eat.

She scooted Howard back to their seats.

After the meal, the overhead lights turned off. Darkness helped Amanda feel invisible and more relaxed. She drifted into a light sleep until the loud arrival announcements woke her up. Michelle stirred. "Mommy," she said, groggy. "I have to go to the bathroom."

She escorted her daughter to the lavatory, but when she scanned business class, Tony was not in his seat. After helping Michelle, Howard buckled her up and Amanda took a walk to get her circulation going. At the front of the business class section, an attendant pulled back the curtain to first class. Tony came out of the cockpit.

What was *he* doing in there? Special invite from the Captain? She rushed back to the lavatory area and stopped at the emergency exit where she looked out the porthole.

Her mind raced. It had all been too convenient—his help too instant. She watched the sunshine outside. London was known for its rain. The grand estates and clumps of trees dotting the ground below reminded her of the beautiful country tours she'd taken with her mother in previous years.

But fond memories gave way to doubts. Who was Tony? And what would happen when she met up with Peter?

She wanted the children and Hillary to have a happy visit. Where would she take them first? Tony interrupted her by leaning over to peer out the same porthole.

"Out walking again?" Amanda asked with a false sweetness in her voice.

"Yes, keeps the blood flowing."

"And what are you working on in London? You never mentioned…"

Tony cleared his throat. "Corporate contracts. They can be quite complicated when crossing international borders."

"American corporations?"

Tony looked at her with impatient eyes. "One you've never heard of. A new business merger between Britain, France, Italy and the US. Difficult cultures to bring together."

She didn't like his dismissive answer.

"Will you have time to shop? Visit Harrods?" he asked.

He was changing the subject. "I don't know," she said.

"Same here. I took my daughter on a shopping spree to Harrods a couple of years ago. Bought her a baby grand." He chuckled, "The shipping cost as much as the piano."

Amanda had no reference for a life like that and remained guarded. "I'm glad your daughter plays. Is Wendy a good teacher?"

"She's quite good, and my daughter is doing well."

If he was a fake, he was a convincing actor. "Time to get back to my seat for landing. Good luck with everything."

Tony looked at her with a warmth that made her feel special. She didn't want to feel that way with a stranger. "Is your daughter okay now?" he asked.

She nodded. "Yes, she's awake and doing fine, thanks to you." She returned to her seat.

They landed at Heathrow with a thud and a bump, followed by screeching tires. Tony waited at his seat and then followed Amanda and the others off the plane. They marched straight to the passport stations and got into various lines. After clearing customs, they pushed their carts outside.

While Hillary lined up for a cab, Amanda turned to Tony waiting at the curb. "Good-bye, Tony, and thanks again for your help." She searched his eyes for the last time, not sure if every-thing he said was a lie.

He lit a cigarette.

She didn't hide her surprise. "You smoke?"

He took a deep drag. "I took it up again when my wife left. My daughter hounds me with anti-smoking literature on a regu-lar basis."

"Good for her," she said. "Lots of luck with that."

"Don't forget my offer if you're up for tea. Just call me at the Connaught." He waved to a man holding up a sign with his name on it.

"Right," she said, her tone laced with sarcasm. When the cream-colored Rolls Royce pulled up for Tony she did a double take. Was this someone who would spike her tea with poison? Or be a threat to her children or Peter? Ridiculous. It's just how the other half lives, and like Tony, it had nothing to do with her world.

He climbed into the car and pulled away. She felt the weight of unanswered questions and unexplained emotions and realized Hillary was probably right. His invitation was a simple meeting for afternoon tea. And besides, he couldn't find her now unless she contacted him. When their turn came, a black taxi pulled up and the driver helped load their bags. "Where to, Mum?" the man asked Hillary who looked at Amanda.

"Hammersmith," Amanda said. "Twelve ninety-five Hammersmith Road."

They scrambled into the cab and Amanda sank into the back seat. The weather changed from sunshine to dreary gray.

The chunky cabby squeezed behind the steering wheel. "Right, Mum. Know London?"

"Bet your boots," said Hillary. "I used to live here, didn't I?"

"Right you are, then. Have you all there in a jif, Mum."

Preoccupied with her thoughts of meeting Peter at the lab, Amanda failed to notice the black Bentley that pulled out and followed them.

CHAPTER TEN

The cab pulled up in front of the Smithson-Bentley lab where Peter worked. The drab four-story building looked plain, but functional. Long brown stains from constant rain marked its gray stone walls. To Amanda, the whole area looked bleak, devoid of trees or interesting architecture. Everything was modern and weather-beaten. Even the pedestrians hurried along with glum faces, their heads bent against the wind. She hadn't seen this part of London daily life before, and it felt depressing and gloomy.

While the cabby unloaded their suitcases, Michelle and Howard rushed into the foyer with Hillary in tow. Amanda joined them after the doorman took their bags. An elevator stood open inside.

"Dad's lab is on the third floor," Howard said, pressing a button in the lift.

"McWheeeee," Michelle squealed, her face lighting up with anticipation. "I'm going to see my daddy."

They stepped out of the elevator and approached a desk guarding the entrance to a long hall. Amanda smiled when the woman sitting there looked up from her work. She guessed her to be in her fifties, neatly dressed in a dark blue suit at least twenty years out of date. "You must be Winifred," Amanda said. "We've spoken over the phone. It's so nice to finally meet you, I'm Amanda Tregnier." She extended her hand. Winifred stood up and with reluctance offered a limp handshake, but no smile.

"This is my friend Hillary Windham, and Peter's children…" She paused. Michelle had dashed down the hall, jumping up to see through the glass that sealed off the research area. Howard stood next to her, searching the laboratory. Amanda turned back to Winifred and said, "I'm sorry. I guess they couldn't wait. They haven't seen their father in a while."

Winifred lowered her face and peered over her reading glasses. "Yes…quite, but you'll have to collect your children at once. This area is off-limits to the public." She sat down and picked up some papers.

Amanda cringed inside at the woman's cold dismissive tone. Embarrassed, she glanced down the long hall. "The children are not a security risk, they're just anxious to see their father."

Winifred looked sullen. "I'm afraid Dr. Tregnier is not here. Had you telephoned first I could have saved you the trip. We've booked you at the Kensington Hilton. Your husband will contact you there." Her eyes shifted to the papers on her desk as if the conversation was over. Hillary retrieved Howard and Michelle.

Amanda's brows bunched together. She wanted to shake the woman. "Peter told me to come here. What about his service flat? I thought we'd be staying there?" She searched Winifred's face for something positive, but the wretched woman's expression remained neutral.

"I don't know what your husband has told you, but we've rented that flat to a visiting scientist. And I don't know where Dr. Tregnier is this week. All I know is—"

Amanda interrupted. "When did he make this new arrangement?"

"He called this morning."

She frowned at the maddening woman. "What about my friend? We'll need another room…"

Winifred gave a brief glance. "I wasn't advised there would be more than you. It's a large hotel and off season—plenty of vacancies, I'm sure. I'll ring up a cab for you." She reached for the phone. "Good bye then."

Furious, Amanda turned and stalked to the elevator. She waited until they were all in the lift and then told Howard and Michelle about their father. She felt awful when their faces fell.

Michelle started to cry. Howard kicked the wall with his good leg. Amanda unclenched her fists to wrap her arms around Michelle. "What a rude, detestable woman," she said. "I have no explanation for any of this."

"We'll find out soon, I'm sure," Hillary said.

In a disheartened tone Amanda added, "Sorry, kids, but we're off to a hotel."

"I bet Dad doesn't even know we're coming," Howard said.

Amanda tried to lighten the mood. "Then it'll be our wonderful surprise."

"Or shock," Hillary whispered, nudging Amanda.

"I brought his favorite Halloween candy," Michelle whimpered, "I saved all my Reese's peanut butter cups for Daddy."

"And you'll always be his precious princess, sweetheart."

The urge to strangle Peter grew so strong Amanda had to stop thinking about him. She focused on the elevator. The warm interior and strong scent of furniture polish on the wood panels made it stuffy. When the doors opened on the ground floor she welcomed the cool lobby air.

Amanda's underarm prickled from heat and nervous exhaustion. Perspiration slid down her side. The notebook slipped and she shoved it back up. She had never felt worse.

Hillary perked up with a cheery tone. "Not to worry, Amanda. We'll get another room. I have to book something anyway. You can share with Peter and the kids can bunk with me." She turned to Howard and Michelle. "Okay pumpkins? Give your Mum and Dad some time to themselves?"

Howard and Michelle nodded with sad faces.

They waited for a cab and it started to rain. Amanda snapped open her umbrella just before the taxi arrived. They jumped in and sped away to the Kensington Hilton.

The hotel had plenty of rooms, but Peter hadn't checked in yet. Hillary booked a double room next to Amanda's. Before ascending to the tenth floor, Amanda bought a variety of Cadbury chocolates in the lobby shop, letting Howard and Michelle pick out what they wanted. Anxious to call Peter, she settled the children into their room and left them watching British telly.

She motioned Hillary to follow her into the hall for a talk in private. "Those poor kids, what a let-down. You doing okay, Mandy?" Hillary asked.

That was a childhood nickname in times of stress. Amanda shook her head. "I'm furious. I almost lost it at the lab. I couldn't stop thinking of ways to murder my husband."

"Totally understandable," Hillary said, patting her arm. "His absence is bloody-awful. But if and when you hear from him, we can make plans for the rest of the stay. Right now I'm going to have a short lie-down and then get some work done."

"Thanks, I'll call you as soon as I know anything."

Alone in her room, Amanda called Peter's cell phone. She got a 'not in service' message. Pacing, she stopped and pulled a few clothes out of her suitcase, tossing them on chairs. Unable to calm down, she drew a bath and poured an entire container of English Lavender bath salts into the water. She drifted into a half sleep until intuition alerted her. And right on cue the persistent double ring of the telephone jangled from the bedroom. She wrapped herself in a large towel, dripping bubbles on her way to the bedside phone.

"Peter?" she answered in a curt tone.

"Yes. Have a good flight?"

Again his voice sounded like a garbled echo in a wind chamber. "Where are you and why didn't you meet me? Winifred was rude, and you still sound terrible. And why is the connection so awful?" She tensed, rubbing her wet hair with the end of the towel.

A pause. "Did you bring my good luck piece?" he asked.

His tinny voice annoyed her and made him sound so far away. She plopped down on the bed and pushed aside the black book lying on the nightstand. "I want to know what's going on first!" She tore the paper off a chocolate bar with her teeth.

"I'll explain in a minute. Did you bring it?"

She chewed hard and swallowed. "Hold on, Peter. Why aren't you here?" He didn't even know she'd brought the children— or Hillary...

"First things first. Did you bring it?"

So angry, her throat tightened and she yelled, "Answer me, or I'm booking the next flight back. How can you do this, Peter? I've come all this way, and you still won't tell me anything. All you care about is your stupid project. Where are you?!"

"I can't tell you. This is critical. I'll send someone to pick it up. Once I have it, I'll tell you everything and then you can go home."

She stood up, clutching the bath towel around her. "Not on your life, Peter. I'm not falling for any more of your promises. I'm here to see you in person and we have important things to discuss. You don't get anything until we meet. You asked me to come here, remember?"

"Now darling, this is no time to argue," he said in a softened voice. "We'll take a trip as soon as some things are settled. It won't take more than a week—two at most, and then we'll go wherever you want."

"You've used the *soon* excuse too many times, Peter. Tell me where you are or I'm leaving."

"Amanda, for God's sake, this could be dangerous. Just do as I ask and then go home. If you don't know anything, you can't be hurt. Understand?"

"No I don't. If you're talking about Rotar, I've met him. Is he dangerous?"

His voice stiffened. "You met Rotar? What did he tell you?"

"Does it matter?"

Peter's breathing sounded like a wheezing foghorn. "Rotar's the one who's caused all this... Never mind. He can't protect you from harm if you don't stay out of it. Wait at the hotel and a messenger will identify himself by giving your middle name. Let him have my good luck piece only if he does that. Then go home and take care of the kids. I don't want anyone hurt."

Her anger escalated. She hated the name Danielle because her father had chosen it. "What man, Peter, and what harm? What on Earth are you involved in? And you know I never use my other name."

"It's just a security code…"

"Why codes? What's all this cloak and dagger stuff?"

"There's no time to explain," he said in an apologetic tone. "Please, Amanda, just do as I ask. The man's a foreigner. I only know him as Goldtooth."

Amanda raised both brows. "You're sending someone named Goldtooth?"

"It's just a nickname."

"You've met him?"

"No. Just do it!"

"Why?"

"This is crucial. Everything will turn out all right if you do as I say."

She sank back against the pillow. Her head buzzed. Were the children in danger? She didn't know what to believe. "I don't know if I can trust you anymore Peter. I want a real explanation."

"Of course, and you'll have one."

"Not later, now! And I hoped you'd found a cure for Howard's leg…"

"I'm still working on that. Sorry sweetheart, losing signal. Have to go."

The line went dead.

She pounded the phone receiver back in its cradle and glanced around the room. The large bed looked cold and lifeless. Above the oversized chairs hung a large painting of two angels shooting arrows at a romantic couple picnicking alongside a stream. The gold and cream décor made the room feel peaceful and elegant, at odds with the heightened stress that was choking her.

She rang the desk clerk and asked for the origin of the call, but he was unable to help. Fighting back tears, she fell back on the bed. Who was Goldtooth? What did the formulas in Peter's book mean? Why did he refuse to meet her? And that croaky voice—so bizarre.

She didn't trust Rotar either. Or his excuse that Peter was shielded by some *other dimension*. Rubbish! Peter was out there somewhere manipulating her with more of his ludicrous secrets. Yet it looked like she had the most important card in this crazy game, and she wasn't about to give it to anyone but Peter himself.

She longed to consult Hillary. Her friend would know what to do and always attacked a crisis head on. But if Peter's warnings were real, she couldn't risk involving Hillary or anyone else.

Come on Mandy, she chided herself. Where's your thinking cap? And just like that she got an idea. She'd go to Harrods, buy another black leather notebook and scribble in some fake formulas that looked real. A shopping trip to Knightsbridge would give her time to think things through.

She broke off another square of chocolate, scowled, and tossed it aside, dialing the room next door.

"Hello?" Hillary's voice sounded sleepy.

"Hil', Peter called and I'm going to meet him," Amanda said. A stretch of the truth but so what? "Order room service for the three of you and get an early night. I'll meet you at breakfast for an update."

"What's happening, Amanda?"

"No time to explain now, I'll catch you later. Are you good until tomorrow morning?"

"Of course, but…"

"Thanks, I owe you one."

She hung up before her friend could argue and hoped Hillary and the kids weren't in danger. How could they be if Peter didn't know they were in London? The rude secretary could care less and would most likely never mention them to anyone. That logic had a few flaws but most logic did when it came to people.

She finished dressing and put on the shell necklace. Their honeymoon shells had become a symbol of diversion and betrayal.

With the black book securely inserted in her leather boot, she filled a small purse with basics: wallet, passport, lipstick, Tic Tacs and cell phone. She left her large bag with the purple rock in her room. She didn't want any interruptions from Rotar or that weird two-tailed cat.

In the hall a stocky man with a black knit cap approached. She felt sorry for the hideous scar on his chin but his mean eyes made her reconsider.

A no-good thug.

She held her breath against the odor of stale cigarettes when he passed. The elevator doors opened. Before entering she glanced back at the man. Scarface hesitated in front of her room and turned enough to catch her staring at him. He continued around the corner at the end of the hall.

Goldtooth?

She shuddered, her head screaming to get away from the hotel fast.

CHAPTER ELEVEN

Tony sat in the decoy car he'd arranged for while waiting to clear customs at Heathrow. Rain streamed down the windows and splattered off the shiny black hood of the Bentley. He peered through the fogged-up windows, keeping his eyes fixed on the Kensington Hilton entrance while talking on the phone.

"I'm reasonably certain this anonymous tip is nothing but a hoax," he said to his superior in Washington DC. "Someone's demented idea of a wild goose chase. Amanda Tregnier is a housewife and mother and most likely knows nothing about the details of her husband's work."

"Stay on her," his boss ordered. "We got another tip. Someone insisting that the crazy scientist has developed a paranormal drug that can alter the human body in some way. And the tipster claims foreign entities are hot on his trail for the formula."

"You're telling me Tregnier's into some kind of biological warfare?" Tony asked.

"Affirmative. Something that could easily be dropped into a drink or mixed with food sabotaging anyone, anywhere, anytime."

Tony frowned. "Any clue as to the identity of the informant?"

"Negative. The call came from a disposable phone somewhere in Europe."

"That's a big area," Tony said. "Do you have any idea where Tregnier might be?"

"There's nothing solid at the moment."

Tony's mind flared, wondering how Dr. Tregnier could cause so much debate over something he had theoretically developed when nothing extraordinary had been revealed at his London lab…

"You still there?" his contact asked.

Tony cleared his throat. "I'm here, but this is disturbing news, if not outright unbelievable. I followed Amanda Tregnier to her husband's lab and then to the Kensington Hilton. As far as I can tell he hasn't met up with her yet. She's got her kids and a friend with her. Not a high security risk in my opinion. But I'll wait a bit longer and hope our elusive doctor shows up."

"Stay on the wife, Tony. She could lead us to this alleged terrorist."

"Terrorist?"

"If he's developing drugs that can alter human beings, he's a threat to mankind."

Tony frowned. "If you insist the information is that credible I'll need replacements to watch the hotel twenty-four seven…"

"You've got it. I'll arrange for a relief team."

"Thanks. Call me if you get a lead on Tregnier's location."

"Will do."

They cut the connection and Tony pondered the latest news. Paranormal activity? Sounded ludicrous but intriguing. Preposterous to think Peter Tregnier could be a danger to global security. Could he be wrong about Amanda Tregnier and her family? A good cover, if that was the plan. Either someone was trying to rattle the US government, or there really was something bizarre going on.

Tony glanced at his watch and decided to go to *The Phantom of the Opera* alone. He'd give the other ticket away. Hoping to catch a nap before the theater he tapped his fingers on the leather seat and waited for his relief to show up.

His plan changed when he spotted Amanda hurrying out of the hotel. The bellman blew a whistle and a cab pulled up.

She climbed in.

"Follow that car," Tony said to his driver.

Part of him worried that she was not who she pretended to be; the other hoped there was a mundane explanation for her trip out alone. "Stay close," he added as the driver wove through traffic,

passing Marble Arch and Buckingham Palace. Pedestrians struggled against the wind, a few making their way into pubs.

The chauffeur looked into the rear view mirror. "Almost missed
that traffic light, sir."

Tony frowned, his mind filled with questions. "Run the blasted
light if you have to! Don't lose that cab under any circumstance."

While they followed behind a red double-decker bus through the
busy streets, Amanda seethed, her nerves raw from Peter's usual
dodge and evade tactics. Her angry thoughts were interrupted
at the sight of a familiar pub. Pangs of nostalgia brought back
memories of her student trip to London years earlier when she
had joined other classmates for happy hour with the locals:

*Bodies jammed around wooden tables covered with beer mugs, the
low-ceiling caverns warm and stuffy from cigarette smoke. Everyone
and anyone could join in on discussions about politics and world
events, or the correct way to drink British ale—warm or cold?*

Amanda longed for the enrichment of those gatherings that
had piqued her interest in other places, especially England. Peter
never shared much other than his research goals and a firm belief
in the reincarnation of shells. He had odd ideas about where
dreams came from and a curious fascination for the moon, but
when she had something to contribute he would nod, tune out
and steer the conversation to the kids.

If she ever located him, she'd force him to take her on a vacation and let him meet the other wonders of life he was missing by
living his life in a test tube. She missed her student days and realized how little she and Peter had in common. She looked around
for other old haunts, but nothing showed up. Her ride came to an
end when she arrived at Knightsbridge.

The cab let her off at the west entrance to Harrods, its familiar pea-green and marigold-colored awnings flooding her with

memories. Crowds of shoppers jostled in and out. Determined, she shouldered her way inside. When the blast of warm air hit her in the foyer, she exhaled slowly, rejoicing in her freedom to wander the one million square feet of high-end shopping without Peter, her kids, or Hillary. She knew she would never get around to all three hundred departments in the world-famous store, but neither did she aspire to the challenge.

She wound her way through the maze of halls and found the stationery display. While looking at leather notebooks she detected a strong scent of Old English after shave close by. She spun around and discovered Tony right behind her.

"What a pleasant surprise," he said, beaming. "You're shopping, too?"

Amanda hesitated. His arrival in this melee of people at this particular time had to be more than chance. Her mother's advice came to mind: *Better to befriend the enemy and not antagonize him until you find out more.* "Yes," she said. "But you don't seem like the shopping type."

"I'm not. Just buying a gift for my daughter. And you?"

"I'm looking for gifts too, but how in the world did you see me in this herd of people?"

"Guess you stood out above the crowd," he said with a laugh.

She didn't share the humor. "I'm not *that* tall."

"No, but you are unique, and exceptionally beautiful. Have you found anything?"

"Not yet."

"Is your husband shopping with you?"

"He's been delayed."

"You're free this evening then? You could have some dinner and see the play… I still have that extra ticket I bought for my daughter."

Did Tony know about the black notebook or see what she was looking at? Doubtful. "Thanks but I don't think so. My husband might arrive at any time. But if his plans should change, I wouldn't mind going out on the town for dinner. What time will you eat?"

His smile was quick. "Six. And the play's at eight."

"Sorry, but the play is out of the question."

"Shall I have my driver pick you up somewhere?"

"No thanks, I'll take a cab. What restaurant?"

He grinned. "The Connaught. Their food is excellent."

"Then I'll either be there at six or leave a message."

He nodded. "I hope to see you. I really want to share my flash-back with you."

She didn't answer and pressed her way through the shoppers to put as much distance between herself and Tony as possible. Fretting, she needed a private place to call Wendy in DC, but first she had to ditch Tony. On the way to the escalator she passed a display of music boxes and decided to look at them later.

From the Food Halls on the lower level she looked up the escalator to see if Tony had followed. He was nowhere in sight. Elaborate presentations of fruit and vegetables caught her eye. In the meat and fish halls, the chilly air and strong smell of raw fish wafted from displays. She left the offensive stench and returned to the main floor.

She had two hours to kill and decided on a manicure. The directory listed a beauty salon and ladies lounge both on the fourth floor. At the lounge she scrolled to Wendy's number stored in her cell phone. She stopped pacing in front of a massive gilded mirror when her friend answered.

"Hello?"

"Wendy? Thank God you're home."

"Who's calling this early?" a sleepy voice asked.

"Amanda. Sorry, I'm in London."

"With Peter?"

"I'm meeting him here, but the reason I'm calling is to ask you if you know an Anthony Ramsey?"

"Tony? Of course, why?"

"I met him on the flight over. What do you know about him?"

Wendy chuckled. "You sound so serious, Amanda. He's a busy attorney and travels a lot. I teach his daughter piano at her boarding school. Her grandfather's the benefactor of my education. What's this about?"

"I was just checking. He's very friendly but I wondered how trust-worthy he is."

"There's nothing to worry about. He does some hush-hush work for the government but very low level. He calls it smoke in a barrel."

"What does that mean?"

"Darned if I know. I gather his daughter's a handful, but she's musically gifted so she and I get along fine."

"Well thanks for the background."

"No trouble. But Amanda, I'm jealous. I love London."

"Don't be. The weather's rainy and stormy."

"And here as well. We're getting tired of it. But I want to hear all about everything when you get back. When will that be?"

"A few days, I think. I'll call you. Thanks a lot, Wendy."

Now she had more mixed information about Tony. From Wendy's glowing report she could eliminate impassioned stalker or devious serial killer. But the government connection bothered her.

The beauty salon had so many employees that a female attendant whisked her into a chair right away. She selected a deep-red polish named *Furious*.

Less than an hour later she stood outside the salon and admired her nails. Glancing around she didn't see Tony. The crowd of busy shoppers forced her to snake her way from one shopping hall to another until she located the stationery department again. The salesman offered a high-grade soft leather black booklet he called a 'jotter'. About the right size, it lacked the conch shell embossed on the front but only Peter knew about that. She paid the exorbitant price and put it in her purse. She'd be 'jotting' all right, jumbling numbers and symbols and anything that looked like formulas. She glanced around but saw no familiar face or figure.

She had time to look at music boxes and wound up a heart-shaped silver box engraved with two roses. When it started to play *Love Story*, she slammed down the lid and moved to a plastic grand piano. After lifting the top, *My Way* tinkled from the keys. The song matched her mood exactly. She bought it for her collection.

She wanted a thank-you gift for Hillary. She'd already purchased several hats for her friend's collection but found a Robin Hood one. Perfect. Hillary was always championing the underdog.

Out of time and a little guilty over her extravagant afternoon, she planned to take the kids shopping and let them choose their own souvenirs.

Outside Harrods, rain from dark skies pelted the sidewalks. She opened her umbrella and waved for a cab. Cars sprayed her boots from puddles. The third cab that passed stopped. She watched everything on the way to the Connaught but in heavy traffic she couldn't tell if anyone was following. While looking for money to pay for the cab she stuck the new black jotter into her other boot. The original was still snug and dry.

Inside the hotel she spotted Tony at the far end of the lobby, talking on a phone with his back to her. She moved toward him in silence. "Sorry, can't talk now," she heard him say. "I'm not sure I agree, and I haven't found him yet, but I'll stay on it." He hung up.

She tapped him on the shoulder. He turned and smiled when he saw her. She stepped back, her thoughts churning while her nerves flared. She offered a reserved smile.

Was he spying on her because of Peter?

Could Tony have been the man in the gray car in DC?

Was Wendy completely clueless about this man?

CHAPTER TWELVE

"You look wonderful," Tony said. "I have a table waiting." His eyes drifted away. "There it goes again…"

Amanda caught his unfocused gaze. "What?"

"I keep hearing wind chimes."

Was he putting on an act? He knew about her musical interests. "You must have music on your mind."

"Yes, well, one can rationalize anything I suppose."

He led her to a small table in the cozy dining room. The understated elegance of the quiet décor matched the hushed sound of low conversation. Nervous, she glanced around at the guests.

"Is everything all right?" he asked.

"Yes," she fibbed, guarding her tongue and thinking of Peter's warnings.

His face flashed disapproval. "When will you meet up with your husband?"

"I'm waiting for word." She turned to the menu. "There aren't any prices. I'm not sure what to order."

He smiled. "Order whatever you like. Can I help?"

Did he mean the menu or her fib? "I'd rather just enjoy this welcomed break."

"But if you want to share anything, I'm a good listener."

She used that against him. "But you wanted to share your vision with me, didn't you?"

He straightened up on the chair. "Let's order first."

Suspicious, she wondered if he'd really had a flashback at all.

"Would you like roast grouse or seared ostrich breast or what I usually have? I'm a vegetarian and they prepare a special meal for me here."

She let the redirection of their conversation slide. "You come here often then?"

He nodded and motioned for the waiter.

"I don't know much about vegetarian food, but I'm game."

He ordered their dinners. When the waiter left she asked, "What brings you to London so often?"

"I have several clients here."

"What kind?"

He hesitated. "Mostly large international businesses— some government."

Her stomach churned. She tried to sound casual. "What branch of government?"

He laughed with a mischievous sparkle in his eyes. "I'm afraid that's too secret to share."

He was making fun of her. The wine steward arrived to fill their glasses. They toasted each other.

"To new friendship," Tony said, eyes glowing at her.

"To mysterious encounters," she said, smiling back at him.

They clinked glasses.

She sipped her wine and began to relax, grateful for a momentary escape from all the stress. The steward filled her glass again.

After their watercress soup the waiter returned with a side salad and the main course. She stared at her plate heaped with what looked like granulated mud pie covered with little red fish eggs. It had an odd smell. "What is this?"

"Planet steaks," Tony said. "Soy meal, tofu, eggplant, red pomegranate sauce and who knows what else. Try it, you might like it."

She continued to stare at the mound but pushed away the salad plate. "That's making me cry."

He looked surprised. "The dressing is loaded with fresh garlic, onions, ground ginger and sunflower seeds. It'll cure anything and cleanse your system."

She laughed and wiped her eyes. "If you want mine, go ahead. It's too strong for me."

She pulled a box of Tic Tacs from her purse. "You'll need these later if you eat that. You're one of the most sophisticated gentlemen I've ever met yet you advocate cleansing my system with garlic and onions in front of these elegant guests."

"Why not? Who needs to impress anyone? We can do whatever we want. My world is very complicated, but yours seems nice and simple. That's not so bad."

"My world is far from simple." She frowned at how her life had suddenly become a hectic maze of obscure events.

"I gather that has to do with your husband?"

"I'd rather talk about you. You haven't told me much about yourself."

"It's difficult."

He sounded just like Peter. "Why?"

"Client confidentiality among other things. But also my ex-wife. A power-obsessed woman who doesn't want me to have any social recognition in Washington. She sabotages me whenever she can, interfering with my career as well as my music world. Unfortunately she uses our daughter to get what she wants." He heaved a sigh. "I pick projects in Europe whenever I can."

He sipped some wine and searched her eyes. "You can see why I envy your life in the suburbs raising two children with your husband. You're lucky, Amanda, and a breath of fresh air for someone like me."

He caught her off guard. Was he trying to lower her defenses? "I can't imagine you envying me, but I'm sorry to hear that you have problems. I guess we all do."

At his silence and sad expression, she stabbed the planet steak with her fork and took a bite. Surprised she said, "This crazy dish of yours isn't half bad. In fact it's delicious…"

He perked up and beamed. "I've always enjoyed it, and the perfect finish to this meal is carrot cake and herb tea, if you have any room left."

"I like your planet steak, but for dessert I want something with chocolate. Lots of gooey fattening chocolate."

They finished their meal in silence. She still had no idea if she could trust him, and it was getting late. "If you're not going to share your vision, I have to get back to the hotel."

"We can talk in the car on the way to the theater…"

"Theater?" she asked in surprise.

He pulled out two tickets. "The Phantom."

She'd longed to see it for years and looked at her watch. Would she regret it later if she caved? "I'm sure Hillary and the children are fast asleep—I guess a few more hours out and around won't hurt anyone."

"Excellent. He got up from the table. "We'll have to leave now."

He signed for the meal and escorted her to his waiting Bentley. The car that picked him up at the airport was a Rolls. Did he have a stable of luxury cars at his disposal? They climbed in back and drove away. She tapped on the seat, waiting for him to begin.

He looked uncertain. "I wanted to tell you this ever since it happened but I wasn't sure if you wanted to hear it."

"Try me."

He cleared his throat. "I'd been listening to a concerto on the flight and got up to stretch my legs. When I first saw you, your beautiful face looked up at me and I couldn't help but stare. Your eyes had such a peaceful look and a memory stirred."

She shifted. "Go on."

"There were tropical forests all around me and exotic birds and a waterfall spraying fine mist into the air. You were running toward the waterfall, laughing and waving at me to join you. Your familiar face was someone I knew well. Musical chimes rang out and I realized the colors in the landscape were all wrong. Strange glittering shades and unearthly hues. Purple skies and the water a brilliant gold. It felt as real as a memory and seemed to go on forever."

She studied him with raised eyebrows. "The chimes could have been part of your concerto and the tropical paradise from a dream."

He shook his head. "I know when I'm dreaming, and it wasn't a dream. I know it sounds nuts, but it wasn't like any place I've ever seen. It was definitely another world."

"Because of the colors?"

"Yes and the plants were strange too. The forest in blues and pinks that vibrated. And the bright sky flashing green with purple clouds."

"You saw all that in a moment?"

"Yes. My thoughts seemed to be energized by something I recognized vividly, yet I knew I'd never experienced it before. So foreign, yet oddly familiar."

She considered the purple rock. Had he been standing too close to her purse and picked up its energy when walking by? But then why hadn't she experienced it? And what about all the others on board? Her smile had been automatic at the time, and she'd felt mildly attracted but nothing more. What was going on?

He continued. "What baffled me was that it felt like a flashback but not from my own memory." He lifted his eyes, perplexed. "It was more like it came from someone or somewhere else but through me."

No wonder he'd been hesitant about sharing. It sounded as crazy as her husband's stories—and Rotar's. "Your subconscious perhaps?"

He shrugged. "Possibly."

The car entered Piccadilly Circus and pulled up in front of the theater. Inside they sat in the orchestra section. The noise and rush of the growing audience distracted her while she gazed around the stunning old-world structure. The orchestra started playing and the lights went down.

She drifted into the mesmerizing music, the magnificent stage sets and elaborate costumes. At times she imagined herself in the orchestra pit playing her flute alongside the other musicians. Between scenes she wondered about Tony. Was he the hero or the phantom? She stole a brief glance. His face was fixed on the stage. He turned to look at her but she shifted her gaze back to the performance.

At the end of the play she and Tony both joined the boisterous standing ovation. She wanted to cling to the magic and remain in the theater, safe and warm, but followed the crowd outside. The wind blasted with a biting chill. "Thank you for an unforgettable evening. That was the best musical I've ever seen."

"I'm glad you liked it."

Guilt nagged her. What if Hillary and the kids needed her? Had Peter tried to contact her? She dreaded relinquishing the book to Goldtooth, but at least now she could hand over a fake one.

"Remember," Tony said, "I can treat you to the best sightseeing tour of London, tailored to your group. All you have to do is call."

She looked around for a cab. "Thanks. I'm not sure of our schedule, but if we can fit it in I'll let you know."

"You'll be here a few days, won't you?"

"I'm not sure of anything lately." She watched theater goers grab one cab after another. "It's late, and I'm tired. Thanks again, Tony. I need to get back."

"I sent the driver home for the night. I'll accompany you."

"No," she said. The curt answer surprised even her. "That won't be necessary."

"But I want to make sure you're safe."

"Thanks and I appreciate the concern, but I'll be fine on my own."

"I hope my family problems haven't upset you—or my strange experience…"

She scanned the street for a cab. "No, it was intriguing…"

He shrugged. "Maybe we're destined to meet again."

She didn't answer that.

He raised his hand to flag a cab and his cell phone rang. "Ramsey." He listened. "Elizabeth, are you all right? It's the middle of the night over here." Again he listened.

A cab stopped and Amanda climbed in.

Tony said, "Catch you later," to the phone and hung up. He leaned in the cab window. "I have a hysterical fifteen-year old arriving in the morning. If you let me take all of you to breakfast, I could use your help."

She smiled. "I know very little about teenagers, and I'm not sure where we'll be in the morning. I have my own team to take care of, Tony. You'll manage, I'm sure."

"Of course. But please call if you have time to meet my daughter. She's energetic and fun and a little unpredictable at times. That's when we call her *Dizzy Lizzy*."

Too tired to laugh, Amanda smiled. "She sounds like a kick. Tell her hi. Good-night, Tony."

"But I don't even know how to reach you," he said.

She waved him off and on the quiet ride back almost fell asleep. If she stayed in London would she find her elusive spouse and negotiate him home? Howard and Michelle needed a father and she could use a husband. Better stick to the plan. Switch books and try to reason with Peter.

The doorman at the hotel let her in. The tenth floor hall was empty.

Anxious to see if Peter had arrived, she hurried to unlock the door. The key jammed. She tried again.

Stuck.

She knocked and pushed at the door.

It opened with a sudden jerk and a large man with dark foreboding eyes stared at her from the half-lit room.

CHAPTER THIRTEEN

Through the open door Amanda saw her suitcases upside down on the floor among scattered heaps of bedding and clothes. Swallowing a gulp, her eyes questioned the stranger holding a camera.

"Who are you?" she blurted. "What's happened? It looks like a storm invaded my room…"

"Hotel security, Kenneth Michaels." His words came out from under a trimmed mustache. "Are you Amanda Tregnier?" The man's Adam's apple pushed his bow tie up and down when he spoke.

"Yes," she said, letting out the breath she'd been holding. "I have to check on my kids next door." She turned to leave but he held up his hand.

"The maid discovered the break-in on her evening stop and we saw that you had two rooms. We checked on your children and they were fast asleep."

"Thank you but I still need to see them."

He nodded and unlocked the door to their room. Hillary blinked awake but Amanda put a finger to her lips. "It's okay, Hil'," she whispered. "Just checking—go back to sleep."

Hillary nodded and closed her eyes. The tension in Amanda's shoulders relaxed. The sleeping lumps on the bed didn't move. Back in her room she asked, "Who did this?"

"That's what we'd like to know. The room on the other side of you is vacant and no one else reported anything. Has Dr. Tregnier arrived yet?"

"My husband's been delayed," she said, cringing inside at the suspicion in his eyes. "Why would someone do this? I don't have anything valuable."

His eyes narrowed. "The intruder got in with a hotel key. Did you give yours to anyone?"

"Of course not!" Her eyes raked the scene and she picked up her large bag. Empty. Its contents lay scattered across the carpet but she didn't see Rotar's rock.

Security man cleared his throat. "Have you any idea who might have done this?"

She suspected Goldtooth but had no choice but to lie. "No. I don't know anyone here and I have nothing anyone would want."

"They certainly made a mess," he said surveying the room. He turned accusing eyes on her. "What's the purpose of your visit to London?"

Her stomach clenched. "I'm meeting my husband. Were any other rooms broken into?"

"No. My staff checked all the floors. What does your husband do, may I ask?"

She realized he wasn't giving up his interrogation. She pushed clothes off the nearest chair and sank into it. "He's a scientist and works for the Smithson-Bentley Lab."

"I certainly hope he's all right." He took more pictures. "The police dusted for prints earlier, but separating new prints from those of previous guests is not an easy task. They'll want a report from you tomorrow—if you're missing any personal effects…" He went over to check the door. "We've re-keyed the locks and prepared another room for you. Does your husband have any enemies?"

She shook her head. Peter may have been behind the break-in and used Goldtooth. *"Dammit Peter,"* she mumbled.

"What's that?"

"My husband should have been here."

"You don't think he had anything to do with this, do you?"

She bridled at the absurdity of the question. "Absolutely not."

He snapped one last photo and bowed. "I meant no disrespect. Questions have to be asked. The general manager advised me to tell you that your stay is complimentary. We pride ourselves on the safety of our guests. And we're very grateful that you're not hurt."

"Thank you. So am I, but I'm extremely tired."

"Your new room is just down the hall. This will be tidied up tomorrow."

She stood and shook her head. "I'll stay here tonight. I want to be near my children and inventory my things."

He frowned. "Wouldn't another room be more suitable?"

Peter could call or Goldtooth could show up…

His discomfort was obvious. "You're the guest," he said, "but I must add…"

"If it bothers you, I'll sign a waiver of liability," she hurried to say.

"That won't be necessary." He pulled out his cell phone. "I'll have security remain outside your door for the night."

"Fine."

After the call he pulled a slim leather wallet from his breast pocket. "Here's my card and telephone extension. There will be a report for you to sign in the morning. List anything missing and let us know if you think of anything or anyone connected to this."

"Of course."

It was unlikely anything would be missing. She hoped the purple rock was still in the room somewhere.

He gave her a new door key. "Please latch the chain from the inside so no one can enter. You're sure you'll be all right, Madam?"

She nodded. "I'm sure."

She saw the doubt in his eyes as he handed her a second key. "In case you change your mind about the other room it will be available for twenty-four hours."

After he closed the door behind him there was a sharp rap. "Put the chain on now, Madam. If you need anything, security is right outside."

"Thank you."

She latched it and pulled the thin leather book out of her boot. Then the blank one.

She glanced under the bed. No rock. She lifted some of the clothes and bedding and shook them gently. Nothing. She whispered, "Dot Comet?"

No response.

"Rotar?"

Nothing from him either.

She slumped down on a chair and realized she couldn't go anywhere until Peter called again. And she had to write fake notes in the decoy for Goldtooth, if and when he showed up.

She bit off the end of a Cadbury chocolate. Other than Tony she knew no one in London. Winifred didn't count. He should be back at his hotel by now. She dialed his number and heard a mumbled hello. "Tony, it's Amanda. Sorry to bother you so late but you're the only person I could call."

"'s all right." He sounded sleepy.

"My room's been vandalized. Everything's a jumbled mess."

"What?" he interrupted, sounding more alert. "Are your kids okay? Have you called the police?"

"They're fine," she hurried to say. "Asleep next door with Hillary. Since no one's been harmed the hotel will report the damage to the police tomorrow."

"Is anything missing?"

"I don't know—it's such a mess." She told him about the hotel security man but didn't mention the missing purple rock.

"I can be there in twenty minutes," he said.

She rubbed her scalp, her eyes burning from lack of sleep. "No thanks. Tomorrow's soon enough. I'm too exhausted to sort through it tonight. It could be my fault anyway. I was supposed to stay here and wait for a call from my husband. Now I don't know what to do."

A brief pause on the line. "I take it he hasn't contacted you?"

"No, and I don't know where he is."

"Was the intruder looking for something?"

"I'm not sure."

"Amanda, I'll pick my daughter up at the airport and come over in the morning. But be careful. Don't open your door to any stranger. Are you sure you'll be all right tonight?"

"I'm locked in at the Kensington Hilton, room 1014. Hotel security is outside my door."

"Good. Stay put and keep the door locked. And please don't start cleaning or clearing things until I get there. As a lawyer I'm trained to examine things. There might be evidence that's not obvious. Let me help you."

She agreed and they exchanged good nights.

Unable to keep her eyes open, she undressed and straightened out the sheets and blankets on the bed. When she snuggled under the covers her mind swirled with dizzying thoughts. The intruder wanted the notebook, so there wouldn't be much evidence for Tony to find. But because Peter had sent a messenger instead of meeting her, Tony was her only ally. Did Rotar zapp himself into her room and take the rock? It couldn't have been Peter, he didn't even know about the purple rock.

She fell into a fitful sleep, waking up tired and achy. At eight o'clock she opened the latched door. A man dressed in a security uniform sat on a chair outside. "Morning sir," she said through the crack. "I'm up and okay. Will they allow you to leave now?"

He stood and gave a slight bow. "Sleep okay, Ma'am?"

"Yes thanks."

"Very good. Not a stir of a mouse all night," he said.

"Thank goodness for that."

She watched him leave and called Hillary's room.

"Morning, Hil'. Everyone sleep okay?"

"A bit groggy. We were just coming over to collect you for breakfast."

"I'm not ready, but I'll shower and meet you in the dining room. Tony and his daughter will be joining us."

"His daughter showed up after all?"

"She's arriving this morning."

"What about Peter?"

"He won't be coming. I'll update you."

"I won't bother to ask why…"

Amanda's voice tightened. "Don't go sarcastic on me."

"Sorry lovey, jet lag's got me. Don't know about you but I'm not sure if I'm on Paris time, DC time, London time or somewhere in mid-Atlantic."

"I'm off my clock too. Would you order me breakfast?"

"Sure. You want the British special: poached eggs on toasted English muffins, O.J. and coffee?"

"Perfect." She heard her kids laughing in the background before Hillary hung up. It cheered her.

Amanda glanced around at the disheveled room, wondering how she was going to explain Peter's absence. She would think of something and pretend everything was okay.

After showering, she wore slacks, sweater and knee-high boots, slipping a black notebook into each one. She'd work on writing something in the decoy after breakfast. Her night gown still lay on the bathroom floor. About to leave, there was a loud knock on the door.

"Tony, is that you?"

No reply.

She moved closer and called, "Who's there?"

A man's muffled voice mumbled, "I luuk for Danielle."

Her middle name—Peter's code. The accent sounded Russian. Goldtooth? Her chest constricted. She needed more time to fake the other book. "I don't have it here, come back later."

He knocked louder.

She left the chain latched and opened the door a crack. The same scar-faced man she'd seen the day before grinned at her exposing a gold front tooth. "I'm sorry," she said, "but I don't…"

The man snapped the chain and burst into the room.

She jerked back, screaming.

He pushed her aside and shut the door. She caught her balance and staggered back. His hard eyes glared into hers and a strong stench of perspiration and alcohol fanned off him.

"Geeve meee yuur husband's seeekrit buuk!"

She leaped across the mess to the bathroom.

He charged after her.

Inside she tried to slam the door but his foot kept it from closing. Backed against the sink she braced her feet against the door, but he forced it open.

He grunted and gripped her throat with big hands, jamming her backwards.

Unable to scream, her hands scrabbled behind her for a weapon.

His breath stank of cigarettes. She swung a fist to punch his face but he ducked his head and laughed. She groped the sink with her other hand. A toothpaste tube and jars fell off the counter until her fingers clutched the can of hairspray. She swung and sprayed into his eyes.

He roared like a wild animal, his face whipping from side to side. He let her go to wipe at his eyes. While he fumbled for the faucet, she dropped down beyond reach and scuttled out of the bathroom.

Halfway to the door she tripped on tangled bedding and landed hard on her shoulder. She got up and tried to run but her ankle caved and she fell again. Her arm throbbed with pain.

Goldtooth stumbled out and blinked, dripping water and moaning like a drunkard. She hobbled toward the door.

He yanked a small container from his pocket but didn't notice the purple rock fall out at the same time. His canister looked like pepper spray. She grabbed her long umbrella off a chair and backed away, pointing its sharp tip at him.

He lunged and aimed the can at her face.

She pressed the umbrella release button an instant before he sprayed.

It sprang open blocking the mist.

He sneezed and wheezed, snorting from his own pepper spray.

She kicked the purple rock under the bed shrieking, "Heeellllllpp…"

Was no one around to hear?

His momentary distraction gave her the advantage. She shoved the umbrella tip as hard as she could at his eye. He went rigid, bellowing like a wounded animal before falling down to roll on his knees. Blood ran down his cheek.

Amanda cried out, "Rotar help me—where are you Dot Comet? Here kitty kitty…"

The two-tailed cat sprang from under the bed in a purple shimmer and hissed at Goldtooth, its fur sticking straight out.

He froze, moaning and holding his hand over one bloody eye socket. His other eye stared fright at the cat.

It pounced.

He raised one arm to back-hand it and missed. The cat hissed and clawed his leg, but its paws went right through his pants. His good eye bulged out in terror. He tried to shake off the cat but it held tight like a floating mirage. Dot Comet sneezed, spraying purple crystalized darts into Goldtooth's pants. He screamed again, trying to crawl away from it.

At a loud banging on the door, Amanda turned. She had to hide the cat. Her eyes swept the room but Dot Comet had vanished along with the chocolate from the nightstand.

Goldtooth held his eye and rushed to the door, yanking it open so fast it bashed back against the wall. He charged at Tony, knocking him onto the floor, then ran down the hall.

Tony yelled, "Stop or I'll shoot." But as he tried to get up the gun got caught in his raincoat pocket. He freed it just as Goldtooth barreled through the fire door and disappeared.

Amanda came out of the room, pointing her umbrella. Tony waved his gun. "Anyone else in there?"

She stared wild-eyed at him. "That brute attacked me!"

"Are you okay?"

She nodded.

"Where are your kids?"

"Eating breakfast downstairs." She held up the umbrella. "I got his eye with the point."

"Good. Did you see any accomplices? Let's call the police."

"Why are you carrying a gun?" Amanda asked.

The elevator doors opened with a loud 'pling'. They both turned to look. A skinny teenage girl with straight blonde hair stepped out and looked from one to the other. "I got bored waiting in the car." She pointed at Tony's revolver. "Creepy vibes Dad, what's going on?"

CHAPTER FOURTEEN

The pepper spray in Amanda's room had settled and the air was breathable again. At the questioning faces on both father and daughter, she chose not to comment. "The others are waiting for me downstairs," she said. "I'll call Hillary and let her know I'm not coming."

Tony shook his head at the mess while his daughter wandered the room without touching anything.

Amanda briefly explained to Hillary what happened. Before hanging up she said, "Don't say anything to the kids." Then she crossed her arms and glared at Tony. "You carry a gun?"

"Yes. For protection."

"From what?"

He rubbed his neck. "It's merely a precaution. My occupation has made me some enemies."

"We're in danger?" his daughter asked him.

"Of course not." He turned to Amanda. "This is my daughter Elizabeth. Or Lizzy."

"Nice to meet you. I'm Amanda."

"Dupes," Lizzy said.

"I beg your pardon?"

"Short for duplicate as in back-'atcha."

"Oh." The latest slang? Howard hadn't picked it up yet.

Tony made one slow circle of the room before letting Amanda gather some of her things. "We need to call the police," he said.

Before she could answer, Hillary and the children arrived. Her friend stared in shock at the room. "Good God—this is what I call a bang-up job…" She sniffed the air. "Pepper spray?"

Howard and Michelle looked stunned. "McCreepers," Howard said.

Amanda nodded toward Lizzy, glad for a distraction. "This is Tony's daughter, Lizzy. She just flew in." She turned to Lizzy. "Meet my son Howard, my daughter Michelle, and my best friend Hillary."

"Hi," Lizzy said. She smiled only a little to keep her braces covered.

Michelle said, "I'm six and three-quarters and Howard's twelve."

"And a half," he mumbled.

"How old are you?" Michelle asked.

"Almost grown up," Lizzy answered. "Fifteen."

Hillary pulled Amanda aside and whispered, "I guess I shouldn't ask where Peter is, or why Tony and his daughter are here, or what happened?"

"Not in front of the kids," Amanda whispered back.

They rejoined the group and Amanda asked Hillary, "Would you mind taking the others out on a city tour while Tony and I take care of this?"

Hillary put her arms around Howard and Michelle. "Whatever the blazes is going on, we most certainly want to go out and do something fun, right kids?"

"Yessssss," Michelle shouted.

Howard grinned.

Amanda asked Lizzy, "Would you like to join them for a jaunt out and about London-town?" She looked at Tony. "If that's all right?"

He nodded. "It's her choice."

Lizzy pulled herself out of the chair. "I came over for a break from the tedious boredom of dealing with those less astute than myself." She glanced at her father. "Like *Mother* who's behaving like a child. A tour sounds cool. I'm in for creepy sure."

"I'm not quite sure about the meaning of all that," Tony said. "And remember that after the tour you'll be going home again."

"Not when you hear about *Mother dearest*, you won't send me back."

He looked annoyed. "This is not the time or place to discuss your mother."

"Will there be time to shop?" Lizzy asked Hillary.

"If we get going right away."

"Have a good time," Amanda said, hugging her kids. "Aunt Hillary has your spending money." She wouldn't worry about them because Peter and Goldtooth didn't know they were in London.

"Cheerio then," Hillary chirped over her shoulder, herding the kids out the door.

While Tony checked the hall and fire door, Amanda scooped up the purple rock from under the bed's dust ruffle and dropped it into her purse.

"Where are the police?" he asked her when he returned.

"I didn't call them. I'd rather wait and kill my husband myself. I'll just need a referral to a good criminal attorney."

"I understand, but that man could have killed you."

"I know but he didn't, so no police."

"What do you have in mind then?"

"Since my husband has left me no choice, I need your help."

"If I can…"

She anguished over her decision but now that Peter had sent someone who tried to kill her, turn around was fair play. And she could always take the book back to DC if Peter never showed up. She pulled the black book from her left boot and sank down on the lumpy bed.

Tony pointed at it. "Is that what the intruder was after?"

"It makes no sense," she muttered. "Peter told me to give the book to a guy named Goldtooth who would know me by my middle name. Then he showed up and broke through the door. What's so valuable that someone would attack me for it?"

He approached to look. "What's in it?"

She flipped through the pages. "These formulas and all the secrecy. I don't understand?"

"Did your husband tell you why he couldn't fetch the book himself?"

"He said he wasn't in London, and his voice sounded garbled and echoed."

"Let me see that," he said, holding out his hand.

She pulled it toward her chest. Peter had betrayed her, but could she really sell him out? "It belongs to my husband."

"You've got to trust someone, Amanda. Either me or the police."

"I can't involve the authorities. Not yet. Goldtooth won't dare come back now. He knows I have reinforcements." She told him about Peter's phone calls and mysterious warnings. She said nothing about Rotar, the purple rock or the two-tailed cat. He wouldn't believe any of that. If Tony turned out to be a fraud, she could use the rock to wish forth a bigger cat. Perhaps even a three-tailed tiger…

Her mood brightened.

She moved to the window and he followed. Reluctant, she let him study the formulas with her.

"I have no idea what these notations mean," Tony said. "We need to locate a physicist."

"Not yet. Peter might call, and I can force him to meet me so long as I have this." She flipped to the last page and saw a row of numbers. "What do you think these are?"

He took the book from her. "A phone number? Let's try it." He started dialing, but shook his head, pointing the phone toward her.

It made strange buzzing tones.

Tony asked, "Perhaps a different country code? If this is a number, where do you think it is? It's not in England or the US."

"Switzerland? Peter's family came from there. Near Geneva, that's all I know." She should have asked Rotar for the location.

Tony asked the hotel operator for the Swiss country code. He dialed the new number and handed the phone to Amanda.

A woman's voice answered in French. *"Allo."*

"Doctor Peter Tregnier, *il est la?"* Amanda said in a bad French accent asking if he was there.

"Il n'est pas ici," an abrupt voice said. Amanda didn't like hearing that he wasn't there.

"Ne quittez pas, s'il vous plait!" Amanda said, asking her not to hang up, but the line went dead.

"She said he's not there and hung up on me." Her mind went into over-drive. "But that means she knows him. I should have paid more attention to Peter's work when he was home. He told me he collaborated with someone, but our time together was so short and the children always came first. Could his colleague be a woman?"

"Possibly, or a landlady. Let's brainstorm. Someone must know where the laboratory is in Switzerland. When we discover that we can go there."

Amanda wasn't pleased. "The information will be at home in his files, but that's no good. And I can't just fly off to Switzerland— it's too expensive. But Winifred at the London lab has to know how to reach the employees. We can go to her office." She looked down at the floor. "I just wish he'd call first."

"Did you try his cell phone?"

She nodded. "Not in service."

"Don't worry about money. I'd be happy to loan you what you need—interest free."

She didn't like that idea at all.

"And I can see your wheels turning," he continued. "But it's not what you think. No strings attached. If we get an address, I could accompany you. A break in my usual tedious routine would be nice. But that's entirely your decision and doesn't affect the offer."

She didn't want to put herself in debt, but now that she'd entrusted him with the mysterious book could she move forward with him? He had baggage from an ex-wife and a teenage daughter, yet with Lizzy's arrival Amanda felt a little safer. She considered the limits on her credit card and could probably borrow from Hillary, if necessary.

"I can't accept financial help, Tony, not even an interest-free loan."

"Are you sure? There's no pay-back deadline either."

"That's very generous, but I'm sure." She would ask Hillary later. She lifted her head in anticipation of a phone call.

The phone rang. Peter at last.

"Hello," she snapped.

"Amanda…" Peter's voice surged through the line like a bubbling hot tub. "Did…messenger…find you?"

"Ohhhhhh yessssssss." She spoke low, allowing her anger to surface. "Where are you?!"

The line crackled and cleared. "Did you give it to him?" His breathing sounded heavy in constricted gasps.

She gritted her teeth. "How could you send a thug like that? He attacked me!"

"What? There was no reason for that, but I did warn you to be careful."

"How dare you Peter. You didn't even ask if I'm okay!"

"I didn't know he would try to hurt you, but you sound fine."

"What do you care? And where are you? I want to see you right now!"

"Impossible. I have an intermediary. I'll send him back."

"Don't you dare or I'll call the police. He could have killed me. Have you gone insane? I want an explanation immediately."

He cut the line.

She slammed the receiver into the cradle and threw back her head, closing her eyes hard. "He wouldn't tell me where he is and his voice sounds like he's in outer space. How will I ever find him?"

"You will, but not by insulting him. Someone has to know where he is."

Amanda snapped her fingers. "Winifred."

"Time to get some answers," Tony said, heading for the door.

"But what about this mess? I'm supposed to sign a report downstairs…"

"Let the manager know you'll take care of that later. Hang up the *do not disturb* sign and let's get going."

"Right." She grabbed her things.

Waiting for the elevator Tony said, "I can probably get an address for that phone number."

"How?"

"I have a connection in Geneva."

"Who?"

"It's confidential."

Was that good or bad? Her worry meter escalated. He was clever at getting to her one way or another. She could handle that so long as it wasn't financial.

They rode to the London lab in Tony's chauffeured Bentley. The building looked as drab and weather-beaten as the day before, the wind whipping leaves and dust through the streets.

In the third floor office they stared at a dour Winifred. She wore the same suit from the previous day. Amanda introduced Tony as her lawyer. Winifred remained reserved with no sign of the usual British cordiality.

"I shouldn't have to ask you twice for the address of my husband's lab in Switzerland," Amanda stated in an about-to-boil-over tone. "I have good reason to believe he could be in danger."

Winifred shook her head. "Mrs. Tregnier, I am of course sympathetic to your concerns, but our firm cannot get involved. I have no authority to give you his location. Dr. Tregnier's work is highly confidential."

Tony stepped forward. "Excuse me but how long have you worked here?"

She cold-stared him. "I don't see how that's any of your business."

"I assume that you have seniority and more or less manage the place, right?"

At her nod he continued. "If a scientist is in trouble, wouldn't it be your job to avoid problems and publicity? What if reporters started digging into your company's affairs? Confidential work might be compromised. A missing scientist whose family is searching for him might be a big headline in the news."

Her eyes widened and then narrowed. Without a word she pulled out her rolodex and wrote down an address. "It's a small lab in Coppet near Geneva. He collaborates with another scientist, but you must assure me complete discretion."

"Of course." Tony cold-stared her back, took the information without thanking her, and they left.

Seated in the back of the car Amanda said, "Thanks. I was ready to shove her out of the way and grab her rolodex."

Tony smiled. "I know."

"And now that I know where he works maybe I don't need to look for relatives."

"Unless he isn't there. And you still don't know where he lives."

"I would assume at the lab. We don't have a big budget."

"You probably won't believe this but I happen to have some work to do in Geneva the day after tomorrow. I could fly there a day early if you want to ride along. There's a private jet for my use."

Wow, he really was in a different league. "That's quite a coincidence Tony but I'm considering taking the kids home."

"You want to cut and run, now that we found a trail?"

"I can't leave my kids here."

"Who said anything about that? There's plenty of room for them and Lizzy too. I might regret taking her—my ex blames me for everything connected with our daughter, but Lizzy deserves a break.

"Is the woman that awful?"

"Worse. It's one battle after another all the time. He glanced at his watch. "Not that I don't want to change the subject but we'd better hurry. How about a quick meal before I drop you off at the hotel?"

"Good idea. I missed breakfast and I'm famished. Are you thinking what I'm thinking? A pub lunch? Steak and kidney pie or bangers and mash?"

"Pub it is," he said. "They'll have something vegetarian—maybe a tasty Welsh rarebit. Then I've got work to do, but I can be back by six. We can all have a relaxing supper together."

"That sounds fun Tony, but I insist on paying for our share."

"I understand—I'll keep a running tab."

They enjoyed a hearty pub meal and afterwards Amanda went back in her room. She raised her nose at the lingering odors of pepper spray, alcohol and sweat. But there was no message light on the phone. She fumed—Peter hadn't bothered to call her back and now she was making travel plans with someone who could be as nefarious as her husband.

CHAPTER FIFTEEN

Tony returned to his hotel room encouraged by the turn of events. The black book Amanda was delivering to her elusive husband confirmed that something unusual was indeed going on. But her stand-offish attitude bothered him. Somehow he had to gain her trust. He wasn't used to being put off by a woman. Was he getting old? Was she that attached to her husband or just play-acting the innocent wife? He'd better find out.

He stared out the window and shuddered at the storm that forced pedestrians to scurry in erratic directions in search of shelter. Cars blasted their horns to get through the congestion. He would have to contact Leo Braun, the American attaché in Geneva. The man was not to be trusted and had only obtained his coveted position because of his influential late uncle, Deiter Braun, but he knew more contacts than anyone else and could be helpful.

Tony picked up the phone and dialed.

Braun answered with a clipped grunt.

"Leo, Tony Ramsey here. How's it going in Switzerland? Heard you've had some stormy weather."

"How the heck are 'ya, Tony? It's frickin' chilly over here. Just lookin' outside makes me shiver. But you're not callin' about the weather…"

Tony gave an inward sigh. "You're right—I need a favor."

"Yeah? Like what?"

"An address. All I have is the phone number. It's probably in Geneva somewhere. Can you get it for me?"

"Of course. Where're you at now?"

"London. But I'm flying to Geneva tomorrow."

"You're comin' here? You know 'bout this freaky incident, too? Jeeezzzzusssss, ya' can't trust anybody."

Tony snapped into high alert. Did Braun know about the anonymous tips? Typical—the field agents didn't know each other's information. In order to learn more he had to lie. "Affirmative. I've been sent to check it out."

"Bloody hell," Braun complained. "I thought this was top secret. It's my territory..."

"I have the same clearance as you, Leo. Want to pool anything of significance?"

"I've already investigated and there's nothing to tell."

"You must have something to report..."

"Sorry to disappoint, but there's no space freak."

Space freak? Was Leo losing it? "I've been assigned to follow-up on this, so tell me everything."

"You're pushin', Tony."

"Hey, unless you want the big guys involved, you better fill me in."

"Pesky politicians," he grunted. "If there really *is* an alien lurkin' around the Swiss countryside, it's my catch. Could be just some nut on drugs. A farmer thinks he saw an aberration of the Virgin Mary. But if there really is somethin' out there, we gotta' keep this *alleged ghost* under wraps and maintain a low profile, understand?"

"Right. I'm coming tomorrow with our without your cooperation, Leo, and I need that address."

"Guess I can't stop you, Tony—I'll have it when you get here."

Tony gave him the number and hung up. Now he had another reason to get to Geneva. What did Amanda say? *My husband sounds like he's on another planet.* Could Dr. Tregnier be the alien sighting Braun referred to? If some unidentified creature was lurking around Switzerland, it wouldn't remain a secret for long.

Amanda had just finished packing when Hillary returned with the children. Howard and Michelle bubbled about their adventure at the Tower of London, adding their own ghostlike sounds to the story. Hillary was disappointed that the Millennium Wheel had been closed due to bad weather, but it had given them more time to shop. Lizzy declared the trip to Harrods their best stop of the day. At a knock on the door, she bounced across the room to let her father in.

"Have a good day?" Tony asked her.

"Yes, Dad." She twirled in a black raincoat. "Like my new Abercrombie and Fitch designer coat?" He smiled and did a thumbs-up. "I got a T-shirt and sexy pants, too." She opened the coat to reveal vibrant colors of metallic paint splashed on a white top over skin-tight black leggings. A copper-colored bag studded with metallic pyramids dangled from her shoulder.

"The latest teenage fashion?" Tony turned to Michelle and Howard. "I take it everyone had a good time?"

They all nodded with enthusiasm.

Michelle pointed to the plaid tam on her head. "Aunt Hillary gave me this to match my plaid coat and a Harrods' teddy bear." She lifted the bear and swung it back and forth in the air. It had Harrods stitched under one foot and wore a plaid vest that matched the hat.

"She's into plaid at the moment," Amanda said. "Her grandmother wore it a lot."

"And I got a wind-up knight," Howard said. He lifted it by its metal helmet out of the shopping bag and wound it up. Soul-crushing sounds came from its gaping mouth while blood-shot eyes rolled around in their sockets.

Amanda contorted her face. "That'll give you 'knightmares' with a 'K', Howard, and give me a headache."

He turned it off. "You just don't appreciate technology, Mom."

"Not that kind."

"I have an announcement," Tony said. "Amanda and I have decided to pool our resources and fly to Geneva tomorrow morning."

Hillary looked shocked. "What on earth for? And what about my little duckies here?"

Eyes teasing, Tony rubbed his chin. "We're *considering* taking them along."

"What about me?" Lizzy demanded.

Before Tony could answer his daughter, Amanda said, "It's okay, Hil', they're coming with us. But after your interview give me a ring. If we're delayed in Geneva I might need you to fly over and pick them up. Could you take them back to DC with you for a few days?"

Hillary shook her head. "Can't—I just got my *big* break, and I've been waiting a long time for this one. Off to Rome day after tomorrow. Biggest scoop of my career."

Amanda's eyes widened. "The Pope?—you're finally interviewing the Pope?"

"Received the call today. Archbishop tomorrow and then on to the Vatican."

"Oh my heavenly angels, congratulations, Hil'." She hugged her friend. "I'm so happy for you."

Amanda told Tony, "My kids brought homework and that'll keep them busy."

Lizzy said, "I can help."

"No, you're going back to school," Tony said.

"Geeeez, Dad. I brought my laptop and arranged with my teachers to send assignments in on the internet. Besides, I'm safer here with you. Mother was going to kidnap me and entrap you."

"I beg your pardon? How can she do that if she already has custody of you?"

"I overheard her plotting with her boyfriend. They were going to take me out of school and keep me home until you came up with…" she hesitated, her eyes shifty and nervous.

"Came up with what?" Tony pressed.

"Mother wants a favor," she stammered.

Amanda caught the warning look on Tony's face. "We'll discuss this later," he said.

Lizzy pouted and sank back into the chair.

He turned to Amanda. "As soon as I get to the bottom of this, Elizabeth will be going home. It's not the high drama it sounds like."

High drama or not, Amanda wanted Lizzy's help with the kids. "If she joins us it might only be for a day or two at the most."

"Yes!" Lizzy jumped up again. "You need a sitter anyway."

"*I* don't need a sitter," Howard made clear.

"Me neither," Michelle echoed.

"Then I can help them with homework," Lizzie added, nodding vigorously. "I'm the best volunteer tutor at school. Especially in math."

"We'll work this out later," Tony said in a grim voice.

They dined at the hotel and then Hillary took Howard and Michelle back to their room to pack while Amanda stopped at reception to sign the hotel reports. When Amanda returned to her room she wrote altered formulas from Peter's notebook into the new fake one. She felt good about her deception and ready to feign reluctance in turning over the counterfeit jotter to a messenger. But no one showed up to claim it, and Peter didn't call.

The next morning Tony and Lizzy returned to join everyone for breakfast. He'd decided to bring Elizabeth along. Amanda gave Hillary the Robin Hood hat from Harrods and then in private shared her concern about the limits on her credit card. Hillary came through with a promise of a loan, if and when necessary. Amanda knew she might meet up with Peter soon and hoped that the extra resources wouldn't be needed. When everyone and everything was loaded into Tony's car, they waved goodbye to Hillary through the windows.

His driver dropped them off at the executive airport. Amanda was stunned by the large custom jet at their disposal. It had the best in V.I.P. travel: spacious seating for six, a bar and a small computer station. The flight attendant looked like a cover-girl model and served them champagne, vegetarian canapés and bubbling apple cider for the kids.

"Nervous?" Tony asked her while they nibbled and drank in their oversized swivel seats.

"Yes."

"What happens when we find your husband?"

"You don't want to know and neither does he," she said, determined to change the subject. Her marital problems were none of his business, and she didn't want to talk about them. She reached into her handbag and pulled out a chocolate bar, the rock glowing inside. Out the porthole flashes of lightning dissected dark clouds. "It's getting bumpy. I hate it when these storms throw the aircraft around." She glanced at Michelle across the aisle, busy whispering to her new bear. Maybe the stuffed animal would calm her daughter.

Tony interrupted her concerns. "I'll rephrase. Are you prepared for what you will say if we do find him?"

"Not sure yet, but he'd better have some good answers."

Tony stood up and glanced out the window. "So do I. And I don't like the look of that sky either. The seat belt sign is back on—I have to lasso my daughter. Where'd she go, anyway?"

"The lavatory, I think. Probably experimenting with some of the damaged makeup I was going to throw away."

He groaned.

"Does it matter?"

"I guess not. I'm going to find her."

"You think we'll be okay?"

"Of course—relax."

Intellectually she knew no one could guarantee a safe flight but emotionally she was grateful for his optimism.

She squeezed her eyes shut. Here she was, flying to Switzerland with a man she just met, his teenage daughter, and her two children who should be at home in school. She crossed her arms over her chest and hoped for the best.

The jet bumped and shook.

Michelle began to squirm and kick.

Amanda traded places with Howard. In a soothing voice she whispered Michelle's favorite story about angels taking care of people in heaven. Amanda's mother had passed away a year earlier and everyone missed her. Michelle constantly asked the angels to watch over her grandmother.

Her daughter stopped kicking.

Tony returned with Lizzy. "Am I creepy beautiful?" she asked, her mouth clamped tight over braces.

Amanda stared at the unrecognizable face of a fifteen-year old who looked exotic enough to be from another planet. Heavy black mascara and eyeliner set off her pale blue eyes. Bright red lipstick bled past the edges of her lips. Was Lizzy trying for Planet Creep, Vampire of Seduction, or just being a teenager? Tony's angry face stopped Amanda from laughing. Howard pinched his face into a look of disgust but remained silent.

The wheels lowered with a rumble in preparation for landing. She tightened her seat belt.

Another jolt of lightning flashed across the sky. She resumed the angel story, forcing herself not to speed it up. Michelle had enough anxiety without that.

The jet wobbled and landed, skidding on the slippery tarmac. She squeezed her arm around Michelle's shoulder until the reverse blast of engines brought the aircraft to a full stop.

Were they heading into more danger in a country where she had no backup? Was Peter in Switzerland or not?

He had no way of contacting her now.

If she found him, how would she explain bringing the kids along, or Tony?

CHAPTER SIXTEEN

Amanda held Michelle's hand as they jostled out of the small private terminal in Geneva. By the waiting taxis, a bronze-colored Mercedes pulled forward and they scrambled into it. Tony up front and Howard sandwiched between Amanda and Lizzy in the back. Amanda pulled Michelle onto her lap while the baggage handler loaded their luggage.

"How far to Coppet?" Tony asked the driver. Lizzy groaned and lowered her face when a teenage boy stopped and gaped.

"He's looking at me like I'm a poopy dork," she moaned.

Tony scowled at her. Amanda handed her some tissues to clean her face.

"Coppet?" the driver answered in a heavy French accent. "*Oui*, yes, that ees on Rue de Lausanne, yust by the lake, *Monsieur*. No more than ten, fifteen minutes from 'ere." The man's hair was graying, his face ruddy and lined, but his alert eyes held a youthful twinkle. "It is a beautiful route. Vould you like the scenic tour?"

"We might arrange that later," Tony said. "Right now we're in a hurry and need to reach Coppet as soon as possible."

They sped away while Amanda checked the rock in her purse and offered squares of Cadbury chocolate to the others. Tony lowered his window and lit a cigarette.

"Dad!" Lizzy protested.

"Not now," Tony said. "Later when it's less stressful."

Amanda gazed out at the scenery and thought back to when she first met Peter. His stories about summers with his grandparents had been passionate and detailed in family and ancestry. At the time she considered his interest in the past linked to his years of genetic research. Yet whenever she suggested they visit the family farm together, he'd stop talking about it and close up as though she'd intruded into something private. Now she had no choice but to surprise him by just showing up.

In Coppet the driver stopped at a petrol station and asked for directions and Amanda noticed a tourist marker advertising the Chateau du Coppet. Peter had a postcard of the historic Chateau pinned to his cork board in the attic at home. They had to be close.

The driver turned onto a private lane and wound down a bumpy gravel road toward the water's edge. He stopped at a weathered gray barn secluded among apple orchards.

"Creepers, that doesn't look like any scientific lab to me," Lizzy said, "just a yucky old barn."

"This is Dad's farm?" Howard asked. "He works here?"

Michelle squirmed on Amanda's lap.

Tony got out. "Wait in the car, Elizabeth."

"You too," Amanda said to Howard. "Stay here with Michelle, please. We'll be right back." She nodded to the driver.

"Bien sur, Madame, of course I vil stay with the young ones."

She followed Tony.

Wind lashed at the trees and leaves fluttered to the ground. She could have left Tony in the car but didn't want to go in alone. Amanda asked, "How do I explain you?"

"A friend of Hillary's? You didn't have the resources to reach him."

His reassurance didn't help. She scanned the property. Beyond the weathered barn a blackened fireplace and smokestack remained from a burned building. Stakes secured a large plastic tarp over the structure's foundation.

The front of the barn faced the lake, a short distance away through the trees. Smoke from its stove-pipe chimney blew strong and fresh in the chilly fall air. She climbed the weather-beaten plank stairs with Tony and knocked on the door. Wind whipped hair into her face. A male voice within asked in French who was there. *"Qui est la?"*

She shouted back. "Peter Tregnier's wife. Is he here?"

The door opened. A man stared at them with a confused expression on his aged face. He looked like a classic photo of Einstein, studious, with hair sticking out all over. Stitched leather patches covered worn elbows on his gray sweater and baggy pants hid short legs. Dried mud caked his heavy work boots. In contrast, her tall, dark and good looking husband looked nothing at all like a scientist.

"I am Doctor Vidollet," he said, extending his hand. "You are Peter's wife?"

One of the names in Peter's notebook. "Yes I'm Amanda. Glad to meet you." They shook hands. "This is an acquaintance, Tony Ramsey. Is my husband here?"

Dr. Vidollet shook Tony's hand and motioned them to enter. "No, but please come in from the cold."

Inside, two long worktables held a vast array of chemical equipment. Tony peered at glass decanters. To Amanda it was just a massive hodgepodge of confusion. A blackboard covered with formulas leaned on an easel. The notations looked similar to the formulas in the black book.

Amanda glanced around the room hoping for a glimpse of something connected to Peter, but saw nothing familiar. Two cots, a couple of sagging easy chairs and a coffee table filled the great room. A black wood-burning stove against the far wall provided heat. The kitchen alcove had an old refrigerator and a vintage stove along with a modern microwave. The industrial sink looked all-purpose. A door stood ajar revealing a small room with a claw-foot tub and toilet.

Overhead a mobile twisted in the air with seven dangling moons. It looked like the one Peter had at home in the attic, but that one had planets. A poster of a full moon reflecting its pale light across Lake Geneva hung on the wall.

"Where is he?" Amanda asked the doctor.

"I do not know."

"When did you last see him?"

"Yesterday evening." He looked away. "Peter came to me for food and warm clothes but he ran away when a neighbor arrived with one of my missing sheep. I am afraid he did not get anything to eat…"

She pressed the doctor. "I don't understand. Why would he run away, and why was he in need of food and clothing? He called me in London yesterday sounding desperate. I have something important that he needs."

Dr. Vidollet's eyes flashed. "Then you know…"

"Know what?"

"Peter said a messenger would bring me something. I am to work on a project for him, but I had no idea he was sending his wife."

Disturbed by the information, she couldn't put it all together. "What are you working on, doctor?"

"I will not know until I see it. You have something for me?" He shuffled toward her.

Tony moved in front of her. "She doesn't have it with her, but she can get it. Why is it so important?"

The old man's face saddened. "You must bring me the formula at once. It might save…," he faltered.

Amanda skirted around Tony. "Save what?"

"I can tell you nothing." The doctor sat down at his desk, moving papers around. Before she could probe further, Tony sneezed.

"*Gesundheit,*" Vidollet said.

"Dust?" Amanda asked.

Tony shook his head. "I'm allergic to animal dander and feathers."

A shuffling noise drew their attention. A plump gray goose waddled out from under the desk. It snipped at the doctor's pants and honked, waddling over to Amanda, flapping its wings.

"Her name is Fanny," the doctor said with a wry smile. "She's old, but a good friend. I saved her from becoming *pate de foie gras* at the local restaurant. She was being fattened up for the hatchet." He drew a line across his neck with his forefinger.

Tony grinned.

Amanda said, "She must be a good companion, Doctor, but do you have any idea where Peter could be?"

Vidollet got up and stacked his papers in a neat pile. They were covered with formulas. The baahing of sheep came from beyond a side door of the barn. Fanny squawked. "My other children," he said, ignoring her question and gesturing toward the side door. "They always come home for their evening meal. I must go and fill the trough."

Annoyed and impatient Amanda said, "Dr. Vidollet, I've come a long way to find my husband. I need answers."

He frowned. "Unless you have something for me I cannot help you." He gathered some hay from a large bin under the stairs leading up to a loft. Tony blew his nose and followed.

"Let me help with that," he said. "I can manage a *few* minutes around animals."

The wind buzzed and moaned as the men lowered their heads and struggled with the hay to get it outside. Amanda shielded her eyes and remained at the open door. Over a dozen sheep waited on a muddy path that crossed the yard. Tree branches swayed in the wind. Beyond the burned house, leaves rustled and a distant bell tinkled. Rotar peeked out from around the corner of a wood shed. She stifled a cry and reached into her bag. The rock felt warm.

She cast a weak smile and he grinned back before disappearing. A strong gust of wind blew in and circled the room. Rotar appeared, flashing his wand.

Shocked, she asked, "How did you do that?"

He bowed and smiled, chubby cheeks crinkling his eyes into slits. "The power of the wind."

The men approached, talking outside. "They're coming back," she said.

"Then I will meet you later."

Her teeth clenched and she whispered, "I need your help, what's going on?!"

He put an index finger across his mouth. "The rock is a transmitter. Let it know where you are and call for me tonight."

Exasperated, she said, "Why didn't you rescue me when I was attacked in London?"

A sudden gust of wind rustled papers on the desk and shook the glass decanters. "Think wonderful thoughts," Rotar said, his words drifting upward.

He vanished.

She scanned the room and loft area, but he was gone. Tony and Dr. Vidollet returned with Fanny.

"Who were you speaking to?" Tony said.

"Myself."

He looked doubtful.

"Did you move my papers?" Vidollet asked, straightening them.

"Certainly not doctor, but the wind did."

The doctor sank into his chair. "You do not understand my work, and I cannot proceed without more information. Where are you staying?"

Tony caught Amanda's eye and nodded toward the front door. "She doesn't know yet, but we'll be back tomorrow. If you hear from Peter, tell him she's looking for him, will you?"

The doctor nodded. "But I doubt he will come back here."

"Why not?" Amanda asked.

He shrugged. "Simple deduction. He already tried to and it didn't work out."

She scowled and said, "If you *should* hear from him, *Herr doctor,* let him know I have to see him."

Vidollet grunted. "You will return tomorrow?"

"Of course."

CHAPTER SEVENTEEN

Peter sulked in the warehouse, upset that visiting his lab the evening before had left him without nourishment. After convincing Dr. Vidollet to let him in, he'd grabbed a hooded nylon parka and leather boots, but ran away when a neighbor arrived. Because the boot-tips pinched his long toes he had used a utility knife to cut them open and was now on his third outing in search of food and water.

He approached the same farm he'd visited two days earlier. His stomach growled and he felt woozy. When the evening sun disappeared behind shifting storm clouds, he longed for the warmth of the farmhouse. But its lighted windows meant he'd have to wait for everyone to go to bed before ransacking the kitchen.

He peered out from behind an oak tree a few yards behind the barn. A sudden slap of wind stung his face, chilling him. Green goose bumps on his skin reminded him of a toad. Not only did he sound like one, he even looked like one.

The shock of glimpsing himself in a mirror at the lab had been huge. A stranger had stared back at him: An elongated head the shape of an eggplant, lidless eyes too big for his face, thin lips and a receding chin pointing toward a boney chest. A devastating image that horrified him.

On the plus side, he still had his powers and he'd already used his finger power twice to charge his cell phone. But although he could call out, he discovered that no one could call in. Was the phone no longer connected to satellite transmission? And if so, was his finger-charge some kind of galactic source that only responded to his own energy when he dialed? The answer was still a mystery. And the special powers he had acquired didn't make up for the loss of his good looks and athletic build.

Another rumble in his stomach.

He sat down behind the broad trunk of the tree, his bota bag feeling heavier than usual. He fretted over his stupidity and agonized that he might be on a one-way journey. He recalled more details of the big change:

When the potion took hold, his mind shifted into an alternate dimension, twirling him into a white abyss. In what felt like seconds, he journeyed through past centuries seeing brief glimpses of life on Earth. He soared through wide-open spaces above natives in primitive tents and migrating groups on tundra-dense forests. Hundreds of reindeer and frozen huts passed by like moving pictures. Then pyramids and lush tropical forests sped past and he saw elephant herds and villages and cows roaming the riverbeds. He even caught a quick glimpse of dinosaurs wandering freely, their heads towering above tall trees. And last, he raced from planet to planet through worm holes and whirling cylinders of space until sharp crystals pricked him and his world went black.

It was just like Rotar had said: *The past is stored inside you.*

During their research together, Rotar claimed to be from another planet called Rotarious and that he had mutated into a human upon his arrival on Earth. Peter considered the statement intriguing but hadn't really believed him or questioned him about it. Now he wished he'd taken the time for a lot of things before experimenting on himself.

Shifting his weight against the tree a sticky tear slid down his face. He remembered what a psychic had once told him: *You have lived many previous lives on Earth as well as in other universes. At one time you were even a notable ruler.*

"Ha! Some ruler! No sign of that," he grumbled.

Pigs squealed from the other side of the barn. He was so lightheaded and hungry even pig slop seemed appetizing.

He moved on wobbly legs toward the back of the barn. After eating, he'd call Amanda in London again and persuade her to turn over the notebook. Howard and Michelle would be safe with Hillary. He'd never warmed to the independent personality of his wife's friend, single and running around the world, yet he had no problem trusting her with his children.

His powerful vision scanned through the barn walls where a hazy image of the farmer emptied a bucket into the pig trough while pigs squealed from the pen. He watched the farmer walk back across the yard to the house wearing a leather jacket. He longed for its warmth. All Peter had was a work shirt, windbreaker and slacks that hung too short. His long skinny legs looked cartoonish, like a big alien bird.

The back door of the farmhouse banged shut. He snuck through the rear entrance to the barn and grunted a greeting to the animals inside. A horse whinnied and turned, but both cows ignored him. Hunger pangs sent spasms through his stomach. He tried not to make noise, but his breathing hissed when he inhaled and gurgled on the exhale. He sank onto the floor in an empty stall, the damp straw soaking his pants.

The smell of wet hay and fresh manure filled the air but he saw nothing to eat. The animals became agitated, and the cow closest to him mooed. Did they sense his energy? His x-ray vision made the cows and horse look ghostlike with skeletal inserts. Pigs squealed from a pen outside and chickens clucked from a coop.

A door slammed at the main house and someone approached the barn. Peter hid behind a bale of hay, his knees crackling. He didn't have the strength to run away, but he could defend himself with fire power if necessary.

At the entrance, floorboards creaked under the farmer's boots. *"Qui est là?"* A male voice asked who was there.

Peter held his breath to squelch the noisy breathing. His face ballooned.

The animals shifted and stirred in their stalls. The man walked around muttering something in French and then left.

When the door to the house banged shut again, Peter gasped, releasing pent up air in a high-pitched sound like failing brakes on a truck.

"Oh my multiple murky moons," he moaned. A wave of nausea came over him. It was still too early for the farmer to go to bed, but Peter had to eat before he passed out.

He dragged his feet in a snail-crawl out to the pigs. The animals snorted and slobbered over their evening meal, the pen shielded from the house by the barn. Mushy cabbage leaves mixed with fodder lay in the bottom of the feed bin. Peter hated cabbage, but climbed into the railed pen with a groan. He could still float a little when he had the energy to flap his arms.

One pig stood apart from the others and made odd sing-song grunts, tilting its head back and forth. It approached and stared at him.

Peter's stomach cramped again. Dizzy, he leaned over the trough and scraped up gobs of sticky food. It stank so much he had to hold his breath to eat it.

"Achhhhhh, wheeew, disgusting." He swallowed the wet lumps. "Oh, my miserable moon puke, this is *awwwfulllll."* The odd pig watched him, rolling its head with curiosity.

He tried to imagine a Thanksgiving dinner of turkey, gravy and stuffing, but it didn't work. The surrounding pig poop and pee made eating even more unbearable. The slop tasted putrid.

He ate the remaining scraps and gagged.

A second trough held murky water mixed with dubious things he'd rather not consider. A faucet hung above it, but the handle wouldn't budge. He turned and twisted it, but realized he couldn't use his fire power for fear of flooding the pen. Moaning, he gave up and scooped the dirty water into his mouth.

The sudden memory of a New Year's Eve celebration with Amanda, drinking bubbly champagne from crystal-stemmed glasses distracted him. "Why, oh why, my many ugly moons have you done this to me?" he agonized, looking to the sky. "In dreams you were my moon mentor and I trusted you. Your moon magic brought Rotar to me. Where's that magic now?…"

He shambled back to the empty stall in the barn. The horse watched him over the enclosure.

"I should try this on you," he told it, patting the bota bag. "Have some fun in this miserable place." From the barn door he scanned the house. The farmer and his wife were upstairs watching television.

Peter could ride the horse to his family's rustic cabin above Coppet. He had considered moving from the warehouse before someone showed up for supplies and discovered him. If he transformed the horse into an alien, would it remain an animal? The horse as it was could solve his transportation needs, but curiosity teased his restless mind. Would an alien horse be more useful?

He twisted the cap off the bota bag and said, "Don't worry, horse. If I'm doomed to live in this alien body, at least I'll have you to share my fate."

The horse snorted.

He found a feed sack by the stall and squirted a hefty portion of the potion onto left-over grain at the bottom.

"Here 'fella, nice 'fella. Some extra supper," he whispered in a croaky voice.

The horse spread its nostrils, sniffed and jerked away.

"Hey, if I had to consume pig slop, you can get past the smell of rotten eggs. Go on, eat!"

The horse sniffed again, then nibbled the grain and blew spurts of snot onto Peter. Repulsed by the sticky mess he rubbed it off with straw. Strange memories came to him. Moon-driven destiny—seven moons ruling a universe—guilt over something he had done.

Had he been exiled from a distant place? Was it possible to go back again? "I am Moonchild," he said to the horse. "From a planet with many moons."

The horse ignored him while it chewed. Peter's attention drifted. Glimpses of a brilliant scientist flashed through his mind. Did he retrograde to a former life and change physically without leaving Earth? Desperate, he hoped to find answers in the silver book. Rotar hadn't completed translating that section by the time Peter finished the formula. If he drank more, would he go back farther to many lives and many universes? Or if he'd taken less, would he have regressed to a cave man? Or a lion hunter in Africa? The unanswered questions were daunting.

The horse jerked its head around and shivered as if electrocuted. Peter backed out of the stall.

The animal sneezed and dripped gold glitter onto the floor. Its brown shiny coat changed into silvery-white hairs. The long tail curled. Hooves turned into large silver-colored webs, and the mane extended into glistening locks. Red flames glowed in its eyes and silver wings popped out from its shoulders.

"A flying horse!" Peter wheezed. "I've created a flying horse!" His laughter sounded like a hyena, but it felt good, tickling his belly. "Can you fly me to my planet?" he asked.

The animal reared and whinnied.

"Was that a yes or a no?"

The back door of the house slammed open. A man shouted something in French.

"Oh, my fickle flying horse," Peter whispered. "How on Earth am I going to hide you?"

CHAPTER EIGHTEEN

The cab drove away from Peter's lab, bouncing over large stones on the gravel driveway. Amanda gripped the handle above the window and clutched Michelle on her lap. When they reached the two lane highway leading back to Geneva, she relaxed.

Lizzy said, "How 'bout some food?"

Howard looked glum. "Yeah I'm hungry, too."

"Where's Daddy?" Michelle asked. "Is he lost?"

"He's fine—we'll find him," Amanda said with conviction in spite of her worry.

Tony nodded. "Your mother is correct. We'll locate your father, perhaps through my contact here. And after we find a hotel we can eat."

"What contact?" Amanda asked him.

"Leo Braun. I told you about him. He's doing some research for me on that phone number."

Red flags nagged her thoughts. "But I didn't want anyone else involved."

"I only asked for an address. He knows nothing more."

"What doesn't he know?" asked Lizzy. "What address?"

"It's business," Tony answered. "Nothing to do with you."

She pouted. "Who cares anyway?"

Amanda fell silent, angry at not knowing how much Tony had shared with a stranger.

Torn between going home or staying, she couldn't decide which was best. Since Peter had no way of reaching her, she would have to find him. But what if the phone number didn't lead to him? Rotar might know what to do.

The driver said, *"Monsieur,* zee same car *be'ind* us on zee main road iz now again in back. I zaw it at zee petrol station earlier.

I thought not'ing of it until now. Zee black *voiture* iz following verrrry close."

Everyone turned to glance out the rear window.

Lizzy fidgeted with her braces. "Cool, this is so *raddy* cool."

"I shoulda' had my sword, Mom," said Howard. "It's in your suitcase."

She clutched her son's knee with one hand, pulling her daughter closer with the other.

"Can you lose it?" Tony asked the driver.

"But of course. It ees only a Renault. Not zo fast az mine."

Tony lowered his voice. "Go ahead. I'll make it worth your while."

"Ang on," the driver said. He gripped the steering wheel and pressed his foot on the accelerator. Headed back to Geneva, the car sped along Rue de Lausanne.

Amanda clutched her children tighter. Tony held onto the handle above his head and turned to Elizabeth. "Is your seat belt secured?" he asked.

She nodded. "Ultra cool."

The driver increased their speed.

Amanda looked behind again and recognized a face. "Tony, that's Goldtooth from London. He has a black patch over one eye." The man's arm poked out the passenger window with a revolver. "My God," she yelled, "he's going to shoot."

"Duck," shouted Tony.

They all hunched over. The driver leaned down and steered the vehicle in a mild zig-zag without pitching them off the road. "I learned dees in zee Resistance," he chortled.

"Radical," said Lizzy with excitement.

Michelle whimpered.

The driver muttered, *"Mon Dieu,* zey must have a custom-built engine in zat little piece of yunk." He passed a truck and three passenger cars, jerking the Mercedes back into its own lane in time to avoid a head-on collision.

"Watch out!" Amanda screamed.

Lizzy slid further down in her seat. "Bad cool," she sniggered.

"You're nuts," Howard said to her.

"You're clueless," she shot back.

Michelle whispered, "I'm scared, Mommy."

"Can you get rid of them?" Tony asked the driver.

"*Certainment.* 'Ang on." He sped up. "I vas in zee underground in Paris az a young boy at zee end of zee war and drove cars and trucks at 'igh speeds escaping zee Germans." He slowed enough at the train station for a two-wheel turn onto Rue du Mont Blanc.

Lizzy shrieked, "Ultimate radically cool!"

Amanda cringed and Michelle clung to her. Howard whispered to his sister. "It's okay, I'll protect you and Mom."

The black Renault followed and closed the gap.

Their car straightened and turned at the next corner onto a small street, maneuvering between pedestrians and traffic. A trolley crossed the street dead ahead. Their driver jerked hard right, cutting across a small park full of street vendors who stared at the car. Amanda closed her eyes. The car clipped a magazine stand selling candy and postcards. Chocolates tumbled to the ground. The worker waved a fist.

"Crashin' bashin' cooooooollllllllll…" Lizzy said in excitement.

Howard made the screwball sign with one finger to the side of his head saying, "Brainless."

"And you're intellectually vacant," she retorted.

"'Old on…" the driver said.

Amanda's heart pounded in her throat. The Renault was three cars behind. "I think you're losing them," she shouted.

"I see more diversions a'ead," the driver added. They sped through narrow streets, cutting corners and driving over curbs. The car swung right, then a quick left into an alley. A sign on a building displayed clocks. Amanda glanced out the back window—no Renault.

"See that clock sign?" Tony asked. "Turn into their driveway!"

The car swung into the plant and swerved into an open court-yard where men were boxing up cuckoo clocks. The Mercedes screeched to a halt, smashing into a table. Workers retreated and boxes crashed to the ground. Cuckoo clocks played amid broken glass and shattered springs. Everyone in the car was thrown forward, then they sank back gasping for air. The driver turned off the engine.

Amanda jumped out with Michelle, grateful the chase had ended. Howard and Lizzy tumbled after her. Michelle clutched her mother's hand. "Don't be frightened sweetie, we're okay now," Amanda whispered to her daughter.

Her eyes snapped in anger at Tony. "That does it. I'm taking my children home. Peter will have to get himself out of whatever mess he's in without my help."

Tony frowned. "Our children are safe, and I'm reporting the license number and description of that car to the authorities. They'll be caught sooner or later. I want to find out who they work for." He looked around at the damage and the grim faces of workers standing across the yard, waiting. "And unless I pay for these clocks, we won't be going anywhere other than the police station."

Tony asked Gaspard to translate and they disappeared into an office, returning with a cuckoo clock and several wrist watches. Tony handed one watch to Howard and another to Michelle. "These have the added feature of two separate dials on the face so you can set one to Washington time and one to local Swiss time."

"Thanks," Howard said. His watch had a black leather strap and a crescent moon on the face with tiny stars.

"Woowwww…" Michelle admired the flying fairy on the face of hers and its pink strap. "I love this…"

He handed Amanda a cuckoo clock. "A souvenir of our escapade." The wooden clock had been carved with angels. Michelle stretched to see and Lizzy came over to look. He gave his daughter a watch with a winged horse on it.

"No, I couldn't possibly," Amanda said, rubbing the intricate carvings before handing it back. "I can't accept this."

Tony shrugged but didn't take it. "It's too late to return it. Give it away if you want."

She looked at the happy faces of her children. "All right—but add it to my tab. Does it play music?"

"It better. It's supposed to play Edelweiss on the hour."

"Thank you," she said, carrying the delicate gift to the car.

Tony shook the driver's hand. "Fine driving, Monsieur. What's your name?"

"Gaspard. But my driving could 'ave been better. Zee bumper and grill are damaged." Looking melancholy, he rubbed the front of the car and shook his head.

"Have it repaired and bring me the bill," Tony said. "I'll be staying a few days and want to hire you. I like how you handled the car. You were in the war?"

Gaspard's proud eyes enlarged. "I waz yust a boy then, but I 'elped my father in zee French Resistance. He trained me in many zings. He waz electrician and zair expert at wiring and blowing up German vehicles. I waz small and they called me zair *petit surprise package*." He chuckled. "I crawled through zee air ducts and wired conference rooms to monitor important meetings. You call it bugging. I had to learn quickly to survive many risks."

Tony nodded. "A man of many talents... I can use someone like you. Will you remain our driver for a few days? I'll pay you well."

They discussed the details. An eager nod and handshake from Gaspard sealed the deal.

Tony added, "There could be more danger. You okay with that?"

Gaspard chuckled. "Nozzing can come close to zee Resistance, *Monsieur;* az long az you pay my expenses."

"You've got it. Can you recommend a hotel?"

"Bien sur."

"Then lead the way, Gaspard," Tony said.

Michelle whimpered, "I want my daddy."

"The man in the car was just trying to frighten us," Amanda told her. "He's just a bully."

"I'll kill him," Howard boasted, "right after I get somethin' to eat."

"What an absurd statement," Lizzy said. "I, on the other hand, am more than ready for a yummy snack and a hot bath."

CHAPTER NINETEEN

At the sound of the farmer's angry voice Peter hid behind the barn door and focused his eyes, prepared to spew fire at the man. The roar of a motorcycle approached from the road. The farmer shouted above the noise until the cycle stopped in the yard and its engine turned off.

Peter x-rayed through the wall.

A teenage boy rolled the bike under the carport next to an old truck. The farmer's voice grew angrier. Peter relaxed when he realized that the boy had ridden the bike without permission. Teenagers, he thought, but then considered his own son, unable to do so many things. The farmer followed the boy into the house, the back door slamming shut behind them.

"Whew. We got lucky, horse." He patted the animal's neck.

The horse nudged him back. Peter gazed at it, focusing his x-ray vision. Organs and blood vessels had twisted into new shapes. "Now there are two new creations on the planet," he hissed. "Me and you."

The crow of a rooster startled him. He tripped and dropped the bota bag on the ground, stepping on it. Some of the potion squirted out into the hay. He picked up the bag and lodged the cap between two of his three fingers, tightening it. A slow process. A squeaking noise came from behind the wall of the barn.

Sounds like a mouse. "I'll get some cheese in the house and let you sample an adventure into my universe," he whispered. "Something I should've done before drinking it myself."

Peter drifted in and out of sleep while waiting for twilight to creep into night. The cows had been milked, their empty sacks dangling under them. He hoped no one else would show up. Outside, it looked late enough to raid the refrigerator.

He x-rayed the house. Upstairs the farmer and his wife lay in bed in a dark room. In another room the son sat in front of a computer wearing earphones. Peter moved to the back door and turned the knob.

Locked.

He pointed a fingernail into the keyhole, transferring a green beam through his nail. The door handle clicked open.

Finger power was proving useful.

In the dim, but neat and orderly kitchen, he found a refrigerator full of food. He filled an old gunny sack from the warehouse with sliced meats, cheese, fruit, leftover potatoes, chocolate, a carton of milk and several cans of beer. To squelch the memory of the foul-tasting pig fodder he ate bites of cheese while gathering the rest.

The chunks were too big for his thin body and he started to choke. He pounded his chest to dislodge the food but was afraid to cough. Too noisy. He kept hitting himself until the cheese broke loose. When able to breathe again, he unbuttoned his shirt and pulled open the garment to watch bits of cheese move slowly from his pharynx toward the esophagus.

Stupid.

A cat stood in the doorway and meowed. Surprised by its unexpected arrival he grabbed a newspaper from the kitchen table and rushed to the back door, hoping the noisy cat hadn't alerted the family.

Outside he pulled the door shut behind him and sneezed. The loud snorting bellow made his ankles quiver. Absolute panic drove him forward as he hobbled back to the barn with his heavy sack and sank onto a pile of hay. No one came out of the house. He ate some salami, slow and easy, and wished he'd had time to look for a warmer jacket. He scanned the newspaper for a report of his break-in two days earlier, but found nothing.

Tempted to experiment more, he dabbed a small piece of cheese with the potion and set it near the wall where he'd heard the rodent. The mouse came out of hiding, sniffed the cheese and began to nibble. But before Peter could block the hole, it disappeared back into the wall along with the cheese.

"The little nuisance has tricked us," he complained to the horse. He tried to coax it out with more cheese, but it didn't work. It was time to go. "We can't wait around here just to see what I've created."

He looped a rope around the horse's neck. "I hope you can take me to my cabin. It's been years since I went there with my grandparents—I don't even know if I can find it." The mountain retreat was part of Peter's inheritance, but he'd never used it. His research consumed all of his time.

"You're like the mythical horse Pegasus," he murmured, studying the animal's features. "What shall I call you? Peg?"

Not a female name, the horse thought. *I am male.*

Peter jerked, almost falling backward. "I can hear your thoughts," he whispered in excitement.

The horse snorted.

"Was that a hint of sarcasm?"

He led the magnificent creature outside and looked up at the dark second floor windows of the main house. All was quiet. The cumbersome sack of food made movement difficult, so he tied the end of the bag onto his belt and climbed up on the fence. "Stand still while I get on," he said.

The mount was awkward, but he settled on the back of the horse with his sack. "Since you're a sire, do you like the name Starbeam? You have wings and you could have come from the stars."

The horse nodded.

"Call me *Moonchild*," Peter said. "I'm from a distant place."

Starbeam snorted and sparkling gold-dust fell from his nostrils.

Peter tucked his legs under the wings for anchorage. The pigs snuffled in their pen, but the piglet he had noticed earlier approached the rail to stare at him.

"I'll feed you some potion, too, pig. When I return to check out the mouse…"

He turned to see the farmer staring down from the upstairs window with an angry face, shaking a clenched fist.

"Oh my fickle moons, we have to get out of here," his voice cracked. "Run, horse, run," he wheezed. "Goooooooooo…"

The horse trotted up the hill with Peter bouncing on his back. Starbeam flapped his wings. "Don't fly yet," croaked Peter. "I might fall off…"

A shotgun blasted behind them. "Oh, my miserable moon madness, he's shooting at us. Fly, Starbeam, Flyyyyyyyyyyyy…"

He kicked the horse with his boots. It wasn't much of a kick but Starbeam bucked a little and spread his wings, flapping and half galloping until he soared into the sky with the grace of a majestic bird. The wind bit Peter's ears, but he cried out with joy. "Wheeee, wooowwww…"

Tall trees appeared ahead. "Keep climbing, Starbeam…"

Starbeam pushed against the wind and climbed, heading straight for the trees.

"Higher!" Peter cried.

Starbeam lifted fast and soared upward, clearing the forest right before contact.

Peter's panic had frozen him into clutching the sack and hanging onto the horse. He relaxed but kept his hold nudging Starbeam westward while searching ahead for a clearing. The clouds shifted and a small ray of moonlight lit the landscape. They flew above woods and scattered rooftops until he spotted a more remote area and recognized his family cabin.

"Over there," he shouted through the noise of the wind. "The cabin off by itself beside the pond."

Starbeam spiraled downward and landed close to the structure.

Peter tumbled to the ground, the food bag on top of him. "Ouch," he groaned. "My alien bones must be brittle."

The weather-worn cabin had one large room with a side door off the kitchen, a well, and a wood storage area on the back. A covered porch ran across the front with double doors.

He looked for the hidden key in the wood shed. An old bucket still hung on a peg near the door but the key was gone. He couldn't waste time searching so he unlocked the side door with his finger.

Too narrow an entrance for the horse.

He led Starbeam across the front deck, relieved when the old wood planks held under its weight. "Watch me utilize my powers," Peter said, zapping the lock.

Starbeam clomped through the opening. *Impressive,* the horse thought.

Four simple beds with folded blankets and pillows filled the dusty room, all but one bed covered with outdoor gear. Peter shivered in the cabin's damp musty air. The wood-burning stove in the kitchen was badly rusted. Gathering wood from the shed, he put three logs in the stone fireplace. "No one around at this time of year to see the smoke," he told the horse. His fire power created flashes of flame that lapped the wood but died away. He kept searing the damp logs with increasing intensity until they caught fire.

"At last some heat Starbeam." He dragged the bag of food inside and set it on the wooden table. "Now I can rest and eat. Remind me to call my wife before I go to bed, okay?"

Starbeam lowered his head in a respectful bow.

"Where are you from, old horse?" he asked, unpacking the sack. He popped open a cold can of beer.

Starbeam didn't answer.

"Do you understand me?"

Starbeam grunted. *You should not consume that beverage.*

"You're giving me advice?" He tipped the can and took a drink. "For your information I can handle beer. So what's your origin?" His burp sounded like a grumpy crow.

Starbeam stomped his hoof. *I hail from Androdon.*

"Androdon…" Peter took another swallow of beer. "Did you have wings there?"

Of course. But where is my food and water?

"I'll get you some water and grass soon. I need energy to do it. It's been a long time since I've had anything good to drink or eat. Here, you can join me if you're thirsty." He poured some beer into an old bowl and set it on the floor. Starbeam drank.

Peter ate slowly and finished his beer. The bubbles tickled his stomach until he giggled, his laugh becoming louder and faster. He sounded like an hysterical hyena.

Starbeam snorted gold-dust from his nose followed by a machine-gunned burp.

"Aaawwwfffuuuullll," Peter said. "How did you like your beer?"

No answer, but the horse licked froth off his lips.

Peter felt dizzy and his body heated up. A powerful surge of hot air filled his head. He got up and tried to flush the confusion from his mind but his feet wouldn't stay on the floor. Frightened, he half-floated toward the bed. He grabbed the wooden bed rail as he hovered over the middle of the cot, his legs rising little by little toward the ceiling.

"What's happening?" he shouted, flapping one arm at Starbeam while clinging to the rail. Starbeam rolled his head and watched.

Peter struggled to lower himself.

The horse snorted and switched its tail.

"You'd better not be laughing at me, horse."

You are rising like all the hot air inside you.

"I didn't know animals could be sarcastic, but you're right. Hot air defies gravity, and I am very hot at the moment." He groaned. "Oh my maniacal moonbeams, I'm a mess, and now I can't get down to take you outside."

You cannot tolerate alcohol if you hail from Rowundum where all energy is fueled by the brain.

"Rowundum?" Peter's thoughts drifted. "I am aware of my intellectual superiority. Perhaps I do come from a place where the mind has greater energy."

Starbeam raised his tail and let out a loud fart like a rapidly deflating balloon. The smell rose toward Peter in the stuffy room.

"Peeeeee—yuuuuuuugh, that's disgusting… And it even smells like beer."

Starbeam nodded and waved his tail. *I cannot comment on your intellectual superiority, but you demonstrate other powers that originate on Rowundum. I have never been there but have heard planetary rumors…*

"But you're a horse. Granted, a flying horse, but you don't know anything about my brilliant research or anything else about me!"

Peter let go of the rail and floated under the ceiling folding his arms and crossing his legs, then commented to Starbeam, "I've ruined my life by following Rotar. It's all his fault. That stupid midget led me into this disaster. I thought he was my friend. He warned me, but not enough!" He burped and moaned.

Starbeam shook his long silver mane.

A sticky tear slid down Peter's pasty skin. "Oh, my blessed moon-god, what I'd give to see my kids again. I abandoned them for what I thought was a good cause."

He wiped his cheek and listened to the steady crackling of logs in the fireplace. When he finally drifted into a half sleep, his breath hissed and gurgled in a steady rhythm.

During the night he descended slowly from the ceiling to a soft landing on the bed. Half-awake, he fell back to sleep and dreamed. It was like the dream he'd had before, except he was drifting inside the giant clear dome, not outside it. Through the dome he saw many moons in the distance. A pungent smell of green grass filled his nostrils. He carried books and laughed as he rushed toward a large glass pyramid.

A tall ethereal being ran toward him waving a hand. "Moonchild," the stranger cried, "you must go back…"

Eureka! I've finally made contact, Peter cried in his mind, focusing intense eyes on the being's face, but he was too far away.

Something wet brushed Peter's face.

He struggled to stay in the dream. A hard nudge to his shoulder demanded his attention.

He woke up.

CHAPTER TWENTY

The pavement in Geneva's old town looked slick from an earlier rain, but the sky had cleared and Amanda hoped the weather would hold. As they drove across the Rhone River into the quaint village, she watched for the black Renault but saw no sign of it. The children had calmed down after the car chase and that provided some relief, too.

Gaspard dropped them all off at the Hotel de la Cigogne, and Tony reconfirmed the driving agreement and promised to arrange for another car. In the palatial lobby of the hotel Amanda admired its Baroque fountain. The interior felt like a lavish grotto. Belle Époque frescos covered the walls and tall stone columns divided the reception area from a lounge. Lizzy, Howard and Michelle hurried to warm their hands in front of a roaring marble fireplace. Tony booked two adjoining suites, both with a living room and two bedrooms. Amanda waited until the desk clerk left to fetch something from an interior room before saying, "Suites, Tony? Isn't that a bit extravagant? I could get a standard for myself and my kids. I need to stay on a budget."

He looked annoyed. "Don't worry, you'll only be charged for a standard room."

That irritated her. He probably had a trust account and was accustomed to luxury. He should have consulted her first. If it happened again, she'd revoke the tab and arrange her own lodgings.

While waiting for their luggage, they gathered in the living room of Tony and Lizzy's suite. Howard grabbed the remote and flicked through television channels while Lizzy set up her laptop on the desk. Michelle hassled Howard until he let her scroll through the programs too.

Tony lit the logs in the fireplace and Amanda let her eyes rest on a bouquet of fresh flowers. They complemented the beautiful antiques in the room and a stunning view from the window. She gazed down at the river where a small park bordered the river walk. Its colorful flowerbeds had been arranged like a well-tended English garden. She felt safe.

Tony joined her. "Nice view. Gaspard chose well."

She nodded. "The rooms are lovely. I hope the kids can get along."

"They're too exhausted not to."

"You're probably right," she said, feeling tired herself.

Tony looked at his watch. "I'm going to contact Braun—see if he's found an address yet."

"Fine," she nodded.

The bellboy delivered their bags, using the connecting door between the two suites to divvy up what bags went where. They decided to regroup in an hour, and Amanda escaped next door to unpack with her children. The living room and bedrooms were similar, both lavish and peaceful. Amanda felt like a queen for a day. She took the larger bedroom with a huge bed fit for a king, and the other room had two beds for Howard and Michelle. Each bedroom had its own bathroom.

Leaving her children to sort out their things, Amanda ran a bath. She relaxed in a tub filled with pine-scented bubbles and closed her eyes. Peter's strange behavior had to be temporary and fixable. She touched the shells around her neck and looked forward to confronting him with the latest Goldtooth story. He'd have to take care of the brut, and she'd make sure of it. The only way she could cope with all the stressful things in her life was to cancel her negative thoughts and believe that everything would be all right. It's what she did whenever she had no control over her circumstances. By the time she finished her bath, unpacked, and dressed for the evening, there was no time to summon Rotar. She'd call him later.

When they all gathered in Tony's living room again, he had ordered hot chocolate, a bottle of brandy and canapés. He added logs to the fireplace and stood in front of the warm flames smoking a cigarette. Lizzy sat curled up in an easy chair leafing through a city guide.

"Dad—you said you were quitting." Lizzy looked miffed.

"I'm working on it."

Michelle coughed.

He put out the cigarette.

Amanda joined Howard and Michelle on the couch.

"I don't know why I bother sending you all the self-help stuff," Lizzy continued, "if you just ignore the advice of every expert on the planet. 'Killer smoke', Dad."

"I know, I know, I'm dealing with the *mental* part."

"Radically cool. I'm counting on you." She lifted her magazine. "I'm going to check out the riding school here. I'm thinking about becoming a vet someday."

"An admirable goal," Tony said.

Michelle blurted, "I love horses."

Howard slapped his bad leg. "Never tried one."

"I bet I could teach you," Lizzy said in a confident tone.

Howard frowned. "No thanks."

Lizzy wrinkled her nose at him. "Oh well, your loss. I'm also thinking of other career possibilities. The diplomatic service, or perhaps an astronaut…"

Amanda relaxed, glad they were talking about something other than violence and Goldtooth. Lizzy's variety of interests reminded her of being fifteen and believing she could do anything she wanted. But marriage and children had changed a few things.

"I'm gonna' be a champion athlete," Howard threw in.

"No you're not," Michelle said. "You're gonna' be a knight, and I'm gonna' be a princess."

"What sport?" Lizzy asked Howard.

"Swimming. I'm gonna' compete in the Olympics."

Amanda stared at him in astonishment. Did Howard even know about the special Olympics? He rarely swam. She knew that not all dreams could come true but it was still important to have them. She'd always wanted to write books on musical therapy for children struggling with illness. The natural music of everyday life experience inspired her. When she drove the kids to school in the rain she would hum a tune pretending the car wipers were violins and the splatter of rain her piano keys. Thunder was a drum roll and flashes of lightning—the sounds of gigantic cymbals. "I always wanted to write books about music," she said. "And one day I will."

"I'm sure you will." Tony poured hot chocolate for the kids and handed her a glass of brandy. He poured another for himself. "A toast to our dreams." They all toasted.

"Did you reach your contact?" Amanda asked him.

"Yes and I have an address. The name at the location is Tregnier."

Surprised she said, "That makes sense; it's probably a relative."

"I hope so." He shifted a log with a poker before refilling his drink. "Let's go there now." He went to the table and spread out a map. "If we don't find him we might at least talk to some relative and see what they know."

Lizzy interrupted. "I want to go sightseeing in a horse-drawn carriage under the romantic old-fashioned city lights." She waved the magazine AD for him to see.

Tony looked up from the map. "Not tonight, sweetheart—maybe later if the weather improves."

"Can I stay here then?" Lizzy asked. "Order in a pizza? Watch Swiss television? I need to brush up on my French."

"Sorry, I'd feel safer if you all came along. It's not far."

"Show me on the map," Amanda said.

"It's here," he pointed, "across from a local cemetery—not far."

"Cemiteree?" Michelle asked, wrinkling her nose.

"McCreepy," Howard said.

They put on their warm coats and left. Tony let the lobby doorman find them a cab.

At the Tregnier address, they parked by the cemetery entrance and Tony asked the driver to wait with the kids. He offered his arm and led Amanda across Boulevard de Saint George.

They climbed the steps of an ordinary brick townhouse and Tony banged the black iron knocker three times. After a long wait a woman opened the door. Short and plump with light-brown soft curls around a full face, her blue eyes questioned them. She looked 'twenty something', and nothing like Peter.

"Do you speak English?" Amanda asked. "Are you the woman I spoke to on the telephone this morning? My name is *Madame* Tregnier—Madame Peter Tregnier."

The woman blinked and twisted the corners of her floral apron. An odor of fried onions filled the entry hall. "Peter Tregnier lives here and I am Marta, but you cannot be *Madame* Tregnier," she said in a heavy French accent.

Surprised, Amanda said, "Does Peter Tregnier have an American relative with the same name in Washington DC?"

The woman's face paled. "My fiancé is American. He is a scientist and his work takes him to Washington."

Amanda's eyes widened and her face reddened.

Marta moved back a step into the foyer.

In the entry a pair of men's boots caked with mud sat beneath the coat rack. Amanda flashed back to Dr. Vidollet's mud-laden boots at the lab. She pushed past the petite woman and marched straight into the living room.

A framed photograph on top of the television caught her attention. Peter and Marta stood holding their skis in front of mountain peaks, a lodge, and other skiers. It was her husband, not a relative. Marta was smiling, her hair pulled back behind her ears revealing opal earrings.

My missing earrings, Amanda fumed. She set the photo back. "Where did you get those earrings?"

"A gift from Peter," Marta said.

Amanda's jaw fell from what she was hearing. Deception upon deception. Her brow tightened. "And how long have you been engaged to my husband?" The strong smell of burning onions nauseated her.

Marta trembled and shook her head. "That is impossible. You cannot be his wife. We are to be married. He bought this house for us."

Amanda jerked her wallet out of her purse and opened the photograph holder. The first plastic sleeve showed Howard, the second Michelle. "Our children," she said, and flipped to an old photograph of herself and Peter.

The woman groaned.

Amanda squeezed back tears. "We were married thirteen years ago," she managed to say. Tony moved to her side, watching them both.

The woman clutched her apron and stammered, "We have been together for almost a year."

"I've been sharing my husband with you for a year? Where is he?!"

Marta shook her head and lifted her shoulders. *"J'ne sais pas."*

"Don't tell me you don't know. Is he here now?"

"Non," she said, shaking her head in emphasis.

Her answer was so immediate and certain that Amanda believed it. "Where do you *think* he is?"

Marta swallowed. "I told you, I do not know…"

Amanda uttered a cynical grunt. Anger surged through her. She glared at Marta. "I've had enough of this. Peter can reach me at the Hotel de la Cigogne, and you can tell him I'll be returning to America and suing for a divorce."

Before the woman could answer she jerked her shell necklace off with a snap and threw it at Marta, most of the shells scattering to the floor. Then she rushed toward the front door. Stopping abruptly, she spun around. "Where did you meet?"

"That is none of your business."

"I think it is. Peter could be in great danger and then you will have no one to marry! Better I find him than those brutes who are looking for him."

Marta remained stone-faced.

"Look, I have something important I need to give him! Help me out here, for his sake."

Marta drew a breath. "I am a pharmacologist at the Kruper Pharmaceutical Laboratory in Geneva. Peter was a guest scientist and given access to some of the supplies he needed. We met there."

"He worked there recently?"

"Yes."

Amanda glared at the woman and left with Tony in tow. The door slammed shut behind them. Tony grabbed her before she ran across the street.

"You may have obtained a valuable clue, but you shouldn't have told her where we're staying, Amanda. You're still in danger."

"Nothing can be more dangerous than what I'm going to do to my so-called husband when I find him. The nerve of him telling me my children are in danger. Another lie upon lie upon lie. I wasn't in danger until I got to London. I could have been killed. Everything's been a lie." She panted, nostrils flaring. "And that woman stole my husband…"

Tony placed a hand on her shoulder. "What if she really didn't know about you? She might be as innocent as you are."

"Innocent, my eye…" She jerked free.

"She could be crying her eyes out right now. At least give her the benefit of the doubt until we know more. Peter's the one…"

"Don't say that name anymore," she interrupted. They approached the cab. It was empty except for the driver. "Where are the children," she screamed at the man.

He shrugged. "The young lady followed the young man into the cemetery. I tried to stop her. Then the little girl ran after…"

"Oh my God," Amanda cried, running toward the massive iron gate. In the moonlight, rows of tombstones cast slim shadows across a bluish ground. Tony was right beside her. She heard a scream. All three children ran out a side gate and across the street. A short man scurried after them into an ally. Tony pulled a gun and sprinted after him. Amanda shouted, "Stay away from my children, I have the book you want!"

When she caught up and entered the ally, it looked similar to the one in her dream. She detected someone behind her. Tony had grabbed the short man ahead and held him to the ground. The sound of heavy breathing chilled the back of her neck. Still running, she spotted a log next to a trash can. Fear, adrenalin, anger kicked in. She scooped up the log and blindly swung around. Impact. Right into Goldtooth's eye patch. He howled in pain. He clasped his eye; she shoved the log into his groin. He crumbled to the ground. Then she kicked him in the ribs, over and over again. He rolled away on his side. "Why are you following us?" she shouted.

"Zee buk. Und ve vant your huzbund."

Amanda jerked the forged book out of her boot and threw it at him. "We can leave now," she said to Tony. The children were at his side. Tony let go of short man.

"Stay away from us or there'll be hell to pay," Tony said.

Short man looked terrified. Goldtooth moaned and remained lifeless on the ground.

Back in the car Amanda shouted at Howard. "How could you leave the car? You endangered everyone!"

"My bad," Lizzy said. "He wanted to look for Tregnier names on tombstones."

"And I found one," Howard said in an apologetic tone. "Pierre Tregnier, eighteen forty-nine to nineteen twelve. *Ne* means born and *mort* means when he died," he threw in, looking to his mother for approval.

Amanda was speechless. She wanted to reprimand him yet he had found another clue. "We'll discuss this later. Let's get back to the hotel."

While they drove, Amanda silently trembled in the back seat as her entire marriage flashed before her. To save money they were still living in the house she'd inherited from her mother, while Peter had purchased a townhouse for another woman. She was married to a Jekyll and Hyde.

She fought not to cry and found it difficult to breathe.

After putting her children into bed, Amanda freshened up and removed the real notebook from under her bra strap. She found Tony smoking a cigarette in his living room. Lizzy had also gone to bed. "Here," she said, handing him the black book. "I don't care what happens to it now."

He took it. "I'll make a copy in the morning for Vidollet."

"Go right ahead."

"Do you want to talk about it?"

She looked down at the floor. "Can we get away from the smoke?"

"Done," he said, smashing out the cigarette butt in an ashtray. He poured two brandies and handed her a glass. "You need an outlet for your anger, Amanda."

"Easy for you to say…"

"I've been there, too. Anger solves nothing."

"What else can I feel? I just learned my husband's doing research on a foreign agenda named Marta!"

Tony looked glum. "Marta isn't the only problem. Goldtooth will discover you've given him a fake book and come after you again."

"Who cares?" she snapped. "All I want is to go home and get a divorce. As quickly as possible."

"I understand, but you have children to consider. Their father is in trouble, and now we have two new clues to follow."

She shrugged. "I want nothing to do with him anymore. I don't know what I'll tell the kids but it's not going to be the whole truth. Not yet. They need to get home first where everything's safe and familiar."

"Will you be able to sleep?"

"Probably not." She took a sip of brandy and put the glass on the table.

"Good night Amanda."

She left Tony standing in front of the fireplace and took a box of truffles with her next door.

In bed she remembered her father leaving her mother. That opened the dam and she burst into tears, wracked with heavy sobs. When her parents divorced, she had vowed not to let her future children grow up without a father. But history had just repeated itself.

Nothing seemed real. Had she ever known Peter? Was their marriage nothing more than brief meetings of a typical family on his occasional trips home?

Her thoughts turned cynical. Aside from the children, her life was a bad joke. What could she tell them about the impending divorce? That their father was living with another woman who was younger, plumper and more docile?

How could he!

She popped a truffle into her mouth and yearned for her mother's loving advice. She'd tell her to be strong for the children, but at the moment she didn't feel very strong at all.

The sound of a police siren outside brought her out of her misery. She remembered Rotar.

Pulling the rock from her purse, she held the sparkling transmitter close to her face and whimpered into it. "Come in, Rotar, I need you." Then she slumped into a wing-back chair.

A soft wind stirred above her head.

Rotar appeared in a swirl of pink, yellow, blue and green smoke. He landed at the foot of the bed and bounced up and down.

"Do you have any chocolates left?" he asked, his face lighting up.

"Thank heaven you're here," she cried. "I'm having a meltdown, and my head is splitting. I'm taking the children home. Peter has a fiancé, and I'm getting a divorce. You'll have to find him on your own. Can't you use your stick and do something? You can have all the chocolates." She gave him the half-full box.

Rotar swished his stick. *"Re-lax-i-don-don,"* he said.

Her face twisted in disbelief. "Re-lax-i-don-don? That's your solution?" Before she could say another word, a soothing warmth relaxed her. She relished the relief until Dot Comet sprang out of the rock, shrieking like a wild peacock.

Panic set in.

"Stop that cat racket, Rotar! The others might hear!"

CHAPTER TWENTY-ONE

Amanda stared at the cat, gripping the chair arms. Rotar stood up and waved his wand. "*Bree-gong-meee*," he commanded. A chocolate flew out of the box. Dot Comet leapt and caught it. "*Re-trac-to-fron-tum*," he added. The cat disappeared back into the rock.

Amanda sneezed. "Can you clear the smoke in here?"

He nodded and muttered, "*Smo-ker-nia Van-is-ium.*"

The smoke vanished. "It was pretty, was it not?" he asked

"The cat act?"

"The rainbow smoke, when I arrived."

She grabbed a chocolate from the box. "I didn't notice—Peter's engaged to another woman."

"Is that bad?" He popped a truffle into his mouth. Melted chocolate ran down his chin.

"Of course," she hissed.

His head fell. "I did not know it was bad. I have been socially disconnected from your cultural habits, so I am in need of learning about such things. But I am concerned that we have not found him…"

"I was counting on you, Rotar. We were in a terrible car chase; some horrible men shot at us and we could have been killed. After we lost them we crashed into dozens of cuckoo clocks. Then I discovered Peter has a secret life. And then the same men went after my children! In a cemetery! I'm shattered, and I can't concentrate." Tears filled her eyes. "And why didn't you rescue us today?"

Rotar leapt up on the bed, looking concerned. "I was out of range on a hasty trip to Spain."

"Spain?"

"Yes, visiting Peter's friend. When she moved she took his cat with her. I thought perhaps she could tell me where he is."

"Peter had *another* woman?"

He shook his head. "I do not think so. She was just his neighbor who retired near Malaga. Did you try to reach me?"

She cleared her dry throat. "Well actually there wasn't time, it all happened so fast."

"I see…"

"But now I need your help to find Peter and kill him."

"You are making a joke?" he asked.

"Oh no I'm not. Well maybe. I don't know. If you can find him, my kids will at least still have a father. I want to move on with my life."

"You are angry about Peter's behavior, I understand that, but I cannot locate him unless he has the purple rock on his person. He is shielded from my tracking device."

"But if you're teleporting yourself through space, can't you just *zap* yourself to wherever he is?"

"My distance is limited and as I told you I do not know where he is."

"Can you really move through space?"

Rotar took another chocolate. "My wand has true magic. It moves me by wind energy." His wide smile exposed a chipped tooth. "I will show you." He twisted the gnarly stick and waved it through the air. Tiny sparks encircled the wand. A wisp of purple wind whirled around Rotar like a miniature cyclone, scooping him up and hurling him across the room into the other wing chair. A scent of lavender filled the air.

"You see?"

She nodded. "But how do you do it?"

"You have to be in the right state of mind. If you believe you are in London, for example, even though you are here in Geneva, you have to advance your mind and visualize yourself there. The miracle of movement or teleportation, is up to you."

"I still don't see how it works."

"Alien commands create frequency waves like a radio. With my wand and the wind I visualize and concentrate on my destination. I can move through time too. That takes a different frequency and my master frowns upon use of it. Going into the future is forbidden."

"Why?"

"Fate. If we go forward to select our future or manipulate our destiny, then what happens to fate?"

"Who cares?" She lifted her arms. "None of this makes sense. I thought I was working toward my destiny in my own way. Why would fate bring me to Peter who has so cruelly deceived me?"

He looked down. "Perhaps there is a purpose you are not yet aware of?"

"I don't believe there can be a purpose for anything so awful."

"My master would say…"

"I don't care what your master would say."

"I think you must hear this even if you disagree. He is Aeolius, Commander of the Wind."

"Your master controls the wind?" She rolled her head to ease a headache. It felt like her cold was coming back.

"On my planet we convert the wind's energy…much like you do here with windmills."

"You come from another planet?" Her thoughts twisted. "Of course you do. Someone with your powers…"

"Do you not have a master commander?"

"Yes, we call him God."

"We call my master *The Wise One*. But he also answers to someone higher." He licked the chocolate off his lips.

"So where does Peter fit in?" she asked.

"My master entrusted me as the keeper of knowledge. I was sent here as custodian of an ancient book—the one you glimpsed on the plane."

"The one in your eyes, flipping through endless pages?"

"The very one. Peter called it the silver book. It is made of *tritolium*, an indestructible substance from my planet much lighter and stronger than earth metals. It contains many secrets and the records of our universal ancestry. The information can never be destroyed. I was instructed to guard this book until humans were ready for the truth. But I made a mistake and thought your world was ready for it. Peter was the brightest and most advanced scientist and researching genetics. I entrusted him with the book."

"You trusted *my husband* with a universal book of knowledge? He can't even be trusted with his marriage vows." She flashed angry eyes.

"At first I merely allowed him a little bit of information. But after I had translated what he wanted most to know, he stole the book."

"Why couldn't you keep it on your own planet? Why involve Peter or anyone else?"

Rotar stood up and paced, eyes fixed on the floor. "That was not my decision and not for me to question. I was lonely here and Peter became my only friend. I would very much like to return to my planet, but now I am serving a penance."

"Penance?"

He stopped pacing, his eyes filled with regret. "I was banished for my mistake and must remain here until I pass the book of knowledge on to someone trustworthy. Then I will be allowed to go home again, if I can find a way back."

"How did you get here?"

"My space ship crashed and was damaged when I arrived."

She went to the window and gazed at the city lights. "I can imagine your angry master wanting the book back, but why should that condemn you to a life on *this* planet? What are you serving your penance for?"

She turned and said, "Sorry...I'm bitter right now. Forget I asked that."

He nodded. "It is hard to speak about my shortcomings."

She slumped back into the chair. "You really gave this irreplaceable book to Peter?"

"Only on loan. To a person of great scientific training and ability. Someone who could unlock the secrets of the universe for all to share." He dropped his head. "But I chose the wrong person and released the secrets too early. Peter has experimented with them in dangerous ways. I must retrieve the book before the anger of Aeolius destroys us all."

"This is ludicrous. Everyone on the planet has to suffer for the mistakes of you and Peter?"

"Regrettably so." He nodded with such firmness that the bell on his hat tinkled.

"How could any commander or leader want that? It would serve no purpose."

Rotar's face was grim. "Aeolius can destroy anyone and everything with the wind. The book of truth has been recorded since the beginning of time. When Peter took it to serve himself the world experienced terrible storms."

She recalled the countless reports of foul weather. "If all this is true, why are there no safeguards?"

"Excellent question," he said, meeting her eyes and pointing at himself. "As keeper I am the primary safeguard but I have failed at my job. The ancient truths were released a millennium too early."

"A millennium? How old are you?"

He looked away, sheepish. "I am fifty-five Earth lifetimes old."

"Which is how many years?"

"Around four thousand."

She closed her eyes again, pressing fingers to her temples. "My life spans milli-seconds compared to that…"

He blew on her forehead from across the room. A burst of cool wind enveloped her head like a soothing balm. The smell of eucalyptus and lemon filled the air and cleared her sinuses. Her headache vanished. She opened her eyes in surprise. "Thank you. Can you heal anyone? You know my son…"

He shook his head. "In some situations yes, but there are complications…"

"I guess I can only hope. But how can you still be living in the same body if you're four thousand years old?"

A smile stretched across his face. "On our planet we choose when we die in order to be reborn. It is part of our growth process. But we must be careful in making the decision to move on. Although we can choose the time of our death, we cannot choose the path of our next life."

In a cynical tone she said, "Most humans would want to live forever."

"I am aware of that. Overpopulation would create congestion and deplete your natural resources."

She nodded. "That's already happening, but I can't think about those problems right now. Do you know what's happened to Peter?"

"I am not at liberty to elaborate. He is in grave condition. The sooner you find him the sooner I can help him."

"Why can't you tell me?"

"Because he is the first human to try such a thing on himself and I do not yet know how it affected him."

"Oh my dear God…" The situation was worse than she imagined. She needed to get the children home and safe. "I'm overwhelmed by all this, Rotar. But I've been meaning to ask, why is your English so good when you live in Switzerland?"

"All languages are stored in my mind."

"All?"

"Many thousands."

Boy, she felt she had achieved something by learning a little French. What a joke. Now she understood the meaning of 'pea brain'. Exhausted, she felt like she'd hit a brick wall and climbed into bed. "Thank you Rotar but I can't deal with any more tonight. I hope you understand."

"Shall I put you to sleep?"

"Yes please. Anything that will help me rest and get my energy back. I can reach you with the rock?"

"Correct. I will keep looking for Peter. If he contacts you, please give him the rock. Then I might be able to help him."

Amanda's eyes widened. "You're not sure?"

"No because his greatest danger is himself."

She frowned. "Isn't that true for everyone?"

"Yes and no. His position is more precarious than anyone else's on this planet. His decisions and his own destiny will either save him or destroy him. The wrong people are hunting for Peter's secrets. I must retrieve the book before they do and confiscate his work."

"Then I'm counting on you," she said.

Amanda was no longer sure she wanted to find her husband. After turning over a copy of the notebook to Vidollet she would be free to go home. And the way she felt, Peter could stay lost or hidden or vanished. Rotar and his magical powers seemed capable of a successful search.

He waved his wand. A mild breeze surrounded her with tiny fluttering lavender lights. Before another thought stirred her mind she fell into a deep sleep.

CHAPTER TWENTY-TWO

Startled by a tap on her shoulder, Amanda opened her eyes. Lizzy stood over her with a mischievous smile. "What's going on?" Amanda asked in a groggy voice. Thick-headed from sleep, she was relieved to see that Rotar had gone.

"It's after nine—we started breakfast without you."

She sat up. The reality of Marta followed by Rotar's revelations still haunted her. She tuned in. "I never sleep this late… Where's your father?"

"Who knows? He ordered lots of yummies and there's coffee for you."

"I'll get dressed."

But Lizzy didn't take the hint to leave. "Your bag had purple stuff all over it," she said. "I dusted it off—what was it?"

Amanda had to collect her thoughts in order to fib. "I don't know." She swung herself out of bed and said, "I'll join you shortly."

Lizzy clamped her mouth shut and left.

Plenty of food remained on the coffee table in Tony's living room. Amanda hugged her children before they scrambled after Lizzy to watch TV in the adjoining suite. They had previously agreed that Amanda's living room would be the hangout for the kids where they could entertain themselves and even do homework but so far no lessons had been completed.

Alone and eyeing her breakfast choices, Amanda lathered heaps of butter and raspberry jam on a fresh croissant. She savored the rich creamy taste. No more dieting. The nerve of Peter criticizing her for any weight gain. Now she knew it was just his way of controlling her by attacking her self-esteem. Defiant, she ate another, washing the food down with hot coffee.

She wondered what to do next. Before she came up with any solutions, Tony returned carrying a paper sack, his face jubilant.

"Enjoy your breakfast?" he asked.

She felt smug and full. "Yes thank you. What's in the bag?"

"Just something for the driver."

She peeked inside. "Another gun?"

"I got it for Gaspard from my buddy, Leo Braun."

"He may not even show up—yesterday was no picnic."

"He's on his way as we speak. You want to solve this mystery before you go home right?" He poured himself a cup of coffee.

"Something tells me to pack up my kids and head back to DC."

"You don't mean that."

"I do, and I don't."

She laced her hands around the back of her neck and leaned her head back. "I have to tell my children about Marta and get hold of…, ahhh, some *miscellaneous* things and take the formula to Dr. Vidollet and then I'll decide what to do about Peter."

She moved to the window and stared down at the river. The water rippled and churned in ominous rhythm beneath gray skies. The weather looked as bleak as her mood. Rotar had asked for her help. Snap out of it, she told herself. She turned. "Okay. You're right. For the sake of Howard and Michelle I'll help their father."

"That's the spirit. I've copied the book, and if you want me to put the original in a safe place, I will." He handed her the notebook as well as the copy.

She hated the sight of both and took them with reluctance. "Let me think about that."

"I also borrowed an eight-seater Suburban from Braun. We'll be more comfortable."

"More gifts from your buddy? Who *is* he?"

"A government contact. He's the one who got Marta's address for us."

"And a government car too?" *How convenient...* An alarm rang, shattering what little trust she had for Tony. "You certainly have the right connections."

"I've handled a few Government legal cases here. The SUV is a favor."

Another story no doubt.

Tony gulped down a glass of orange juice. "I had two nasty telephone conversations with Elizabeth's mother. Lizzy was right—my ex is using her as ransom."

"That's awful. What kind of mother does that?"

"It's to aggravate and upstage me. Her own misguided sense of importance makes her jealous." He looked at his wristwatch. "But enough about my ex. Gaspard should be here by now. Let's get the others. When we deliver the information to Dr. Vidollet, perhaps we'll get some answers. If we're lucky, Peter might even show up."

Or unlucky, Amanda thought. She didn't know if she wanted to see him. She gathered her purse next door and when she returned with the kids, Tony was watching television. He was about to turn it off when a special news report interrupted the program. A male reporter spoke in French and she understood most of it.

"We pause our normal broadcast to bring you this story just relayed to us about a strange-looking creature spotted by a farmer in the Coppet region yesterday evening. The unidentified intruder broke into their family home and stole food as well as the farmer's horse." A cutaway showed the barnyard, structures and a man standing outside with his wife and son.

"The eyewitness claims the mystery visitor was not recognizably human and believes what he saw was an alien life-form—a ghostlike being flying away on the back of a winged horse."

The reporter stopped and cleared his throat. "The local police have searched the area and found nothing that resembles what the farmer saw, but anyone who notices anything unusual should call the police immediately or contact this station."

Amanda put her hand to her mouth and muttered, "That's crazy, a flying horse? Who'd believe that story? That farmer must be snorting Swiss cheese! This can't have anything to do with our mission…"

"I hope not," Tony said.

She closed her eyes in dread. "I have an uneasy feeling about this. Let's hurry and get over to the lab right away."

CHAPTER
TWENTY-THREE

Gaspard maneuvered the white Chevrolet Suburban through the busy streets of Geneva and headed for Coppet. Somewhat over-sized for the narrow streets, its roominess comforted Amanda. The children got along in the far rear.

Amanda agonized over Marta and Peter. Did Howard and Michelle suspect anything? She shifted next to Tony in the center seat and gazed out the window. Autumn leaves blanketing the boulevards reminded her of DC. A black Renault in the next lane startled her, but it wasn't Goldtooth's car. Looking around she saw nothing suspicious. She reached into her purse for the purple rock.

It wasn't there.

Ohhhh…noooo… Her mind traced back to the bedroom. It had been on the nightstand when Dot Comet jumped back inside. Was it there when she got up? She didn't remember. Did Rotar take it with him?

At Coppet Gaspard turned into the long driveway leading to the old barn. The place looked quiet.

She got out with Tony and asked the children to wait in the car. Michelle and Howard had books to read and Lizzy had brought along a fashion magazine.

In the dull morning light the barn appeared older and more weather-beaten than the day before. Its door stood ajar but when Amanda knocked, no one answered.

"Hello?" she shouted.

Tony pushed open the door, motioning her to stay back, but she followed him inside. Glass decanters and papers lay across the floor and pantry food from kitchen shelves had been tossed around or smashed. Dresser drawers hung open and clothes were strewn all over. A faint moan drifted from the cot across the room. Dr. Vidollet lay sprawled on it with dried blood caked to his forehead and pillow.

"Doctor…" she cried, rushing to his side. "Tony, we need to call for help. And please get me a wet cloth, the colder the better."

He nodded and headed for the sink while pulling out his phone.

She felt the doctor's cold hands and took his pulse. Very weak. The pillow under his head was askew and she adjusted it, noting his dull eyes and ashen face. "We'll get you to a hospital."

The doctor rallied and raised his head. "No, please, I am fine," he mumbled. "Two men…one with an eye patch, the other small and fidgety. They hit me and ruined my lab."

More fallout from Peter. "I know who they are."

Tony brought a wet cloth. "You're sure I can't get you to a hospital?" he asked Vidollet.

He shook his head. "I told you, I am fine."

Amanda cleaned the doctor's wound. "It's too chilly in here for him. Could you light the stove Tony? And boil some water for tea?" She perused the room. "What a mess."

Before long Dr. Vidollet sat at his desk sipping hot tea. He looked frail, but his eyes glistened and his color had returned. She wrapped a blanket around his shoulders while Tony took care of most of the mess.

"Doctor, some answers please," Amanda said.

He looked sad. "You brought Peter's book?"

"Yes, and I'll give it to you but first tell me what his notes mean."

The doctor nodded, trembling. "The information contains the formula for an antidote to a chemical drug that transforms the human body…" He looked away and shook his head. Tears filled his eyes.

"How?" she asked. "What does it do?"

"This is a terrible thing. The potion Dr. Tregnier has devised reveals a person's distant past. Previous lives—in other places."

"What places?" asked Tony.

"Planets…universes…" He became more agitated.

She turned and whispered to Tony, "That news report on TV where the farmer saw something alien, could it be?"

He didn't comment and asked the doctor, "Are you talking about hypnosis?"

"No, there is no hypnosis involved. This goes far beyond sub-conscious memories."

The doctor's pet goose waddled across the floor and honked. Tony sneezed and shooed her away.

Vidollet covered his face with his hands. When he pulled them away, he looked stricken. "I do not know how much your husband has shared with you or if you will even believe me."

"Try me," Amanda said. "Peter has shared nothing."

"He was obsessed with the idea that we are reincarnated beings from different planets genetically bred to look human while living here on Earth." The doctor rubbed tears with his sleeve. "Some of the knowledge came from the silver book."

"What silver book?" Tony asked.

"He called it the Silver Book of Knowledge, filled with remarkable information from the past. He got it from the midget."

She stared at him. "Are you talking about Rotar?"

He nodded. "You know him?"

"Who's that?" asked Tony. She remained mum.

The doctor sniffed and sipped his tea. "Peter was working on a new drug to treat schizophrenics. One day a small man knocked on the door." He nodded toward the side door that led out to the sheep. "Only three or four feet tall he looked like a middle-aged gnome. He brought the silver book to share with us. It contained many formulas and a strange language he had to translate. At first he would only let us study it for short periods of time. But Peter showed great interest and stayed up day and night to experiment with some of its data."

"Rotar's the midget?" Tony glanced with suspicion at Amanda. Vidollet nodded.

She ignored Tony. "Doctor, the men who did this to you are after the formula for the antidote. I brought the book to London and was attacked. The two men you described chased us yesterday. And again last night. I gave them a fake one, but they probably figured it out and then came here."

The doctor looked at her in alarm.

"Where did the midget get the book?" asked Tony. "And why'd he bring it here? Peter's a scientist and no doubt a pragmatist. The midget must have been pretty convincing."

"Mon Dieu, he was. I have spent my life as a scientist. I should not have let Peter collaborate with someone or something unknown. The small man told us that the formulas in the book were harmless and came from an ancient recipe developed by his ancestors. I did not take him or the book seriously at first. But Peter did. He was fascinated and never questioned the little man's story."

The doctor put his hands over his eyes and moaned. "Rotar said certain combinations of formulas could transport the mind into other dimensions and reveal the progression of life. One day he helped Peter mix a complicated brew. I recognized only the laurel leaves and mercury. The mixture put Peter into a trance-like condition and afterwards he showed me unusual chemical combinations and formulas insisting they had been communicated to him from another reality. He hoped that mixing Rotar's ingredients with his modern drug might produce even greater scientific results." The doctor shook his head. "Peter wanted total recall of his previous lives."

Amanda stared at the doctor, aghast. "Is that possible?"

Dr. Vidollet shook his head again. "I did not believe it, but the drug elevates the electric currents of the brain to a higher frequency. In this altered state impossible things can happen. For instance, the physical body can dematerialize and travel through time. That's what Peter said. He took so much of the formula that he recreated a life on another planet. He told me all this when he was here a couple of days ago."

She squelched an outburst.

Tony said, "It sounds far-fetched, doctor, but true or not, why did the midget bring the book here?"

Shame clouded Vidollet's face. "I wondered the same thing. The midget said the village gossiped about our research. He often hid in the loft to watch us work, but we did not know it until much later. When he introduced himself he said it was time to share his secret with talented scientists who could reveal the truth about existence. We were quite taken in by his humility and sincerity. He provided information that took us far beyond anything known to modern-day science. Peter spent most of the past year working with him."

Overwhelmed by the details Amanda became impatient. "Where is Peter and what's wrong with him?!"

"You do not want to see him," the doctor said, wincing. "He looks ugly—truly ugly. Lumpy green skin and a hairless pointed head. Very large eyes and a small mouth, but I am not sure what his nose looked like." He rubbed his forehead. "He was here for such a short time."

She gripped her chair seat.

Vidollet continued. "Peter has altered his DNA and you have the antidote. He said some of the ingredients came to him in part from conversations he had with the moon when he was in a trance-like state. He claimed he had often tuned in to information somewhat like a radio transmitter does. Peter considered the moon his mentor and through the midget he finally made contact. To me it is insanity."

"You've got that right," Amanda said, remembering Peter's late nights in the attic talking to the moon.

"It's absurd," Tony said.

She cleared her throat and shook her head. "The doctor is telling the truth as he knows it."

Vidollet added, "Your husband does not look human anymore and he is in great danger. He is aging rapidly. He has only been transformed for a week and is already older than me. If we do not hurry, he will die."

She clutched the chair tighter to steady herself. "Peter is old? Do you have a photograph of him?"

The doctor shook his head. "No, I tried to take one but discovered my camera had no film. I did not reload it after my wife passed away...more than two years ago... I should have been prepared..."

"I'm sorry for your loss, doctor," Amanda said. *He's still grieving, poor man.*

Tony asked, "Was Peter the alleged creature we heard about on the news?"

The doctor shrugged. "I have not seen the news lately, but the two men were looking for the silver book."

"They'll want the real formula for the antidote too," Amanda said, "and probably Peter, as well."

Vidollet shuffled over to the kitchen and grabbed a bag of cookies. Fanny waddled behind him. "Here you are, *ma petite.* A cookie for my little feathered friend."

"Fannie eats cookies?" Tony asked.

"Oh yes, even the peanut butter ones Peter brings from America."

"That figures," Amanda muttered. "Your goose eats my homemade cookies. At least Peter didn't share them with Marta."

"Marta?" Vidollet asked.

"Yes, I just learned that Peter has a fiancé in Geneva."

"Another woman?"

Tony cleared his throat. "Let's not go into that now. Has Peter made any more of the formula he took?"

"Such sad news, but to answer your question, he has some of it with him in a bota bag. I do not know if he can make more. There are certain conditions that must be met."

"Such as?" asked Tony.

The doctor broke another cookie and placed a small piece into Fanny's beak. "Peter made preposterous claims. According to him the crescent shape of the lake is a factor and the crescent phase of the moon. Also the unusual tidal fluctuations on the lake during moon phases. These things had to coincide when the drug was taken. But he grew impatient and made a trial run during a full moon. The formula worked fine, according to him."

"Except for small details like mutating in an alien form," said Tony.

"A drug for psychotics mixed with a midget's formula from an ancient book and the moon?" Amanda asked. "That's crazy."

"Perhaps not," the doctor replied. "The new formula Peter developed was blended with herbs and minerals from the soil of this region. More specifically from the ground of the southern range of mountains, which are also crescent-shaped. It was written in the silver book. There is a local myth of the lake's tides and the new moon… Peter believed that he had to come here to connect the clues. In part, he was right. By working here, he encountered the midget. But perhaps the formula would have worked anywhere if the right mix of minerals and herbs combined with his regressive drugs were accurate."

"Everything he's ever done is pure *myth*," Amanda said.

Tony asked the doctor, "Do you have any of the formula here?"

"No, Peter took what he had with him except for some of the phlenamium drug he claimed to have made. I have hidden a small amount and will need it for the antidote."

She looked at Tony. "I'll give him Peter's book so he can start working on the antidote. But he needs a safe place to work."

"I can arrange that," Tony said to the doctor.

Vidollet shook his head. "I cannot go anywhere else. If Peter is right, I need the herbs and minerals of this area as well as the lake."

Amanda went into the small bathroom and removed the copy of the notebook from her boot. The original was tucked safely in the other one. Vidollet took it from her and began reading.

"Tony," Amanda asked, "do you think my husband has turned into an alien from another planet?"

"I don't know. There could be all kinds of intelligent life out there."

"Why do you think that?"

Tony's eyes intensified. "From reports of Earth sightings—"

"What does that mean?"

"UFO sightings, for example, and evidence of ground markings and chemical residue that science can't explain. Alien life is quite possible, although it hasn't been proven."

She looked doubtful. "What's your stake in all that?"

"Even lawyers can have other interests…"

A part-time musician who believes in alien life and has friends in the government. She took an extended breath. "My brain's a little scattered right now. Since the doctor needs to stay here, can your buddy provide supplies and security for him?"

"Yes to both, and security's already on the way."

She flinched. "How did you know we'd need them?"

"I didn't know about the poor doctor here. Otherwise I'd have sent someone out last night. But when I copied the book this morning, I took the precaution of telling my connections about the trip. Just a safety measure after our ordeal yesterday. Security was offered and I accepted."

"You mean there's someone watching us right now?"

He nodded. "They promised to be discreet."

Her discomfort elevated and her breathing increased. "Without consulting me again? I'm dumbfounded by this, Tony."

"We're American citizens in Switzerland, and we've been fol-lowed by *two goons,* one of whom attacked you in London. Don't you think a little protection is in order with our without your permission?" He sounded annoyed. "In light of what happened to Dr. Vidollet…" He trailed off and looked away in disgust.

The doctor clutched Fanny, staring blankly at the papers on his desk.

Full of doubt and suspicion, Amana squeezed her hands in frustration.

"In view of this latest development I'm going to ask them to stay and protect the good doctor," Tony continued, adding in a sarcastic tone, "If that's okay with you?"

"Since you've already arranged it, but you must realize that the only way I can help Peter is to keep it secret."

Tony shook his head. "That's fantasy thinking, Amanda. But the security team won't reveal anything—they're well trained."

She snorted. "People are notoriously fickle, even well trained ones. But since Dr. Vidollet needs security, do I have your word their presence will remain confidential?"

Tony scanned the yard through the window and nodded. "You have it. You can't do this on your own."

Her eyes darkened. "I know I can find Peter. I'll explain later. And if security is already here, can you also help Dr. Vidollet with what he needs for the antidote?"

"He need only make a list," Tony said in a brusque tone.

Vidollet looked up and said, "I want to give you the silver book for safekeeping, but you must guard it with your life."

Amanda went still. "You have it here?"

He nodded.

She and Tony watched Vidollet open the oven door and remove a foil-covered baking pan.

"Peter told me where he had hidden it," the doctor said. "Good thing because I dry my socks in here. What if I had turned it on?"

He handed her a bundle sealed in foil. Under the foil she saw the edges of tissue paper but didn't disturb the wrapping.

"You must be very careful," he said.

In spite of its large size it felt no heavier than bubble wrap. She found a cloth shopping bag near the table and set the package inside, shouldering the bag. "We'll find a safe place won't we?" She locked eyes with Tony's, waiting for his confirmation.

"Of course."

A car horn sounded outside. "Is that Gaspard?" she asked. "The kids!"

Amanda bolted out the door. Tony reached for his revolver and followed.

A green sedan with a government seal on the door approached the lab. She didn't recognize the two men inside. The one on the passenger side lay slumped with blood seeping from his head. She screamed and ran for the Suburban, reaching for the rock in her purse. *Forgot—not there—where's Rotar?*

Gaspard leaned over the hood of the SUV, aiming his gun at the military car.

"Don't shoot, Tony shouted. "They're with us."

Gaspard pulled back.

Inside the van Amanda saw the children crouched on the floor. She put a finger across her lips and gestured for them to stay down.

The government car stopped. The freckle-faced driver jumped out and ran to Tony. "Two men shot at us. I've radioed for an ambulance."

The driver looked ashen, his voice echoing with fear. "You okay, Ma'am? We had you covered but those guys ambushed us."

Amanda panicked. *First get the children out of here…*

All three kids jumped out of the car. Lizzy had the purple rock in her hand.

"Get back in there right now!" Amanda shouted. "And stay down!"

Michelle stared doom at Elizabeth and yelled, "*Ze-he-brak.*"

"What?" Lizzy looked at Michelle in confusion. The rock started to glow. "Yipes," Lizzy squealed, dropping it on the ground.

Howard waved his walkie-talkie. "It's going berserk again, Mom. Is Dad trying to contact me?"

"No," she yelled. "In the car quickly, all of you!"

Something sharp jerked her sideways and she heard the echoing retort of a gunshot ring out from the woods. Her skin burned. The children screamed. Colored stars danced in front of her eyes. Amanda's knees buckled and the bag slipped from her shoulder. Slumping to the ground, the scene around her faded to black.

CHAPTER TWENTY-FOUR

"Bloody mess," Braun said to Charles from the back seat of his government-issued Mercedes. On his way back to the farm outside Geneva he stewed over the news of a second sighting and hoped to uncover something of value to him. He had never taken Joseph Reinholt for an alarmist or a nut-case. The man gave every indication of being a credible source, yet a warning stirred in Braun's gut. He couldn't figure out why.

As Charles sped through the Swiss countryside, Braun felt no closer to a resolve. The discovery of the footprints two days earlier was all he had. "Can't you drive this thing any faster?" he bullied Charles. The two men he'd sent ahead to the site had called and reported strange noises inside the farmer's barn. He was anxious to get there before the whole country showed up.

At the familiar location, Braun spotted four Swiss policemen huddled together in the rain, guarding the area. Fortunately, the local authorities had given him their total support along with an unspecified amount of time to investigate the farmer's claims. The police didn't want to lose face if the reports turned out to be false. Seeing them there bothered him, however. The likelihood of their silence about the investigation was highly improbable. Rumors usually travelled faster than facts.

He popped two antacids, chomping on the wafers until the car came to a full stop. Then he threw his stout legs onto the hard ground and climbed out.

The two American aides, Jack Wilder and Bradley Green, met him at the entrance to the barn. Dressed in security-force uniforms they stood at attention.

Braun wrinkled his nose at the smells from inside. "What've you found?" he asked.

Wilder spoke first, the older of the two with a wide face and broad shoulders, his flat nose reddened from cold. "The farmer is out rounding up his cows but he confirmed that around midnight he saw something strange fly away on a horse. He swears the horse had wings and a silver glow. He also said his back door was damaged and he's missing a lot of food from the kitchen. His horse is gone too."

"That's what the media reported. Go on."

"Like I said on the phone, the farmer heard an unidentifiable sound in the barn this morning, but we haven't located anything. We both heard loud squeaks and scratching noises from behind one of the walls but we couldn't see anything."

Braun spoke quickly, not hiding his impatience. "The damage to the farmer's door should have alerted the entire family, yet they didn't hear anything. We'll need to analyze the door. And if he says he heard something in the barn, we need to locate the source—now! This is the second alleged sighting he's reported and I want some answers."

Green, his rigid manner matching a sharp nose and ice-blue eyes, spoke up. "Sir, there is one thing. I was just about to check out a strange liquid substance inside…"

"Show me," Braun demanded, following Green into the barn.

Green pointed to the thick greenish-brown globs of liquid clinging to some of the hay strewn along the floor near an empty stall. "I was going to take a sample in for analysis, sir."

"Do it. And see that the lab puts a top priority on it."

Green filled a plastic bag with the gooey mixture and sealed it. Braun pulled a small can of Lysol from his coat pocket and sprayed the air around him. "This place is probably infested with germs." He put the can away and asked Wilder, "Where's that noise you mentioned?"

Wilder led him to the area next to a stall. Braun cocked his ear against the wall to listen, detecting a low scratching sound and heavy wheezing.

"Could be a rat," Wilder said. "Stuck inside the wall."

"Pull the boards away," Braun ordered, popping another antacid into his mouth.

Green searched the barn and found a crowbar. He jammed it into a gap, leveraging one of the boards away from the wall.

Braun's face reddened. "Faster, you idiot—it might have an escape tunnel!"

Green used the heel of his boot to smash down on the crowbar. The board ripped off.

Startled, Braun stumbled backward and froze, fixating on what looked like a two-foot long rodent making a shrill noise. It hissed and snarled, ogling him with red and yellow eyes. A thin purple tongue extended between long fangs. Large brown warts covered its hairy body.

Before Braun could grab his can of Lysol to spray it, the creature jumped past him and scampered out the back door. Pointing at the bizarre animal, his voice trembled. "C…c…catch that *thing*! And bring it back alive!"

Wilder ran after it.

Braun tried to follow but his legs wobbled like jello. He bumped into Green, biting his tongue and losing his balance. When he got up his hand was covered in wet manure. He shouted to his driver.

"Charles, get my wet-wipes—and hurry up, dammit…" Waiting, he held his hands in the air and hung out his bloody tongue.

Wilder chased across the field after the creature. Then he suddenly stopped and shouted, "It's running up the hill into the woods, sir."

"Keep going," Braun yelled with a lisp, his tongue a burning pain.

Charles brought wet wipes from the car and cleaned him off before spraying his hands. "This is a matter of international security," Braun shouted. "There could be more of those ugly beasts out there. Go after it!"

Both aides continued the chase while he fumed.

A light rain hampered visibility.

The creature was nowhere in sight.

Braun threw the wet-wipes on the ground and ran to the car, motioning Charles to follow. He jumped into the back while Charles slid with care behind the wheel, patting down his impeccable black uniform jacket.

"Forget your friggin' coat," Braun yelled, "and get this car moving! Head for the woods."

Charles turned. "But sir, my Stella is the finest in the Geneva fleet. Those fields will ruin her."

Braun felt his blood pressure rising. "I'll get you another one. Just put it in 'go' and light a fire under this thing—Now!"

Charles grunted and drove. The heavy car broke through the hard ground and skidded on wet grass, bouncing over stones and into holes. Fresh cow paddies sprayed away from the wheels. A barbed wire fence ahead blocked their route.

Charles whined. "We have to stop."

"Ram the fence," Braun ordered. "Hit the pedal!"

Charles increased speed but not enough to break the wires. Spikes scraped across the hood and windshield in high-pitched screeches, slowing the car to a stop. Braun's teeth tingled from the sound.

"Sir," Charles moaned, "the ground is too soft."

"Flatten it," Braun ordered, leaning across the back of the front seat to catch sight of the animal.

The wheels spun but remained imbedded in deep mud while barbed wire wrapped the hood.

"My car is ruined," Charles wailed.

Braun sank back into the seat.

Failure was not an option.

Ever.

His mind tortured by the beast's escape he shrieked, "Get this tank turned around so I can requisition a helicopter and a team of hikers. And we'll need nets and dogs. Big hungry huntin' dogs. That ugly *critter* ain't from this planet, that's for certain."

Renewed excitement rippled through him. His voice lowered. "Once we capture this thing it's *show and tell time*, Charles. I won't forget your services either. I take care of my friends. That government sissy in Washington will stop breathing down my neck once I hand over this furry freak. Let's go catch us a space monster."

CHAPTER TWENTY-FIVE

The following day Braun headed back to the farm to look for the mysterious rodent. He barked at his driver. "We're late. Gotta' see if the troops have found that freaky monster yet."

Charles patted down his ill-suited hair piece and said in a glum tone, "Yes sir."

Braun knew that Charles detested aggressive driving, his personality avoiding controversy whenever possible, but he wasn't going to get into a pity-party with his driver. "Faster, Charles. You can't be a sissy when it comes to get up and go. This is a Mercedes, dammit. Just slam it, will you?"

Charles sped up and the farm came into view.

A helicopter sat waiting on a clearing near the barn. Braun greeted the pilot who informed him the rodent had not been captured. Braun climbed on board and pointed, "Fly me over there, toward the men."

The chopper ascended and flew into the morning sun, circling over the field. The wind had calmed, but Braun ignored the weather, peering through his binoculars for any sign of the *thing*.

Someone had leaked the sighting to the press. Back at the barn half-a-dozen reporters crowded behind a barricade held back by the same four Swiss officers from the day before. "I knew this would get out," Braun grumbled. The pilot couldn't hear through the noise. "Stupid sensationalists," he added.

Braun watched his troops scour the terrain. Twenty American and Swiss security men combed the fields on foot, some leading dogs on leashes. "My men will find that little runt. If not, we'll catch it with the Humvee."

Braun had ordered the powerful sports utility jeep to navigate the fields. Its commanding officer hung halfway out the side window of the agile vehicle, scanning the ground with binoculars. The men beat through the bushes, swinging axes and cracking open logs.

Braun shouted into the radio to the officer of the black Humvee, "Use the dogs you morons, they'll sniff it out."

The copter turned and Braun saw Charles near the barn dusting off his loaner car. The black Mercedes was a temporary replacement without bullet-proof windows. Stupid twerp wouldn't have a life without his cars.

Braun ordered the pilot to circle above the trees in view of an area beyond the forest. He spotted a few vacation cabins, surprised by the smoke trailing from one of the chimneys. He would have the pilot bring him back later to check it out.

When the pilot banked and swooped back toward the farm again, Braun's stomach turned queasy. Charles waved frantic arms and pointed to the barn. The police strained to control the reporters from swarming in.

"Fly closer to my driver," he shouted to the pilot, gripping the seat of the chopper. Charles continued to wave and shout.

The helicopter blades stirred the grass, whipping Charles' hair and blowing off his toupee. He scrambled after the hairpiece.

Braun shouted to the Humvee on his walkie-talkie. "I think the runt's in the barn—get the troops back here!"

He told the pilot to land, but before they touched down, Joseph Reinholt ran out of his house with a shotgun.

What the heck?! I told him I'd protect his livestock… Leaning out of the chopper, he shouted to Charles. "Stop that idiot!"

Charles ran bald-headed toward the farmer catching up with him at the barn entrance. The two men struggled over the gun.

The rodent darted out the rear and charged across the field, heading straight at the approaching Humvee and the troopers on foot.

In an angry voice Braun shouted into his walkie-talkie, "Get that freak—somebody throw a net over that mini-monster!"

The farmer shoved Charles to the ground and aimed his gun at the animal.

"Grab him…" Braun yelled.

Charles kicked the farmer's leg and knocked him off balance at the moment he squeezed the trigger. The shot blasted through the passenger and driver's window of the new Mercedes, shattering both. Charles closed his eyes and hung his head.

"Bloody hell," Braun cursed, watching the rodent escape. At chaotic shouts from the reporters he turned to see them knock down the barricades and shove the police aside. They chased after the creature snapping photos while the authorities ran after them.

The helicopter lifted off again and hovered over the rodent as it fled the hunting party. The noise of the blades aggravated Braun's explosive temper.

He motioned the Humvee to follow.

Its driver increased the speed of the SUV, crushing small rocks and spraying dirt. The officer in command hung out the window and shouted to the troops. Braun listened on the walkie-talkie.

"We've got it cornered," the man yelled. "Bring those nets boys!" To his driver he shouted, "Slow this thing down!"

The Humvee reduced speed.

One of the men on foot stumbled and lost grip of his dog. The German shepherd sprang after the creature. "Stop that dog. Shoot it if you have to," the Humvee officer yelled.

A foot soldier aimed his handgun at the dog. The deformed rat made a u-turn and doubled back toward the Humvee. It turned so fast that the dog rolled over and lost time before charging again.

"Don't run over it," the officer shouted to his driver.

The rodent continued toward the oncoming vehicle. The foot soldier fired at the dog.

He missed.

The gunfire startled the rodent. It bolted under the Humvee.

Instead of stopping, the SUV accelerated and sped out of control, ramming through a fence and crashing into an oak tree.

Braun watched in horror. His inner radar told him all was lost.

He ordered the pilot to land near the crash. Out of the chopper and fuming, he surveilled the situation. All that remained of the alien monster were green and red bits and pieces strewn across the ground. The strangest *thing* he'd ever witnessed had been reduced to what resembled flattened Christmas popcorn. He glowered at the officer in charge who grumbled something about his driver hitting the gas pedal instead of the brakes.

Reporters flashed photos from a few yards away. Braun waited for the Swiss police to escort them back to the farm. He paced in front of the men until the journalists were out of earshot and then said to his men, "I'll see that you never get another decent assignment in your entire careers, you nitwits."

He popped another antacid into his mouth and pointed at a man wearing heavy horned-rimmed glasses. "You there, get some plastic bags and see that you pick up every last bit of that thing. Get some helpers!"

"Yes sir." The man hurried away.

He gazed at the others; a wicked smile lit his face. "And since you've blown this here field trip today, you can bloody well hike your feet off." He pointed toward the woods. "Head on through there and I'll meet you on the other side at the first clearing."

The men groaned and started to climb. Braun returned to the chopper and flew back to the farm. Charles sat on the back steps of the house holding his wet toupee. "Car-crazy clunk-head!" Braun told the pilot. "Put her down so I can assess the damage. What a mess."

"Yes sir."

"And after I disinfect, we'll head up to that cabin in the woods. But let's give the troops time to get there first."

"The cabin with the smoke, sir?"

"That's the one."

CHAPTER TWENTY-SIX

"What do you want?" Peter asked Starbeam, annoyed by the intrusion in the middle of his dream. He wanted to return to the alien who had called out to him. He'd never gotten that close before.

I must relieve myself, Starbeam thought.

Peter swayed from his bout with beer and slid off the cot, taking the horse outside. When he crawled back into bed he grumbled, "Don't disturb me again—I have a hangover and my head hurts, but I need to get back to my dream."

He fell asleep and was back on his planet. Dressed in a clean silver robe, his body felt strong and healthy. The air around him smelled soothing, like sunshine on newly-cut grass. But when a sudden breeze blew a putrid odor from a large glass cauldron, he grimaced. Turning away from the pot, he faced an angry-looking tribunal of men sitting behind a floating glass table. Their eyes accused him, boney fingers pointing while their toothpick legs and small feet dangled beneath floating chairs. What could be the source of their power?

Behind the strange beings, glass houses in the shapes of pyramids, cubes and small domes stretched away beyond large open windows. The buildings floated on cloud-like puffs of white smoke. High overhead, a gigantic transparent dome enclosed the entire village.

It's like a giant greenhouse, he remembered, with artificial solar lamps to illuminate the interior. A monstrous fan the size of a two-story building circulated the air.

He began to recall life on his former planet and brightened. As a scientist, he'd researched ways to control the tidal fluctuations of the seven moons and been instrumental in rescuing the planet from destruction.

When the tribunal leader banged a glass gavel on the table, Peter's excitement dampened. The man glared at him. Three beings sat on either side of him wearing robes decorated with moons, stars and planets. They had long slender bodies and oblong heads with bulging eyes. A long white beard made the leader look like an aged warlock. His pointed hat held a star-shaped gemstone that glistened in the artificial lighting. When his pupils enlarged, they changed from green to red. He fixed eyes on a small transparent pyramid floating in front of the table, forcing crystallized power to surge through a curled wire at the top of the pyramid.

Sparks flashed.

An interior triangle glowed with a red and yellow range of compressed energy. A burst of white smoke shot into the air from the top wire and out through a network of lines crisscrossing the village.

The energy source. Peter realized they were all born with power in their eyes. Smaller pyramids covered the fields and lined the pathways. He had helped develop those too.

A male being dressed in a plain gray robe stood on a floating ladder stirring something in the large glass pot Peter had seen earlier. Steam from the mixture surged upward, invading the fresh air with a sour smell. A murky mist clouded the domed ceiling high above him.

The leader pointed a finger with an extended purple nail at Peter. About two inches long it curled at the end.

Peter began to perspire and his legs weakened. The foul smell was getting to him.

The leader spoke, his voice croaking and reverberating through the air. *"Oox-oer-ri-op! Plec-tac-fun, Yetz. Fik-owli-pia-moff."*

Peter looked at him in confusion. "Can you speak English?" he asked in a clear voice. It was the first time he had spoken to anyone in his recurring dream.

The man glowered at him before adjusting his lower mouth and neck. He clicked, clacked and clucked as if changing channels. "Very well. You have deceived your brothers and therefore you must die."

"What do you mean?" Peter whined. "What have I done?"

The tribunal leader stretched out his arm and touched Peter with the tip of his nail. The electric shock made him stumble backward. "You have offended the moons," his accuser said in a wavering tone.

Peter regained his balance; his throat became tight and dry. "But how?" he stammered. A jolt of energy from the leader's eyes hit Peter's right knee. His legs buckled and he fell to the glass floor. "Ouch!" he moaned.

"You were supposed to repent, but you chose to serve yourself," the leader said. "You took credit from your brothers. You are greedy…" The man's voice grew louder and his words echoed in the great space. *"Greeeeeee-deeeeeeeeee…"*

"You're wrong," Peter cried in anguish. "I am your beloved Moonchild. I've been searching for you all my life."

Something wet nudged his face. He opened his eyes.

The morning sun cast light into the small cabin.

Starbeam's nostrils blew gold dust on him.

Peter groaned in misery. He was back in his deformed body and his smelly clothes were soaked with sweat. He pushed Starbeam away and sat up, holding his aching head between his hands. "What a nightmare," he mumbled in a tinny voice.

The winged-horse nodded. *You were agitated and speaking rapidly.* Starbeam farted and dropped excrement onto the wooden floor. *Excuse me.*

"Phew…" Peter looked over the edge of the bed. "It's green and purple with silver specks… Is that space dung?" he asked, sliding off the bed.

I tried to hold it. I am not accustomed to confined spaces.

"Thanks a lot." Peter covered his nose.

What gibberish were you speaking?

"Gibberish? I was about to die on planet Rowundum." He got up and gathered the newspaper he had stolen from the farmhouse, using it to clean up the mess. After dumping it in the garbage bin behind the cabin, he led the horse outside. "I'll take you to water and then we'll go into the woods where we won't be seen."

At the pond Peter scanned the mountains in the distance. The sweet smell of wet grass overwhelmed his senses. "This euphoric aroma is why I came to Switzerland," he said to the horse. "It's the smell from my former planet." He cleared his throat and looked around. "I don't know if my ancestors on Rowundum can hear me, but it feels like everything I say can be heard in space somewhere. Could it be true?"

A gust of wind slapped Peter in the face. He winced. "Where'd that come from? There wasn't any wind a moment ago…"

Starbeam lifted his shoulders in a horse shrug and said, *Everything you think and do is recorded…*

"Moon rubbish. No one can possibly hear me."

Starbeam arched his head and thought, *Don't be so sure…*

"What do you know about it?" Peter asked. "Tell me."

The winged horse ignored him and drank from the pond.

And drank.

And drank.

"Leave some for the ducks," Peter said. But Starbeam continued until satisfied.

The odd pair walked back to the cabin and Peter confided, "I used to long to remember my past, but now all I want is to forget. I always believed my dreams were my true reality and this life only a temporary shell to support them. How wrong I was! It's a good thing I woke up from my nightmare before learning more. And all this trouble because of Rotar's book. I should have thrown it away. But now I desperately need it so I can sell it to my foreign partner."

At the front porch he patted Starbeam's neck. "I thought I had achieved my life-long quest. I stepped into the looking glass and found the answers but the power does me little good while I'm stuck down here. The transformation is killing me."

Starbeam nodded.

"But I can still win," Peter assured. "I just need the antidote."

He sat down on a pile of firewood and pulled out his phone. "You were supposed to remind me to call my wife." He started to dial but his sensitive hearing picked up unfamiliar sounds in the distance. He stared across the meadow and scanned the forest with his long-range vision.

An army of men moved through the woods toward him. "Oh my furious, fickle moons," he cried. "They're coming to get me. It's an invasion!"

He jumped off the logs and hobbled to the kitchen where he grabbed the pillowcase and scooped up the remaining food and drinks. He saw no sign of his visit other than cold ashes in the fireplace.

Struggling with the heavy food sack, he clambered onto the horse, guiding it toward the forest. The loud noise of a helicopter in the distance scared him. "Hurry Starbeam, but don't fly. Don't want that chopper to see us."

The horse galloped.

Peter clutched the rope, bouncing up and down. The food bag pounded his leg. He hoped to make it to the trees without falling off.

"Almost there," he cried, "faster—faster…"

Starbeam sped across the open field and into the shelter of the woods. "Whoaa…whoaa…" Peter said, pulling hard on the horse's mane.

Starbeam stopped abruptly, jerking Peter forward, then backward. He laid flat on the horse's back and looked up through the trees. The chopper cleared their tops, flying toward the cabin.

He sat up. "That was close Starbeam, but we made it. Let's keep going and get away from here, but be careful."

The horse snorted, swinging his head up and down while trotting along the uneven path. "This is hazardous ground," Peter warned again. "Not for klutzes."

I'm not a klutz, Starbeam thought. *You are…*

He ignored the comment, directing the horse along the upper ridge of the woods and away from the army of men. The two aliens continued in an easterly direction crossing four streams before they found a small clearing sheltered by trees. Peter dismounted and tied Starbeam to a branch in a grassy area where he also gathered wood for a fire. Then he made a bed out of pine branches and rested on his soft creation. Willing himself to relax, he felt detached from both of his worlds. The seclusion of the forest hid them and not even his former planetary lords could threaten him at the moment. But the reality of his situation dampened his mood and while waiting for dusk to light a fire, he ate some of his food and sipped milk.

Starbeam nibbled grass.

When the sun finally sank behind the tree tops, Peter focused his gaze on the pile of wood he had gathered until the twigs and branches caught fire. "Not bad," he said to Starbeam. "You are obviously impressed?"

The horse kept eating.

"Okay horse. But if it gets cold, you'll appreciate my fire power." Starbeam snorted.

"At least I know now how I got these powers," Peter rambled. "And you acquired your gold dust and wing power from Androdon."

He suddenly remembered the aborted phone call. Dialing Amanda again, he waited for the hotel to answer. When the call went through to her room, it rang and rang.

No answer.

He called back and learned that she had checked out. He tried her cell phone, but it went straight into voice mail. Frustrated he said to Starbeam, "My wife has probably taken my book with the antidote back to DC. Can you fly me there?" he asked. "Of course you can't. I'd die. So what do I do now?"

Starbeam pawed the ground and grabbed the rope in his teeth, pulling it free of the tree. While flexing his shoulder muscles, he waved his curly tail, snorting gold crystals over the fire. Peter watched the sparkling dust particles settle, leaving only blackened wood.

Starbeam nudged him, thinking, *Climb on.*

Curious, Peter grabbed his supply sack and mounted. "Where're we going?"

You'll see.

The horse advanced from a trot to a canter. Peter gripped the rope. A fallen tree lay ahead in their path, too high to jump over. "Watch out…," he yelled, closing his eyes.

Starbeam flapped his wings and lifted into the night sky, clearing the obstruction easily. Radiant stars twinkled, and a crescent moon glowed among them. As they ascended higher, Peter wanted to reach up and touch the stars, but didn't dare let go of Starbeam's neck. Wind stung and pounded him, but he held on.

Starbeam circled and headed toward Coppet. They flew over Peter's favorite landmark, the Chateau du Coppet, its multiple stone chimneys rising into the dark night. The horse turned toward Lake Geneva. Peter shouted, "Oh, my happy, freezing moon-face. Are we going to my comrade? Hurry Starbeam! Vidollet can help me contact Amanda!"

Starbeam thought nothing, accelerating in speed as he zoomed toward the lab.

CHAPTER
TWENTY-SEVEN

When the barn came into view, Peter yelled to Starbeam. "How did you know where to take me?"

Your energy is there, Starbeam thought.

In a majestic swoop the horse landed under the cover of trees away from the barn. Peter slid off. "Whew, you did it." He started to tie him to a tree, but remembered Starbeam could just untie it again. "Stay here, understand?"

Starbeam nodded.

The plastic tarp covering the foundation of his ancestral home flapped in the wind, catching Peter's attention. A longing simmered through his weak body, savoring the memory of his grandmother's waffles smothered in butter and home-made jam. But he had no choice but to reject his craving and instead focused his x-ray vision on the barn.

Two guards stood outside by the front door. What were they doing here?

Holding his breath, he crept between the sheep toward the trough. The animals shifted out of the way, their bells clanging. He stayed low, hoping the mild disturbance would go undetected.

Near the side door he listened for any sign of the security guards. Then he focused again and saw only the hazy image of Dr. Vidollet inside, leaning over a table mixing ingredients into a large glass decanter. The coast was clear. He rushed into the lab. "Doctor, I'm back," Peter hissed.

His partner lifted eyebrows in surprise. "Peter—you look even worse than before. I hoped your experiment would wear off. You do not look at all like the reporters described you and flying on the back of a winged horse? Is this true?"

"I'm afraid so, and now the military is after me."

"Your wife is looking for you too. She brought your notes for the antidote." He shifted back to his papers.

"She's in Geneva? Wonderful. Is it done?"

Vidollet looked up with angry eyes. "I should not even be concerned about your antidote."

"Why not? What's wrong?"

"Who is Marta?"

"How do you know about Marta?"

"How do you think?"

"Amanda?"

The doctor nodded.

"Moon curse—I must call Marta at once, but where's Amanda now?"

The doctor's eyes went dark. "She was shot after bringing me the formula."

"My wife was shot?!"

"Grazed by a bullet. A sniper in the woods."

"Is she all right?"

"She will be fine. Her friend posted the guards."

"What friend?"

"Mr. Ramsey."

"Who's he?"

"An American attorney, but I think there is more to him than that. He seems to have unlimited resources."

"So where is she?"

"She did not say."

"But you're preparing my antidote aren't you?"

"I have started to work on it."

"Thanks." Peter heaved a noisy sigh. "I've come for the silver book. And food. Something I can take with me."

The doctor stared, blank-faced. "I have cookies if you want, but I no longer have the book."

Peter gasped. "Where is it?"

"I gave it to your wife for safekeeping. Two men broke in to steal it." He pointed to his bruised forehead. "Do you know who they are, Peter—these thugs?"

He hesitated. "I do have other colleagues, but they wouldn't hurt anyone…"

"Obviously not." Vidollet looked away.

"Blast the jumping moonbeams—I'm sorry you were harmed but I need the book. What should I do?"

"I must finish this. Come back in two days. As for the silver book and the whereabouts of your wife, that is none of my concern."

Vidollet shuffled over to the cabinet where he kept Fanny's cookies and handed them to Peter. Fanny came out from under the desk squawking and flapping her wings. Peter grabbed the cookies and started to leave. Fanny pecked at his leg.

The front door opened with a bang. A tall muscular guard stood in the doorway pointing a revolver. "What's all the noise?" He looked at the doctor, then at Peter. "What the blazes?"

Peter rushed out the side door, half floating, half hobbling in the direction of the trees. He fumbled with the sack tied to his belt, whistling for Starbeam in a sound so high-pitched that birds screeched and flew out of the trees. The winged horse trotted toward him. Peter heard the guards shouting, their pounding feet drawing closer.

He pulled a can of beer from his sack and gulped the bubbly liquid, emptying it. Some slid down his chin. His head flashed hot and he began to rise. A bullet whizzed past his head. Starbeam took flight.

"Moaning moons, we're both dead," Peter cried.

Starbeam circled overhead, and Peter reached for the rope, but it was too far away. "Come get me," he shouted to the horse as Peter continued to rise.

Someone shot again. Another miss.

Starbeam flapped his wings and nose-dived toward the guards, blowing gold dust on their handguns. When the powder blanketed the weapons, the guns stopped firing.

The men looked confused, clicking their revolvers again and again. Starbeam flew toward Peter who caught the rope and hung on tight, his body swaying as he dangled in the air. Starbeam flew down to a long bare limb on a dead tree.

Take hold of the tree, Starbeam thought, hovering over the limb. Peter grabbed it and hung there while the horse flew underneath and picked him up on its back.

Peter wrapped the rope around himself to keep from floating off the horse. Pleased to be back in control, he focused his fire power at the confused-looking men. Flames from his eyes burst in front of them. He blasted fire, again and again. A flame hit the guard's arm setting his uniform on fire. Starbeam blew gold dust and put it out. Peter waved to the guards and smiled while they shook their fists at him. He directed Starbeam to leave. "I don't know what that stuff is, but I'm sure going to find out. I could make a *fortune* with you."

The rope kept Peter tied to the horse while they flew back to the forest. "We're in big trouble now, Starbeam. Those guards will report us, but don't worry. I'm almost free and so are you. I'll be back in my own body soon."

They landed at the same sheltered spot in the woods. Starbeam clamped his teeth on the rope while Peter built a fire. When he sat down, he weighted himself with heavy rocks and waited for the beer to wear off. "Your gold dust is intriguing Starbeam."

It has many purposes, the horse thought.

"You're a rare find… You fly, and you have magical gold dust. But why on earth—I mean, why in heaven's name would you wish to be reborn on this planet? You were only an ordinary work horse here."

I was admired on my former planet, but I wished to come here to find my true love. I have good bloodlines, but of all the horses I met in the vast fields of Androdon, I never encountered the horse of my dreams…

"I didn't know horses could love."

All beings can love, so I dreamed of a new life here. Love was rumored to be a condition of existence on Earth… I wished to be mated with my true love forever…an eternal commitment, like humans have…

"We try," Peter stammered, "but few make it because…well my father, for instance, was never faithful to my mother, but… never mind."

Starbeam continued. *My father was a legend…the sire of his day…a magnificent flying champion with a supercharged, wide wingspan. He won every air race and achieved many planetary records. But I inherited my mother's smaller wings, and he went on to sire more offspring…* A gold tear leaked from Starbeam's eye. *You have not met your true love?*

"Yes…but I blew it. Let's focus on you. Have you found love here on earth?"

Starbeam dropped his head. *No. Destiny brought me to a farm where I was the only horse. I still had no one… I wanted someone who needed me for myself, not my genes…*

Peter looked up from the fire. "It seems the complications of relationships even stretches into the universe," he said. "I had that love you came here for, but now I don't know…"

You are lonely too?

"Desperate is more accurate, but I'd rather not talk about it right now. I prefer to rest."

Peter laid down, adjusting the rocks around him. Starbeam's story triggered his own guilt and shame. He had to make things right again with Amanda. But what if she no longer loved him? Drifting into a light sleep, he prayed that his dreams wouldn't take him back to Rowundum.

CHAPTER
TWENTY-EIGHT

Amanda woke in her hotel bedroom and looked around. Disoriented, her side hurt. The bandages wrapped around her waist restricted movement. When the room came into focus the blurry figure of a woman dressed in a white uniform moved to her side.

"The bullet was shallow," she said in a French accent. "Not much damage. You were very lucky, *Madame.*" Her voice sounded childlike from a petite body with short dark hair that framed a cherub face.

The devastating scene at the lab in Coppet flooded Amanda's thoughts. She remembered clutching Rotar's silver book and calling out for him.

Her vision cleared and she tried to sit up but stopped when she felt a dull pain in her side. "My children, are they all right? And Lizzy?"

The nurse placed a hand on her arm. "You need not agitate yourself, *Madame.* Everyone is fine. The children are watching television."

"I want to see them."

"You have been sleeping for nearly twenty-four hours. *S'il vous plait*, you must calm yourself." The woman took something from the nightstand. "The pain medication has worn off." She handed Amanda two pills and a glass of water. "Something for the discomfort."

Amanda swallowed, but was not in the mood to relax. She could handle a little pain. She still hadn't told her children about Peter. A sudden knock at the door was followed by Michelle and Howard rushing into the room.

Amanda smiled. "It's so wonderful to wake up and see my two favorite people on the entire planet." She shifted and sat up.

"Are you okay, Mommy?" Michelle asked, afraid to hug her. "Tony said you just needed to sleep."

Howard grasped her forearm. "I should've protected you, Mom."

"I'll be fine. What matters is that we're all safe."

Howard's face contorted with anger. "This is because of Dad, isn't it?"

She asked the nurse to wait in the living room and then slid out of bed. Her head a bit woozy, she wobbled to the wingback chair in front of the window and made herself comfortable. She gestured Howard and Michelle to sit on the floor. They listened to her abbreviated version of Peter's living arrangement with a friend in Geneva. She left out details of Peter's physical condition and told them their father was part of an experimental research team designing and testing space suits and gear. She added that government officials were trying to find him in connection with his work. Then she planted the first seed to prepare them for the impending breakup of the family.

"So, my darlings, it's very important that we continue to look for Daddy, but he may have to stay in Switzerland for a while. He might not be able to come home right away."

Michelle's eyes opened into sad saucers. "Why not?"

Howard interrupted. "How come they can't find him? Where'd he go?"

"I'm not sure, but I'm going to find out."

"But you won't go away, will you Mommy?" Michelle looked ready to cry.

"Of course not sweetie." Amanda struggled to hold back tears.

In a frantic tone Michelle pleaded, "Promise you won't ever leave us, Mommy?"

"Never, ever, my precious…"

Howard clutched his knees and hammered the carpet with his heel. "Dad told me he'd be home for Halloween. Now he'll probably miss Christmas and my birthday, too. What's going on? Why's he livin' here with a friend?"

She looked at her hands. "I don't have all the answers but I think it's less expensive that way... And he still loves you very much."

Michelle got up from the floor. "No he doesn't. He's a big fat liar." She ran out of the room.

Howard stood and clenched his hands. "Dad told me it didn't matter that I was crippled. He said I was still his warrior son, a brave and mighty knight. He's full of it."

"No Howard, he does feel that way about you and that will never change. But right now there are other things that haven't turned out the way he planned. Try to understand."

"I don't want to understand! I just want my dad..."

"I know, but what if he's in trouble and needs our help?" She felt terrible for her children and hated lying to them but they weren't ready for the whole truth. She stood up. Where's Tony and Elizabeth?"

The change of focus worked. Howard said, "Lizzy's glued to her computer as usual, and Tony took that funny-looking book to some specialists."

She gasped. "Oh my jumbled stars, he had no right to do that without permission. He probably took it to his contact." Even more reason to find Peter as fast as possible. "Hold my hand, will you Howard?" With his help, she shuffled to the bathroom to wash up. He steadied her as she slipped on slacks and a sweater. When she leaned over to lace her red high-tops, she winced, but anger over the missing book drove her to ignore her wound.

With coat in hand, she picked up her bag. It felt heavy. She rummaged inside and discovered the purple rock. *Where did that come from?* She remembered the scene back at the lab and realized Lizzy must have put it back. Howard stood guard over her.

"You're not leaving, are you Mom? Can I go with you?"

"Sorry, but I need you to stay here and watch the girls."

"But that nurse is here; you can't go out by yourself."

"I'll be fine."

She munched on a chocolate and handed the box to Howard. "Help yourself but don't ruin your appetite."

Howard nodded but his heavy brows lifted in concern. "Mom, if Dad doesn't come home, you'll need me more than ever. I want to come with you."

"I know, and of course I need you, but this is something I have to do by myself. I'll be fine, don't worry." She felt confident, knowing she had the rock and could summon Rotar.

Howard sulked and followed her through to Tony's living room where Amanda greeted the nurse and sent her home. She addressed the others. "Go ahead and order room service if you want. Just don't leave this suite under any circumstance." With a quick kiss for her two children, she waved to Lizzy and left, bumping into Tony in the hall. He looked excited but frowned when he saw her.

"What're you doing? You can't go out in your condition." He took her arm and tried to maneuver her back inside.

She pulled away and groaned from an ache in her side. She stared him down. "Where's the book?" she demanded.

He glanced down the hall looking nervous. "Can we talk inside?"

"No. I'm leaving. Let's use the elevator."

They walked down the hall and waited for it in silence. Once inside, Tony spoke first. "I just got back from the hospital. The security officer who was shot is going to make it. He might lose an eye, it's too soon to tell, but he's coherent and on the mend."

"Thank heaven for that," she said. "I've told my children a little about all this. They think their father's working on some bizarre space equipment and might have to remain in Switzerland. I'm going back to the lab now to see if there's been any sign of him."

Tony looked skeptical. "This could be very dangerous, Amanda. Not a situation for amateurs. If Peter shows up we'll hear about it. We have to consider our children's safety."

She huffed with impatience. "I know you're trying to be helpful but it's *my* husband who created all these problems. I owe it to my children to help him. He's still their father."

Tony looked irritated. "What can you do on your own with two kids? You were just shot, and it could have been fatal. Don't you realize what's at stake here? Not just for us but for the future of the planet? If your husband's theory is correct, we may not even be a common race of human beings!"

She was fully aware of the risk yet something urged her on. She needed to contact Rotar. "Of course I know, but Peter's in danger and I have to do something."

Wincing at a sudden spasm of pain, she pointed a finger at him. "Who are you and who do you work for and where's the book?"

The elevator opened at the lobby. They walked outside. She fumed, waiting for an answer.

He lit a cigarette.

"The book?" she asked again.

"I thought Leo Braun could help translate it. He's got more resources than I do."

"Did you arrange to join me on my flight?"

"We met because of your daughter's panic attack, remember? But if not for her, I would have found some other way to meet you. I was attracted."

"Was?"

"I'm not sure how I feel anymore."

"My wedding ring meant nothing?"

"I was so dazzled by you that I didn't see it at first."

She glared at him. "I don't believe you."

Tony said, "Braun's been looking for Peter too." If he doesn't find him before…" He looked away.

"Before what?"

He met her angry eyes. "Before someone else does. Peter's formula could be lethal in the wrong hands and extremely valuable on the black market."

Amanda's expressed her vehemence. "No government involvement. I owe him that much. I don't care what he's done. He's the father of my children and out there alone and probably scared."

Tony's voice tightened with annoyance. "This is absurd, Amanda. How can you hope to do what experts with manpower and equipment are having trouble accomplishing?"

She raised her chin. "I won't know until I try."

"If you continue to investigate at least let me go with you."

"And bring your government buddies along?"

"No, I give you my word on that. We'll go underground and do this together and if questioned we can be sightseers. I'm diverting you with tourist attractions."

"There's just one problem Tony." She looked hard at him. "What good is your word?"

His neck flushed red. She'd never seen a reaction like that from him. "Are you blushing?"

"No, but I'm upset." He took a nervous drag on his cigarette.

Maybe he had a conscience after all. "Okay, we have a deal. But if I still find your motives questionable, we part our ways."

"Agreed."

"And I'm going to get that book back."

"I understand."

"And I'm bringing the kids along. Let's go tell them."

"Are you crazy?"

"Not at all. I have a plan."

Back at the suite Tony went straight to the hotel phone. "I'm going to call room service, we need some real food." He ordered raw vegetables, fruit and a variety of sandwiches.

When he hung up Amanda said, "Sounds good, but food won't get the book back." She addressed the group. "Okay team," Amanda added, "Are you ready for my secret weapon?"

Howard and Michelle stared up at her from the couch in silence. Lizzy swiveled on the computer chair.

Tony smirked from his perch in front of the fireplace. "Secret weapon?"

"I'll show you after we all vow to keep this among ourselves. Ready?"

Curious expressions crossed their faces and they nodded.

"This isn't a game," Amanda added. "It's serious and keeping your promise is vital."

"I certainly agree with that," Tony remarked.

"Wait here, I'll be right back." She grabbed her handbag and went to her own suite.

CHAPTER TWENTY-NINE

In the privacy of her bedroom, Amanda took out the purple rock and held it like a walkie-talkie. "I need you, Rotar."

A moment passed. A flash of light exploded.

Surrounded by a mass of rainbow-colored smoke, Rotar appeared and bounced onto the bed, chuckling in rapid snorts. He waved his stick and the smoke vanished.

"Thank the stars you're here Rotar," Amanda said.

"I have been waiting for you. I was afraid you had gone home." He somersaulted and landed on the floor with a loud thud.

She fixed eyes on him. "I was shot at the lab but I didn't have my rock and couldn't call you. Dr. Vidollet was attacked and two security men were hospitalized. Where were you?"

His eyes enlarged, flashed light, then retracted into mysterious dark pools. "I am extremely sad to learn of this. I was in the Far East."

"Far East? When we're desperately trying to locate Peter?"

"Yes, well, I had to deal with a storm. A monsoon was threatening a small island populated with fishing villages. The storm may have been caused by Aeolius, so I held it back which required several hours and a lot of magic. But I finally diverted it out to sea. You may have seen it on the news. The reporters said the change in the storm's direction was a miracle. So now I am a miracle worker." He changed the subject. "Are you still injured?"

"A little, but I'll be okay." She held her side.

He aimed his stick at her wound. *"Cor-ec-ti-um Hea-li-um."*

The dull pain vanished. When she raised her arm, nothing hurt. She peeked under the bandages. Not even a scar.

"Thank you! I want to know how you did that, but we have more important things to do first. I need your help and it's time to meet the rest of the team."

"I have already had the pleasure of meeting Master Howard."

"Yes, and now I want you to meet the others. We need your magic…your powers…your wisdom…your knowledge…" She gulped down her fear. "We're desperate."

Rotar began to pace. "Do I look all right?" he asked, adjusting the point of his hat.

She smiled. "You look fine. Are you feeling a bit shy?"

He nodded.

"Don't worry. They'll love you." She took his stubby hand and returned to Tony's living room.

Tony stared dumbstruck at Rotar.

Michelle jumped up and down, pointing and giggling.

Lizzy whispered, "I knew something freaky was going on."

Howard said, "You've come back, and you're really for real."

"His hat's just like the one in the attic," Michelle shrieked.

Amanda said, "Quiet please. This is my friend, *Rotar.*" She introduced each of them by name. Rotar removed his hat and tufts of thick-mottled orange-yellow hair stuck out.

"How do you do," he said. Faint ripples of pastel colors rolled across his face. He replaced the hat on his head. Its bell tinkled.

Tony circled Rotar, studying him. Rotar bowed and smiled, eyes squeezing together, cheeks flushed. The rainbow colors rippled across his face faster and brighter.

"McWooooooow," Michelle said, stretching the word. She ran over to him. "Can I touch it?" He let her stroke his cheek.

Howard just watched.

"What's the stick for?" Lizzy asked. "Is that…like…a funky homemade sword?"

"Don't be rude Elizabeth," Tony said.

"A cane?" she mumbled.

Rotar showed them the wand. "It is not a cane and much more than a sword."

He pointed his stick and it sparkled. *"Van-iss-iu, Max-i-milliam,"* he uttered. A strong gust of wind filled the room. They covered their faces. Rotar disappeared. The wind subsided.

"Where'd he go?" Howard asked, stunned.

Amanda tried to remain calm. "I don't know…"

The wind returned and they braced against its force. An ashtray crashed to the floor and a flower vase fell over. Rotar re-appeared with a man dressed in leather body armor. Wood basket-work tied the leather together and shells adorned the young man's chest plate. He carried a sword and stared at them in puzzlement.

"Awesommmmmmme…" Howard whispered.

Rotar beamed. "I am not supposed to travel through time, and I have never brought forth anyone from the past before. But Peter told me of his son's admiration for knights. I thought I might try it just this once."

The knight wandered the room looking terrified.

Amanda found her voice. "Rotar, can you calm him?"

Rotar waved his wand and the knight relaxed.

"How'd you do that?" asked Howard.

He grinned. "It is quite simple really. In what you call hyper-space, one can walk through walls, see through solid things, become invisible. It is an interaction between parallel universes. I brought him forth with my electro-magnetic energy waves, a little like your radio waves, then I tune my mind into the knight's world. I picture him, locate him, and I communicate with him. Do you see?"

"You mean like mental telepathy?" Amanda asked.

"Yes."

The knight leaned over the desk and touched Lizzy's computer. Then he peered out the window.

Amanda shifted her gaze from the knight to Rotar. "This knight seems totally unfamiliar with our time. Where's he from?"

"He's from England," Howard piped up. "Probably King Arthur's court. I can tell from the armor."

Amanda asked Rotar, "Why aren't you supposed to move in time? If you go into the future, you could see the results of our search for Peter, learn the outcome, and return to rescue him."

"Oh, no. I am serving my penance on this planet for that very reason."

"What happened?" Amanda asked.

Rotar looked down in sadness. "I tried to go into the future to learn the progress of medical research because I wanted to be tall. But I was caught and my master was very angry. Movement in time is forbidden. We are not allowed to disturb the natural progress of the universe. We can move through space from one place to another in current time, but that is all."

The knight bent down to look under the shade of the table lamp. He squinted at the light bulb, touched it and jerked his hand away.

Amanda asked, "Will you get into trouble for bringing forth this knight?"

"Most likely, but I will send him back before his life's course can be altered."

"Good," she said. "Please do it now."

"Not yet, Mom," said Howard. "I want to study him."

The knight scanned the room, confused but no longer terrified. He looked in his late teens with an overgrown beard and thick coarse hair down to his shoulders. "Where, pray tell, am I?" he asked, placing a cautious foot on the thick carpet. "This is a jester's folly, is it not?"

"Wow, he talks," Howard shouted. He went to the knight and reached for his sword, but the knight drew back. Howard smiled. "It's okay," he said in a confident voice. "I only want to look at it."

The knight eyed him, wary.

Howard leaned forward to examine the medieval sword without touching it.

The knight held up a hand to block him.

"It looks heavy," said Howard. "Can I please just *hold* it? I want to check the weight." He grinned, eager eyes flashing. "I won't hurt it."

The knight backed away. "And who be ye?"

"I'm just a kid who loves knights. I always dress like a knight on Halloween. I have a wooden sword. I'll let you hold my sword if I can hold yours?" He grabbed his sword next to the fireplace and waved it in front of him.

The knight looked skeptical but unsheathed his sword and handed it to Howard. Its weight jerked Howard off-balance. "It's so heavy," he said. "Can you make one just like it for me, but lighter?"

The knight looked insulted. "I am nay a sword-smith."

Amanda pleaded. "Rotar please take the knight back where he came from before anything happens."

She noted Rotar's obvious fascination. "In a moment," he said.

While Howard examined the sword, the knight stared at the television which was airing the news. "What is yon magic box? Ye practice black arts here?" He moved and touched the screen, pulling away when the faces moved. "The man is small and flat—as flat as a painter's canvas, yet he moves and speaks. He is inside? Or be this a painter's trick?" The knight put his arms around the TV to lift it.

Rotar pointed his magic wand at him. *Re-trac-to-fron-tum Max-i-mil-lium!*"

In a cloud of smoke the knight disappeared from the room along with the television set. Michelle ran to her mother. Howard stared at the empty table where the TV had been. "Neat," Howard said in a shaky voice.

Rotar sighed. "My knight will wake up believing he had a bad dream. But how he will explain the strange box, I do not know. It will show no magic in his world without electricity."

Lizzy picked at her braces. "We're busted. That weird dude stole our TV."

Excited, Howard dragged the sword with both hands. "Can I keep this?" he asked.

"Certainly," Rotar bowed.

"No you may not," Amanda burst out.

"It is of no concern," Rotar assured. "The Knight can acquire another, but I will lessen the weight of this one. *Van-iss-ium Weigh-tum,*" he commanded.

Howard beamed, "It's lighter now," waving it and lunging at the wall.

"Howard, be careful," Amanda cried.

"Mom, you have to see how it's worn and used."

"I see. But practice when you're alone, not with others around."

"I want to be a knight!" Howard shouted. "Can you make me into a real knight, Rotar?"

"Absolutely not," Amanda said.

Rotar shifted from Howard to Amanda. "I must go back and retrieve the television. I do not want a twenty-first century artifact to change the course of history. Then I would never finish serving my time here on your planet."

With the swish of his stick, Rotar disappeared. His hat jingled. Within moments another tinkle announced his return. "This television weighed nothing during transport," he explained. "But now it is heavy."

He struggled not to drop it.

Tony helped him set it on the table. "The knight was still wondering what had happened to him," Rotar said with a chuckle. "I whisked it away quickly."

Tony said, "I'm impressed, Rotar. You must be the dwarf Dr. Vidollet spoke of at the lab. We can certainly use your talents." He turned to Amanda. "How did you find him?"

"Rotar found me…"

"How?"

She shrugged, keeping the purple rock and Dot Comet to herself.

Tony nodded at Rotar. "Then you can find Peter for us?"

He shook his head. "Unfortunately, as I have already explained to Amanda, in his present condition he is protected, and I cannot penetrate his essence. He is shielded by a field of energy beyond my powers."

"So," Amanda added, "our first goal is to retrieve the silver book. Are you all willing to help?"

Tony's face closed. "It's safe with Braun."

"You have found my book of knowledge?" Rotar asked.

"Yes," Amanda said. "Dr. Vidollet was hiding it and gave it to us for safekeeping, but Tony has taken it to his associate here in Geneva."

Tony quickly added, "You must understand that this involves international security."

"It doesn't matter," Amanda interrupted. "Right is right. We have to get it back from Mr. Braun."

Tony shot an annoyed look. "Be reasonable, Amanda. The building is heavily guarded."

"I'll need help, but I know I can do it," she said. Waiting for Tony to argue further, she suddenly raised her hand. "I'll answer that."

And right on cue the telephone rang.

"*Allo?*" She heard heavy breathing on the other end.

"Amanda, thank God." Peter's voice sounded static and chopped up by an echo chamber.

"Peter, where are you? I've been looking everywhere for you."

"I've spoken to Marta," he said. "I'll make it up to all of you, I promise. But you must return the silver book to Dr. Vidollet. It's critical. If I don't give it to…"

"Listen to me, Peter," Amanda said in a frantic tone, "Your promises are empty. I won't return anything until you tell me where you are. I can help—"

"No," he interrupted. "Just return the book… It's promised to someone else. Then go home to the kids. You're in way over your head, Amanda. For once in your life listen to me."

"The book belongs to Rotar," she argued. "He can help you, Peter, and the kids—"

"I need that book," he interrupted. "It's crucial. For God's sake Amanda, just do it. My life's at stake here... "

The line went dead.

She slammed down the receiver. "He had the nerve to hang up again," she said, letting out her anger. "All he wants is Rotar's book—life and death for him, of course. No one else counts."

At a loud knock on the door Elizabeth dashed across the room. "It must be room service with our food," Lizzy said. Rotar was showing Howard how to hold the sword correctly.

Tony rushed after her saying over his shoulder. "Hide Rotar," but Lizzy had already flung open the door.

A young steward pushed a food cart inside. At seeing Rotar he stumbled on the carpet. The cart jerked and the trays slid over the edge. Rotar pointed his stick to stop them in mid-air and slid them back onto the cart. Wind tousled the waiter's hair. He backed away, displaying a stunned expression and rushed off.

Tony leaned into the hall shouting, "Just a magic trick—there'll be a tip waiting for you."

Amanda fidgeted. "He'll tell everyone."

"I hope not," Tony said. "Let's eat, shall we? I'm starving."

Rotar stood on tip-toe and eyed the food. He took a roast beef sandwich. "Do you have blood pudding? That is my favorite."

"Holy McYuck," Howard grimaced. "Blood pudding?"

"You have never tried it?" Rotar asked.

"No way." Howard wrinkled his nose. "Where do you live, anyway?"

Rotar's eyes fell. "I reside in a cave. It is not as pleasant as this hotel."

Michelle put her hand on his arm. "Can I see it sometime?"

"Of course but it is small and damp. Roots grow through the walls and the ground floods on occasion. I do not think you will like it."

"Sure I will," Michelle said.

"Sounds cool," added Howard.

Rotar looked thoughtful. "Perhaps."

They attacked the food. Lizzy returned to her computer. Tony followed her and offered a sandwich. "You must eat something."

"I'm on a diet, Dad."

"Try." He handed her the sandwich. She took it with no enthusiasm.

After the meal Amanda said to Tony, "It's settled then, tomorrow we retrieve Rotar's book."

His eyes went dark. "How do you expect to accomplish that? Braun won't hand it over, you don't have security clearance, and you're still wounded."

"No I'm not, Rotar healed me." She inched up her sweater, just enough for the others to see. "Look, the wound is gone and no pain, either."

Tony appeared awestruck. "I'm not sure I can even grasp this."

Howard and Michelle gawked in silence and even Lizzy turned to look.

"But I am able to go get my book," Rotar said.

"I was hoping you'd say that," Amanda said.

"Too dangerous," Tony threw in.

Another red flag alert. Was he stealing Rotar's book just like Peter?

"I only need to know the location," Rotar said.

"Done." Amanda said, smiling with confidence. "Tony will write it down for you, won't you Tony?"

Tony's face went grim.

"I will see you tomorrow then?" Rotar asked.

"You're welcome to stay here with us, Rotar," Amanda said. "Is that okay with you?"

"In a real bed?"

"In my suite. The couch converts into a bed. Is that problem?"

"No. I shall be extremely careful and most grateful."

Amanda cast a comforting smile, glad to know that he felt at home with them. Howard and Michelle beamed. They seemed happy with the arrangement too.

CHAPTER THIRTY

Braun approached his secretary in the foyer of his office located on the seventh floor at the American Bureau of Intelligence. Unlike the building which had a plain stone edifice and a lobby designed in modern tones of silver and white contrasted with black marble and black leather furniture, Braun preferred a traditional décor which made him feel part of American history. Mahogany antiques polished to a high sheen accompanied the American, Presidential and Swiss flags, standing on poles. He also had a trophy secretary. Tall, with a long blonde braid down her back. A distinctive dimple made her look younger than she was.

"Where is my historian?" Braun growled, startling his assistant.

She blinked and then smiled politely, exposing a gap between her front teeth. "He should be here by now. Perhaps traffic?"

"Traffic? When I am in possession of the most significant find in the history of the world?"

Fuming, he returned to his office and continued washing each tiny leaf of an overgrown fichus tree. A pine smell of disinfectant filled the room. The silver book lay open on his oversized desk.

Tired of the task, he plunked down in his chair and studied the strange symbols printed in gold script. The yellowed paper had a parchment quality to it.

At a tap on his door he looked up. "Professor Gerard has arrived," blonde-braid announced. She accompanied him to a chair and then backed out of the office, closing the door.

Braun reached across the desk and they shook hands. "Glad you could finally make it," he said in a snide tone.

A slight man, the professor looked frazzled, wind-blown and parched. His short dark beard covered pink skin that was flaking and his stare was intense through thick glasses. Braun regretted touching him and used a wet wipe to clean his hands.

"And this is the book you mentioned?" the man asked, clearing his throat.

Braun handed the man a bottle of water and chuckled. "Much more than a mere book, my friend. Can't make out any of it, but I can assure you it is not a record from this planet."

The professor took a sip of water. "And how did you come to that conclusion?"

Braun could see that the professor was doubtful. "I'm not at liberty to share all the details, but we tried to copy it, photograph it, scan it, and it can't be duplicated. Also, one would deduce from its thickness that it weighs four or five pounds, yet it's light as a feather."

"Mon Dieu. May I have a closer look?"

"Of course. But as I told you over the phone, you will sign this confidentiality agreement first. This is top secret. Not a word of this leaves my office."

The professor nodded and signed. Braun called his assistant in to sign as a witness. When the legalities were done, the eager historian moved to the other side of the desk. He perused the open pages and then carefully lifted a page with trembling fingers. "This is incredible."

"Yes, I savor its uniqueness," Braun said. "I believe there is information in here as to our very existence," he added, "as well as evidence of life on other planets. And I'm hoping that sooner or later you will fill in the what, why, when, where and how…"

The visitor said nothing, leaning closer to the foreign script. "I will need colleagues to help me. I'll have to move the book."

"Not possible. Anyone who studies this will do it here. We have a lab in the basement as well as research rooms. Anyone you select will be approved by me first and comply with the same restrictions."

The professor blinked and pushed heavy glasses up his nose. He was obviously not pleased with the arrangement. "May I use the men's room a moment?"

Braun hesitated. "What for?"

"To alleviate myself. I was detained in traffic for nearly an hour."

Braun waved toward the door. "My assistant will show you. It's down the hall."

When the man was out of the room, Braun swiveled around in his chair and looked up at a black and white photograph of his mother taken years earlier. A stout woman with a somber expression sat in a chair, while a young Braun stood next to her. His lips were rigid, his eyes stern. "I'll show you Mother. You were wrong about me. When I unlock the key to this treasure, I'll be world famous."

An alarm went off in the building. "What the hell?" Braun gasped.

He got up to go see. Blonde-braid shouted through the door. "Fire!"

Braun smelled something burning. Curling smoke swirled into the room from out of nowhere. He waved his arms, swinging around in a circle, trying to clear the air. The scent now hinted of lavender. So did the color of the smoke, changing from gray to blue to purple. The air too thick to see clearly, he thought he saw someone small like a boy move next to his desk. The book lay open on top. It was safe. No it wasn't. It disappeared right in front of his eyes. Not possible. He leapt at the desk to cover the book with his body, but it was no longer there. Instead his chest landed on a collection of small vintage cars that had belonged to his father. The sharp metal stung his skin. A security guard rushed into the office. Braun raised himself up and tried to appear calm.

"You all right sir?" the guard asked, waving away smoke.

"Fire. There's a fire in the building."

"No sir. We checked all the floors. Only smoke is in here. Did you set off the alarm? A cigarette or cigar?"

"Of course not! Get out. Turn off that damn alarm."

"Yes sir."

Braun stared at his desk, now void of his treasure. He dropped onto hands and knees and looked under the desk. No book in sight. Furious, he stood and called out to blonde-braid. "Where the hell is the professor? Don't let him out of this building!"

She entered his office. "I saw a small man."

"The professor?"

"No, smaller, wearing leather clothes. He smiled and tried to hush me and then he disappeared."

"Impossible."

"And he had a nice smell. Like flowers. How could he vanish like that?"

"Lavender?"

She nodded.

Braun's cheeks turned red. His eyes bulged. "I don't know what's going on but he can't just disappear. Lock up the building and don't let anyone leave until you locate the little thief."

"Yes sir."

Amanda paced Tony's living room, waiting for Rotar to return from his trip to Braun's office. Tony sat at a table flipping through the morning newspaper. The children were next door doing homework. Amanda poured herself a cup of coffee and focused on the TV. A female reporter stood in front of a small church in Coppet, adjusting her scarf. The wind tore at her long hair. About fifty onlookers crowded her, one of them dressed in minister's clothing. She spoke in French. Amanda nudged Tony for his attention.

"We are live at the Coppet Community Church where we continue our report on the break-in at a local farm two nights ago. After reporting a claim made by a farmer of seeing a non-human being and a flying horse, Swiss authorities and American investigators continue to withhold information." The camera cut away to an aerial view of the farm.

"Reporters at the scene yesterday managed to break through police barriers and photograph officials chasing after an unidentified creature. The animal, described by a reporter as *outer planetary*, was unfortunately crushed under the wheels of an American sports utility vehicle used by investigators. In spite of several attempts, the farmer refuses to comment further on the matter."

The reporter sniffled and cleared her throat before continuing.

"The church pastor has met with a few of his parishioners to pray over these alleged revelations and has called for a meeting to debate the possible religious significance of these claims. A gathering will take place in front of the American Consulate in Geneva this afternoon at four o'clock. The location may have been chosen in order to achieve as much international exposure as possible.

"One of the earlier accounts claimed the sighting was an apparition of the Virgin Mary. Whether this is indeed a hoax or something never witnessed before, the rest of us look forward to the unveiling of whomever, or whatever, is causing this upheaval in our usually serene and peaceful village. This is Madelaine Genaux, reporting live from Coppet."

Amanda set her coffee cup on the table. "Peter will be caught for sure now." She saw the wheels turning in Tony's expression.

"If it really *is* him," he said. "We still don't have hard evidence, although it seems likely. The media hype has gathered a few locals, but it's hardly international exposure."

"It will be," she said. "Peter needs the antidote. This publicity and the guards stationed at the lab will only spook him."

Tony didn't comment.

"And where's Rotar?" she asked. "He should be back by now. I'm worried."

"He hasn't been gone long enough yet. Try to remain calm."

"Easy for you to say. What if Braun has already translated the book's secrets or Rotar got caught?"

"I doubt Braun has had time to translate anything, and as for Rotar, I don't think anyone could catch that guy unless someone rendered him unconscious."

"Well? Something could have happened to him. I'm scared, Tony."

"Let's give it a little more time."

"And if he doesn't show?"

"He'll show."

"I can't wait. I need my rock."

"Rock?"

"It's a homing device."

She pulled it from her purse and slumped on the couch while Tony watched. "Come in, Rotar. This is urgent."

An explosion of smoke appeared. Rotar swayed on the carpet for balance. He clutched the silver book. "What is it? I was at the farm looking for Peter."

"You got the book!" Amanda cried.

"There are guards at the farm. Not a good idea, Rotar," Tony said.

"I am aware."

"Did you see any sign of him?" Amanda asked.

"No."

"Did Braun or anyone see you?" Tony asked.

"Perhaps, a very attractive young blonde, but she is not a concern. I created a lot of smoke for cover."

"Oh my stars, I'm sure Braun will be furious."

"And the rock?" Tony asked Amanda, nodding at it.

"It belongs to Rotar," she said. "Works like a transmitter."

"Of course," Tony said in a cynical tone.

"We have to put the book in a secure place," Amanda said.

Tony raised his shoulders. "The hotel safe?"

Rotar cast serious eyes under bushy brows. "I will need it for my research."

Amanda and Tony both pondered a moment. Then Tony said, "I can put it in this fancy designer bag," he picked up a black and gold bag advertising Swiss Truffles. "If I hang this inside one of my suits in the closet and jam things against it, no one will be the wiser. You'll have access whenever you want."

Rotar nodded.

Amanda worried about the plan. "I don't know."

"Rotar can move it or secure it in the safe later if he likes. Let's try this first."

She looked to Rotar for confirmation. "That will be fine," he said.

Amanda heaved a huge sigh. "Okay, now that that's settled, let's gather the others and go. There's a gathering at the American Embassy at four, but I want to visit Marta and her lab first. Peter might be there."

CHAPTER THIRTY-ONE

Amanda didn't like Tony's idea of leaving the silver book in his suite, but she put off her distrust yet again in deference to their cause. After everyone dressed to go outside, they were stopped by an agitated manager in the lobby. He slicked back dark hair with one hand while his right eye twitched. An arrogant smile revealed nicotine-stained teeth. He glared at Rotar. "Are all of you registered here?"

Tony smiled. "We certainly are. Is there a problem?"

The room steward stepped forward and pointed to Rotar. "This man—he did something."

"Our friend is a magician," Amanda hurried to say. "An illusionist."

Tony was quick to add, "We can find another hotel if there's a problem. There are plenty of vacancies this time of year."

The manager shifted and slicked back his hair again. *"Non, non, pas de problem,"* he said. He started to leave, saying something to the steward in French, then turned and watched Tony with suspicion.

"Walk slowly," Tony told the group in a low voice, "like everything's normal…"

Rotar turned and pointed his stick at the two men muttering something inaudible. Both men vanished.

"What did you just do?" Amanda blurted.

Tony whispered, "Calm down and keep walking."

Rotar smiled innocently and followed them outside. "I will tell you in a moment."

A cold wind blasted them as they climbed inside the Suburban. Amanda and Tony settled into the middle seat with Rotar while the kids piled into the rear.

When they drove away from the hotel, she poked Rotar. "Where'd they go?"

He looked down, sheepish. "I only sent them into the kitchen while passing a teen-weeny cloud through their minds to erase the memory of our talk."

"You can do that?" she asked. "Just erase the entire scene?"

He nodded. "With magnetic powers. But it is not dangerous. Sort of like blowing a puff of smoke through a strainer, that is all."

Flustered, she said, "Your magic is attracting attention—you need to control it."

"Very well."

She introduced Rotar to Gaspard.

They stopped for a quick lunch before Gaspard dropped them in front of the pharmaceutical building where Marta worked.

The group clamored into the lobby and Amanda stopped to check the purple rock in her handbag. Tony took the others to the waiting area. "Let's try to leave Rotar out of this," he said. "The less exposure the better."

She saw some of the visitors and staff staring at Rotar. Then Michelle grasped his hand and sat down with him on the couch.

A young brunette at the front desk checked her lipstick in the mirror. When she noticed Amanda and Tony waiting, she pursed her over-sized full lips and extended her chest, smiling at him. "May I help you?"

"We're here to see Marta Meyer," Amanda said in a calm voice, although her insides were anything but calm. "She's an employee."

"And you are?" the receptionist asked in a heavy French accent. She adjusted her sweater and flashed Tony a coy glance.

"Amanda Tregnier."

Ms. Full lips dropped her smile. "You are related to Dr. Tregnier?"

Another stab. The woman knew her husband, but not her. She held her tongue. "Yes, I'm visiting from the US."

"I see." The receptionist made a phone call.

In a few moments Marta entered the lobby through double doors. Her eyes radiated contempt. "What do you want now?"

Amanda remained firm. "What did your company have to do with Peter's discovery?"

"I cannot tell you," Marta said, lips clamped tight.

"Why not?"

Marta muttered under her breath. "If Peter is found—"

"What do you mean, *if?* He must be found!" Amanda said. But that meant he wasn't here.

Marta's eyes hardened. She turned and held open the swinging door, motioning Amanda and Tony to follow. A long corridor with polished floors led to offices on the left and glass-encased laboratories on the right. An elevator faced them at the end of the hall. Marta led them into a small office and closed the door. "A scandal would be bad for our company," she said.

"But Peter will automatically be connected to you and this lab. Surely you realize that?" Amanda argued.

Marta nodded. "I suppose so."

"So it's imperative that I learn as much as I can and find my husband quickly before anyone else. Don't you see?"

No reaction from Marta.

"Look," Amanda pleaded, "just tell me what the connection is at this lab."

Marta paused and nodded toward the entrance to the long hall. She led them into an empty lab, bolting the door behind them.

In a storage room she used her key to unlock one of the cabinets, removing a small clear bottle of white powder. "This is Peter's. It's called Pflenamium. It's a new drug he developed.

Tony studied the bottle. "What does it do?"

"It's a regressive drug. It releases the mind's memory beyond normal time-span and possibly to pre-birth if one takes enough of it."

Amanda gasped. "Peter took this?"

"Yes, but he said that by itself it only unveils certain memories like traumatic incidents."

Dumbfounded, Amanda asked, "Then what did he do? How did he get into his current predicament?"

Marta put the bottle down. Her voice quivered. "He called this his root drug and combined it with a formula in a secret book brought to him by a small stranger."

"Rotar," she whispered to Tony.

Marta continued. "By combining the two formulas, Peter proved that the subconscious has the ability to physically recreate what it remembers." She trembled and stared off into space, her voice faint. "This is a horrible thing."

Tony shifted his stance and moved closer to her. "Why on earth would he experiment on himself with such a thing?"

"Peter believed we all originate from one source and contain within us the total energy of the Universe. We are only temporarily separated from that source each time we are reborn into a new body. He claimed that if we can go back far enough we can tap into our unlimited knowledge which was his objective."

"My God…," Amanda mumbled.

Someone banged on the door. Marta waved for both of them to follow.

Tony slipped Peter's bottle into his coat pocket.

Marta unlocked the door to a man in a gray suit. He brushed his neatly-trimmed mustache with one finger and cast hard eyes at Marta. "Who are these people and what are they doing in here?"

"This is our Managing Director, Mr. Stefan Andersen," Marta said, her voice wavering. "My visitors are Peter's relatives. They are looking for him and insisted on seeing for themselves that he is not here."

"You brought them inside for that? What nonsense…" He turned to Tony and Amanda. "What is it you really want here?"

Tony moved in front of Amanda. "Peter's aunt is very ill; we're looking for him."

"I think not," Andersen said. He pulled a cell phone from his pocket and punched a number. "Meet me. First floor hall," he demanded to someone on the other end.

"We're leaving," Tony said and tried to pass him.

Andersen blocked the way.

They stared each other down.

Amanda skirted around both of them and left the room. In the hall she stopped and fumbled in her purse for the rock, pulling out a plastic container of Tic Tacs instead.

Andersen grabbed her arm.

"Let go!" she cried, jerking her arm from his grip.

The elevator door at the end of the hall opened. Goldtooth stepped out. He ran toward them, pointing a finger. A back brace was wrapped around his waist. "Dat ees zee voman vat kicked meeeeee."

Amanda dropped the box of Tic Tacs on the floor. They scattered like small pebbles.

Goldtooth lost his footing on the Tic Tacs and fell on his face. A gold object from his mouth skipped across the slippery surface.

At a shrill cry from inside Amanda's purse, the two-tailed cat sprang out, pouncing on the Tic Tacs.

Tony stared, slack-jawed.

"What the blazes?" Andersen shouted, pressing back against the wall away from the hissing cat.

Dot Comet skidded on the linoleum spraying tic tacs everywhere while sliding toward Goldtooth. Protecting his face with one hand he cried, "Eet ees zee devil cat I tell you 'bout."

Andersen stretched out to grab the cat, but couldn't clutch it. He grasped again, but his hand went right through its body.

He slammed back against the wall.

Dot Comet shrieked and spewed purple smoke into Goldtooth's face, making him cough and gag and then sprayed a purple sticky substance on Anderson's hand.

Goldtooth slid and skidded back the way he came. Anderson ran down another hall shouting for help.

Dot Comet started after Goldtooth but Amanda pulled a chocolate bar from her bag and tore off the paper. Frantic, she called the cat and waved the treat. "Here kitty, kitty."

Dot Comet turned and saw the chocolate. She tossed it into her bag and Dot Comet leapt inside after it.

She snapped the purse shut.

"Crazzzeeeeeee voman," Goldtooth shouted, holding a hand in front of his missing gold tooth, one eye still covered with a black patch.

Amanda spotted the tooth on the floor and kicked it toward him. Then she bolted back to the lobby with Tony right behind.

Marta followed, her face pale and scared.

Elizabeth gave a disinterested glance at their return. Amanda grabbed her children by a hand, casting a weak smile at Rotar. She turned to Marta. "You're in trouble now because of us…"

Marta shook her head. "I do not understand what happened back there and I do not wish to know unless it can help Peter."

"Are you sure you'll be all right?" Amanda asked again.

Marta nodded. "Yes, if you leave immediately. Andersen will yell at me but he wants Peter and knows that I am the only contact."

Marta stared down at Rotar. "Are you the small man Peter spoke about?"

Rotar nodded.

She huffed and hurried back to the work area.

Tony hustled everyone into the Suburban. Amanda and Rotar remained outside. Out of earshot from the kids, Tony said to Rotar, "You know about the two-tailed cat?"

"Of course—Dot Comet lives inside the purple rock."

Tony stared at him. "Of course."

Amanda said, "At least we know who Goldtooth works for."

Tony nodded. "Useful information, but we have to get out of here now. We haven't heard the last of those two." He patted his pocket. "If Andersen discovers Peter's concoction is missing he'll be after us in an instant. And if he believes what he just saw in there, he'll want the cat too."

They joined the others waiting in the car. Amanda turned to the kids in the back. "No Peter yet, kids… Sorry."

Howard and Michelle stared gloom out the windows. Lizzy watched the passing scenes.

After circling a bit and watching if anyone was following, they decided no one from the lab had managed to organize a pursuit car. Amanda reminded Tony of the rally downtown. Gaspard drove them to the American Consulate where the event was in full progress. They joined a crowd of about a hundred people. A religious leader with a gentle face shouted into the microphone, his words angry.

"And if the world is to believe in this preposterous political stunt, then we must fight back. This is a hoax, organized by manipulative political leaders who want to weaken the church's position in society. There is no UFO in Coppet, and there is no extraterrestrial being from outer space."

The crowd clapped with uncertainty.

"We are children of God," he bellowed, "and because we are, the truth will prevail."

A man shouted back. "What if this turns out to be real?"

The minister shook his head. "It is not, but if it were, the world would be greatly affected and we would have to react accordingly."

The same person raised his voice. "Isn't that just another form of demagoguery? Aren't you saying that religious leaders with limited knowledge are trying to control our spiritual evolution?"

The moderator answered, "Absolutely not! We need to be responsible citizens and adhere to church doctrine. This fantasy creature is nothing but a hoax."

Amanda pushed her way through the crowd amazed that so many people had gathered to debate the existence of her husband. She wanted to get up on the podium and tell them all to go home—that a scientist had just experimented irresponsibly and given rise to a bizarre but unintentional experiment. She moved toward the steps debating whether or not to speak up when Hillary stepped out of the crowd and blocked her way.

CHAPTER THIRTY-TWO

"I thought you were in Rome," Amanda said to Hillary.

"I saw the news report this morning on CNN. My boss flew me over for the rally. And why haven't you returned any of my calls?"

Hillary's mood seemed to match her black hat. "I'm sorry, we've been really busy," Amanda stammered.

"And where's Peter? Weren't you going to meet him in Coppet?" Tony stepped up and said, "That was the plan."

"I've spoken to him," Amanda added. "Things are complicated."

"When haven't they been," Hillary mocked. "If I'm still your friend, Amanda, you can jolly well tell me what's going on!"

"I can't," Amanda said in a sad voice.

The rest of the group caught up and interrupted the strain between them. Hillary looked down at Rotar in puzzlement. "Hil', this is Rotar," Amanda said. "A new friend of the family."

"How do you do." Hillary shook his hand, waved hello to Lizzy and then hugged Michelle and Howard. She stood back and snapped a group photo. "Thanks everyone. I always collect pictures from my travels."

Rotar had shielded his eyes from the flash but not in time. Pages of text rippled across his eyeballs. "Whirrrrrr...boii-iinnng..." came from his throat. "The light set off..."

"Never mind, Rotar," Amanda said.

Hillary looked up from her camera.

Rotar turned away and his eyeballs returned to normal.

Hillary shifted confused eyes back to Amanda. "Strange noise...so what *can you* tell me about this mystery?"

Amanda attempted a lighthearted tone. "Not much, but we're on our way to dinner. Care to join us? I'm dying to hear about your meeting with the Pope."

"Sounds enticing—but you're evading me again. I'm here for a story and I want the exclusive."

"Later, Hil'," she told her. They walked toward the car. She didn't know how to avoid the 'Peter' questions. "You can ride with us—we've got room."

Gaspard recommended *Les Armures*, a twelfth century restaurant decorated with regional antiques. Tony invited him to join them for dinner. A plaque commemorating President Bill Clinton's visit hung at the entrance.

The maître d' seated them at a round table for eight. Above them the ceiling had been painted with a 17th century fresco. The children sat between Gaspard and Rotar. "This is the best food in town," Gaspard said. "Stewed hare with noodles is their specialty."

Michelle made a face. "I want *begetarian*."

"Vegetarian, dear," corrected Hillary.

"I want steak," Howard said. "I'm hungry."

"And I want nothing," announced Lizzy.

Tony looked annoyed. "You will eat something, Elizabeth, even if it's just soup. I don't want an anorexic daughter."

"Well, Dad…you abuse your lungs every day…"

"I'm fully aware that I'm not a good example…"

Rotar looked up from the menu. "I would like Steak Tartar."

"Me too," Howard said. "What kinda' steak is that?"

"Raw meat," Rotar answered with a smile.

Howard made a face. "Yucko!"

Gaspard chuckled. "It is delicious, served with an egg yolk on top, capers and chopped onions."

"Triple yucko," Howard said.

They ordered their meals, chatting and eating while the courses were served. The room filled up with customers. Amanda asked Hillary to share her experience in Rome.

Hillary's eyes softened. "I was in *awe*. His Holiness had an aura of peace and tranquility around him that I could actually *feel*. He used an interpreter of course, and as though he had heard my prayers, he spoke of his desire for world peace. And when I asked his opinion on human rights he expressed our need for multi-cultural tolerance and priorities in education, science, and technology for greater economic advancements."

She raised her palms in reverence and continued. "He was so contained, Amanda, so sure of his own presence and so totally in a state of grace that I almost expected him to perform a miracle." She looked away into space.

Amanda waited, spellbound.

Tony listened.

Hillary returned her focus and continued. "When I reluctantly finished the interview, I felt charged with renewed faith that we *can* reach the needs of everyone on this magnificent planet."

In a momentary silence at the table the others stared at Hillary. Amanda said in a hushed voice, "That was beautiful, Hil'."

Hillary smiled, her eyes dazed, and shifted on her chair. "Now it's your turn. Was that supposed to be Peter in the news?"

Amanda swallowed hard and glanced at the children eating and chattering amongst themselves. "Let's order dessert, and while we're waiting, Gaspard, will you show the children some of the antiques?"

"Of course."

They ordered and Gaspard escorted the trio out beyond the dining room. Tony leaned toward Amanda to listen. With a glance at the other guests Amanda whispered. "Why do you think that was Peter?"

Hillary whispered back. "I can't seem to think of anything else. He's a scientist. He's always secretive about his experiments. You've been here for days and still haven't met up. I have so many questions. What's he done?"

Amanda kept her voice down. "Peter found a treatment for psychotic patients that regresses their memory to reveal the source of their problems, that's all. So what are you worried about?"

Hillary's eyes cast disbelief. "There are a lot of religious questions to be addressed," her friend said. "Whatever Peter is up to,
it might be disastrous to the world."

"Why?" Amanda said more abruptly than intended. "If there
really *is* an alien like the story infers, I'd be *fascinated*. I'd love to
know if there's life elsewhere."

Hillary gave a conciliatory nod. "Having just visited with the
Pope, I am reminded that even the Roman Catholic Church wears
a double garment of science and faith. They admit that there can
be more than one avenue leading to the truth. But the mystery
remains and we become doubtful because we want to actually
see God, and witness first-hand proof of UFOS and aliens." She
blinked and stared at Rotar across the table.

Tony spoke in a low voice. "You're correct, Hillary, the
Catholic Church has been studying the stars for centuries. It
started when they were formulating a calendar over four hundred
years ago. Now they collaborate with a University in Arizona and
share their observatory. They call their telescope the *Pope Scope.*"
He chuckled.

"Interesting, Mr. Ramsey," Hillary said. "I'll have to check
into it."

"Fascinating," Amanda added, eyeing Tony. "How do you
know this?"

With a teasing grin he said, "I know a little bit about a lot
of things."

Hillary went on. "I understand some strange things are happening here but if there is in fact an alien in Coppet, the discovery
could create division and fear. People need the teachings of the
church to guide them—that's what has helped civilize the world."

Amanda said, "I agree that we need guidance, Hillary, but
what would change?"

Hillary wiped her mouth with a napkin before answering. "If
Peter has created a drug to become this non-human we're read-

ing about, then the world will turn to chaos. Believe me, people will panic."

"I understand your concern, Hil', but you could put a twist on this and point out the awesome implications of such a discovery, *if* an extraterrestrial is indeed living on Earth." Amanda looked at Rotar. He nodded but kept quiet.

Hillary's expression was blank. "How?"

"Explain that it might just be possible for the soul to reincarnate somewhere else, other than Earth."

"I suppose it's a possibility, if one believes in reincarnation," Hillary said.

Amanda pressed on. "And if this truly is a new discovery, we're reaching into worlds that might teach us more about our spirituality and extend our frontiers—to past lives as well as future incarnations. With new scientific discoveries we may be exploring the universe."

Hillary looked pensive. "But we do that already with the space program."

Amanda sighed. "Not through the Pope Scope or space exploration—I'm talking about the *spiritual* universe."

Hillary wriggled. "I'm not sure I can accept any of this. If Peter has tampered with our soul or manipulated it in some way, then he has violated God's law. It's not up to us to meddle with spiritual design."

Amanda felt frustrated. "I understand what you're saying, Hil', but try to put your beliefs aside for a moment and think about all of us as one, with powers that all of us possess. Perhaps even miracles…"

Hillary shrugged. "I'm sorry but I can't."

Amanda turned to Rotar. "Will you tell her what you can do?"

Rotar looked around at the guests. "Now?"

Amanda nodded. "Explain who you are and where you come from."

"It is easier to show her," he said.

Amanda raised a brow. "Here?"

Rotar touched his stick hidden under the table cloth and stared at the coat of arms hanging on the wall to their left. Swords flanked either side and a metal suit of armor stood in the corner next to beveled glass windows. *"Blo-kum-pat-ski."* A funnel of wind blew toward the wall hangings and the swords switched sides, shaking the coat of arms. The plaque fell to the floor with a loud crash. Guests and staff turned to look.

"Rotar, we're in a public restaurant!" Amanda cried through clenched teeth.

"You rigged that ahead of time," Hillary told Rotar.

"Magic, I guess," he grinned. The suit of armor leaned forward in a bow—then straightened.

Amanda saw Gaspard standing at the entrance to the dining room with the kids in tow. They stretched to see.

Gaspard shrugged.

The guests stared in silence until nothing more happened and then resumed eating. The waiters looked cautiously around and continued their tasks. The maître d' rushed over to Tony with knotted eyebrows, his mouth pinched. "What is going on here?"

Tony stood up and gave a polite smile. "Just a newly developed gadget from America. We're applying for an international patent. It's a remote control mobility device. I apologize for testing it in your restaurant…we were just trying to demonstrate it to a client." He nodded toward Hillary. "Would you like an investor's prospectus?"

"Non merci," the maître d' said. He hurried away.

"That was quick thinking," Amanda said, noting how easy it was for him to make up a believable story. She turned to Hillary. "So, what do you think now? I'm sure Rotar didn't mean to frighten you, but we need your help."

Hillary's jaw sagged. *"My* help? This is freakish. Rotar can do this? I need *your* help, Amanda. I need more information before I can adjust a lifetime of research."

She nodded. "I was hoping you'd understand. All right, I'll get you a story, if there is one… but I'm not confirming one way or the other."

Hillary let out a big breath. "I've just seen powers that are *inhuman*. Where does Rotar come from? And the sightings…?"

She offered a weak smile, touching Hillary's arm in an effort to acknowledge the frustration. "Later, Hil'. Right now we need your help, and Peter needs your help. If nothing else, at least give us time. You can help by delaying harmful press."

Hillary adjusted her hat. "I have to think and pray and have a serious chat with God. I'm staying at the International Hilton. Please let me know if there's any more news about Peter that I can use in my column. This is big…this is *really* big."

The waiter returned with the dessert orders and Gaspard brought the children back to the table.

When they got up to leave Amanda said, "Let us drive you back to your hotel, Hil'."

Hillary eyed Rotar. "I think I'd rather take my own cab. No offense, Rotar, but I need some solitude." She thanked them for the meal and left.

Rotar blinked through sad eyes. "I did not mean to upset her."

Amanda gave a compassionate smile. "If anyone can achieve a higher consciousness, she can. I've known her most of my life."

"What's higher consciousness?" Howard asked.

Lizzy scowled. "It means progressive thought—like an awakening from stupidity, hint hint…"

Tony interrupted, "Howard asked a very good question, Elizabeth."

Howard asked again, "What is it Mom?"

Tired, Amanda said, "There's a power within us, a knowing of things that we can't explain. Some people call it wisdom. But there's also intuition that lets us know there's more to our world beyond our basic senses—coincidences that occur at precisely the right moment. Does this make sense to you?"

Howard pondered. "I think so. Like when you know the phone is going to ring right before it does."

"Exactly. I listen to my intuition instead of fearing it."

Michelle spoke up. "Yeah, like my friends who visit me at night. Some of them are angels and talk only to me. They tell me not to be afraid and that I'll be a princess one day. I'm going to be a real princess, Mommy…"

Tony smiled. "And on that note, *your highness,* let's call it a night."

Tony carried Michelle, half asleep, to her room. Amanda helped her undress.

"Good night, all of you," Tony said, tilting his head for Amanda to follow. She blew a kiss to Howard, then waved good night to Rotar and followed him to his suite. Elizabeth disappeared into her room.

Amanda saw a box of truffles on the floor. Alarmed, she picked it up. "Someone's been here," she said to Tony.

"The maid comes in to turn down the beds."

She went back to her own room, trying to remember how she'd left her things. Rejoining Tony, she said, "My bathrobe's been moved, I left it on top of my suitcase." Her thoughts jarred. "Check the book!"

He dashed to his room. "Still there," he announced from the closet, smiling when he came back. "The maid could have cleaned off the table and forgotten to put the box back."

"I doubt it. I have this eerie feeling that someone's been here. Could have been Andersen or Goldtooth—we made fools of them at the Kruper Lab today."

He shook his head. "Braun's the best suspect, but security here is very strict. I think you're over-stressed. The book's safe and sound."

"Thank the lucky stars for that," she said, sinking down in the easy chair. "But if someone was here looking for it they'll come back."

"Marta knows where we're staying too," he said. "Perhaps she discovered the drug is missing…"

She looked up. "You still have it with you?"

"In my pocket."

"We have to hide it somewhere else. And find a better place for the silver book."

"I prefer to keep it close. It's safe with me and the book is fine."

Her dark eyebrows pinched together. "I guess I can go through everything in the morning to see if anything's missing. I'm too tired to deal with it right now."

"Good. You need to relax." He poured a brandy for her and another for himself. His eyes met hers. "You were magnificent today."

She blushed. "You too."

"I enjoy helping you."

"But I don't know how I'll ever repay you. And I have a husband out there—."

"You're married to a…sorry, it's not my place…"

She took a sip of brandy. "I can't go there with you Tony."

The displeasure in his face was obvious. "Why put up a wall?" he said. "I'm going against my country because I care enough to help you."

"I thought you were here because it's the right thing to do?"

He took a deep breath. "Maybe we're being naïve. We're playing with fire here, and it could backfire on both of us. Is Peter worth it?"

She flinched. "He's brilliant…" she paused, "in his own way."

She could see that he wasn't buying it. He moved to the fireplace and lit a cigarette. "I don't understand why you're so loyal to a man who cheated on you…"

"Love can do that. But you're fogging up my logic."

"You have no logic."

"You don't know me well enough to say that."

"I'd like to know you better,"

In despair, she grabbed her box of chocolates from the table. "That's not going to happen."

"Why not? People change their destinies all the time. This was forced on you. Why not exercise your free will?"

She stared at him hard. "I'm exhausted and I can't think. I'll see you tomorrow."

He flicked his cigarette into the fire and gulped down his drink. Without a word he went to his room. She took another sip of brandy. Maybe it would help her go to sleep faster.

Amanda stood alone at her bedroom window, staring at the dim glow of a crescent moon veiled by misty fog. How would humans react if the mystery of the Universe was revealed for all to understand? Would love prevail? Or chaos?

She closed the curtains and fell into bed. She felt locked in a vacuum between the husband she no longer had and the stranger tugging at her. Moisture filled her eyes. But before she could anguish further, she fell into a deep exhausted sleep.

CHAPTER THIRTY-THREE

The next morning Amanda looked around again for evidence that their suite had been tampered with. Her intuition nagged her but she couldn't be certain. She let it go and went to the dining room where the others were already having breakfast. The children chattered among themselves while they ate. Rotar slurped up a spoonful of porridge. Tony read the morning paper. The waitress took Amanda's order, glancing at Rotar between each slurp. When her food arrived, Amanda picked at her waffle, feeling anxious. She noted more chatter than usual amongst the guests exchanging the morning newspaper.

Tony showed her a copy. "This is getting serious," he whispered.

A cartoonish drawing depicted a strange-looking being with a large pointed head and thin wispy body waving from astride a flying horse above the trees. Powder drizzled from the horse's nose onto the guards on the ground. "My God, this can't be," she muttered.

"More than one witness saw it," Tony added, looking grim.

"How do we get to Peter with this kind of publicity?"

Tony shook his head. "I'm surprised it hit the International press without more concrete evidence, but don't forget that the other two sightings were reported on TV."

Amanda ate a little but was anxious to get rid of the kids so she could continue her conversation with Tony. When they finished their meal Amanda said, "Lizzy it looks like you're done eating. Will you take Howard and Michelle upstairs please? Rotar can stay and finish his breakfast."

Lizzy looked at her blank-faced. "Are you getting rid of us again?"

"I want to stay," Howard said. "I can take care of anything you need, Mom."

"Me too," Michelle added. "I want to stay with Howie."

Amanda smiled lovingly at her kids. "I know, but go get some homework done and we'll join you soon."

Reluctant, they left. Rotar continued eating.

Amanda read the newspaper accounts about the confrontation at the laboratory in Coppet. The report must be true or near the truth. It ended with a commentary she read aloud to Tony and Rotar.

"After a third sighting of extraterrestrial beings in less than a week and claims of a space rodent encounter, (the photograph too vague to substantiate), we predict over-zealous imaginations have been combined with irresponsible journalism. The Swiss police at the farm where the alleged space creature was photographed have no physical evidence of anything alien. Investigators have been tipped that a small scientific facility in Coppet might be a haven for drug dealers. An American security officer stationed at the research lab claimed gold dust blown from the nostrils of a flying horse rendered his weapon useless and fireballs from the alien's eyes burned him. But this eyewitness has refused further comment on the incident. Scientists believe these claims of flying horses and alien beings are either fantasy or a hoax. Are we to believe in this sensational reporting or could it be the result of some hallucinatory drug misleading the citizens of Switzerland into false hysteria? You decide."

Amanda let out a long sigh. "It was written by Hillary Windham." She closed her eyes and smiled. "This will give us some time."

Tony tapped a finger on the table. "Not much. We're not the only ones looking for Peter, and they won't give up."

"Then we have to get to him first before there's another sighting."

Tony gazed at her, his expression troubled. "Washington will react to this even on thin evidence. Do you know what that means? My reputation and my connection with you?"

She could think of nothing comforting. "What is your job really?"

"I'm a consultant, but my work is top secret. I can't discuss the details—sorry." He shifted in his chair. "But my involvement with you is purely a personal choice. I want to help."

She made no attempt to hide her frustration, but when she thought of her children and how much they needed their father, she regained her courage and drew in a deep breath. "I don't want to jeopardize your career. I'll take my kids and move to another hotel and disassociate ourselves from any trail we've made for those horrible men from the Kruper Lab as well as Braun and Marta."

Tony shot an annoyed glare. "I can't let you go out on your own. You'd get into trouble in a few hours without me."

"We can manage," she argued. "And we have Rotar." She looked at him and smiled as he put down a cup of hot chocolate.

He beamed back. "Of course, I am *Rotar the Mighty.*"

"And we might find more clues at the County Hall of Records. I prefer to take the kids home but I can't give up yet."

"I can retrieve what you need," Rotar said.

"There are lots of records and time-consuming research," Tony said.

"My God, we'll never find him in time," Amanda moaned.

"I am aware of the name Howard located at the cemetery. It will only take a moment."

Rotar got up and sauntered into the kitchen. Amanda looked to Tony for assurance. "Do you think he can act that quickly?"

Before Tony could answer, Rotar returned holding a few sheets of paper. "I made copies too."

Amanda looked at him, awestruck. "Is there anything you can't do? Never mind, no time now to get into it. Let me see," she said, spreading out the lists. Tony leaned over to look.

"Here's a name of someone who at one time lived in Coppet, Jacques Tregnier. It might be a relative. The current address is in Verbier."

"An exclusive ski resort," Tony said. "Two, three hours by car."

"Perhaps this man knows Peter?" she asked in a hopeful tone.

Tony frowned. "If he's close enough to be a cousin, Braun's probably been there already."

"But if Braun's busy chasing down the silver book, maybe he hasn't gotten to Peter's relatives yet." She looked to Rotar for affirmation, but his expression was non-committal.

Tony shrugged. "We could fly there. If he's related he might know where Peter might hide."

Her eyes questioned. "Are there regular flights to Verbier?"

"We can go by private helicopter. I have free access."

Anxious to meet the person and avoid a long drive, Amanda went along with Tony's suggestion. Tony called Gaspard who agreed to accompany them to Verbier. He would also arrange for a helicopter and pilot.

When the threesome entered Tony's suite, Michelle ran to her mother. "Mommy, Lizzy showed us how to go on line. I know how to send my own messages on a computer," she announced, buzzing with excitement.

"That's wonderful, sweetie, but did you and Howard get any of your work done?"

"I finished a lesson in my workbook—Howie did some too."

"Good for both of you. I'll check it later."

Tony asked Lizzy, "Did you find time to work on your own assignments?"

"Didn't need to. I'm waaaaayyyyy ahead. I've completed most of the work for the entire school year—it's the accelerated program."

Rotar uttered a soft cough. "I can teach you many things—er—if you are bored," he said.

"What kind of things?" Lizzy asked in a snippy tone.

Tony's eyes warned her to behave. So did his tone. "Lizzy?"

Rotar squeezed his eyes shut and opened them again. Miniature reams of paper with writing on them flipped through his eyes page after page.

Lizzy leaned forward, her eyes boring into his. "Wow that's fantastic! If I had you as my tutor, I'd be the best student in the world."

He chuckled and closed his eyes.

Amanda asked for their attention. "I thought you'd have more time to do homework, but our plans have changed. I have a surprise."

All eyes were glued on Amanda while she filled them in on the trip to Verbier. Eager to fly in a helicopter, they grabbed their jackets and hurried out of the hotel.

When airborne, Gaspard shouted over the noise of the chopper. "We are lucky, zee weather eez with us at zee moment. Thees eez one of thoze memorable days in Switzerland."

The majestic Alps glistened against a blue sky and Amanda found the beautiful scenery a momentary distraction from her anxious thoughts. When the village of Verbier came into view, white alpine-style structures dotted a long steep valley nestled between high mountain peaks. The air looked crystal clear but a dark sky loomed in the distance.

After landing, they rented a car from an agent who also gave them directions to the home of Jacques Tregnier.

"I'm nervous," Amanda muttered when she saw the house.

Gaspard pulled to a stop in front of a two-story chalet not far from the entrance to the cable cars. Amanda asked the others to wait while she approached the house with Tony. He banged the knocker hard against the carved wooden door.

A man appearing to be in his seventies opened the door. She saw a family resemblance and flushed. "Are you Jacques Tregnier?"

"Yes…" He studied her face, then Tony's.

"Are you related to the Pierre Tregnier who died in Geneva, and Peter Tregnier who lives in Washington DC?"

The man sported a tangle of receding gray hair and stared at Amanda with soft eyes under white eyebrows on a weathered face. He slumped with poor posture. "I am Peter's second-cousin. And you are?"

She flashed a quick smile. "Mrs. Peter Tregnier from Washington. I'm Amanda. How do you do?"

He shook her hand and stammered, "You must come in."

She pointed to the car. "Peter's children are with me, and our driver, and two other guests. This is my friend, Tony Ramsey."

The man looked at the S.U.V and then back to Amanda. "Please bring everyone inside."

Tony left to get the others. Waiting in the foyer, Jacques Tregnier asked. "Tell me about Peter. It has been months since I have heard from him. We used to ski together, but he was with someone else. I must apologize for my confusion. He is no longer with Marta?"

His question triggered Amanda's temper. Was she the only one who didn't know about her husband's fiancé? "I didn't know about Marta until a couple of days ago."

He looked away. "I am sorry to learn this. I was not aware."

"Please don't say anything in front of the children."

He nodded and flashed a smile when the others arrived at the front door. "How do you do?" he said in a jovial tone. "I am your father's cousin but you may call me Uncle Jacques."

They all sat down in a comfortable living room and Jacques offered refreshments. The room was filled with hand-carved furniture upholstered in earth-toned plaid. A middle-aged woman Jacques introduced as his housekeeper brought coffee, cookies and hot chocolate. A fire roared in the copper-hooded fireplace. When a cocker spaniel bounced into the living room wagging its tail, Tony sneezed. The dog jumped onto Jacques' lap.

Amanda asked him, "Can we talk privately?"

"Of course." He turned to his housekeeper. "Helga, please take the children and La La to the kitchen. He turned to the kids.

"There is a model train that runs all the way around the room near the ceiling. Helga will turn it on for you."

Howard stood up. "The dog's name is La La?"

"Yes."

"Cool name," he said. "We got one at home named Pluto."

Uncle Jacques chuckled.

The minute the others were gone Amanda asked, "Do you live here alone?"

He nodded. "My wife passed away seven years ago and we have no children." He nodded at the sound of a small motor and a train whistle followed by the happy shouts of the kids and dog yips. "An unfortunate disappointment for both of us."

Amanda said, "It isn't all fun and good times with children but I'm sure you know that." She changed the subject and filled him in on Peter's research in general terms. He listened with intense interest. After a slight hesitation he spoke.

"I am not aware of Peter's current projects. I am a retired chemist from the Bodenfluhn Pharmaceutical Company in Geneva."

He paused to light his pipe.

Amanda waited, anxious to learn more.

He continued. "Peter had progressive ideas bordering on genius. Or *insanity*, depending on your point of view. We shared our work on occasion but he became so obsessed and impatient that I finally withdrew my help. His work was too risky. I have not seen him since then. Are you here to confirm my fears?"

Setting her cup on the table, she ignored the question. "Do you have any idea where Peter might be?"

He thought for a moment, then told her about Coppet. "The barn is all that is left of the family farm. The house was destroyed by fire. There is also an old family cabin in the mountains nearby, but I do not even know if it is still there."

Bingo. They'd come to the right place. "I know about the farm, but can you give us directions to the cabin?"

"Is he in some sort of trouble?"

"It's all conjecture right now—we're not sure," Amanda said.

"Oh dear…" Jacques blew out a puff of smoke. "I will draw you a map."

Tony collected the others.

When finished, Jacques handed her the sheet of paper. "I also wrote down my telephone number." The others gathered in the foyer and Tony gave him his contact information too.

"We're so grateful for your help," Amanda said, clutching the map. "I'm anxious to find Peter. Thank you for you hospitality."

"And I am honored by your visit. Will you please keep me informed and call me if you need anything? I feel responsible in some way. I did not stop him when I saw that he was exceeding the guidelines of scientific exploration."

Amanda shook his hand. "You're not the only one. His current research partner told me the same thing. He feels bad about it too. But Peter was determined and no one could have stopped him."

"We'll be in touch," Tony said, shaking Jacques' hand.

"Thank you. I hope you will find him."

Uncle Jacques opened the front door and gasped, closing it again. *"Mon Dieu,* the sky has darkened and the wind is howling. It looks like early snow. You cannot travel in this weather, and as you see I have plenty of room for all of you to stay." He pointed upstairs toward more rooms.

"We'll try to get back to Geneva today," Tony said, "and if we can't, we'll come back here. Is that all right with you?"

"Of course but this is dangerous weather. Transportation will be shut down."

"If it is, we'll see you later and make new plans," Amanda assured. "Good-bye and thanks."

They returned to the small airport where the helicopter pilot informed them that all aircraft had been grounded due to an impending snow storm. He was going to get a room for the night and would contact them in the morning. Tony arranged to cover the cost and the pilot left.

They gathered in the waiting room and discussed whether to go back to Uncle Jacques or find a hotel. Amanda felt disappointed over the delay. Time was critical in reaching the cabin before anyone else.

Rotar listened and pulled on Tony's sleeve for attention. "I can get us to Geneva in seconds if you will allow me the pleasure," he said, boastful.

"Safely?" Tony asked.

"I don't know," Amanda said, her doubt-meter elevating. "Perhaps it's best to spend the night with Uncle Jacques…"

"It is just a wisp of time," Rotar added. "No problem."

"No problem?" Amanda said as her jaw dropped. "Am I losing my mind? We're considering the risk of some outer-galactic space travel because of a snow blizzard?"

"I can also check out the cabin for you," he said, with a smirk on his face.

She stared at Rotar. That would save time and time was golden right now. She was certain he wouldn't do anything to harm them, and if something went wrong he'd fix it, wouldn't he? She blinked. "Okay then, tell us *how.*"

CHAPTER THIRTY-FOUR

Amanda's thoughts ping-ponged between the safety of Uncle Jacque's house and Rotar's offer to transport them through space and time back to Geneva. "This is ludicrous, Rotar, cabin or no cabin, how can you guarantee we'll arrive safely? Peter's not worth risking our lives."

He held a confident smile. "We all hold hands and close our eyes and I use my powers to get us there. You will feel nothing… actually you might feel a little like compressed pudding but you will be there in less than a flash."

"Just like that?" Amanda asked, worry creasing her face. "Regardless of how large or small we are?" She glanced at the children.

He nodded. "Size makes no difference. It is sort of like folding the line and eliminating the space. Understand?"

"No, not at all." She'd just about had enough of his simple explanations.

"He's quoting Einstein," Elizabeth said with assurance. "Something about the fourth dimension of time and space…"

Rotar beamed. "We will continue the physics lesson later Miss Elizabeth."

She nodded with an eager smile.

Rotar grinned. "Dipping dimensions…"

Michelle jumped up and down. "Dips of detentions," she giggled.

"McDippy," Howard groaned.

"If it's so simple," Amanda said, "why not just get rid of the storm?"

"I can rescue people in a storm but I have no power to stop it. My master will not allow that."

"But you diverted the storm away from the Asian fishing village," she argued. "You told us that."

"Yes but only until everyone was safe. If I do the same here, do you not think people will question the sudden retraction while we fly away? I am not able to hold it off forever."

Amanda knew he was right. She cleared her throat and looked at Tony. He shrugged.

"Very well," she said. "Does the entire team agree?"

Lizzy gave a brief nod, Howard and Michelle did the same, but Gaspard looked worried.

"Gaspard? Would you prefer to wait here until the storm passes?" Amanda asked.

"*Non*, I come with you, but it eez difficult to accept. Like witchcraft."

Tony said, "Think of it as advanced science, Gaspard."

Amanda took her children by the hand. "Let's go around the corner and do this while the terminal's empty." She asked Rotar, "Have you ever transported so many at one time?"

"No, but that is of no concern."

She shuddered. "I'm trusting my children to you, and my friends…"

"You will all be fine," Rotar said.

They clasped hands and formed a circle.

"Anything else we need to know?" Tony asked.

"You might feel a slight pressure on your chest or body as you dematerialize and then it will go away as you rematerialize," he said with authority. "Now close your eyes and hold on tight."

Before anyone could react he said, *"Van-iss-ium Ge-no-via!"*

Clutching Howard's hand on one side and Michelle's on the other Amanda felt herself being squeezed like cake frosting out of a funnel and forced through airless space. Something pressed the bridge of her nose and she tried to inhale but her nostrils were clogged. She tried to open her mouth, but couldn't.

The unbearable pressure panicked her but it only lasted an instant.

She squirted out of the tunnel, the pudding-like feeling firming up as she reappeared. The others stood beside her.

"You may open your eyes, now. We are in Geneva," Rotar said.

She gasped and inhaled the sweet air, recognizing the private airport. Then she scanned her body to make sure she was back. The others did the same. Michelle clutched her mother's arm, squeezing her eyes shut again.

"You actually did it," Amanda exclaimed, wiggling her fingers and then hugging Michelle. "Is everybody okay? Remember, this is very—I mean, *very*—hush hush."

The children nodded; Tony appeared deep in thought. Gaspard looked relieved.

Amanda shuddered in the frigid wind. "It's cold. Let's get off this runway fast."

They hurried to the parking lot where they'd left the Suburban earlier in the day. Inside the car Amanda fretted in silence. What just happened? She felt totally wasted from nerves and scientific eccentricities and alien magic and God only knows what else. She checked her watch. Less than a minute ago they were in Verbier. Mind-boggling.

"Do not agitate yourself Amanda," Rotar said.

Gaspard said, "My wife must not know about this space travel. She will never let me out of zee house again. Zis will remain our secret, yes?"

"Of course," Amanda said. She turned to the youngsters. "And you all understand that for our protection we can never discuss this experience with anyone other than ourselves, agreed?"

The kids nodded.

"Would you like for me to check out the cabin?" Rotar asked.

"You know where it is?" Tony asked.

"Just show me the map."

"That will get us back to the hotel sooner. It's late," Amanda said.

"Then wait here a moment."

Rotar stepped out of the car and waved his stick. All eyes stared at the spot where he vanished. Suddenly he reappeared, scattering flakes of snow on the ground. His arms were wrapped around a newspaper with something inside.

Gaspard opened the door for him. The newspaper smelled foul. Tony got out and had a look. "This looks like animal dung, but it's green and purple with silver specks in it."

Rotar nodded. Horse excrement. The flying horse."

"You saw it?"

"No, there was no one at the cabin. But the fireplace still smelled of smoke and I found this behind the shed. The paper is dated two days ago."

"So if you can find the horse, you'll find Peter?"

Rotar shook his head. "Peter's brain waves are tuned to a frequency so high that I cannot pick it up. I also suspect that his planet is much farther away and has alienated itself from other planets in the universe."

Tony asked, "You mean they can block communication like a planetary firewall?"

"I am almost certain they have enclosed their planet within a protective sphere. If the horse is from a closer star with free-flowing energy, I might be able to find it, but Peter's energy is blocking everything."

Amanda looked at him, dejected and tired. "This is hopeless. Can you put that awful-smelling stuff in the rear, Gaspard?"

"Yes, and package it up for me later so I can have it analyzed at Braun's lab," Tony added.

Gaspard held his breath and took the newspaper to the rear of the SUV, stretching the stench as far ahead of him as he could.

When they left the airport, Rotar said, "All is not hopeless, Amanda. But I need to return to the lab tomorrow. Dr. Vidollet will perhaps have the antidote ready, and Peter will have to go there."

"Not alone," Tony said.

"But I am most capable…"

"We can't let you risk this by yourself," Tony added.

"But I have my powers," he argued.

"It could be dangerous," Tony insisted. "I can't allow you there on your own even with powers."

"But I can search without detection. How will you avoid the guards?"

"Rotar's right," Amanda said to Tony. "Coppet could be hazardous for us."

Tony grunted. "We'll figure something out. Rotar and I can work on it."

"Last time I was shot there," Amanda said in a tired voice. "I don't want to go back."

Lizzy spoke from the rear. "I have an idea, Dad."

"I hope it's good."

"Well?" Amanda pressed.

"We can hide among the sheep while Rotar checks out the barn."

"That might be a little too close," Tony said. "We have to find a way to temporarily discharge the guards and allow Peter access to the antidote if he shows up."

That's when Amanda realized what Tony was doing. Furious, she turned on him. "You just want to capture him for the government. He'll become a human specimen!"

Tony's eyes went dark. "Would you prefer that Andersen got him first? A prisoner for his sophisticated lab?"

She felt trapped. "If you go with Rotar, we all go with Rotar. But the children will stay out of sight and out of earshot and out of gunshot range."

Her trust in Tony shrank. She reminded herself to proceed with caution and take nothing for granted. Rotar would have to protect Peter.

CHAPTER THIRTY-FIVE

Peter slept in his hiding place in the woods. His breathing became erratic and he dreamed of the rat he had fed with the potion. Had someone found it? Was it stuck behind the barn wall and starving to death? He woke up, shivering. The campfire had burned out and Starbeam stood at his side. Peter touched the branches beneath him to confirm he was awake and cradled his head between his hands. "I was dreaming about the rat in the barn," he moaned to Starbeam.

I heard you...

"I hope it's still alive. And it's freezing—I have to go back to the farm and find a warm jacket and more food. Then I can check out the rat."

Starbeam nodded.

By midmorning they set out for the farmhouse. When they reached the edge of the woods he left Starbeam and continued on foot.

Peter watched the farm from behind an oak tree and used his x-ray vision to scan the house. The farmer and his wife were inside. It was a weekday so he assumed their son would be at school. The wind nipped at his ears and his teeth chattered. He considered sneaking into the barn but just then the couple came out of the house and drove away in their truck. He half skipped, half floated across the field into the barn, cheered by his good luck. Cheer turned to gloom. Torn wall boards lay on the floor with debris scattered around the hole where his experimental mouse had gone into hiding. "Darn, somebody found you, rat," he said in a gurgled voice. "I hope you got something to eat." He sighed, wondering if the farmer had it or perhaps the authorities. He had to be extra careful.

A new horse smaller than Starbeam and female looked at him from its stall. He tried to pet it but it shoved him away, whisking its tail against his face.

"Bonko-stars," he whispered. "I could change you into something magical. Maybe you wouldn't be so standoffish if you met Starbeam." He chuckled at the absurdity of the match.

Pigs squealing in the pen outside reminded him of the foul tasting food he had eaten in his desperation. He went out to visit the lone pig that had watched him before. It scampered toward him.

"I'll try the formula on you, little pig, before I go into the house."

The pig grunted and opened its mouth.

"Hold still," he said, squirting a large portion of the sticky liquid from his bag. "I'll be back in a few minutes."

The pig oinked and swallowed.

He hurried into the house and found a leather jacket in the hall closet. He took a moment to snuggle in its warmth. Then he ransacked the fridge pulling out a few carrots and a lone apple. He saw nothing cooked that he could take, and the milk carton had already been opened. It would make a mess. There was no time to search the pantry. The farmer could already be on his way back and would certainly alert the police when he discovered his jacket missing. But if Vidollet was ready with the antidote, Moonchild would soon be non-existent.

He returned to the barnyard and spotted the farmer's motorcycle in the carport. Shifting his gaze from the motorcycle to the pig, he was taken aback. The undersized pink pig had transformed into a black motorcycle pig...

"Wow, my distant moonbeams of utter fantasy," he hollered. "Have I actually created you?"

The pig nodded and thought, *I have always wanted to go fast like a motorcycle...*

Its skin had darkened to a purplish black color. On its back sat a small black saddle with a silver horn topped by a red button decorated in stars. The pig's beady eyes had become orange head-lights. A red lightning bolt ran down its forehead onto a stubby snout with black and silver nostrils. A ring of small reindeer horns crowned its head entwined in a dish-like circle. Two sad-dle bags hung over its rump and exhaust pipes ran along its back, curving under the hind legs. Chrome wheels replaced its hooves.

"Mighty moonbeam magnificent…" Peter cried. "I daresay I'm delighted with my fanciful potion."

He bellowed alien laughter and led the pig out of the pen. "With four wheels instead of two you look more like a peculiar ATV, to me. And those fantasy reindeer blades on your head—are you a helicopter? What the blazes are you?"

The pig smiled, *I wish to go fast and fly. I want to surf the jet stream.*

Peter stared at his creation. "Surf the jet stream? I don't think so. Let's just try out your new wheels for now."

He stuffed the pillowcase of supplies into a saddlebag and climbed onto the pig's back, raising his legs and kicking his heels.

Nothing happened.

He looked for something to trigger the pig. The red button on the saddle horn pulsated in flashes of gold and silver colors. He extended a long boney finger and pressed.

A high-pitched engine revved into action.

He gripped the saddle horn and edged it forward with care.

The born-again 'ATV pig' jolted into action, spinning its wheels across the barnyard toward the garage.

Peter jerked the horn to the left to avoid impact. The pig swung away from the building and raced toward the woods.

"Yippee-aiy-aaaaayyy—ride 'em cowboy…," Peter gurgled in excitement. He spit up green slime. "My own little dirt bike! But you're much more than that. Wait 'til Starbeam meets you. He might be jealous when he meets my little screech pig on hot wheels."

The pig geared down and rolled along the bumpy terrain. Peter relaxed. "Soon I'll be human again and I'll have the only flying horse and four-wheeled pig on the planet…"

Outside the Hotel de la Cigogne, Braun got out of his car and fumed over the disappearance of the priceless silver book. He had gotten up before sunrise and decided to take matters into his own hands. Neither his chief of security nor his secretary had come up with anything.

Adding to the mystery, the vanishing dwarf he'd seen in his office never surfaced. A magician perhaps? Something very odd was going on.

In the lobby he startled the night clerk, a boyish-looking young man plagued with acne. The clerk looked sleepy and ready to end his shift. The two were alone, so Braun didn't bother to lower his voice.

"I will make it worth your trouble to provide me with certain information," he stated in a hard tone.

The young man scanned the lobby. "I don't understand sir."

"I want to know everything about Anthony Ramsey and the Tregnier woman he's traveling with. They're both staying here, according to him. I want you to keep an eye out for anything unusual, that's all."

The clerk looked suspicious. "I'm afraid we have a privacy policy and pride ourselves—"

"Skip the pride!" Braun said, slamming a wad of Swiss francs on the counter. "This is a matter of international security. You don't need to know anything else."

The young man stared at the money and produced a weak smile. "Yes sir," he said, slipping the bills into his pocket.

"And you'll ask other employees, discreetly of course, for information about the group. Perhaps they've stored something in the hotel safe, or there is strange activity in their room."

He glowered at the boy and handed him two more bills along with his business card.

The clerk nodded, but looked nervous.

Braun suppressed a smile, turned, and rushed out the front door where his driver waited. "Money can accomplish many things," he said to Charles while making himself comfortable in the back seat of the dark blue Mercedes. The car was a loaner while the other two were under repair.

"I hope it pays off," Charles said in a gloomy tone. "I don't see how a suburban housewife with two children can be much of a threat…"

Braun grunted at his driver. "That so-called 'innocent house-wife' is married to a renegade scientist. And I don't trust Ramsey either. He's supposed to be watching her and taking her family on scenic tours. What bunk. The bribe will get me information and then we'll see who has the bargaining chip in this curious intrigue."

He reached for his wet-wipes and cleaned his hands. "Money germs all over myself. It's disgusting—filthy bacteria everywhere."

"Wouldn't you rather wear gloves sir?"

"No. They accumulate dirt inside."

Charles asked in a tired voice, "Where to now, sir?"

"Back to the farm. I want to talk to that imbecile farmer again. And then return to headquarters to question the lab technician. There might be something interesting to report to Sam Henry in Washington. Got to keep stallin' him until I can get my stolen property back. We've got a busy day ahead of us, so spin 'em, Charles, spin 'em fast…"

Charles groaned. "On our way, sir."

"And keep your eye out for a news stand."

"Very well sir."

CHAPTER THIRTY-SIX

Peter sped toward the forest on his new A.T.V pig. Trees loomed ahead. "Whoa pig," he cried, pulling back on the saddle horn but the wind whisked his words away. "Slow down," he shouted again.

The pig didn't respond.

The trees drew closer and Peter pulled harder on the horn. But instead of slowing, the pig's headlights started flashing. A vertical rod extended the crown of reindeer horns about four feet above its head. The horns flattened into blades and whirled into action.

The pig roared like a helicopter and lifted into the sky.

"Oh my magnificent moonbeams, you really can fly," Peter shouted.

They cleared the treetops with ease.

"Can you also find Starbeam from up here? He's a flying horse."

The pig flew in a zig-zag pattern along the edge of the forest until Peter saw Starbeam. The horse looked up and took flight.

Peter guided the pig to follow. When they reached the clearing at the campsite, Starbeam swooped and landed in his usual graceful style. The pig hovered over the campsite kicking up pine needles and debris as it gently set down.

The aliens greeted each other in a friendly way. Starbeam snorted and lifted his wings, then bent one leg and bowed to the pig.

The pig squealed and smiled.

Peter dismounted while the animals studied each other. He took a moment to admire his creations and decided he might transform an entire menagerie of animal life when he returned to normal. It would make circuses obsolete. Bloated with pride he dropped his sack and lit a fire. Telepathic thoughts entered his mind from both space animals, their communication reverberating like an echo chamber.

You have joined me to find your way home, thought Starbeam.

Finally, the pig thought back. *Ever since I was a piglet I have yearned for the power of a four wheeled motorcycle. I watched my owner riding away on his. Now with my whirly blades I am free to fly into the sky and seek adventures anywhere.*

"Oh my scary moon-flights," Peter said in distress. "I'm not sure I can let you do that."

The pig looked curious. *You are welcome to join me.*

He shook his head. "I need you here. You can't leave yet. It's very important."

Annoyance crossed the pig's face.

Peter thought of a distraction. "I haven't named you yet. What shall I call you? Heaven's Angel? Star Angel? Moon Angel? Or Whirly Pig?" He chuckled. "What do you think?"

The pig looked up at the sky. *Too cutesy...*

"Are you a girl or a boy?"

The pig thought, *I'm a girl and I can fly as delicately as a butterfly or roar across the fields like a truck.*

Starbeam broke in and thought, *Butterfly...truck...speed... motor bike...all terrain...what about Hummerfly?* He snorted.

*That sounds good...*the pig thought.

"Then Hummerfly will be your new outer-planetary name," Peter said. "And this is Starbeam." He sniggered at the two foreign animals. "Oh, my goosey moon bumps, I'm introducing a pig to a horse. What next?"

I have reconsidered my name, the pig thought. *I like Humfly better and it's shorter.*

"All right. Is that your final choice?"

Yes. Humfly... She smiled and hummed like a small machine, *hum, hum, hum, Humfly will fly away...* She turned her wheels and twirled in a circle, lifting one shoulder and then the other. In a grand finale she raised her rump into the air, dropping it with a thump. She revved her voice into low and bellowed in a guttural voice, *hurrumphhhh…*swishing her rear end back and forth, twirling her crown. *Hurrumphhhh, hurrumphhhh, hurrumphhhh…Love that rhythm…I'm gonna' fly me to the stars…*

"Maybe I'm crazy and hallucinating all this," Peter said as he sat down by the fire and opened his sack. "It's getting dark and I'm starving. I only have one apple."

Anything's better than pig slop, thought Humfly

"Enough," Peter said, putting out the carrots for them to eat.

Humfly turned to Starbeam. *Wanna fly?*

Starbeam shook his head.

Humfly revved her engine. *Too 'fraidy' horsey to race? Comon' let's try it.*

You'll crash. And you're no match for me.

"Stop it, both of you," Peter said, annoyed. "We have to fly to my lab. My antidote should be ready by now."

He frowned at Humfly. "You make too much noise when you fly fast. You can ride with me on top of Starbeam. His wings are quiet."

He led Starbeam to a fallen log. Humfly used the whirling antlers to elevate herself onto the horse's back. From atop the log Peter climbed into the pig's saddle.

"I feel like royalty perched on a throne!" he shouted. "If we can get safely past the guards, I know a secret place to hide. But we have to be very quiet."

He suddenly recalled times past when he had boasted too much too soon and jinxed his plans.

"Never mind. Let's see what we find when we get there. Time for takeoff—start flapping, Starbeam."

Starbeam began with a trot, then a gallop until he lifted into the sky. They approached the farm and Peter's sharpened vision detected media vans and groups of people camping near the lab entrance. They looked like reporters and visitors, a few dressed in religious robes. Before they were close enough to be spotted he directed Starbeam to land in a grove of trees on the opposite side of the property.

The wind trashed branches and whipped leaves that scattered to the ground. Starbeam swooped down but clipped a branch with his wing. In the rough landing Peter and Humfly fell off. The storm blanketed the noise.

"There go more of my extraterrestrial bones," Peter cried, trying to stand up. "And it looks like you've hurt your wing, Starbeam, but I can't do anything about it at the moment. Stay here both of you while I check things out." He pointed to a covered foundation and blackened chimney. "That's what's left of my ancestral home."

Receiving no reaction from the horse or the pig over his loss, he kept the painful memories to himself and in a serious tone said, "And don't move around or make noise. There are armed guards and media cameras and people everywhere. I'll be back as soon as I can."

He turned and half jumped—half floated into the darkness.

CHAPTER THIRTY-SEVEN

Braun sat at his desk fuming over reports that Peter Tregnier hadn't shown up at the cabin in the woods. And an early morning visit back to the farm had met with an angry farmer insisting the outer-space thief had struck again. His motorcycle jacket was missing along with food and one of his pigs.

But without evidence, Braun was at a standstill.

His mind churned, trying to make sense of the puzzle: the horse, the pig, the jacket, the food, a pulverized space rat and Dr. Tregnier. He made arrangements for a subordinate to watch for suspicious activity at Joseph's farm, but wished he had thought of it earlier.

Braun was cleaning his desk with a wet-wipe and waiting for the preliminary report from his lab technician when the telephone rang. His secretary had gone home for the night so he answered. Still in a foul mood he shouted, "Braun here…"

"It's Sam Henry, Leo. Calling from DC. How the heck are 'ya?"

Agitated, Braun wiped his brow with the dirty cloth. "Blast," he muttered.

"Beg pardon?" Sam asked.

"Uh, nothing. Would you hold on a moment?"

"You don't want to put me on hold, Braun. I might start thinkin' you're up to something. Like something no good." He had a hyena laugh.

Resentful, Braun fumbled for a new wet-wipe and rubbed his forehead. Kissy-ass Sam Henry was a CIA body snatcher— a hatchet man who shot first and asked questions later. He got away with it because of some internal reform he had suggested to the President's ethics review board. Now the golden boy could do no wrong.

"You still there Braun?"

"Apologies, Sam. How can I help you?" He swung around in his chair and tossed the wipe into the trash.

"What the blazes is going on over there? The newspapers—"

"Think nothing of it," Braun interrupted. "Some imaginative reporter's been blowing things out of proportion, that's all."

"Well then, suppose you tell me what *is* going on…"

"Yes sir. Just a nutty scientist who thinks it's Halloween."

"What about the *alleged* experiment? And Tony Ramsey? Are you keepin' an eye on him?"

Braun popped an antacid into his mouth. "Ramsey latched onto Tregnier's wife and they're touring together. But I don't know, Sam. I'm not sure about Ramsey."

"What do you mean?"

He detected doubt in Sam's voice but decided to play the blame-game anyway. "I think he's working with the wife on his own."

After a moment of silence, Sam said, "I've always thought of Tony's loyalty as unimpeachable."

He cleared his throat. "I'm not certain, but I'm working on retrieving the evidence as we speak. And my lab is—"

"You have specimens? What kind?"

"Don't know yet, sir. I'm waiting for a report."

"Call me when you do. And I don't need to tell you the President's concerned about all this hype. He's got paranormal fanatics, clergy and government leaders houndin' him. If any of this stuff's true there's no tellin' what might happen. Especially with a crazy scientist on the loose. You're gettin' cooperation from your Swiss counterparts?"

"Yes sir. I've got security stationed at the lunatic's lab now. We're doing everything possible to track this down."

"Well good, Leo. I'm hopin' this is the result of some *pot party* or somethin'. But just in case, I'm sending over a couple of agents. Ernie Bauer and Jack Bloomfield. They'll report to you day after tomorrow."

"Sir, I don't need reinforcements yet…"

Sam had stopped listening. "They have their orders and they're bringin' some state-of-the art equipment to ensure that no one lets this mysterious thing get away."

"But there's nothing mysterious about it."

"The President's waitin'. Don't let him down."

"I understand, sir."

Sam hung up. Braun slammed down the receiver and wiped perspiration from his brow. The offensive bureaucrat was always squeezing him. He swung around in his chair and looked at the photo of himself and his mother. "I'll show him, and you too, *Mommy dearest*, that I'm not a screw up."

The phone rang.

"Hello," he shouted in a cranky tone.

"Rudolph, sir, from the lab."

Braun shot up in his chair. "You got something?"

"I think so. Can you come down?"

"On my way."

He rode the elevator to the basement. Sitting across from Rudolph, he dropped a smug smirk from his face. The lab technician, wiry, with boney hands and protruding knuckles, adjusted his rimless glasses in a modest way.

"I am puzzled by the findings sir. Still inconclusive, of course," Rudolph said.

"In what way?"

"These chemicals in the hay that you sent me are foreign and as far as I know have never been identified."

"Can you guess what they are?"

The tech removed his glasses and rubbed his forehead. "This formula could be capable of altering the mind in some unnatural manner. It is very potent, whatever it is."

Ecstatic, Braun got up and shook Rudolph's hand, ignoring the man's shyness. "Think you can duplicate it?" He grabbed a wet wipe from a container on the desk and wiped his hands.

Rudolph studied the papers. "I can try, but some of the elements don't make sense."

Braun shuddered at the potential of Peter Tregnier's discovery. "Stay on it. Call me if you come up with anything."

Rudolph looked up. "I'm already sleeping down here, sir."

"Good. That's 'above and beyond' loyalty and I'll see that you're taken care of."

"Thank you."

"Don't let me down."

"No sir."

He started to leave the lab but stopped and turned around. "By the way, I'll need some of that hay sample from the barn."

"Sir?"

"For an associate in Washington," he lied. "Put a little in a plastic bag for me. I'll have it sent by special courier."

"Of course sir."

Rudolph transferred some of the material into a bag, leaning close to his work as though his glasses weren't strong enough. "And the remains of the rodent? You want some of that too?"

Braun shook his head. "No…well, yes. On second thought I'll send both over. Have you analyzed the pillow hairs we found at that vacant mountain cabin? The one with the fresh fireplace ashes? Are they human?"

Rudolph looked bewildered. "Fraid not. They could be a wig of some sort but they're not like any man-made materials either…"

"Nonsense! Someone's playing Halloween tricks here. What else could they be?"

"I don't know sir. The unknown fibers contain levels of radiation, but I can't offer any conclusions."

Braun's mind buzzed from all the unanswered questions. "Keep on it," he said, trying to remain calm, "and let's give Washington a little of everything to look at. For a second opinion."

"Good idea sir." Rudolph prepared three labeled plastic bags of specimens.

Braun took his loot and patted him on the shoulder. "Keep up the good work."

Back in his office, Braun locked the samples in his safe. Then he took a nap, waiting until midnight to head back to the Hotel de la Cigogne.

A little after twelve o'clock, Charles yawned and drove like he was in a funeral procession. He was not happy about the late trip.

Braun squirmed and fretted in the back seat of the car, unable to shake his anger over the imminent arrival of two men from Washington. He needed more time.

The weather outside matched his mood: foggy and soggy. "Turn up the heat," he shouted. Charles jerked and swerved.

"And mind your driving—I'm thinkin' back here."

"This is my third car in less than a week—I have to get used to it."

He ignored his chauffeur and worried about the two agents arriving. When they learned about the squashed rodent it would get back to Sam Henry. Braun would face ridicule and scrutiny, the things he hated most. Throughout his school years and military service he had been misjudged many times. He would have to continue to blame whatever he could on Ramsey.

Charles pulled up in front of the hotel and slammed the brakes. Braun popped an antacid into his mouth and fumbled with the door. Perspiration covered his forehead. The cold wind bit his face.

He rushed inside.

The night clerk stood behind the counter.

Braun came right to the point. "You learn anything of value to me?"

The young man shifted his eyes around the lobby, his face grim. "One small item, probably of no significance."

"Let me be the judge of that!" Braun growled.

"My girlfriend is a room maid," the clerk said. "She said there is a small man living with Mr. Ramsey and the Tregnier family."

Alarms rang in Braun's head. "A boy or a man? The Tregnier woman has a son."

The clerk shook his head. "No this is an older man. A midget. A bit overweight."

The man in the smoke in his office? He had to check it out. "Anything else?"

"Not that I know of, but there is a rumor amongst the staff…"

"Yeah? What?"

"The small man is a clever magician."

"How do you know that?"

"He stopped food in midair from falling off a service cart."

"How'd he do that?"

"With a magic wand."

Braun's brain flew into fast forward. But he had to keep mum. "Yeah, sure."

He handed the boy some Swiss Francs and said, "Anything more on that or anything else, call me."

The boy nodded.

Rushing out of the hotel, Braun fumed. The little man was real. And Tony was in on it. Probably in cahoots with the Tregnier woman and her crazy husband. Somehow, they'd stolen the book. Magician, huh! He had to get into their rooms and find out more before the stateside reinforcements arrived. And when they did, he'd have real facts to implicate Ramsey.

CHAPTER THIRTY-EIGHT

Peter watched Starbeam fold his wounded wing close to his shoulder and worried. What would he do with the horse after making contact with Vidollet in the morning? He couldn't just fly away on Humfly and leave him there. But all he could do at the moment was hide and rest.

He tiptoed toward the plastic tarp. A twinge of nostalgia came over him, recalling his summer visits. His father had refused to return to Coppet, too absorbed with his work as a nuclear physicist at Georgetown University. At the age of twelve Peter lost his mother to cancer and his father sent him to Coppet on summer vacations. Just before Peter's twenty-first birthday his father died in a freak automobile accident and a short time after he inherited the Swiss property. His grandparents had provided him with many fond memories, even though the main house had now burned down.

He turned away from the flattened plot and scanned for guards. The outline of a man stood inside the barn. Dr. Vidollet sat hunched over his desk. Peter counted two more men outside on the other side of the barn by the parking area where curious gawkers huddled in the cold. He could enter the basement unseen. He lifted a corner of the tarp and found the staircase.

Concerned that the wind might carry his wheezing breath, he scooted down the first few steps and pulled the tarp over his head. No way could he get Starbeam and Humfly down such steep stairs.

He tested the wood for rot and loose nails. Each step on the brittle boards supported his light weight. Out of sight and safe for the time being, he scanned the dark musty cellar with his night vision. The dampness blurred his view, yet even in the dim light he saw years of neglect. Cobwebs and dirt covered various pieces of furniture and multiple rows of shelving that once stored canned foods and supplies.

He wiped his eyes.

A half dozen glass jars of fruit remained on the top shelf of a heavy built-in cabinet. Gray with dust and their lids corroded and rusty, he wondered if the peaches were still edible.

He found an old chair, its cane webbing broken in patches and dragged it over to the shelves. When he climbed on, the chair wobbled. He re-balanced, and when his footing felt secure he stretched to grab the jars on the top shelf but couldn't reach them. The basement held no other possibilities. He tugged on the shelves attached to the wall and pulled himself onto a higher shelf. But just when his knee made contact, the board crunched with a groan. Its screws pulled loose from the wall and the cabinet fell away, throwing him backwards. Jars and shelving tumbled in a loud crash on top of him. Dust clogged the air.

Pinned to the floor, Peter moaned in pain, struggling to breathe.

He rolled a little to one side and opened his leather jacket. Green blood seeped through his shirt. Weak from lack of oxygen, he dragged himself from under the pile, inch-by inch across the dirt floor. The wood scraped his wounds.

In what seemed like an eternity he stood up on shaky legs and checked for broken bones.

None.

Peaches and broken glass lay scattered on the floor. He picked one up and checked for glass shards, wiping off the dirt and popping it into his mouth.

It tasted sweet, mixed with dirt, its flavor reminding him of metal, but he didn't care.

Ravenous, he ate another and another. Syrup dripped down his chin. He ate all the peaches and while looking for more food, discovered a double door behind the shelving. The opening looked wide enough for a horse and cart. He surmised earlier owners had sealed it for security.

He tried to open the doors but they stuck. Using a rusty pipe, he jammed it into the crack and pried them open. But instead of daylight, he entered into a dark tunnel. A blast of damp air chilled him.

The green ooze seeping from his chest meant he had to proceed quickly. He set a chunk of shelving ablaze with his fire power and held it like a torch while moving through the wet passageway. A smaller tunnel branched left but he followed the airflow. His wet feet grew numb before he reached the exit. When he pushed through the thick bushes outside he saw that Starbeam and Humfly could easily get into the cellar.

The orchard to the west obscured his view of the lab but the sound of sheep bells clanging meant he wasn't far away. By the lake an old dock held mooring rigs. Perhaps the tunnel had at one time been a supply route or even a means of escape…

He hurried through the apple trees and found Starbeam and Humfly. When they were far enough away from the guards, Peter stopped to examine Starbeam's wing. "You may not be able to fly me back to the woods, Starbeam. And since Humfly roars like a real helicopter we'll have to stay here until you're better."

He didn't wait for an answer. "Follow me. We have to hide."

He lit the same torch and guided them along the dark path through the tunnel. Humfly's chrome wheels squeaked on the wet ground.

When they reached the basement, Peter pointed to his chest, sopping wet with alien blood. His boots were soaked. He found an old tarp and some rags to wrap his chest and protect the wound. Then he made a bed out of the tarp.

"There's a guard inside the lab," Peter told them, lying down. "Vidollet comes out to feed the sheep in the morning. I'll signal him at that time to bring the antidote here."

Starbeam nodded.

Humfly snorted at Peter. *Whatever…*

"Anyone have a better idea?"

I'm a flying all-terrain vehicle. I want to rattle and race. I want to fly like a big-pig-mama across the stars. She stared defiance at Starbeam.

Peter looked at her. "You're stubborn, aren't you? Starbeam's injured and I'm wounded. I could be dying. I need you to stay here and help me. You can do your big-pig-mama thing later, okay?"

Mama-mia star-poop to you too, thought Humfly. She turned away and dropped to the floor, wheels sprawled, and huffed.

"Let's get some sleep," Peter said, but got up in alarm. "Moon-blast, I forgot—I have to hide my bota bag with the potion."

He found a secure place under the stairwell. "I'll just turn this bucket upside down over the bag."

Starbeam snorted but Humfly turned away.

Peter went back to his makeshift bed. "Starbeam, wake me up early, okay?"

Starbeam flapped his left wing. *Very well.*

Oh brother, thought Humfly. *Starbeam's nothing more than a butt dart...*

Humbly reminded Peter of the constant bickering between Howard and Michelle. But he couldn't think about his family. He needed to rest and heal. Tomorrow he would contact Vidollet and be transformed back to normal. He'd be more famous than anyone on the planet.

Dear moon, my god and commander, help me restore my life, Peter prayed. *Please heal Starbeam's wing so he can fly again. I'd be very grateful. And please in the name of the universe and all eternity make the antidote work.*

Tears slid over lumpy skin and pointed cheek bones. "I want so much to see my human face again," he whispered aloud.

Starbeam nudged his shoulder.

A calm filled the room.

Peter hoped it would be his last night on Earth as an alien.

CHAPTER THIRTY-NINE

After her argument the evening before over Tony's insistence that he accompany Rotar to the lab, Amanda had tossed and turned most of the night. She woke up tired and immediately began to worry again, but she didn't know what to do about it. Dressing quickly, she nodded to Lizzy and the kids who were eating breakfast and went to join Tony and Rotar next door. At hearing the phone ring she stopped at the cracked door and listened.

"Thanks for calling me back," Tony said. "Da, da." He nodded, listened a moment and hung up.

Amanda's heart skipped a beat. That sounded like Russian. Gut-wrenching doubts nagged her. She tromped into the living room and shot accusing eyes at Tony. "Who was that?" she demanded to know.

"I called a friend about Andersen. They know of him. And Goldtooth."

"You have Russian friends?"

"Affirmative."

She looked to Rotar for comment but he shrugged and stood from the table. "I will go next door and eat before we leave for the lab."

She shot angry eyes at him. "And why aren't the winds subsiding, Rotar? Have you looked outside at the weather? You have your book now."

He responded in a sad tone. "I do not know. Perhaps Aeolius will not relent until Peter is no longer an alien."

"What's that got to do with anything?"

"He abused the secrets in the book."

Amanda couldn't think straight. "Then we'd better find him. You can go eat."

Tony grunted. "You're being very hard on our small friend today, Amanda."

"I'm angry. Sick of this weather and your constant surprises. Who am I running around with, the American version of James Bond?" She stared him down.

He looked annoyed. "Hardly."

"You never mentioned you spoke Russian."

"My father encouraged me to learn. He said one day we'd either have to fight them or join them. I spent a summer in Moscow as part of an international music program and took an intensive language course. Then I continued studying while at the Air Force Academy."

She sank into the couch. How would she ever protect Peter if Tony had so many powerful connections? "You're a fraud," she snapped. "And you lied to me."

"I did not."

"Lies of omission Tony, all these hidden details." She wrapped her arms around herself.

He sat down on the chair opposite her and tried to catch her eyes. She looked away. "It's going to work out for the best," he urged.

More fiction. "Why should I believe you? Give me one good reason not to go to the Swiss police and tell them what you and Braun are up to? His security team's as treacherous as you."

"And risk harming Peter?"

"He's already at risk because of the two of you."

Tony raised his hands. "I would never harm you or your family. You've got to trust me."

"Why?" she retorted, feeling trapped by Tony and Peter both. She ate a truffle.

"Bear with me—I have good connections."

"Like who?"

"I'm not at liberty to say just yet, but soon."

"Then I'm not at liberty to trust you either. And I doubt that 'soon' will ever get here. Your manipulation infuriates me. You defend and defer…no, you detour and divert, or rather you detain and desist, or resist. I'm so angry I'm not even coherent and furthermore I don't care."

He tried to suppress a smile. "I understand."

"No you don't, but what difference does it make? You've lost all credibility with me."

In a gentle tone he said, "If it helps any, I did decipher your garbled rationale."

"It doesn't."

"You're so angry Amanda, and it seems you use chocolates to divert issues yourself."

Her glare could have flash-frozen a buffalo. "What do you know about it?"

"That perhaps losing your father through divorce and now Peter…"

"One has nothing to do with the other!"

Tony looked deflated. "Perhaps you drew Peter into your life to resolve some unresolved issues with your father?"

Amanda bolted out of the couch. "Stop analyzing me! That's what Peter did. Neither of you are qualified."

Tony stood up and shrugged. "Just a thought. But we can't waste time arguing. Let's get going." He picked up his overcoat. "I've arranged for a boat to take us to Peter's lab. A surprise visit—undetected."

She frowned. "I'm not going anywhere with you until I get some real answers about your Russian friends." The sound of the television caught her attention. A female reporter stood at the entrance to the lab in Coppet. Wind whipped her hair while she fought the force of a storm and struggled to speak.

"The press lingers outside the heavily guarded laboratory in Coppet, hoping to catch a glimpse of Dr. Francois Vidollet, the scientist who we believe is being protected by American and Swiss intelligence. UFO enthusiasts have joined tourists and religious groups, many of whom suspect the two governments are hiding an extraterrestrial being right here in Coppet."

An aerial view showed the barn with guards posted on all sides. The camera swept in on different groups with close-ups of curious spectators. Some appeared angry and trying to rally the crowd.

Amanda threw the couch pillow at the TV. "Now we'll never get in. What'll we do?"

"Rotar can help us," Tony said.

The reporter continued.

"It has often been rumored that the United States Air Force as well as European military have hidden evidence of UFO sightings from the public. The international ecumenical community seems anxious to debate the ramifications of how the discovery of an extraterrestrial being would affect the world-view of religion. We have been informed that a demonstration is scheduled for tomorrow morning in front of the White House. Simultaneous demonstrations will take place at the US Consulate in Geneva which will be in the afternoon, local time."

"I want to go to that," Amanda said.

"I doubt we'll be back in time," Tony said, "but what concerns me more is the increased exposure in Washington that is sure to spread elsewhere."

Before Amanda could comment, Michelle, Howard, Lizzy and Rotar rushed into the suite. Michelle hugged her mother. Howard laid a protective arm around Amanda's shoulder. Rotar hung back, looking shy.

"What a wonderful greeting," she said, lightened by their arrival. Her face fell when she turned to Rotar. "I'm sorry Rotar. I didn't mean to be so rude. Forgive me?"

Rotar nodded with a smile in his eyes.

"We need your help today, Rotar," Amanda added. "Let's get ready kids. We're going to the lab. Anyone not back in five minutes with jackets on and hands scrubbed gets to stay here and do homework!"

They dashed toward their rooms. Rotar flipped his stick at their backs, *"Freez-i-um,"* he said. They stood frozen in place. "This will save us some time." He waved his stick again. *"Ker-klean-i-ko."* The wind swished around until they sparkled with cleanliness. *"Dres-i-um Levi-tar-pet,"* he added, and they were dressed in warm jackets. One more wave of the stick and they unfroze. Michelle giggled, Howard grunted and Lizzy laughed. Rotar chuckled, flapping his arms as though the wind tickled him.

Amanda grabbed her coat. She muttered to Tony in passing. "This discussion is not over."

Gaspard drove them to the quay where a twenty-five foot cabin cruiser waited. When they boarded he asked, "We are all seaworthy, *mes amies?*"

"That means *my friends*," Howard said, grinning with pride.

Gaspard nodded and smiled. The boat's gangway swayed in the wind and they held on to the rails until safely seated inside.

The ride was bumpy and Gaspard used a navigational map to find the right pier. The dock was out of view from the farm. After mooring the boat, Tony said, "Gaspard will go first and signal when it's safe for us to follow. And no one must make a sound. The wind will help hide the noise but we still have to be careful."

"This will be just like keeping a secret," Amanda said. Michelle put her finger across her mouth to silence everyone.

Howard stood and wobbled. "Let me out. I hate boats…"

Lizzy jumped up, bumping Howard aside. "Excuse me, but ladies go first."

"You're not a lady, you're a McFlirty, McSlurpy," Howard shot back.

"Silence," Amanda hissed through clenched teeth.

Gaspard crept up a small incline, motioning the others to follow. They moved through the orchard and tall grass, approaching the guarded area. Then they got down and crawled. The wet ground smelled sour. When they closed in on the barn, Tony motioned for everyone to stay back.

"I want to go with you Tony," Amanda whispered.

Tony shook his head. "You have to stay here with the kids. Gaspard will come along."

"Don't forget me," Rotar said.

Amanda looked at him. "Rotar, you can stay and watch the kids while I go with Tony and Gaspard to the lab."

Rotar looked perplexed. "I prefer to go with Tony. What if Peter is there?"

"I'm sorry," Amanda said, "but we can't all go and you're the best one to keep the kids safe."

"Very well," Rotar said. "I will wait here."

Tony did not look pleased. "I'd like you both to wait here."

"No way," Amanda said. "If my husband is in there, or nearby, I want to be the first one to find him."

"Your choice," Tony said, shrugging. "But it could be dangerous."

"I'm aware of that, and I'm going with you!"

CHAPTER FORTY

While waiting for Amanda and the others to return, Rotar decided to check on his home. He waved Howard, Michelle and Lizzy to follow and crawled toward the boulders. At the entrance he put a finger to his mouth and said in a low voice, "I will show you where I live but we must hurry."

He led them through the bushes into the tunnel and to his damp cave. Water dripped from the ceiling. A candle flickered on the table. He picked it up by its brass holder and held the flame high. "This is my home—I call it Planet Alley."

Rocket parts sat in neat stacks against one wall. Additional components had been disassembled and converted into a table, stool and other furniture. A Christmas angel dangled from a tree root in the ceiling and book shelves filled a corner. "What do you think?" he asked.

The kids looked around, spellbound. In an unsure tone, Howard said, "Yeah, ahhhh, it's neat…"

"It's spooky," Michelle muttered.

Lizzy scrutinized the room. "It's ghastly, but has possibilities—a fireplace, satellite TV, stereo equipment, a modernized kitchen and some designer bedding would help."

She moved over to a box sitting on a side table. "What's this, an outer-space microwave?" She pointed to the metal box with a glass door. Curly probes and colored knobs covered the top and sides.

"It's a dingle dipper," Rotar said.

"A what?" Lizzy eyed the large gold button on the top left, then the silver matching one the right. "What happens if I push either of these?"

"Do not touch," Rotar said, but too late. She pressed the gold button. Bright crystals sparkled and small white snowflakes whirled around inside the compartment. Colored powders mixed in with the frozen flakes. "Quick!" Rotar said, "What is your favorite ice cream? State it clearly."

Lizzy looked at him odd. "Chocolate, why?"

Brown powder swirled.

"And topping?"

"Caramel I guess."

"Anything else?"

"Like what?"

"Flavors? Hurry!"

"Marshmallows, whipped cream, I don't know."

Rotar watched foreign symbols run through the small panel on the front and stop. He pressed a silver button. "I have sent in your request."

Howard and Michelle stared at the box in silence. A frigid mixture of something gooey filled a small holder. The machine dinged and donged and the door opened. Lavender smoke puffed out of the cavity and a perfect ice cream cup sat on a tray.

"How?" Lizzy asked, casting a stunned expression.

"It is a voice-activated dingle-dip machine. It can make any ice cream your palate desires, chocolate, strawberry, peanut butter, lime, licorice, bacon, pickles…"

"Pickle ice cream?" Michelle asked, screwing up her face.

Rotar nodded. "Anything you ask of it."

"Far out," said Howard.

Lizzy dipped the small spoon that came with the cup and licked. "It's steamy scrumptious for sure! I should have asked for sushi, one of my favorite treats. Do you have a patent yet?"

Rotar shrugged and shook his head.

Howard cross-eyed his pupils and stuck out his tongue. "Sushi? You're cracked."

Lizzy snorted. "And you're an under-educated troll. My best friend is from Japan and she introduced me to a more *sophisticated international* cuisine.

"So? You're talkin' about raw-fish ice cream," Howard argued.

"What would you know about gourmet food anyway, but now you both have to taste this." Lizzy passed the ice cream cup to Michelle and wandered the cave while the others were eating. "It must be lonely in here Rotar—I'd go bonkers."

Rotar smoothed out the sheepskin covering his rocket bed. "I had a friend once. He brought me books to read. Books were scarce, you know."

Lizzy frowned. "Scarce? They're a dime-a-dozen and most of the old ones are giveaways."

He lifted his eyes to the shelves along the wall. "Now they are, but at that time…"

"How long ago did your friend visit you?" Lizzy asked.

He thought a moment. "It was about two hundred years ago, or perhaps three—I do not remember, but he died."

Michelle looked sad.

"But you have us now," Howard hurried to say.

Lizzy picked up one of the leather-bound books and turned a few pages. "I'll bet these are valuable."

"Perhaps," Rotar said. "Some are written in Latin and French, others in Old English. I read them between feeding the stray cats that visit me on occasion."

Michelle remained still, her eyes fixed on the candy in a wooden bowl. The multi-colored bite-size pieces glowed, emitting miniscule sparks. She reached for a blue one, held it a moment and then popped it into her mouth.

"Stop," Rotar said, but again he was too late. Michelle lifted her face into a beaming smile. Her eyes twinkled and she began to giggle. She laughed and laughed in a high-pitched noise that made Howard cover his ears. He grabbed a red one and ate it, breaking into uproarious laughter. Rotar reached over to grab the bowl but Lizzy leapt in front of him and popped a yellow candy into her mouth.

"What are these things?" she asked while chewing, mimicking the uncontrollable laughter that filled the cave. When the boisterous frolic finally stopped, Rotar answered.

"Merry berries," he said. "They enhance my tune-ups by tickling my personality when I am feeling low." He clutched the bowl. "I have been here so long that I have been forced to ration down to one berry on the occasion of my year-change."

"What's that?" Lizzy asked.

"My birthday. And I do not have many berries left, so I must ask you not to eat any more."

"When's your birthday?" she asked.

"I never know. When I acquire another scale, I age."

Howard screwed up his face. "Scale?"

"My Rotarious skin is scaled and covered by my Earth skin."

"That's awful," Lizzy said. "I can't even comment on how you'd ever moisturize something like that."

The three children stared at Rotar in silence. On the shelf next to Howard, an egg-carton shaped box began to shimmer in rainbow colors. "Cool colors," he said, taking it. "What's inside this weird thing?" He opened its lid.

Rotar took it from him. Purple velvet lined the box with a dozen depressions. Silver starfish-shaped pendants sat in each indentation. One was missing. "This are precious heirlooms from my planet."

Lizzy leaned down to study the eyes that pulsated white crystals from their centers. Howard extended a finger to touch, but Rotar pulled the box away and rubbed one of the glass eyes. The yellowish color changed to orange and then to red. "These are Eternity Eyes."

"What's that?" Michelle asked.

"It is a token only to be given to a true friend," he said, grasping the pendant on the chain around his neck. "This one was from my mother."

"One's missing from the box," Howard said.

"Yes, I gave it to my 'book' friend."

"You've only had one friend, ever?" Lizzy asked.

Rotar nodded sadly. "The pendant is only to be shared with a forever friend."

"How long is forever?" Michelle asked.

"For eternity," Rotar said. "And one cannot give it until the commitment is mutual."

"Mind frazzling," Lizzy said.

"Brain freezing," Howard added. "I don't know anyone I'd want to be friends with forever, except maybe my dog, Pluto, and most of the time, my mom."

"Me too," Michelle said, nodding.

Lizzy looked frantic. "I doubt my dad would give me one. I can be a pain at times."

"You got that right," Howard said in a huff.

"You're a McJerk," she retaliated.

"McSnot," Howard shot back.

Michelle held hands over her ears. "You're both McMental!" she blurted.

Rotar frowned at them. "Enough of this. You will have many friends in your lifetime and perhaps even as many as a dozen, if you are lucky." He placed the box back on the shelf. "Now we must leave."

He picked up the candle and carried it into the dark tunnel. A mild scent of lavender followed him. The brass shimmered pink, purple and gold. Lizzy meandered into the tunnel offshoot.

"I want to explore," she said. "Where does this lead?"

Rotar moved to her side with his candle. "Nowhere. It ends up ahead."

Howard followed them dragging his leg through the mud.

"Wait for me," Michelle whimpered. Howard stopped and took her hand.

The wind will blow that thing out," Lizzy said, nodding at Rotar's flickering flame while continuing through the tunnel.

"What thing?" he asked.

"Your candle."

"Oh no, this is my infinity candle."

"Your what?" Lizzy stopped.

"I brought it with me from my planet. It never goes out."

"Never ever?" Michelle asked.

"You're joking," Lizzy said.

"Neat," Howard commented.

Lizzy inspected the candle. "We could market something like this."

"Perhaps," he said with reluctance, "but it will go out eventually..."

Lizzy's eyes questioned him. "But you just said..."

"It will go out when I die."

Lizzy frowned. "Let's change the subject."

Michelle nodded.

Howard shrugged with impatience.

"I understand," Rotar said, squeezing his eyes together. "But I do not think we should go any farther. It is wet and cold in here and the others will be looking for us."

"Wait," Howard said. "I think I see something."

"What?" Michelle asked.

"A door," Lizzy said.

"It is nothing," Rotar grumbled. "Just the basement of a house that burned down."

Lizzy pushed open the door.

Rotar followed her into a dark room waving his candle.

Howard and Michelle pressed after them.

Lizzy pointed, "The flying horse!" She rushed over to the animal.

"What's that pig-of-a-looking-thing over there?" Howard asked.

The sound of loud breathing echoed from the floor.

"What's that?" Michelle asked, her eyes fixed on something asleep on a pile of rags.

Rotar grunted. "Children, I believe we have located your father."

CHAPTER FORTY-ONE

Rotar looked around the dark, dank and smelly cellar. The three children gawked at the strange figure sleeping on crumpled tarps. Howard pointed. "That's not my dad," he stated with firm conviction.

The pig grunted, shifting on the floor with a squeak; the horse switched its tail back and forth bowing its head.

Rotar looked with sadness at Peter. "This is your father in his new form." He placed the candle on the floor.

Curled up in a fetal position, Peter's slow breathing resembled a high-pitched fog horn. Dried green fluid covered his dirty clothing.

Howard backed away. "This freak smells."

Michelle whimpered, "That's not my daddy."

Lizzy petted the winged horse in a feverish motion.

Howard stammered, "Why are you lying to us? I bet you don't even know my dad. Take us back to Mom."

Michelle stared at the sleeping creature, big tears pooling in her eyes. "That's a monster. I want my real daddy." She backed away.

Howard took his sister's hand. "We're leavin'," he said.

Rotar raised a hand to stop him. "I am afraid it really is your father and he is in urgent need of help."

"Maybe it's him," snorted Lizzy. "This is the flying horse in the news. But what's that thing over there on wheels?"

Rotar turned to the pig and cocked his ear to listen. "Very well," Rotar said. "The pig tells me that Peter rescued her from the farmer and she is now an ATV pig, whatever that is."

"All terrain vehicle," Howard said in a huffy tone.

"But she can also fly," Rotar added.

"How do you know?" Lizzy asked.

"She told me."

"I didn't hear anything," Michelle whined.

Rotar smiled. "I can hear her thoughts."

They stared at the pig and at the horse. Michelle looked back at the creature asleep on the rags. "That's a Halloween ghost," she cried, covering her mouth with one hand.

Peter woke and sat up with difficulty. His wheezing voice had a shrill metallic echo. "Howard and Michelle, what are you doing here?"

"Daaaadddddd?" Howard stammered.

Michelle stared with frightened eyes. "You're not my daddy."

"I know I don't look like your father, but I am. I'm known as Moonchild now from a planet with seven moons."

"Holy McAlien," Lizzy said. Her jaw dropped and her mouth gaped.

Peter asked Rotar, "Why did you bring them here?"

Before Rotar could answer Howard said, "He didn't, we found this place by accident."

Peter's stare held obvious contempt. "This is all your fault, Rotar."

Rotar shook his head. "I warned you and warned you but you refused to listen."

Howard fidgeted. "Is it really you Dad? What happened?"

Peter looked away from them. "I thought you were at home with your aunt Hillary."

Howard stomped the floor with his shoe. "No Dad, we came with Mom to help find you. You gotta' come home and get fixed."

"I don't think your mother will let me."

"Why not?"

"It's too complicated to explain."

"I don't want him," Michelle said. "I want my real daddy."

Rotar focused sharp eyes on Peter. "This is not the time to discuss these matters."

Michelle blurted. "Tony's getting the 'antelope' for you."

"Antidote," Howard corrected.

"Who's Tony?" Peter asked.

Lizzy stepped forward. "My father. He's a highly notable international attorney. He has important connections and liaisons in multiple countries. He's helping Amanda, and so am I."

Peter turned to Rotar. "A teenager said all that?" Before anyone could respond he continued. "You started this nightmare. Now I need to reach Dr. Vidollet. Tony or no Tony."

Rotar answered. "We are waiting while the others contact him."

"Good. And I need the silver book as well."

Rotar circled the room. "This is a grave situation, Peter. The book does not belong to you and you no longer have any right to consult it."

"But what if my antidote doesn't work?" Peter said. "I might need it."

Rotar shook his head with sad eyes. "Let's hope it works. I need the silver book to return to my planet."

Peter grunted. "It was my intention to contribute something significant to the world. But you never told me I could get stuck here as an alien. You should have."

"Agreed. But you were not interested in listening to me. I thought I had found a friend, but you only wanted to exploit the information I brought. I released the book at the wrong time in history. I allowed my heart to rule my head and thought I could cheat the calendar."

"So it *is* your fault," Peter accused. "You gave me the book that ruined my life."

Rotar shook his head. "You did the ruining all by yourself. But for whatever curse has befallen you, I am truly sorry."

Peter said nothing.

Rotar pointed to the horse. "We read about the flying horse in the paper. It is capable of destroying guns?"

Peter grinned. "I call him Starbeam. He blows gold dust from his nostrils and communicates telepathically. And I might look frail right now, but I have powers too. I can see through walls and ignite fires with my eyes."

"Nifty," said Howard.

"And the pig?" Rotar asked.

"That's my other experiment on a slop-yard animal. Humfly wanted to be a flying motorcycle. But all four of her legs turned into wheels so she became an ATV, created by yours truly, Doctor Moon Magic." He chuckled. "What do you think?"

"Doctor Moon Magic?" Howard questioned. "You sound like a guy in a carnival."

"Well son, right now I look like someone from a circus sideshow so I guess the name fits. I happen to like it. Feel free to call me that."

Howard looked down, sullen. "Gee thanks."

Rotar said, "Howard, your father has acquired many different personalities through his regression. You will need to view him with different eyes now."

"I get it," he replied, turning away.

Rotar turned to Peter. "As you already know, I am the keeper of knowledge. Starbeam comes from Androdon, a planet millions of light years away where everything living has wings."

Peter said, "He told me. What about Humfly?"

"She hails from the dark planet of Zotnar."

Rotar turned to the pig. "There is much darkness where you come from but you can be good or bad, it is your choice. With your new power I caution you to be very careful how you choose to use it."

Humfly looked at Rotar and thought, *I dream of flying through the universe with my whirly-wheel.*

Rotar shook his head. "You will not go far with that equipment, but you could travel pretty far on the jet stream of this planet."

Peter interjected. "We can work on that later. Just hold your horses or your pig wheels or whatever."

I'll take it into consideration, Humfly thought back.

"What did you just agree to?" Howard asked, "I only heard your side of the talkin'."

Rotar said, "Humfly wants to fly into the universe but has agreed to remain in Earth's atmosphere for the time being."

"Oh is that all," Howard sneered. "If a pig can fly, I want to go where I have two good legs." He patted his bad leg.

"Enough," Peter said. "No one is going to experiment or go anywhere, understood?"

"Yeah…" Howard muttered, looking dejected.

Peter asked Rotar, "What about me, oh keeper of all knowledge?"

Rotar stood straighter. "I am Rotar the Mighty. We must get you the antidote and return you to your Earth form."

Peter snorted. "If you're so mighty, why can't you just fix me?"

Rotar crossed his fingers behind his back. "My powers are limited. But I can show you something I can do." He drew an imaginary circle through the small cellar with his stick. A strong wind stirred the dust causing them to cough and gag, but the wind replaced the putrid smell from Peter's body with a scent of lilac. The green blood on his chest vanished, and so did the scrapes and cuts.

"Stop, please, my eyes," Peter shouted.

The wind calmed and Rotar bowed. "I am Rotar the Mighty. I move in the wind."

Peter lowered his hand from bulging eyes and looked down at himself. "If you can heal my wounds, why can't you use your power to return me to normal?"

"We are working on that but I will need to consult the silver book."

"Then you'd better hurry. There's not much left of me."

Rotar gazed at the ground in serious thought. Michelle crouched in front of her father, inspecting his face. Howard joined Lizzy and stroked the horse. "Be careful with Starbeam, her wing is wounded," Peter said.

A loud shot popped outside.

"Something's happening at the lab," Peter shouted, his eyes frightened. "I have to get the antidote." He pulled on Rotar's arm to get up.

"Let me handle this," Rotar said in a worried tone.

"I'm coming with you," Peter insisted.

Rotar turned to the children. "Stay here, all of you. Do not leave this cellar. I will return for you."

Michelle looked terrified and Howard dazed. Lizzy stopped petting the horse and just stared.

"Are Mommy and Tony okay?" Michelle asked.

"Of course," Rotar assured. He turned to Lizzy. "Elizabeth, will you watch the others please?"

"I'll watch myself," Howard said.

"I'm scared," Michelle said.

"I'll take care of her," Howard said with authority.

"Very well," Rotar agreed, "but you must all remain quiet and touch nothing. I repeat—nothing. Do you promise?"

They all nodded. Peter stood up and Rotar helped him regain his balance.

"I could ride the pig," Peter suggested.

"Too noisy."

Rotar hustled Peter through the tunnel in skipping-like steps. When they reached the outside he swirled his stick. The wind surrounded Peter with energizing crystals. As soon as he could walk by himself, Rotar moved ahead saying, "Hurry up."

"Wait," Peter said, stretching his ear in alert. "Something's terribly wrong."

CHAPTER FORTY-TWO

"Stop," Peter said to Rotar. He clung to a tree and assessed the situation. He spotted Dr. Vidollet and two other men standing in the sheep pen with Amanda. A guard held Amanda's arm, waving a gun at the others. One of the men sneezed several times, agitating the sheep. Dr. Vidollet petted the animals to calm them. Peter hissed at Rotar. "Do something you insufferable midget."

Rotar looked annoyed. "Their secret rendezvous with Dr. Vidollet did not go well."

"So do something!"

Rotar continued to study the area but said nothing.

Peter scanned the barn. He saw one man inside and two others beyond it holding back onlookers who pressed against the barriers by the road. He shifted his intense focus to a stack of firewood by the back door.

Flames erupted.

The guard holding Amanda shouted, "Fire! Get some water over here fast!"

"Blow those creeps into outer space," Peter demanded of Rotar.

"I cannot while he is holding Amanda."

Flames stretched toward the eaves. Peter panicked and hissed at Rotar, "It's spreading! Blow it out!"

A guard bolted out of the barn with a bucket and scrambled toward the lake. Two other guards came around the building searching for containers. One of them grabbed Dr. Vidollet's pail, dumping the grain before running after his colleague toward the lake.

"Save the formula, it's inside the barn," the man holding Amanda shouted to the others.

"Let go, you brute," she yelled, punching and kicking.

He maintained his grip and backhanded her head.

Peter heard Amanda's scream and focused his eyes on her captor's leg. The guard's pants caught on fire. He dropped her arm and ran, shouting for water.

Amanda turned toward Peter and looked curiously at him; then replaced curiosity with revulsion. He wanted to say something, but she turned away. He shifted his stare to the fire. "Somebody save the antidote!" he squawked, sounding like a crow.

Flames engulfed the building. Peter yelled at Rotar, "Blow it out you simpering slow-poke…"

Dr. Vidollet gripped his chest. "Fanny is trapped inside!" He moved toward the burning barn sobbing. "My work will be destroyed."

A tall man Peter presumed to be Tony grabbed his arm and held him back. "Doctor, you can't go in there."

"Rotar!" Peter shouted.

Rotar waved his stick at the building. *"Tor-un-dia Fla-wisk-ium!"*

A wind storm headed west like a furious funnel, increasing in force with a drum-roll sound of thunder. Flames blew across the barn and the weathered planks cracked and broke from the pressure.

Guards returning with buckets of water were blown back toward the lake.

Another guard bounced across the field hitting a tree before he collapsed. The storm blew sightseers and reporters away from the main road. Camera equipment flew weightless through the air. People hung on to each other while crawling to their cars. Some vehicles turned over. A nun rolled into the field screaming.

"Not so hard," Peter shouted.

The wind blew out the flames but tore the barn off its foundation, scattering its contents across the property. The furniture, the doctor's notes, and even the kitchen appliances blew away along with the lab equipment.

"You've destroyed everything, you fool," Peter cried. "I'm doomed."

"My goose," Doctor Vidollet whimpered. "My Fanny is gone."

The doctor's vintage stove tumbled across the parking lot and landed on its side. The oven door swung open and Fanny jumped out, squawking and flapping her wings. The doctor smiled and wiped his tears, calling the goose to him. He grabbed her and checked on his woolly flock. "My children are all right, my precious children…"

"My life!" Peter said, pointing at Rotar. "What do we do now you crazy carrot-head?"

"You should not speak to me like that."

"You're an imbecile. I wish I'd never met you."

"You started the fire. You were too impatient."

"And you created a hurricane!"

"Aeolius created the hurricane. My commander is very annoyed and perhaps overdid it."

"Commander? What're you talking about?"

"Don't answer that," Amanda said.

Peter's eyes blazed. "It doesn't matter. The antidote's gone."

A reporter crept toward them with a camera. Peter poked Rotar's arm and pointed. Rotar swished his rod. The man rolled backward until stopped by an overturned taxi. "We must leave now before he wakes up," Rotar said.

"Guards by the lake are coming," Amanda said, nodding at the men.

Rotar aimed again and directed the wind at them. Waves hurled the men into the water. "By the time they reach land we will be gone."

Amanda glared at Peter. "We've got to get out of here before the entire world converges on us, but where are the children?"

Rotar said, "Peter and I will show you."

"You left them alone?"

Rotar shook his head. "They are watching the horse and the pig."

"What?! We've got to hurry!" Amanda turned to a man Peter did not recognize. "Gaspard, you'll help Dr. Vidollet with his goose?"

Gaspard nodded.

The man who had sneezed so violently caught up with Peter. "I presume you are Peter Tregnier. I think I can help you."

Peter already disliked the man. He grunted and eyed him from top to bottom. "You're the infamous Tony? Your daughter told me all about you."

"My daughter's a bit precocious, I'm afraid. I was merely helping Amanda in her search."

"So how in this murky moon-madness can you possibly help me now?"

"All is not lost," Tony said. "I have the original of your little black book with the formula for the antidote."

Peter's face lifted in joy. "Get it, and we can go to my hiding place and work in peace. We'll need equipment of course." He turned to Amanda. "You and Dr. Vidollet can get that for me and then we'll start over."

"Why should I help you?" she said in an angry voice. "I don't even know who you are."

He cringed. "I'm still your husband."

"You certainly are not! You're a hideous creature and no more than a stranger to me. Ask Marta for help. Our marriage is over."

"I understand that you hate me Amanda, and I'll make it up to you, I promise. But I'm still the father of our children and we have to get to work at once."

"He's right," Tony said. "We've come this far. He may not deserve it, but you owe it to your children to help him."

Amanda gulped air. "Stay out of this Tony, and don't tell me what I owe my children! I resent this and no longer care what happens to Peter."

Peter tensed and wiped tears with his sleeve.

Tony raised his hand and shushed everyone. "I hear sirens. We've got to hide."

Rotar motioned the group to go ahead. "Follow Peter. I will stay here and contain the authorities."

A gust of wind tousled Rotar backward. He steadied himself. "Aeolius is agitated. Go!"

Peter led them toward the cave, the guards and rubble fading from view.

The sky darkened. Thunder crackled through the air and rain pelted the ground. Peter stopped, motioning for silence. His acute hearing alerted him to sounds from the orchard.

He x-rayed through the rain and saw Starbeam walking toward the main road. His wing was tucked to one side, and two young women sat on his back. The small female in front had large eyes in an oval face and long blonde hair curled to her waist. Her sheer pink empire gown revealed a slender body and her hair sparkled like tiny flickering stars. The taller one behind her wore an Elizabethan riding habit. She had dark hair tucked beneath a wide brimmed hat with a long peacock feather. Both girls looked drenched. Howard shouted through the trees. "Come back, Michelle and Lizzy. Starbeam, bring them back…"

Peter choked. "Michelle? Lizzy?"

Amanda gasped. "Oh my God! Somebody do something!"

Looking frantic, Tony sprinted toward the horse.

Peter called out, "The horse is hurt and can't fly. We can reach them." He coughed and wheezed, following Tony. Amanda ran after them.

The noise of a helicopter alerted Peter. Humfly flew out of the trees, chasing the horse. The pig hovered over the girls, then passed the horse and turned to face Starbeam.

The storm blew Humfly sideways into the trees.

She struggled to bank.

Her whirly blades snagged a branch and she crashed to the ground.

The horse clip-clopped to the main road.

A large truck parked on the shoulder backed up and nearly ran over Starbeam. Two men got out, one wore an eye patch. They threw a net over their catch and shoved the horse and girls into the rear of the vehicle.

Amanda cried, "Rotar help us! It's Goldtooth!"

The men pulled down the door, securing their catch.

"Stop!" Peter shouted. But the storm swallowed his words.

"Those are women, not girls," Tony yelled. "They can't be Michelle and Lizzy."

The truck rumbled and drove away. Everyone stopped running. Gaspard and Dr. Vidollet caught up.

Rotar bounded across the field, zapping himself next to the others, but the wind tossed him off balance. He stumbled and hit his head on a boulder. He lay motionless on the ground.

"Get up," Peter barked. "We need your help!"

Rotar moaned, sparks darting in his half-open eyes. Amanda grabbed his stick and squeezed his fingers around it. "Wake up Rotar. Please wake up!"

His eyes closed.

Amanda took the wand and pointed it toward the road. *"Stop-i-us Truck-i-us,"* she commanded but nothing happened. *"Break-i-um Down-i-um!"* she cried. Again nothing. "Hocus pokus," she muttered under her breath. "It's useless."

Howard caught up with them and clung to his mother. "We found a leather juice bag in the cellar," he blurted. "They didn't drink much 'cause it tasted awful." He panted and gulped for air.

Peter said to Howard, "I hid my bota bag in the cellar so nothing like this would happen." He avoided looking at Amanda.

Tony raised an angry fist at the sky and asked Howard, "What happened to them?"

Howard said in a trembling voice, "They transformed right in front of me and changed into medieval clothes. They said the horse told them to find Dad and get the antidote."

Amanda looked shocked. "You mean the girls are grown up? It's not just a trick?"

"Not a trick Mom! They're different, but you can still see that it's Michelle and Lizzy. Their eyes and stuff like that. But what if they stay that way?"

Amanda groaned. "Now those brutes have our girls and they're not even themselves!"

"Mon Dieu," Gaspard said.

Tony nodded. "Yes, 'my God' is right. They must have been staking out the farm to catch Peter and the infamous winged horse."

"What can we do?" Amanda wailed.

"First we have to get out of here," Tony said. "Let's put Rotar on that thing over there." He pointed at the ATV pig.

Tony hoisted Rotar into the pig's saddle. He used Rotar's belt to hold him in place and rolled him through the grass behind Peter.

"The girls could be killed!" Amanda said frantic.

"I don't think so," Tony said. "And the sooner we get to a safe place the better."

Amanda screamed at Peter. "It's all your fault you monstrous reptile!"

Peter had no idea how to resolve the crisis and led the group toward the tunnel. Gaspard followed alongside Dr. Vidollet who clutched the goose close to his chest.

Peter's eyes stung from the wind. He had nothing but contempt for Rotar but was relieved that the antidote would now be essential to transform the girls as well. Amanda and Tony would have to cooperate. He was certain of that, once they got over the shock.

At the entrance to the tunnel Peter turned and saw the others fighting the wind. Rotar looked rain-soaked and remained immobile. But the burdens that jammed Peter's thoughts no longer mattered in light of a throbbing fear for his daughter, the peculiar teenager and his injured horse. They were dealing with new bodies, under a time crunch from exposure to Earth's atmosphere and held captive by foreign thugs. He understood first-hand the grave danger they were in and wished he could somehow blast the universe into oblivion.

CHAPTER FORTY-THREE

Amanda sat cross-legged in the small cellar, wrinkling her nose at the musty smell of mold, mildew, rot and wet clothes. Anxiety inflamed her thoughts. She stared at the glum faces around her. Peter wheezed while Howard and Gaspard remained silent. Doctor Vidollet held Fanny under his arm. The goose and the ATV pig eyed each other with equal curiosity. Her husband was an unrecognizable monster, so outlandish she couldn't look at him, yet she wanted to study his alien features and would have, had the absurd creature not been her husband. She cast a cold sneer at his pathetic face and looked away.

Tony paced back and forth, glancing at Rotar who was still unconscious on the floor.

"He has to wake up," Amanda moaned. "My little girl is gone."

"So's mine," Tony said, his face contorted with anger.

"They must be soaked and cold and scared." She hid her face with her hands, convulsed by an uncontrollable fear. A feeling of helplessness consumed her while tears puddled, leaking down her cheeks. She blamed herself for not taking the children home.

And now it was too late.

Tony knelt down to check on Rotar.

He stirred and groaned.

Amanda moved next to him and wiped her face. "Rotar please wake up. We need you," she pleaded.

His eyes opened. Tiny particles darted around in the pupils. He uttered something garbled, then chuckled and closed them again.

Peter sneered. "It's useless."

Amanda cast an irritated look at her husband. "He's injured." She touched Rotar's shoulder. "Rotar?" she said in a gentle voice.

Rotar's eyes opened again, wider this time. Numbers and symbols scrolled through his pupils.

A pling sounded. Then a plong.

"Sounds like a slot machine," Tony said.

Numbers continued to flash through his eyes, stopping to highlight and moving on.

The activity stopped.

Rotar shook his head and stood up. "Whew," he said. "What a nightmare…"

"That was a dream?" Amanda asked.

"Not really. My mind had to reboot. It takes time."

"You're okay now?" she asked.

"I certainly hope so."

She doubted that very much, but continued. "Before I tell you all the devastating news can you dry us out? It's freezing in here."

"My pleasure." He waved his stick, muttering something. A chill whipped through the room. Snowflakes fell from the ceiling.

"Stop," Amanda cried. The others hugged themselves, heads down. Tony brushed snow from his shoulders.

"My extreme apologies," Rotar said. "It seems that things have gotten a little mixed up."

The wind howled.

Amanda's teeth chattered. "*Pleeeeezzzze.*"

Rotar hit his ear with the palm of his hand. Then the other ear. His eyes glazed. Formulas and numbers scrolled through his pupils, then a red flag and more numbers, followed by a *blonk* sound. He squeezed his eyes shut and opened them again, waving his stick. "*Wa-run-ti-um Ex-pan-sior,*" he commanded.

The snowflakes vanished and a warm wind filled the room with heat.

The group relaxed.

Rotar fanned his stick across them and dried their clothes.

Amanda thanked him. "Are your powers a bit off?"

He nodded. "The back of my head aches but it will pass."

"We'll get you to a doctor," Tony said.

"No, I will work on it. If I had my book…" He didn't finish the sentence.

Tony's face said it all: grim and grave. "We'll be back to the hotel soon and your book. Right now I'm concerned about you and your powers."

Amanda cleared her throat. "If you're feeling better Rotar, we need your help to find Michelle and Lizzy—they've been kidnapped and they've changed. They drank some of the potion."

"They took Starbeam too," moaned Peter.

Rotar's tone was filled with guilt. "This is my fault."

"There's no time for blame," Tony said. "Your talents are needed. Stefan Andersen is involved in this; those men with the truck work for him."

He looked at Amanda. "We learned that yesterday at the Kruper lab. But since Peter formulated his Pflenamium drug at Andersen's lab, Stefan has the formula. Now all he needs to exchange the girls is Peter and his formula for the antidote. We're in serious trouble."

"That's an understatement," Amanda said. "But I'll do whatever it takes to get my baby back—and quickly."

Peter stood up. "We must make more of the antidote right away."

Amanda leapt to her feet and moved in front of him, her mouth inches from his face. "I'm sick of hearing about your problems. Always you, you, you… Take your freaky self to some other planet and never come back! This is about Michelle and Lizzy."

Peter backed away. "I can help them when I get back to my earthly body. And they'll need the antidote too."

Her eyes blazed. "When we get them back! And if you hadn't experimented in the first place…"

"Stop it both of you," Tony interrupted. "Arguing won't help to solve any of our problems."

"Then what will?" Dr. Vidollet asked, letting go of Fanny. The goose flapped her wings and squawked at Humfly. The pig snorted and oinked back.

Amanda said, "By now they know that the antidote I threw at Goldtooth is a fake. Let's give it to them in exchange for the girls."

Tony shook his head. "They'll demand to have both Peter and his black book before they give them up and even then they might change their minds and keep the girls for experimentation. It wouldn't take them long to figure out how to create world havoc if they catch Peter. I have a better plan than that!"

"Like what?" Amanda asked.

"Not now," Tony said in a harsh tone.

She looked to Howard. "Where's the potion the girls took?"

He stammered. "Uhhh…Michelle has it with her, Mom."

She closed her eyes in horror. "Now those miserable men have that too! They don't need Peter any longer if they already have the potion." Her angry eyes pierced Tony's.

"Then we'll have to hurry and stop them," he said with a forced smile.

Howard's eyes lit up. "Can I help?"

"You certainly can," Tony said. "The authorities will search every inch of this place looking for us so I need you to go with your father and Doctor Vidollet to Verbier and stay with Uncle Jacques. Since he's a chemist I'm sure he can provide the necessary supplies for a new antidote."

"So you've met my cousin," Peter said. "He's brilliant, is he not?"

"Yes well, he told us he never condoned your questionable experiments."

Peter scowled. "Listen Tony, whoever-you-are. Don't talk to me like that in front of my son. I prefer to stay here and work at my ancestral home."

Rotar chuckled. "There is not much left now except this cellar…"

"But there are conditions here that might help," Peter snarled. "It was you who told me about the unique herbs of this region."

Rotar nodded. "That is true but you can take samples of soil and herbs with you."

Peter frowned. "Very well. We stay with Uncle Jacques. How do we get out of here?"

"We'll go by motorboat," Tony said. "Once we're back in Geneva I'll book a helicopter."

"I'll have to gather the samples first," Peter said.

"Fine, do it."

Tony removed the small glass jar of Pflenamium from his pocket and handed it to Peter. "I got it from Marta's storeroom. Will it help?"

Peter took it. "I suppose I should say thanks."

"I can't leave without Fanny," Dr. Vidollet said.

Tony gave a brief nod. "Take her."

"And my pig…" Peter added.

Tony shrugged. "If your cousin agrees…"

Peter and Dr. Vidollet left to collect herbs and soil. Amanda said to Tony, "What about the girls?"

"We'll get them back."

"But how do we find out where they are?"

"I'm on it."

She cast doubtful eyes at him.

Tony looked at Rotar and winked.

Rotar smiled.

"What about Dad?" Howard asked. "He'll attract attention at the airport."

Amanda said, "We'll find him a disguise—a ski outfit and ski mask. It's early in the season but it will have to do."

When Peter returned with what he needed, they left through the tunnel. Rotar stopped in front of his cave and swished his stick. A rock wall appeared, hiding its entrance.

"What did you just do?" Amanda asked.

"It is a hologram. A false image of a wall. Air will still circulate into my home but no one will know it is there."

"Amazing," Amanda said.

"Indeed," said Tony.

The group gathered outside and prepared to dash through the rain to the boat dock. The sky had turned dark and wind lashed the trees. Out in the open with guards and media nearby, dread filled Amanda's thoughts. The absurdity of Tony's boastful solutions hit her. And Rotar's claims of 'mightiness' were probably his way of justifying his limited ability to help. Her husband's insatiable quest for notoriety infuriated her. None of them could assure her of anything. Not only were the girls in the hands of criminal brutes, they weren't even the same girls!

She wanted to scream and demand that they find Michelle and Elizabeth immediately.

She wanted an antidote that worked.

Instead she cried in silence and prayed to stay calm and focus on a speedy resolve.

CHAPTER FORTY-FOUR

At the small private airport in Geneva Amanda waited while Tony made arrangements with Uncle Jacques. He finished the call and put his phone away. "He's going to take them all in," he said.

"I'll be indebted to him forever," Amanda muttered in a weak voice, still numb and dazed by the crisis that wouldn't leave her thoughts.

She hugged Howard and they said their good-byes at the helicopter pad. Tony, Amanda and Rotar headed back to the hotel. When they tumbled out of the SUV, Tony asked Gaspard to wait for him. Amanda started to ask why, but couldn't focus, so kept quiet.

In the hotel lobby, guests and staff stared at Rotar. The manager spotted Rotar and moved toward them.

Rotar twisted the top of his stick and whispered, *"Flee-um-dum Desk-ku-ri-um."*

The manager turned and walked like a robot toward the check-in desk. He struggled to reverse his steps but couldn't. When they reached the elevator, Rotar mumbled something and the manager relaxed but appeared upset and confused. The elevator doors closed.

"That stopped his advance," Rotar said inside the lift. "I intended to cheer him up with phantom tickles but I must have picked the wrong command again."

Tony suppressed a laugh but Amanda felt too upset about the girls to find anything funny. "He's a nuisance Rotar, but please be careful. We need to keep a low profile. The girls are our first priority."

"I know," he said. "May that man be plagued with a thousand head-lice until he has no more greasy hair left on his head…"

"You mean that?" she asked.

"No. Just tickling my thoughts searching for my personality."

"Your personality?"

"I feel cloudy, like a veil inside my head is making me sad. I was searching for my picker-upper to remove it."

She frowned. "You can do that?"

He nodded. "The cloud will pass," he said.

Amanda lifted a brow. "No lice?"

"No lice."

"Glad to hear it," Tony said as they entered his suite.

He prepared to go out again. "Will you and Rotar be okay for a while? I have to borrow Braun's computer."

"For what?" Amanda asked.

"Information."

"What information?"

"I don't know yet, but I'll find it. I also want to retrieve some of Starbeam's green dung from Braun's lab."

"Why?"

He looked exasperated and raised his hands. "Because we now know that the alien horse is real. I want some samples."

"You don't trust Braun?"

"We shall see…"

"And your plan, Tony?"

"When I get back." He turned away from her and hurried out the door.

Amanda paced across the room in anger, popping a chocolate into her mouth. She should have gone along but he hadn't asked her. She should have insisted. Rotar munched a crisp apple, splashing himself with spurts of juice.

She gave him a hand towel. He put it down and swished his stick. Tiny colored bubbles surrounded his face. When they popped one by one, he was clean. "Would you like me to do the same for you?" he asked.

Amanda closed her open mouth and shook her head. "I can't even begin to think about the advantages you have with your magic right now. I'm too frightened for the girls."

"We will find them. Do not worry."

She had her doubts about his confidence and changed the subject. "Are you feeling any better?"

Rotar nodded. "The tickle has left my legs and is now scanning my stomach. I am being cleaned out and tuned up. The cloud will be found and deleted." He glanced at the TV. "My brain tells me to turn on the television."

Her eyes questioned him.

He blinked twice at the screen and it turned on.

A special news report covered the latest devastation in Coppet. A male reporter stood in the middle of the wind-damaged area. Rescue workers loaded injured people into ambulances. The reporter spoke at a rapid pace, his tone anxious.

"The latest trauma here in Coppet has fueled rumors that some unknown power is responsible for the disaster which has left a building destroyed and onlookers severely wounded. We are under public pressure to confirm reports of extraterrestrial forces in the area. The residents of Coppet are demanding an official explanation of these recent events and protection for their village which has been under surveillance for more than a week now. Stay tuned for more information as it comes in about the destruction that has occurred here today."

Amanda dropped down on the couch and hugged her sides, staring wild-eyed at Rotar. "This is terrible, and it's all Peter's doing!"

Rotar joined her. "You must relax," he said in a soft tone. "Peter is not the only one to blame. I used my wind power."

She threw up her hands. "Relax? The entire world is descending upon Coppet now. Tony can't fix this. We're doomed—my little girl and Lizzy are gone and they could be dead!" Tears flooded her eyes.

Rotar eyes widened. "Do not worry about the bigness of the problem. We must focus on what to do." He blinked, snorted and chuckled, then broke into a series of giggles.

She stared at him, bewildered.

He covered his mouth. "The cloud is gone but the probes tickled my laughter." He wiped moisture from his eye and said, "Please do not distress yourself. The world will take care of itself and we will find the girls."

"I wish I could believe you," Amanda said.

"I am more concerned by the wind. Now we must return two animals and three humans back to Earth people. Until we do, my penance will not be completed."

"But why are you still serving a penance?" she asked. "What good is your suffering?"

"It is self-inflicted. I was the honored keeper of knowledge and as I explained earlier, I tried to cheat destiny by going into the future to obtain a discovery that would alter my genes. I came here to prove I could learn patience and wait until the correct time to pass on the book. Now I do not know if I will ever go home again."

Amanda frowned. "I'm sure it's your destiny to return to your planet. And in a way you're lucky. At least you know where home is. Some of us don't know where we're going next."

His face became serious. "I cannot reveal the future for you even if the information you seek is in the book."

"Can't you just peek a little?"

He shook his head. "It is forbidden. And I must stay here as long as required until your planet is ready for the truth."

"Are you saying you will never die?" she asked.

Rotar looked at her. "While I am here I will not die."

"How can that be?"

"That is how I am made. I can outlive your children, your grandchildren and your great grandchildren if I must. But when

I return to my planet I will die when I am ready. And perhaps be reborn as a tall being."

Her mind boggled. "But what if you're reborn short again?"

"Then I would live out that life as I am. But who can say? I am hoping that my work here will ultimately reward me with my wish."

He bit into his apple. "I thought Peter could make something that would help me grow. The secret is in the book somewhere but I have not yet found it."

"And what about the girls? Will they have powers?"

"Were they alien?"

"I don't think so. They looked human, Elizabethan era, but it was dark."

"Then they will not have powers."

More frustration. The girls wouldn't have a way to protect themselves from their captors.

The door banged opened and Tony rushed in. "Have you ordered anything to eat?" he asked.

She folded her arms in front of her. "Who can eat in the middle of this crisis? When do we get our girls back?!"

"I'm working on it, but we have to eat in order to think." He dialed room service and ordered a cheese tray, French bread, fruit and a large tureen of soup.

Angry that he could dismiss the emergency and order food, Amanda stood frozen and stared out the window at the street below. "I'm full of anxiety and you're ordering food. My patience is running out. What's the plan Tony?"

"First we get Andersen."

Her eyes remained fixed on the street scene outside. "How?"

"We're going to kidnap him."

She swung around and saw his smug smile.

"Gaspard has agreed to hold him captive at his house," Tony added.

"You're taking this evil man who has kidnapped our children to a taxi driver's home in the suburbs?"

"Let me finish. We'll use Andersen as leverage for the girls."

Her frustration rose. "We don't even know if anyone wants him."

"We do. I obtained a lot of information. There's a lot more to Mr. Andersen. His dossier traces him back to Sweden. He was educated at the University of Stockholm in chemistry, then two years at Brown University for a master's degree. He worked in a small lab in Ohio and then at another in Illinois. After that he disappeared for a few years. There's no record of him working or living anywhere until he popped up at the Kruper lab. His passport is Swedish but he's not Swedish at all."

"What is he?" she stammered.

"Russian."

She glanced at Rotar for moral support. She couldn't imagine kidnapping anyone, but since Michelle and Lizzy's abduction, turn-around was the only way to get them back. "I could end up in prison for this," she groaned. "That would be great for my kids. A jailbird mother and an alien father."

Tony placed his hands on her shoulders. "I would never let that happen."

"You can control the Swiss judicial system?"

"Trust me."

At a knock on the door, Tony opened it. The room steward entered with a cart and arranged the food. He was the same young man who had served them before. When finished, he eyed Rotar and backed out of the room, closing the door. Tony poured red wine into three glasses. Amanda wanted more information but instead he sat down and buttered some French bread. Rotar slurped cream of broccoli soup. How could they eat under the circumstances? "Tell me more Tony, I can't wait."

"All right, but you're not going to like it." He set down his bread. "The intel linked Peter to Andersen."

She stared at him, shocked. "Linked? How? You think Peter's a Russian spy? The connection might be totally innocent—he worked there, remember? It's where he met Marta."

"I know, but Peter may have made a deal to sell his discovery, if and when it worked, in exchange for the clandestine use of Andersen's lab. Then when Peter went into hiding, Andersen may have taken matters into his own hands."

"But when they couldn't catch Peter and the horse they kidnapped our girls."

"You got it."

"Could Uncle Jacques be involved?" she asked. "Do you think Howard and Dr. Vidollet are in danger?"

Tony shook his head. "There's no reason to link Uncle Jacques with any of this and I have two men watching his house. They'll be safe."

Another red flag. "But your guards might lead Braun straight to Verbier."

"Not possible. I've enlisted them from another source. They have no connection to Braun's office."

"I want to call Howard."

"I already did. He's fine."

She wanted to believe him. Her mental stability depended on believing him. "You better be telling the truth. So how do we get the girls back?"

"An exchange."

"But how will you get word out once you have him?"

"I've thought of that," Tony said. "I have connections in Russia. They'll pass along my proposal. Andersen's superiors will want him back for the potion and the Pflenamium. They'll try to get Peter and the antidote too. If pressed to the wall we can offer them Peter's formula for that, too, but let's use one negotiating tool at a time."

"So when does all this happen?"

"First thing tomorrow morning."

Rotar looked up from his soup. "May whoever has kidnapped the girls become famous by having a disease named after him…"

Amanda stared at him in surprise. "You mean that?"

Rotar nodded. "Selfish people destroy the future for everyone. Greedy people should come back in the next life as water buffaloes." He slapped his knee and laughed.

She asked Tony, "So how does your grandiose plan work?"

"Leave that to me." He eyed Rotar. "Think you're well enough to help me?"

Rotar nodded. Amanda shook her head and cast doubtful eyes at both of hem.

Tony raised his glass of wine in a toast. Amanda was reluctant to toast anything but lifted her glass. Rotar grabbed the bottle from the table and began drinking. The wine spilled down his chin.

"To a successful ambush," Tony said.

"To rescuing Michelle and Elizabeth," she corrected.

Rotar raised the bottle into the air and burped. "To ancient souls and the swift return of loved ones."

They drank in unison to each of their wishes.

CHAPTER FORTY-FIVE

Braun stood on the roof of the Hotel de la Cigogne and peered over the edge to the street below. A shower cap protected his bald head from the pelting rain. Angered over the destruction of the lab in Coppet and the failure of his security team to locate Dr. Vidollet, he was certain Ramsey had something to do with the doctor's disappearance.

Through friendly persuasion in the form of money, he had obtained the exact location of Tony's hotel room from the night clerk and spotted the window he was looking for. Wearing leather gloves, he tied a rope around his waist and signaled his driver who stood back from the ledge. Charles pulled on the long rope and nodded that it was secure

"This is crazy, sir," Charles called to him. "You could be killed."

"I know what I'm doing. Just do your part."

Charles stammered, "You sound too angry for this, sir."

"Mind your own business."

Braun fumbled with the rope and eyed the window-sill below. "I'm almost certain Ramsey was in Coppet—he's probably hiding Tregnier's wacky partner inside."

"Why?" Charles asked. "He's the one who asked for security at the lab and he's been cooperative all along. And you said he's been with the Tregnier woman twenty-four-seven."

He gave Charles a sour look. "We don't know which side he's on, you fool. How do you know he won't take credit for this finding, if and when we catch up with Dr. Tregnier?"

Charles rolled his eyes. "Why not let the new agents handle this? Isn't that why they're coming?"

"I can't trust them either," he said. "They could be Ramsey's backup. He could have called Washington and requested them to spy on me. This is my territory and no one's going to interfere."

"As you wish."

Braun adjusted the rope around his waist and stared at this chauffeur with cold eyes. "You don't understand. I've failed. The old doctor at the lab, Tregnier and the flying horse—they can't just vanish. Ramsey knows what's going on. In the meantime my reputation's sinking fast. And someone has the silver book. I've got nothin' without it. Don't you get it?"

Charles shrugged. "Not really."

Rainwater seeped down Braun's face but he pretended not to care. "Is the rope looped around the pipe?"

Charles nodded.

"Then just hang on to it," Braun snapped.

Charles let it slip through his hands while Braun inched his way down the wall, his back and waist burning from the tight cord around his middle. "I'm gonna' get this guy," Braun muttered.

He reached for foot support but slipped on the narrow edge. His hands trembled as he scaled down the wall. Rain clouded his vision and a stench of algae from the river blew into his face. Reaching for the window pop-out molding, his gloves were too thick for a good grip so he pulled them off with his teeth. The revolting taste of the germ-infested leather gagged him.

While he slowly and methodically made his way along the ledge toward Tony's suite, his stomach knotted. Looking down at the street below, it rose up toward him. He turned away and shook free the dizziness.

At Tony's room, moisture fogged the window. He peered inside, squinting to see. Ramsey and a woman sat at a table. Tregnier's wife, no doubt. A midget with wild orange hair and a plump face sat with them. "The man in my office. He stole my silver book! I got him! I got 'em all!"

He reached into his pocket and pulled out a listening device. The small gray box had a transmitter attached to rubber suction cups. He pressed the cups against the corner at the top of the window. The midget got up and waddled to the other side of the room. Braun pressed his ear to the glass but the traffic noise below drowned everything else. He cursed himself for leaving the head-set in the car.

Amanda noticed Rotar's agitation. "What is it?" she asked.

Tony stopped eating. "Something wrong?"

"There is a stranger outside," Rotar said.

Tony reached for his raincoat slung over the chair and pulled out his gun. He headed for the door.

Rotar shook his head. "Not the door, the window."

"Impossible," said Tony, glancing at the window.

Amanda turned around to look. "Are you sure?"

"The man in the office when I retrieved my book is hiding by the window."

"Braun," muttered Tony under his breath. "I was just there. He certainly moves fast. And a good actor, too. Didn't give me a hint..." He put a finger to his lips. "When I count to three we'll dash into the other suite."

"And then what?" Amanda whispered.

"One thing at a time."

"I have a better idea," said Rotar.

"We can't hurt him," Tony warned. "Much as I'd like to."

Rotar pointed his stick toward the window. "*Trans-fer-ium Lak-u-muncia!*"

The wand sparkled, and a small gust of wind coiled like a miniature tornado, passing through the dual pane window.

They rushed over to see.

Flying through the air Braun's voice echoed, the rope twisting like a serpentine behind him. The wind tossed him around and around above Place Longemalle, past the Promenade du Lac, and like a diving kite plopped him head-first into Lake Geneva.

"Can he swim?" Rotar asked.

"I have no idea," Tony said.

Amanda searched the stormy darkness but saw no sign of Braun in the water. "Help him, Rotar," she cried.

Rotar waved his stick again. *"Mir-cul-um-toff Kert-zi-um!"*

The wind scooped Braun out of the water and tossed him close to the dock. A round life buoy landed on his head.

"He'll be back," Tony said. "We'll have to stay one step ahead of him."

"What time do we go after Stefan Andersen?" Amanda asked.

"Gaspard's picking us up at seven. Set your alarms for six."

"I don't know if I can sleep with all this stress," Amanda said. "I want to check on the others in Verbier and talk to Howard."

"They might be asleep. Everyone was fine earlier and settled for the night."

"Where will I sleep?" asked Rotar. "I want to be on alert now that the American man knows where we are."

Amanda said, "You can bunk down on the couch right here."

He beamed. "Thank you. I will watch the window and the door."

"And I'd like to sleep in Lizzy's bed for the night," Amanda added. "Don't feel comfortable all alone next door."

"Good idea," Tony said. "You'll both be okay now? Get some rest?"

Amanda shrugged. Rotar nodded.

"Good night then," Tony said, going to his room.

Amanda arranged bedding on the couch for Rotar. A log fell in the fireplace—she watched it in a trance-like state. The medieval sword leaning against the side of the mantel disappeared. "Rotar did you see that? Howard's sword just vanished."

"No…"

"I swear I just saw it disappear…"

"Fatigue is playing tricks on you. Perhaps Tony moved it."

She nodded in confusion. "That must be it."

"Good night, Amanda. Magical dreams," Rotar said, making himself comfortable on the make-shift bed. Jumbled symbols scrolled through his eyes and his lids closed.

"Sleep well," she whispered.

She left the door slightly open to the living room were Rotar slept. His loud snorts and snores kept her awake. Some night guard he turned out to be, envious of his ability to sleep. She thought of the girls. Were they asleep somewhere and warm? Desperate to know that they were safe, she began to pray.

CHAPTER FORTY-SIX

A pale moon veiled the village of Verbier in eerie shadows. The dark clouds threatened an early snow. Howard, Peter and Dr. Vidollet had met Uncle Jacques at the runway, loading Humfly and Fanny out of view in the back of his SUV.

At Uncle Jacques' house La-La, the cocker spaniel, greeted them with hysterical barking. Fanny flapped her wings and chased the dog around the house. When Humfly followed the activity, La-La turned and attacked the pig. The frustrated housekeeper contained the dog in her bedroom while Vidollet took Fanny to the basement lab. Howard helped move Humfly to the back porch where the housekeeper gave the pig a meal of apples and left-over greens.

The second floor guest bedrooms were shown to everyone and Dr. Vidollet started working on a new batch of antidote downstairs. Howard joined his father and Uncle Jacques for dinner in the kitchen. Peter nibbled, saying nothing, and Uncle Jacques ate quickly. Howard stirred his bowl of beef stew, removing the sliced carrots and turnips. He worried about his sister and Lizzy.

"You must eat dem," the housekeeper said in broken English. "Dey are goot."

"I hate carrots," he told her. "Turnips even more." He crinkled his nose.

Uncle Jacques took a tray of food to Dr. Vidollet. Peter left most of his supper uneaten and half walked, half floated upstairs to make a phone call. Howard resented being left alone with the housekeeper.

"My dad looks like a turnip," he muttered. "Who's he calling anyway?"

The housekeeper ignored him and cleared the table.

Annoyed, he went upstairs and leaned against the carved wooden door of his father's room. He had to listen hard to understand Peter's gurgled words.

"We're working on the antidote now," Peter said. "I won't tell you where I am until I've tried it. Then I'll sell it for the right fee."

Howard's eyes widened and his breathing quickened.

"Five million US dollars in a numbered Swiss account. Take it or leave it."

Howard wanted to yell at his father but kept his mouth shut.

"I'll get you the silver book in due course, Andersen, but either way, my fee is the same. I'll pass over the antidote when the money is deposited—not before."

Silence.

Peter wheezed, gasping for breath and said, "That's extortion. You even think of selling my daughter to a Siberian experimental lab and I'll see that you burn in hell. You saw what I did to the barn? You won't have a building left if you harm one hair on their heads. I'll turn your blood into Russian borscht, your kidneys into…" Peter coughed and gagged.

Frightened and feeling helpless, Howard had to tell his mother. Anger flooded him and he hurried to his room. In his parka pocket he could feel the bota bag. He had taken the potion away from Michelle in the basement hideout and lied to his mother, believing his father might need it in Verbier.

Across the hall in Uncle Jacque's room Howard looked for money. From a wallet on the dresser he pulled out some Swiss francs and stuffed them into his jean pocket.

The wooden floor creaked as he crept past his father's room but he kept going, hoping no one would hear. Downstairs he tiptoed to the front window and glimpsed a guard sitting in a car by the front gate. He hobbled to the kitchen and heard the housekeeper speaking to both doctors in the basement. Deciding it was safe to leave by the back door, he found Humfly on the back porch snorting and chewing her meal.

"Want to take me to the train station?" Howard asked in a joking tone. He knew she couldn't fly him all the way back to Geneva.

She nodded.

"Okay, but don't make a sound. I'll push you away from here before I start your motor."

He led the pig outside and rolled her down the steps. Then he grabbed Humfly's chrome exhaust pipes and swung her wheels around to the uphill side of the house.

It started to snow.

"Stay quiet," he said, pushing her along a small street toward the ski resort.

The bitter cold made his nose run.

Leaking tears, he tried to shake free the awful thought that his father was a traitor. After a few blocks he stopped and climbed on, pressing the silver-and-red button on top of the saddle horn.

The engine roared.

The ring of reindeer horns on Humfly's head began flashing like radar control. Her eyes became bright headlights, illuminating the street.

His heart skipped a beat and he clung to the saddle horn.

When Humfly didn't move, he pushed the horn forward. She jerked ahead. He pulled back and she stopped.

He edged the horn carefully ahead and her four chrome wheels whirled into action. They sped up the incline with ease. Howard cheered out loud and squinted through the chilling snow that bit his face. When they approached a large mountain resort, Howard looked for a road sign to the main village.

He directed Humfly left at the next intersection and they sped down a steep icy incline. He pulled back on the horn. Humfly's chrome exhaust pipes back-fired three times and a heavy stench of cabbage filled the air. "You ate too much of that green garbage!" Howard moaned.

Humfly didn't slow down.

Howard jerked and pulled on the horn, but the wheels continued to skate downhill, faster and faster skidding toward a fast-food restaurant at the bottom. He yelled, "whoaaaaaaaaaaa—heeelllpppppppp…"

But Humfly continued sliding out of control. Her headlights began flashing on and off like a car's hazard lights.

"Humfly, stooopppppp…" he shouted against the wind.

Lights flashed on top of Humfly's head. The horned disc righted itself and a rod extended above Howard's head.

The reindeer blades whirled and flashed.

Humfly whizzed toward the diner at full speed. Three teenage girls standing outside scrambled out of the way. One of them stabbed buttons on her phone.

Just before impact with the building, Humfly gunned her pipes and lifted off the icy street, flying into the sky.

"We're too high—I'll fall off!" Howard screamed as the pig headed higher. "Let me down," he yelled.

Humfly slowed and hovered above the train station. "Not here, over there," Howard shouted, pointing to the far end of the parking lot. The pig swooped down and landed with a jolt, throwing Howard to the pavement.

"That hurt," he wailed, picking himself up. "You can't come with me—go back to the house."

Humfly cast wistful eyes at the stars. Her horns whirled into action and ignoring Howard, she soared into the sky.

High above him the pig slowed, dropping something green that hit the ground, splashing Howard's legs. "Gross," he groaned, and tried to stomp the liquid off.

Humfly rocketed into the dark night.

"Come back, Humfly!" Howard yelled. "You can't leave!" His head fell, wondering what he was going to do—stole the potion—stole Uncle Jacques' money—ran away—lost the pig… No one would ever believe him.

He wandered the parking lot searching the sky but the snow-fall obscured his view. There was no sight of the pig. "You have to come back Humfly," he choked, knowing the pig couldn't hear him.

Scared and angry he shouted, "Find your own way back then. See if I care!"

He wiped his nose on his sleeve and tramped toward the train station. Did he have enough money for a ticket to Geneva? Stabbing the snow with his boots, he'd stow away if necessary.

CHAPTER FORTY-SEVEN

Howard kept his shaking hands out of sight while the man at the ticket counter eyed him with suspicion. Disheveled hair and colorless skin accentuated a tired face. Howard calmed down enough to hold out the money for the agent. "Geneva. How much is it?"

Mr. Paleface took some of the money and handed over his ticket along with his change. The departure time was in thirty minutes. Relieved that he had enough money, Howard rushed away but dreaded the wait.

He paced back and forth across the station floor, fingering the bota bag. Then he stopped at the window to look for any sign of the housekeeper or Uncle Jacques. They could have already discovered he was missing. He closed his eyes and crossed his fingers, hoping they wouldn't show up.

Impatient, he went into the men's room and locked himself inside a stall. Several ants crawled through a crack in the wall. He sat down on the toilet seat and put his good foot in front of the insects. They stopped, wiggled back and forth along his shoe and climbed over. He grinned when they took a new path across his foot.

He pulled out the bota bag and unscrewed the top, squeezing a little of the green fluid onto his shoe. Three of the ants stopped, investigated, and then nibbled the syrupy liquid.

Tiny sparks darted around the ants. One ant swayed, then raised up weaving on its hind legs. Fang-like teeth popped out of its tiny mouth while the body grew into the size of a humming bird.

"Awesome," Howard whispered.

The second ant began to waver. Long teeth and an enlarged head appeared first, followed by a growing body that looked more like a deformed spider with a shiny hairless coat. Both ants sprouted long tentacles and blew bubbles from their mouths, jumping like oversized grasshoppers. The third ant sprouted bright pink wings and a long silver tail that made snake-like rattling noises when it wiggled. Its eyes blazed with red centers.

Howard stood up and leaned against the back wall to watch the strange creatures hop across the floor. They jumped higher and higher. The ant with the pink wings circled above his head. He ducked and waved his wool cap to capture them, but they moved too quickly.

The alien insects would attract attention and he still had half the time to wait. He dashed out of the men's room and walked through the terminal, halting at the sound of tire screeches and car doors slamming outside. Through a window he saw the housekeeper with a security guard. He panicked and rushed back into the men's room.

Fear jammed his thoughts.

If he drank some of the potion, could he fly away?

He locked himself into the same stall and placed his money and ticket on the floor. The three ants hopped in zig-zag patterns around him. Ignoring them, he sipped from the bota bag. The taste made him gag. Swallowing a little, his chin quivered. "Let me have wings so I can fly out of here," he whispered.

Two of the ants nibbled on his paper money while the third flew around the stall and nipped at his hair. He brushed it away. It landed on his train ticket, eliminating something black.

Shoving the ants aside, he grabbed his ticket and money and stood up. His mind whirled. He swayed, sinking deeper and deeper into a dark hole streaked with flashes of light. Bright crystals surrounded him.

Frightened, he watched his hands change into large hairy extensions of his wrists. His insides twisted in pain; his veins felt like stuffed sausages.

He grew taller, and his clothes changed to leather body armor tied together with wooden basket work. Shells decorated the chest piece, and tights covered his legs. A sword materialized in his right hand.

He stared at unfamiliar moving pictures in his mind. A blacksmith shoeing a horse and two men fencing in a courtyard. He knew the behavior of a gentleman in court and the taste of warm frothy ale. His body filled with the brave spirit of a grown man. He looked down at his straight and muscular leg. *My leg!* He shouted in silence.

The visions continued: a beautiful fair-haired maiden running toward him in a meadow abloom with daffodils, then the same young woman lying still in the grass. Sorrow entered his heart.

Another man, dark and sinister, clutched a sword and rode away on a black horse, his leg cut open with a long gash. Howard stood in a field, his sword splattered in blood.

Are these the thoughts of a knight? He stared at the ants. "Who am I?" he asked in a deep voice that startled him. "Do you know the answer?"

He worried that he hadn't taken enough potion to acquire wings like Starbeam or powers like Rotar. But he was afraid to drink more of the foul-tasting mixture.

One of the ants thought in a sing-song lilt, *you're a knight, you're a knight...*

"I can hear your thoughts—my lord, I *am* a real knight..."

He opened the stall door. In the mirror above the sink he saw a young man with a beard and thick hair to his shoulders. His dark eyes stared from a dry, tight complexion. He resembled the knight Rotar zapped into the hotel room. Am I the very same, or his twin? He pulled the sword from its scabbard and admired it.

An old man in shabby clothes staggered in and wavered in front of the urinal. He smelled of whisky and stared blank-faced at him. Howard tensed and said, "I need your coat, Monsieur. I am on my way to a costume party. I will pay you one hundred francs for it." He held out the Swiss money, flapping it. The man gawked.

"*S'il vous plait*, please, *votre manteau*. One hundred francs for your coat…"

Did the knight speak French too? Or was he Howard at the same time, remembering his French lessons?

The man snatched the money and removed his coat.

Howard put it on while the man headed for the stall with the alien ants. "You'll want to use a different one," Howard urged.

The man's eyes popped at the sight of the creatures and he cursed in French.

Howard ignored his crude outcry and hurried out the door.

He slowed down when he saw the guard and housekeeper talking to the ticket agent. Striding past them, he kept his eyes straight ahead, hiding his sword. The boarding ramp was right outside. When his back was to the others, he exposed the sword's position, ready to attack.

At the train a hand grabbed his right arm. He turned to look down at a small chubby train-station patrolman with mud-brown teeth and a knowing grin. Howard pulled away but the man held on.

"What is it?" Howard said to the security agent in a huff. "My train is departing…"

The man pointed where Howard's hidden hand held the sword and said something in French, shaking his finger. He reached for the lapel of Howard's coat but Howard the knight grabbed his wrist in an iron grip and shook his head.

"You may not take eet en board," the agent said.

The guard and maid approached. Howard scowled and handed his sword to the man. "Take it then. Give it to your children," he said in a cross voice.

The agent took it, gloating over his prize.

Howard jumped on board and watched the housekeeper and security guard talking to the agent who shook his head and raised his hand up high to indicate tallness.

The train whistle announced their departure.

Howard heaved a long sigh and relaxed. According to the posted schedule he'd be in Geneva in about two hours. The interior of the train felt warm and stuffy, so he let his coat fall open, revealing his medieval clothing. He made his way along the narrow aisle to the first class section, speaking to the passengers staring at his tights and unusual boots.

"'Tis the season of hauntings and ye are missing out on the medieval magic," he barked. A wide grin split his ruddy new face.

CHAPTER FORTY-EIGHT

Amanda lay in Lizzy's bed tormented by thoughts of the girls. In desperate need of sleep, she couldn't unwind. At Rotar's peaceful snores from the living room she tried to breathe in rhythm with his noises. But just when she was about to doze off, there was a tap at the door.

Rotar continued snoring so she got up and slipped on a hotel robe. Through the cracked door she saw Tony.

"Sorry, but the front desk just rang," he said. "I must have been on the phone when Peter called. He left a message."

Enraged at her selfish husband she lashed out at Tony. "That conniving monster! I was trying to get some sleep. I'd like to pluck every alien hair out of his pointed head—one at a time!"

"I can't let it get to me or I won't be able to function," Tony said. "Don't let the circumstances defeat you, Amanda, we're doing all that we can." His eyes filled with compassion. "You need to call him back—it might be important."

"It better be."

She used the phone in the living room and dialed. Rotar's snorts and snores continued. Someone answered. "Is that you Peter?" she asked.

"What took you so long?" he hissed. "Howard's gone."

"What do you mean, gone?" Her eyes widened. "Gone where?" She felt blindsided and pressed a clenched fist against her forehead.

Tony pointed to his bedroom and waved his hand next to his ear, indicating he would listen in. The extension clicked.

Peter explained Howard's disappearance, the missing pig, and the failure of security to locate either of them. Her knees buckled and she slumped down on the edge of the couch. Her vision blurred.

Rotar woke up and rubbed his eyes.

"They better find him!" she shouted so loud that Rotar jumped from the couch.

Peter wheezed into the phone, "The pig can fly Amanda."

"Oh my flying, frazzled mind," she moaned. "Howard doesn't know how to handle a fast moving vehicle, much less *fly* one. You're a terrible father, Peter! You couldn't even keep track of your son for one day!" She banged the receiver into the cradle. Her hand trembled and tears swam into her eyes.

Rotar blinked sleepy eyes at her.

"Why did I risk the lives of my children for a no-good crazy scientist?" she asked Rotar. But before he could answer, Tony returned.

"I'll send Gaspard to the Geneva train station," he said, "and have my men in Verbier look everywhere. Obviously they're not the best security or this wouldn't have happened."

Amanda's mind cramped. "That outrageous pig on four wheels probably convinced him to sneak away. Howard might be off on a joy-ride and not realize he could be killed." She rubbed her head in furious motion. "I should've gone home after being shot at the farmhouse. I'd still have my children. Everything in my world has collided. I have nothing left."

"Don't go down that road," Tony said. "We have to remain calm. Howard's resourceful. We'll find him."

"I *am* calm," she shouted, sucking in a deep breath. "All right, I'm *not* calm. How can I be, he's my little boy."

Rotar broke his silence. "What happened?"

"We don't know," Amanda said. "Howard's missing."

"That is indeed bad news." He closed his eyes. "He will come here."

"Why did you say that?" she asked.

Rotar blinked; crystals danced in his misty eyes. "Have faith in him. He is a big boy and he will find his way here."

"What if you're wrong?" she said. "And what about Michelle? And Elizabeth? They're all children."

"Rotar can only guess," Tony interrupted. He went to his bedroom to make the calls.

She looked at Rotar with pleading eyes. "Can you find him?"

Rotar stared at the floor, his eyes distant. "I cannot detect his energy or the others. As I explained earlier their altered beings are from another dimension and shielded from me. The potion is powerful but Michelle and Elizabeth are young. They can hang on. I do not know the age of the horse but I will maintain hope for the flying creature as well."

"But you seemed to connect with Howard a minute ago?"

Rotar shook his head. "I am not sure. It is my intuition that tells me he will come here; I cannot detect his energy. Tony is right; I am guessing. But it is a good guess and I do not think I am wrong."

Close to despair she felt about to collapse. "My God, Rotar, do you mean he might be dead?"

"We must wait and see."

She shot up straight. "No. I can't do that or I'll fall apart. Where's the purple rock? I should have given it to Howard."

Rotar looked away. "I gave it to Peter so he could call me if he got into trouble. But he called you instead."

"That selfish arrogant excuse for a man," she screamed. "I never want to see him again even if he changes back to normal."

Tony came back and said, "I could hear you through the bedroom door. Please calm down Amanda. Gaspard is on his way to check the train station and the airport. The guards are on alert and looking everywhere. I know we'll find him."

"I'm trying to be grateful for all the help," she said, "even though Rotar's powers are so limited."

Rotar blushed in dark rainbow colors and zapped on the television. The last news broadcast of the evening was about to start.

Amanda remembered the sword that had disappeared. "Tony, did you move Howard's sword?" she asked.

He glanced at the fireplace. "No, but it was there earlier."

"The sword vanished in front of my eyes."

"What?" Tony asked.

Before she could explain, a news alert caught their attention. A female newscaster sat at her desk in the studio with a screen behind her showing aerial shots from the ski resort of Verbier. Amanda pointed a shaky finger. "Look…" The newswoman spoke in French, but everyone understood.

"We begin our broadcast tonight with this exclusive report from Verbier, where yet another mystery unfolds similar to those we have reported from Coppet."

There was a cutaway to a diner where a reporter stood next to a young teenage girl. "We are experiencing an unseasonably early snow here in the ski village of Verbier which has become a frigid setting for some earth-chilling news." She turned to the nervous teenager who leaned on one hip and chewed gum. "We are interviewing Miss Maddy Millhausen, a local resident. Please tell us what you saw."

The girl kept chewing and moved the lump of gum to the other side in her mouth. "Yes, well, I was in front of the restaurant with friends, and suddenly this weird-looking pig…"

"A real pig?"

"No…well, I don't know. It looked like a pig but it had wheels instead of hooves, and a lightning bolt on its forehead, and these huge lanterns—sort of like headlights, for eyes, and a boy riding on its saddle…"

"And what did it do?" the reporter asked, her expression doubtful.

"Ahhh, it scared the—you know what—out of us. It was coming really fast—like out of control, you know, but just before crashing right into us it flashed some weird horn thing and then took off like a helicopter." She pointed up at the sky.

The reporter cleared her throat. "Your friends saw this as well?" Before the girl could answer the news alert returned to the lead reporter in the Geneva studio.

"I am interrupting this broadcast to report that an unidentified flying object has been sighted by air traffic controllers at the Geneva Airport. As yet they have not made contact with the aircraft, but Nato Alliance forces are investigating as we speak. We will bring you further details as we receive them. We now return to Verbier."

Amanda shut off the TV. "What if the girl's story is true?" she moaned. "Has my Howard flown away on that monstrous pig?" She looked to the others for comfort but got none. "Now the world will converge on Verbier. And Leo Braun will find Peter and Dr. Vidollet."

She sank down on the couch and cradled her head.

"Let's hope that's not the case," Tony said, "but until we learn more, all we can do is get some rest. Rotar has good instincts, so let's trust him."

Drained and exhausted from fear, Amanda wanted to go to her room and scream away the anger and frustration and dread. Someone knocked at the door. "Who's that at this hour?" she asked.

Tony took the gun from his coat pocket and moved to the door. She followed him, but froze when he held out his hand to keep her back.

"Who's there?" he asked, leaning against the door.

"It is I," a man's voice said. "Howard, Duke of Cornwall".

Tony opened the door but no one was prepared for what they saw: A ruddy muscular knight—the same one Rotar brought forth a few days earlier.

Rotar waved his stick at the figure. A small tornado whirled around the man pinning him against the wall.

"I am Howard I tell you." He struggled to break free from the invisible force.

"May a thousand frogs eat off your face if you are not." Rotar slapped his knee and laughed at his own curse.

"But I am," he wailed in a deep voice.

Amanda stared at him in astonishment. "If you're really Howard, where do I live?"

Frantic, he shielded his eyes from the wind. "We reside in Washington DC," he said. "You play harmonious music on your flute late at night, sometimes while you bathe. And you favor chocolate even though you are always dieting."

She turned to Rotar. "Free him."

Rotar flipped his stick and the wind subsided.

She inspected the knight up close. It couldn't be.

Howard almost fell into her arms. She led him to the couch.

"I drank the potion in order to escape on the train," Howard said. "I overheard father speaking to someone with the surname of Andersen. He was negotiating a monetary proposition and demanded a great sum of money. But he warned the man not to harm the girls. I had to come and alert you."

Howard handed the bota bag to Tony. "I had this all along and I am sorry I was untruthful, Mother, but I thought Father might have need of his magical beverage."

Flabbergasted, Amanda stroked her son's thick hair. Then she slapped the thigh of his no-longer crippled leg. "How could you drink the potion when you saw what it did to the others?!"

Howard winced. "I had no choice."

"Are you a knight or are you my Howard?" she asked.

"I am uncertain. Perhaps both. It is confusing."

She knew that his voice would change one day but not quite this fast…

Tony raised eyebrows while sniffing the potion. "Howard's information confirms what I found out about Andersen and Peter."

She sat down abruptly and placed her hand on the coffee table to steady herself. "Are you all right?" asked Tony.

"I just realized Peter may have sent Andersen's side kick to London to kill me."

"I doubt that. There's nothing in your husband's past to warrant such a conclusion."

She eyed Tony and her voice elevated. "There is in the present! Peter said he'd send someone who would know my middle name and Goldtooth called it out through the door. Peter was involved in the greedy scheme all along…"

She grasped her head with trembling hands and shut up. She'd just exposed Howard to some stark realities about his father.

Tony said, "The man may have acted on his own impulses and overstepped the assignment. Thugs often do that. You can't assume that the attack was arranged."

She jerked upright. "Oh, no? Don't forget Peter was expecting to become world famous and couldn't lead two lives anymore. Everyone would have found out."

She looked at Howard. "I'm sorry, but you might as well know why your dad isn't coming home. The person he's been living with in Geneva says she's his fiancé."

Howard pounded the floor with his heel. "I knew there had to be a serious reason Father could not come home." He stared into space. "He is nothing but a mere boor. A royal class, no, an *imperial* royal class boor."

"Let's wait and hear Peter's side," Tony said. "Another possibility is that Andersen could have given those instructions."

Amanda's throat tightened. "I could care less about who did what to whom!" She looked at her son. "We need to change you back, Howard. We need the antidote."

"I know Mother. I am aware of your maternal need to protect me but I feel different and I know things I did not know as a child. This is not my world or time. I am from England and live in a castle. It feels strange to recognize things of this day, but I feel awkward and out of place." He glanced toward the fireplace. "Where is my sword? I left it here and am in need of it."

Amanda frowned. "It was here earlier but then it vanished."

"I had a sword with me," Howard said, "but I was forced to relinquish it to the train agent."

"Did that other sword look like the one you had here?" Rotar asked.

"The very same."

"Then you drew it to you when you projected the energy from the regressive potion. It belonged to you all along but I am afraid it is the only one."

"I accomplished such a feat?" Howard scratched his head.

"I saw it disappear," Amanda said. "But what about your wooden sword?"

"That is nay a sword for a knight. Not even adequate for firewood."

Rotar nodded. "I agree. But now to explain, when the potion activated your powers you entered another dimension void of time and space. Then you manifested this body and clothing and brought the sword to yourself. Simple magic."

Howard looked doubtful. Amanda felt drained. "I can't cope with this. You always say it's quite simple but to me it's quite complicated and unnerving and has brought nothing but grief and strife into our lives. I have no desire to save Peter from himself anymore. We need the antidote and we need to get the girls back."

Rotar stirred. "The flying horse will protect them."

"I hope you're right, but I'm too tired to think," she said, yawning. "Let's go to bed now Howard. You remember your room, right?"

He nodded. "But what is happening?"

"Tomorrow morning we have a plan to rescue the girls."

"May I assist?" Howard asked.

"Perhaps," she said with a weak smile and turned to Tony. "Will you let everyone know Howard's safe?"

He nodded.

"Come on, Howard. Good night all."

Weaving from exhaustion, she followed her son to their suite next door, making sure he was safe in bed for the night. Reminded of their early morning call to kidnap a Swiss citizen, she collapsed into bed, quietly sobbing for the girls and the unfathomable situation her husband had inflicted upon both her children.

CHAPTER FORTY-NINE

Amanda shivered in the predawn, brushing her wind-blown hair away from her face. The designated lookout for Tony and Rotar, she hid in an alley. They'd positioned themselves at the side of the Kruper Pharmaceutical building within view of the entrance. Howard waited across the street in the doorway of a tailor shop, his medieval suit hidden under Tony's overcoat. Gaspard sat parked in the temporary loading zone.

Amanda felt relieved when she saw Tony fingering his revolver in his trench coat pocket. Dressed in a leather jacket, Rotar polished his stick. Traffic increased, and the morning sounds of a city awakening became louder. Employees arrived, climbing the wide steps to the main entrance of the lab.

Twenty minutes passed. Amanda's nerves flared, gripping her throat. What if he wasn't in town? But just as she tried to swallow her anxiety a shiny black Mercedes pulled up to the curb.

Tony nodded to her.

She snapped to attention and gripped her cell phone.

Stefan Andersen sat in the back seat next to a man who looked hefty enough to be a bodyguard. The bulky snub-nosed driver got out and opened the door for the two men. Tony whistled to Gaspard parked a few yards behind and dashed across the courtyard toward Andersen. Rotar ran after him.

The driver spotted Tony and drew a gun. Rotar pointed his stick at the man. *"Trans-fer-ium, Man-i-toff,"* he commanded. A small tornado-like wind swirled around the revolver and rotated it into the air. It landed across the street a short distance from Howard. He scooped it up.

The driver rushed up the stairs toward the building but Rotar tripped him. He fell and smashed his forehead against the cement step, slumping down motionless.

Andersen and the other man got out of the car. The sidekick waved a revolver. Tony pointed his gun at Andersen. "Rotar?" Tony shouted.

Rotar swished his stick again and the bodyguard's gun sprang from his grip, landing next to Howard. Gaspard pulled up behind the Mercedes. "Get in," Tony ordered the two men.

Andersen gave him an acid look. "I'll do nothing of the sort." He twisted his mustache. The other man pulled a sharp knife from his boot and thrust it at Rotar, stabbing him in the left shoulder.

The blow knocked him backward.

Tony kicked the man between his legs. The body guard buckled and grasped his groin. Amanda ran to help Rotar.

"Are you okay?" Amanda asked.

"I think so," he stammered, pulling the knife out and pressing his hand against the wound. A liquid oozed out.

"Cover it, you've got gold blood," Tony whispered through clenched teeth while holding his revolver on Andersen.

Amanda clutched Rotar's shoulder, squeezing above the wound and wrapping a long neck scarf around it.

A faint siren sounded in the distance.

Tony said in a low voice to Rotar, "Can you get these two into the back seat? We're drawing a crowd."

Rotar winced and pointed his stick. "*Re-trac-to-fron-tum Mo-bi-lia.*"

A strong wind whipped around the two men and blew them backward toward the car. Gaspard already had the back door open. The two men tried to resist but a persistent tornado tossed them into the back seat. Tony slammed the door shut and jumped into the front, pointing his gun at both of them. They drove away.

Amanda led Rotar across the street to where Howard waited. A few spectators stared but did nothing.

The siren grew louder.

Examining Rotar's shoulder, Amanda's heart chilled. Howard leaned down to study the wound.

Two security men from the building scrambled down the steps toward the injured driver. Howard started to cross the street holding a gun in each hand. A police car pulled in behind the abandoned black Mercedes. "Howard stop!" Amanda cried. "Rotar we have to get out of here," she added.

He lifted his stick to utter a command but Amanda held up her hand. "Hold on, I have an idea." She grabbed the two guns from Howard and dashed across the street toward the police shouting, "He's a Russian spy. We took these weapons away from him." She pointed at the driver. "And we have reason to believe they're manufacturing chemical warfare supplies inside that building…" She handed the guns to one of the police officers.

The two security men from Andersen's staff turned and ran back inside. One officer shouted orders into his phone and grabbed the injured driver who was awake and trying to get up. The other policeman leapt up the stairs into the building.

Amanda hustled Howard and Rotar around the corner out of view. "We did it!" she panted. "Do you think Tony and Gaspard are all right, Rotar?"

She expected some sort of all-knowing answer but instead he looked blank-faced. "We shall see."

Not a good response. "Are you okay?" she asked him.

He nodded. "I will be fine. Watch this."

He placed his right hand on the wound, palm down and closed his eyes. *"Corec-ti-um Heal-li-um."* A funnel of wind circled the cut and tiny red and yellow crystals swirled with sparkling energy. The bleeding stopped and the skin closed. Then he held his hand over the hole in his shirt until the threads spliced back together. He did the same with the slit in his jacket. The leather closed up.

"Wow," Amanda stammered.

Smells of warm bread from a bakery across the street reminded her they hadn't eaten. Tony would take Andersen to Gaspard's house. They had time for breakfast. "We need to get out of here and find someplace to eat," she said, waving for a cab.

When seated in the back of a taxi and heading for Old Town Amanda said to Rotar, "I'm impressed. You even mended your clothes."

He smiled. "My powers are more advanced than yours but you also have this ability contained in your energy."

She thought for a moment. "If Peter was ill or wounded you could heal him, right?"

"That is correct. But he is an alien and I cannot fix that."

"And Howard's leg when he becomes a boy again? Can that be fixed?"

Rotar looked unsure. "I will attempt to guide him but I cannot guarantee it."

His doubtful answer gave her a semblance of hope but there was no time to think about it.

The cab driver dropped them off at a small café where they waited for their food to be served. Excited but tired, Amanda smiled. "Thanks to your help Rotar, we now have something to trade. How are you doing Howard?"

He grunted. "I need a sword. It is my honorable duty to rescue my sister."

She shifted on her chair reluctant to go into Howard's past, yet curious. "We'll get you a sword. But do you recall what happened when you were a knight?"

"My recollections are scattered and incomplete," he said in a grown-up voice. "But I believe Michelle was also my sister in a former life and I fear that I may have let her down."

"Why do you say that?"

"I saw a man slay her. I skewered the man's leg but he rode away and survived. I am certain the girl in my memory did not live. It is now my destiny to save her in this life."

Rotar smiled and nodded.

The waitress arrived with warm cinnamon rolls, eggs, bacon, fried hash browns and hot chocolate. Rotar stared at the food with a sad face. "You're thinking of your mother?" Amanda asked.

"Yes, she made cinnamon rolls for me when I was young."

Amanda tried to lighten the mood. "Perhaps you can soon go home again and reunite with her."

"But what if she did not wait for me to return?"

She winced at the pain in his eyes. "Mothers can wait forever," she said softly, then wondered if she could wait forever to find the girls. The reality of the situation twisted her insides.

Were the girls taking care of each other? Would the swap for two kidnapped Swiss citizens succeed? Was Howard capable of rescuing them?

Overwhelming anxiety panicked her. She stared at her plate, but couldn't eat.

CHAPTER FIFTY

Amanda paced in her living room while waiting for word from Tony. He'd been gone over three hours. When he entered the suite, she rushed toward him. Howard and Rotar looked up from the TV. "You're safe," she cried. "What about the hostages?"

"They're secured at Gaspard's house."

"Any news of the girls? "

"Not yet, but I've arranged for the exchange in the morning."

Her anxiety intensified. "Did they say anything about the whereabouts of the girls? What if your plan fails?"

"No confessions, but I'm confident that my contact will convince their Russian superior to make a trade."

Filled with unanswered questions she blurted, "Who's watching Andersen now?"

"I have two men stationed at Gaspard's house and they'll bring them to our rendezvous at the music museum in the morning."

"What music museum?"

"I have a friend there. Made a few donations over the years. He's the curator and lucky for us, it's currently closed for renovations. He made it available to me."

That seemed suspect. A group of Russian thugs meeting at a museum? But then again if the authorities were looking for them, no one would suspect that location. For this to work, they needed complete privacy. "And where's Gaspard? What about his wife?"

"They're staying here. I booked them a room down the hall. Lotus wasn't pleased, but she understands the severity of the situation. I think if I hadn't been there to interrogate Andersen myself, she would have bopped him with her stir-fry pan. She's quite a little dynamo.

"Asian?"

He nodded. "Chinese, and very capable."

Amanda's mind whirled while Tony motioned for them to follow him to his suite. He warmed his hands at the fireplace and turned, casting grim eyes at Amanda. "I spoke to Dr. Vidollet."

"And?"

"Peter's back to his human form. The antidote worked."

She slumped onto the couch. "I don't know whether to cry out in joy that the antidote works or curse Peter for his good fortune. He's really back to normal?"

"My father is himself again?" Howard asked.

Rotar's eyes shifted back and forth across the carpet as though in serious thought.

"He's human again," Tony said. "Vidollet will send some of the antidote down tomorrow for Howard and the girls. And for the horse and pig too, if the runaway ever turns up."

The news stunned Amanda. "Thank God, there's hope for the girls and Howard."

Tony cleared his throat. "Now Peter can return to his normal life…"

She flashed angry eyes and clenched her fists. "Not with me, he can't. Peter may be out of the woods but Howard, Michelle and Lizzy aren't! And the cursed wind is still torturing the planet."

Howard spoke up. "My mother has fairly spoken. My father is no longer worthy of our affections. But Tony, what if the law enforcement traces your vehicle to Gaspard's domicile? The timing of your plan could be in jeopardy."

Tony looked impressed. "Good point, but the Suburban is now here at the hotel and the two men guarding Andersen have a vehicle that not even Braun knows about. There is nothing to lead anyone to the temporary holding place."

"Magnificent," Howard said. "We are free to make the exchange. And further assistance for my father will not be required?"

"That's correct," Tony answered, "but there's something you all need to know about Peter…"

Amanda snapped. "I don't want to hear it. We're going out to buy a new sword for Howard. There's an antique armory shop here in Old Town. Are you coming with us?"

"Of course. Let me just—"

"Wait." She raised her head. "Would you please answer the telephone?"

Tony looked confused, but she wasn't in the mood to explain her hidden talents.

It rang.

He lifted the receiver. "Ramsey here." He listened. "I'll call you right back," and hung up. "Excuse me," he said, and went to his bedroom.

She asked Rotar and Howard to go get ready and then hurried to Lizzy's bedroom where she lifted the extension phone, cupping her hand over the handset.

"Cut the sarcasm, Sam," she heard Tony say. "How'd you know I was here?"

Who's Sam? She took in a deep breath and held it.

"Leo Braun told me," the male voice on the other end said. "I've been trying to get a line on that freak sighting of a flying horse and Braun helped me. Now we got an unidentified flying space pig and alien insects at the train station in some ski resort called *Verbeer* or something. The press is going crazy. What the devil's going on over there, Tony?"

"I don't know what you're talking about."

"Don't give me that line of garbage. It's all over the news. Braun claims you're working for the other side."

"Alien insects and a space pig?" Tony asked, sounding incredulous. "And Braun's calling me a traitor? That's crazy and you know it! Why do you believe that little toad anyway?"

"Braun says you've been withholding evidence in order to make a deal with the Russians."

"That's ridiculous. What kind of deal? Maybe that's what he's doing. I'm just trying to stay one step ahead of him."

"You and Braun are on the same side and don't forget it."

"Maybe you should remind him of that. He's been involved in some pretty strange things. Amanda Tregnier has much better contact with her husband and I'm getting close to locating him."

"Braun claims you're hiding some outer-space creature at your hotel and it flipped him into the lake."

"Pure fantasy. He must be hallucinating. My room's on the eighth floor, Sam. If he flipped into the lake from here he'd be dead. Like I told you before, he's been irrational lately."

"He didn't sound irrational but consider yourself warned," the man continued. "I'm going to get to the bottom of this one way or the other. I've sent over two men, Ernie Bauer and Jack Bloomfield. Braun will bring them over to you in the morning."

"I can't meet them until Wednesday Sam, I'm completely tied up tomorrow."

"Then untie yourself and be there. By the way, your ex says hello and hopes you're enjoying your time with your daughter." He hooted a nasty laugh.

"No regards back," Tony replied in a voice tight with anger. The phone banged down to a dial tone.

Amanda hung up and stomped into the living room. "Sam?"

Tony looked furious. "He's the guy dating my ex-wife. I had to deny everything in order to buy us time."

She eyed him, skeptical. "Admit it! You work for the United States government!"

He sat down and laced his fingers. "It's more complicated than that and I can't divulge—"

"Of course not," she snorted. "Heaven forbid you should trust someone you're supposedly working with, even if they've been trusting you."

He closed his eyes. "Aside from all the alien stuff we've got a situation. Two more agents are on their way and Braun is on our tail. We better get an early start in the morning." He stared into space. "My 'ex' be damned… I'm not going to let her onion-brain of a boyfriend ruin our mission."

Amanda's chest constricted. "I'm scared, Tony. Until we get Michelle and Lizzy back it's impossible to think!"

"It's already set up. We'll leave at dawn and make the trade before Sam's agents show up."

She moved to the window and peered at the long, puffy layers of agitated clouds. Howard and Rotar returned from next door. She turned and frowned. "It better work," she said.

Rotar spoke up. "Howard and I will help."

"Yes Mother, I only require a sword."

Tony asked Howard, "Do you know anything about space insects in Verbier?"

Howard's face fell. "I must confess that I experimented with some ants while waiting in the lavatory."

Amanda's thoughts spun. More space creatures to deal with. She offered a bleak smile. "Howard we're not going to get into that right now. We have a mission and I'm counting on your help as well as Rotar's tomorrow."

Howard held up one hand. "I will do everything in my power to save my sister and damsel Elizabeth."

"Bravo then, we move at dawn," Tony said, heading for his bedroom.

"You're not going out with us?" Amanda asked.

He turned. "If you don't mind waiting a moment, I have to make a quick phone call first. It's important."

"Calling who?"

"My sister."

"I didn't know you had a sister."

"It's a family matter—I'll only be a minute."

She looked at him, doubtful. Another surprise, but she didn't try to listen in.

They gathered their things and waited. "I hope we're discreet enough," Amanda said. "I'm tired of people staring at us."

"Do not worry about that," Rotar said.

"We'll need your help tomorrow," she said.

His face brightened. "You will have wind power the size of a tornado."

She visualized the devastation at the lab in Coppet and her eyes widened. "That's what I'm afraid of. You don't have much control over your powers, do you?"

"I became modestly over-zealous at the farm."

"Modestly?"

"I promise not to use so much power the next time."

"Good idea."

She turned to Howard. "You should be fine with Tony's overcoat. If anyone asks, you're going to a costume party."

Howard nodded. "It is done." He let the coat hang open.

"Please button it," Amanda said. "Let's not go out of our way to invite questions."

Tony reappeared. "Ready?"

"How's your *sister?*" she asked in a sarcastic tone.

"Let's go," he said in irritation, escorting them out the door.

CHAPTER FIFTY-ONE

While waiting outside the hotel for Howard to get directions, Amanda thought of Peter. Her husband was now free to continue his life with Marta while her own life had become a shamble. She wanted to kick him all the way into another galaxy.

Howard came out and disrupted her anger. "The antique shop is not far from here. We can go by foot," he announced.

Tony nodded. "The wind has calmed a little. Let's do that." While walking he asked Howard, "Any problems?"

"The manager asked who I was. I think he preferred I take leave of the hotel but I informed him that I was your guest."

In a tired voice Amanda said, "Let's hope it doesn't lead to more problems."

Tony asked Rotar, "How's your wound?"

"He healed himself," Amanda broke in. "I saw him do it."

"Impressive," Tony said.

"He said we can all do it if we learn how to use the full potential of our minds."

"That makes sense," Tony said. He quickened their pace. Rotar scurried after them to keep up.

They found the antique store on a narrow cobble-stoned alley in Old Town. An oval black and gold sign hung over the door with shiny brass fixtures and beveled glass panes. A bell tinkled when they entered the tiny shop.

Antique armaments adorned the walls and furniture filled the interior. An elderly man dressed in a red uniform jacket from the French Revolution era sat behind the counter concentrating on a ledger. Through questioning eyes he looked up at the group. He gave a curt nod and returned to his ledger. Tony followed Howard to a sword display on the wall. Rotar shuffled straight to the antique pistols and rifles at the back of the store. Amanda went with him.

Rotar slid his stick along the weapons and sparks followed his wand. The guns began to vibrate and shift. He lowered his stick. The rifle moaned in a low raspy voice. "Return me to my magnificent Versailles," it said.

The pistol hanging next to the rifle heaved, relaxed and said in a wispy, whiny voice, "Take me to my master in London."

Rotar snorted at both weapons.

Amanda poked his arm and whispered, "What's going on?"

"I awakened them to check their ancestry and authenticity. I have muted them again." He scrutinized other weapons.

Howard studied the swords mounted in rows on a red velvet wall. Rotar shuffled over next to him. Amanda followed. "I think that it the correct timeline," Rotar said to Howard.

"How do you know?" Tony asked.

Rotar lifted his stick. *"Wak-i-um Cen-trup,"* he said in a low voice.

The sword shimmied and arched toward Rotar. A mouth appeared at the center of the grip where the handle crossed the blade. "Where is my master?" it asked in a hollow tone.

Howard gaped. Tony gasped. Amanda squeezed together tight lips.

"Who is your master?" Rotar asked.

"A legend of his day," it said in a reverberating voice. "A knight of the Round Table."

Rotar grinned. "Good." He swished his stick and put the sword back to sleep.

Tony said, "I'll go speak to the owner."

Amanda followed him to the register.

"I'm interested in an antique sword," Tony said to the man who looked up from his work

The proprietor peered at Tony and said, "I have many old swords."

"I understand, but the one I want is from King Arthur's time—Sixth Century England."

He glanced with curiosity at Howard and Rotar. "Is there a special occasion?"

"It's Halloween in America," Tony said. "The young man's an actor and needs a sword to go with his costume." He winked at Amanda.

"An authentic sword would be expensive," the man said.

Tony shrugged. "It has to be genuine."

The man clicked his false teeth. "Excuse me?"

"A *real* one."

"*Bien,* fine." He led them over to where Howard held a long sword encased in a jeweled scabbard. When Howard pulled it out the blade glistened. He waved it in the air, twisting and pointing it with precision. Then he lunged forward and almost pierced the wall. The proprietor winced.

"This is the one I must have," Howard said.

Tony asked the man, "How much?"

"Thirty-five thousand francs, *Monsieur.*"

"We'll take it."

Amanda gulped, "What?!"

She pulled Tony aside and whispered, "You can't do this, it's too much. When Howard returns to normal he won't need it. This is totally unacceptable."

Tony kept his voice low but firm. "It's a gift from me and the memory for Howard will be invaluable."

"But he's only twelve…it's too extravagant."

"I don't have a son. Let me do this for him, please."

She thought of the bracelet her mother had given her as a little girl. She planned to give it to Michelle on her seventh birthday. Peter had never given Howard anything of significance but could she let a stranger do that? Undecided, she looked at Howard the knight. He held the sword in a caress and his face glowed. She turned and nodded at Tony.

Rotar tugged Tony's sleeve. "I wish to purchase this musket."
Tony chuckled. "Whatever for?"

"I like it."

"Will you use it?"

He nodded. "I have a plan."

Amanda looked at both of them. "If that gun works it could hurt someone or damage something."

"Do not worry," Rotar told her.

"Okay," said Tony. "But it's heavy. Can you carry it?"

Rotar nodded. "I will manage. Thank you."

Tony paid the man for the weapons. Outside the store Howard beamed. He wore the sword on his belt. Rotar carried the musket in a canvas bag slung across his shoulder.

Tony said, "Let's have an early supper and then go over the plans when we get back to the hotel."

Everyone agreed, and they found a quaint pub farther down the street.

A generous tip to the stout proprietor allowed them to bring their antique weapons to the table. They ordered a quick meal and Rotar and Howard did most of the eating. Rotar slipped the pepper container into his pocket before leaving, but offered no explanation.

Outside Amanda said, "Why did you steal the pepper, Rotar?"
He smiled. "I will return it later. Do not fear."

Amanda had to admit that of all the things to worry about, the pepper caper belonged at the bottom of the list.

At the hotel Gaspard brought Lotus with him to Tony's suite and introductions were made. Amanda had to admit that the petit woman with sharp dark eyes and an ornate Asian clasp fastening her hair into a bun, was far from docile. She jumped in with suggestions at every step of the rendezvous plan. But after strong protestations from Gaspard, Lotus reluctantly agreed to wait at the hotel until the mission was completed. When finished with their meeting, Amanda shifted on her chair, uneasy. "I hope Leo Braun isn't outside eavesdropping again."

Tony moved to the window. "I doubt he'd try such a fool-hardy thing twice." He scanned the street below. "There's no sign of him."

"I have a feeling he's nearby. Maybe I'm just nervous."

"We all are," Tony said. "Let's get some sleep. We have an early morning."

Before getting into bed, Amanda found the stuffed angel on Michelle's pillow and took it with her for comfort. She prayed for a safe and swift exchange at the music museum. She hoped Humfly would find her way back or was somewhere safe from capture. Picturing the girls, she squeezed the angel and sent thoughts of love and safety to them both.

CHAPTER FIFTY-TWO

Amanda sat in the backseat of the Suburban twisting her hands. It was still dark outside and the museum hadn't opened yet. Howard yawned while sliding his fingers across the scabbard of his new sword. Rotar sat on the other side of her, holding his musket. Gaspard turned down the radio and said to Tony, "Europe ees experiencing zee coldest autumn in recorded history. Much wind damage 'as been reported, especially to fishing boats and private yachts. Zee same ees 'appening on your east coast in America and Canada. And Japan 'as lost two ships at sea. Eet ees terrible, dees weather."

Rotar cleared his throat. "Then we must succeed today and change everyone back to human again."

"You got that right," Tony agreed.

Amanda asked in a sleepy voice, "When will the agents arrive with Stefan Andersen, Tony?"

"The girls will be delivered at nine-fifteen. When they're here I'll call my men to bring Andersen. They're on stand-by a block away."

She glanced at her watch. "Half an hour until it opens. I'm so nervous. What if the Russians don't bring the girls?"

"Not an option—they need Andersen."

Rotar stirred. "May Stefan Andersen and his men itch from mosquito bites for ten years."

She nodded. "I agree, but only after we get the girls back."

The clock crept toward nine. The director who was also the head curator opened the door to the museum and waved them in. Tony slipped out of the vehicle and the others followed. He turned to Gaspard. "You have your gun?"

He nodded and drove around to the back of the building.

Their group stepped into a small foyer and headed to the main viewing room. Its damp polished wood floors had a pine scent from cleaning fluid. Antique instruments circled the room. Scaffolding and tarps in an adjoining display room indicated renovation was in progress but there was no sign of workers. A guard showed up for his shift. The director introduced him to Tony.

"We're meeting someone here and then we'll be out of your way," Tony said. "It might be best if you stay in the staff area until our business is done."

The director nodded to the man and leaned his head toward a door hidden under the main staircase. "You have my permission to watch television this morning."

The guard shrugged and disappeared through the door. The curator said, "I cancelled the workers today. You are free to hold your meeting. I will return around noon to lock up. Just call the guard if you need anything."

Tony nodded and the director left the facility.

The rumbling noise of a truck sounded at the rear of the building. Brakes grated and the engine quieted. "They're here," Amanda said in an anxious tone. She rushed toward the back windows to look.

Tony caught up with her. "Patience," he whispered. "I'm expecting two Russians."

The front door of the museum opened. Two stocky men entered—one of them overweight and pale, the other un-kept and muscular. Both wore black leather jackets and jeans. Tony shoved Amanda behind him. They met in the middle of the great hall.

She kept her eyes fixed on both men and struggled to breathe.

"Yuu arrre Antony Ramsee?" the pale man asked in an accent. He had heavy dark bags under his eyes and a double chin.

Tony nodded.

"I am Thor," he said. "We received your message via your east-west communicator, Mr. Stransky. He was very persuasive."

Tony shot stern eyes at the man. "You have the girls out back?"

"Dah vomen and dah horse are en zee truck. Ver is Stefan Andersen?"

"Andersen will be along in a few minutes," Tony said. "I want to see the girls first."

Thor led Tony to the rear window where they could view the parking area.

Like a robot, Amanda followed them.

The driver of the truck walked to the back of the vehicle. Thor tapped the window with his knuckle and nodded for him to roll up the rear door.

Amanda strained to see.

Goldtooth hovered in the rear looking snarly. Michelle lay curled up on an old mattress covered partly by a blanket. Elizabeth stood by the horse.

Tony dialed his cell phone. "They're here. Bring Andersen." He hung up.

A black SUV drove into the parking lot behind the museum. Amanda gritted her teeth at seeing Andersen and his bodyguard in the rear seat but held her anger. It wasn't time yet.

When they'd parked, Tony turned to the Russians and said, "We can make the exchange now."

Thor stepped to the back door. It seemed like slow motion to Amanda. Howard followed, fingering his sword. "Stay back," she hissed, but he continued. She looked for Rotar and spotted him backing away. Then he slipped into another room and disappeared. She caught up with Tony and Howard, trailing behind the Russian.

Tires screeched in front of the building. Car doors slammed. Leo Braun charged into the museum with two men. Amanda's heart pounded, her mind went numb. How had he found them?

"Stop," Braun ordered, pointing a gun at them. He wore a bandage around his head and his left arm hung in a sling.

"How...?" Amanda muttered.

"What the blazes?" Tony demanded.

Thor's angry face turned to Tony. "Yuu invite reinforcements? Stransky swore this vuud be between us—off the record." He slipped his hand into his pocket. So did his partner.

Tony stared in anger at Braun, "How did you know about this?"

Braun smirked and said, "I've had you under surveillance and now I have witnesses to corroborate your treason. Meet Jack Bloomfield and Ernie Bauer."

Jack, the taller one, kept one hand hidden behind his back while patting down his hair with the other. Stout Ernie kept both hands behind his back. They said nothing.

Tony glared at Braun. "I should have guessed you'd find a way to eavesdrop."

Braun laughed. "Thought you could throw me into the lake and get away with it, huh? My wounds prove what you did." He pointed to his bandaged head. "I heard you plotting this little scheme and got every word on tape. Now it's my turn to throw you all into a garbage dump. More appropriate than Lake Geneva don't you think?"

Amanda couldn't stand it any longer. "We're here to rescue lives!" she yelled. "You're ruining everything, you fool!"

Braun waved the revolver at them. The two men flanked him on both sides. "I think not. You're all under arrest."

Amanda went ballistic. "My daughter was kidnapped and is out back being held in a truck. This is monstrous! I won't take orders from you or anyone else."

Tony raised his hand to hold her back and shook his head at Howard.

Howard set his hand on his sword. The men with Braun noticed. So did the others.

The two Russians drew their guns.

Tony warned Braun. "You don't know what you're into, Leo. We don't need a Mexican stand-off. Stay out of this." He pointed the gun inside his pocket, the barrel bulging beneath the fabric.

Braun sneered. "You just don't want me to ruin your little scheme of selling out to these caviar creeps…"

The Russians stiffened but held their guns steady on Braun. "Ve vill deel vit yuu," Thor said.

"Oh yeah?" Braun sneered. "I'm taking the girls, the freaky flying horse, Andersen and all the rest of you. There'll be no exchanges today."

CHAPTER FIFTY-THREE

Amanda reeled at the horror of Braun's interference. "You're threatening the life of my daughter," she screamed. Ready to run at him, Howard grabbed her. "Let go!" she cried.

He held on and whispered, "You will have your chance Mother, but not now."

She stopped struggling but still seethed with anger.

Tony said, "There'll be consequences, Leo. Sam Henry…"

"Sam Henry be damned!" Braun snorted.

Thor looked disgusted. "Dis ees how Americans keep der deel?"

Braun waved at his two assistants. "I don't have to play fair. Do your stuff boys."

From behind their backs Jack and Ernie pulled out strange firing weapons. Long-barreled guns with wide nozzles and a large compartment beneath each grip. They adjusted a small sighting scope and pressed something along the sides.

Tony aimed his gun at the men.

Wild with anger, Amanda reached a boiling point. Where was Rotar? And why couldn't the guard hear the ruckus? Was the TV that loud? The men out back would be unaware of the situation inside.

Ernie Bauer aimed at Amanda Tony and Howard; Jack Bloomfield at the two Russians. Without warning, Braun's men shot their weapons emitting a film-like substance that billowed into a big shield, enclosing each group against the wall. Tony shot back but the bullet failed to penetrate the oozy substance. The structure was about eight feet high, wrapping around them like a large diaphanous tent. It hardened instantly.

Icicles of pain stabbed Amanda's head. She banged on the see-through wall. It had an opening at the top that they couldn't reach. "I'll see you locked into a germ-infested den of rattle-snakes," she yelled at Braun.

Howard drew his sword and sliced at the solid film but couldn't cut through. The two Russians banged their guns against the hard wall inside their own prison and gave up.

Braun's face erupted into roaring laughter. "This is state-of-the-art stuff. Better than old-fashioned nets, don't you think? Instead of catching flying alien insects, I got myself some bigger bugs…"

Tony hit the wall with his fist. "You're over the line, Braun. The Russians will hunt you down. Don't be an idiot."

"Who's gonna' know if I kill you all?"

Bloomfield looked at Braun. "You can't do that sir. It's not part of our assignment."

Braun's eyes narrowed. "Shut up and follow orders."

Tony said, "You really think I don't have back up?"

"Ha-Ha," Braun snarled.

"Yuu 'tink ve come vitout reinforcements?" Thor added. "Ve vill see you eeten alive by hungree volves for dees outrage."

Entrapped and agitated Amanda couldn't see any way out of the situation. And where was Rotar?!

Braun gloated and maintained his arrogant stance. "We'll be roundin' up the rest now boys."

Tony pulled the bota bag with Peter's potion from his pocket.

"What's that?" Amanda whispered.

He twisted the top off the bag. "A swig of magical powers," he said in hushed words.

"Speak up," Braun demanded.

Tony said, "Did you tell your DC agents about the silver book? The one with the secret formula you were keeping for me? I heard you offered it to the Russians for twelve million dollars. But then you lost it. Did you tell them about that little deal gone sour Leo?"

Braun winced but recovered at once. "Good try Tony." He glanced at his men. "He's lyin'. He's hiding a little alien runt at his hotel who stole the book from me. Tony's the bad guy here."

With Braun distracted and Howard busy examining the wall, Tony squirted a large dose of the potion into his mouth.

"Me too," Amanda said to him.

"Let me handle this…"

"No!" she whispered through gritted teeth.

Tony handed her the bag.

She twisted her face from the foul taste but swallowed as much as she could.

"What're you doing?" Braun demanded.

"What do you care?" Tony said. "If our bullets don't penetrate this thing, neither do yours."

Braun looked uncertain. "That's an assumption. You want me to test it?"

Amanda felt a tingling sensation inside as if she was falling and losing herself.

Tony said to Braun, "You'd better run. Your agents will have to arrest you."

"You got no proof," Braun huffed.

Tony began to transform, his hair growing into white strands of silk. Amanda's mutation started also.

The others in the room stared at them in shock. The Russians looked like they had just seen a ghost. So did Jack and Ernie, but tried to hide their reaction.

"My agents are in the car out back," Tony said in an echoing voice. "They'll be happy to tell Jack and Ernie all about you, Leo."

Braun jerked his arm from his sling and backed toward the front of the room. He pulled a plastic bag from his pocket and shoved something that looked like dirty hay into his mouth. Chewing and choking, his face twisted into a contorted mask.

Wings sprouted from Tony's shoulders and his clothes changed into a white robe.

Amanda felt her energy accelerate. Everything around her slowed to a standstill while her mind sped through time. She looked down at herself and saw a silver robe on a long thin body and felt the weight of wings on her back. A fragrant smell of wild flowers filled her with an overwhelming sense of inner peace. She recalled waterfalls streaked with rainbows above fern-clad cliffs and blue forests dotted with pink foliage.

"My name is Verilla," she said in a hollow voice that startled her. "I am the village priestess on Androdon. We worship God in nature and eat only natural foods." The flush of warm fluid filling her veins made her smile. She looked at Tony.

"Your wings are magnificent," she said, "and your translucent skin is like crystal. You look ageless, even though I see years of wisdom in your blue eyes. Your name is Teppen, the village wise man and I have known you always." When she blinked, long lashes touched her warm cheeks.

He smiled back. "And your eyes shine like silver. I remember you, Verilla."

"I play music on a lute," she added. "When I hear the sweet sounds of my playing I can float."

The Russian agents stared speechless. Howard put his sword back in its scabbard. "The walls are too slippery to climb," he whispered. "Let me have more of that potion so that I may have wings too."

Tony shook his head. "Sorry, but I don't want to risk any more regression."

Jack and Ernie pinned Braun to the floor but pulled away when he began to transform. His teeth changed into long black spikes. Growths dotted with hairs covered a bulky face while his head swelled to the size of a basketball. The pupils of his eyes turned red, and his hair grew slimy and long, matching the rubbery material of his black clothes. A bitter odor of burnt rubber permeated the room.

This time Jack and Ernie didn't try to hide their astonishment.

Braun stood up and waved a sword at the group, its long steel blade glistening. "I am Toller from Zotnar, the planet of darkness," he said in a deep voice.

Jack fired the special weapon at him but it was empty. Ernie stepped forward and grabbed Braun's arm. "Get your filthy germs away from me," Braun told Ernie, "I'm going to win this battle…"

Ernie let go.

Tony fluttered his wings and lifted off the floor. Amanda did the same and they pulled Howard up between them. Fluttering her own wings, she felt an immediate lift and tried to raise Howard by his other arm. Tipping forward and backward, she held her spine rigid to secure her balance. Howard dangled in mid-air, his cheeks flushed from the strain.

All three rose above the shield. Braun pushed Jack and Ernie away like toy dolls and lunged at them with his sword. He almost slashed Howard when they cleared the top.

Tony stopped fluttering his wings. "Blast," he said. "We'll have to lower ourselves again."

The three of them descended into their prison, Howard landing with a heavy thud. A tear slid down Amanda's face. "We're trapped."

Tony shushed her. "Keep the faith Amanda, here comes the cavalry."

Rotar peeked into the room from behind the foyer door and aimed his musket at Braun's back. "May a trillion sneezes plague your destiny for five generations," he cursed.

Braun whipped around but Rotar had already pulled the trigger. A blast of granulated pepper shot through the air exploding in Braun's face.

Rotar laughed and slapped his knee. "I have always wanted to do that."

Amanda understood now why Rotar had been hoarding pepper from the restaurants.

Braun sneezed so loud it knocked him over and shook the musical displays. Amidst tinkles and squeaks and moans and groans he sneezed again and again, cutting his leg with his own sword. Black blood trickled through the cut in his rubber pants.

He dropped his sword and revolver. Gray drool seeped from the corner of his mouth. "You're the measly midget who stole my silver book," he growled in a deep voice.

Rotar grinned and nodded. "I cannot steal what is mine."

"Who the devil are you?"

"That is not your concern."

"Tell me," Braun demanded between more sneezes.

Rotar smiled. "I think not."

Amanda and Tony fluttered their wings and lifted Howard between them, floating out of the shield. Bloomfield grabbed for Braun's gun but Rotar waved his stick and blew it out of his hand. He shuffled over to the weapon and picked it up, pointing it at both men. They raised their arms.

The floating trio landed. Rotar chuckled. "You have changed," he remarked. "A wonderful transformation."

Still sneezing, Braun scooped his sword from the floor and turned toward Amanda and Tony. Howard rushed across the room and swung his sword, knocking Braun's from his hand. He toppled him to the floor and pressed the tip of his blade against Braun's black throat.

"Sneeze again and I vow to slice and dice you into the tiniest of fragments," Howard threatened in his mature knight voice.

Rotar smiled and waved his musket at Jack and Ernie. "I believe we can rescue the girls now."

CHAPTER FIFTY-FOUR

Amanda had to reach the girls. She fluttered her wings and floated toward the back door with Tony right behind her. "Hurry, Tony."

A noise of a high-pitched motorcycle outside shrouded her words. Humfly bolted through the double doors with Peter on her back. The red lightning bolt on the pig's nose pulsated in orange and green. Amanda stopped and gawked, shocked by Peter's decline. His parka hung open, revealing a bone-thin body and he looked human again, but old and gaunt with gray hair and wrinkled skin. "What's happened?" she cried.

"That's what I wanted to tell you," Tony said. "He's aged."

Braun's movements caught Amanda's attention, but too late. He grabbed his sword from the floor and swung, knocking Howard's sword out of his hand. He pinned Howard against the piano and snickered.

Amanda half danced, half floated toward her son. "Do something, Rotar." Her voice sounded wispy.

The Russians banged on the wall of their see-through prison. "Ver have yuu been?" Thor growled to Peter.

Braun stared at the motorcycle pig and Peter. Howard kicked the sword out of his hand. Braun shoved Howard aside but Howard grabbed his own sword and held it on Braun.

Peter clung to the circle of horns on Humfly's head. "I learned about this rendezvous and with the help of Rotar's rock, he came and got me. But I wanted my own transportation. We found Humfly back at the farm and she brought me here."

Thor growled in a bitter tone. "You ver to sell the eemformation to us. Now vee learn dees midget has zee book and the American traitor and the others are vierd creetures. Vee make deel vit yuu but yuu deliver not'ing."

Peter's hands trembled as he climbed off the pig's saddle. Struggling to draw breath, his voice was feeble. "You've sampled my potion," he said to Amanda and Tony. "Enterprising, if nothing else." He pointed to Braun. "I take it you're Braun, the one who tried sell the book for your own gain. Unless I decide to share the antidote, you'll die, you miserable beast."

Howard held his sword steady against Braun. "Father it is I, Howard. I am now a knight."

Peter looked at him with tired eyes. "Your leg is well and strong, son."

Howard nodded. "My dreams of being a knight came true, but Mother and Tony have wings and they hail from a distant planet."

Amanda floated in place, scrutinizing Peter's deterioration. Tony moved next to her. Peter said, "Well now we have the antidote, so everyone can reverse the process before they grow old like me. I didn't expect anyone else to be affected."

Braun bellowed with laughter, "You don't scare me you measly shrimp. You gonna' let your son fight your battles for you?"

Tony floated across the room and stopped in front of Peter. "You cannot match his strength," he warned, glowering at Braun.

Amanda cried in a hollow-sounding voice, "Peter, for heaven's sake, stay away."

"No!" Peter moved around Tony and aimed a knife at Braun. "It was my book and my formula and my discovery." He hurled the knife into Braun's chest.

Braun laughed and yanked it out from the thick material of his vest. He pushed Howard aside and swung the knife back at Peter, cutting him across his waist.

Peter slumped to the floor, bleeding. Howard bolted at Braun and sliced his ear with his sword. Then he stabbed him in the side. Braun dropped to his knees, black blood flowing from the wounds.

"Father," Howard cried, "I will beckon assistance for you."

Peter groaned and motioned him to come closer. "Enjoy your life, son." He picked up the purple rock that had fallen from his pocket. "Give this back to Rotar. It's too late to help me now."

"You must not perish, Father," Howard pleaded. "Why did you do this?"

Peter's eyes lingered on his son's face. "Remember when the moon was so far away?" He drew a raspy breath. "Of course you don't. You were born in the space age. When I was young the moon was beyond the reach of mankind. But then astronauts walked on it and after that the moon was very close. It's all a matter of perspective."

"But of what significance is that?" Howard asked.

Peter's voice weakened. "It's curiosity that makes great scientists. I dreamt that my previous world was ruled by seven moons and for a brief moment I returned there… The past is too far away for most people, but I proved that the past is very close… closer than I ever imagined."

Howard mirrored the anguish in his father's eyes. "I have experienced the same Father and have now become who I was lifetimes ago. But I must return to the present in order to live. Why did you bring this discovery to our planet?"

Peter attempted to smile. "My dream was to become famous by closing the distance between this life and the past. I wanted to be important."

"But you *are* important, Father."

Amanda floated to his side. "I'm so sorry, Peter…"

"It's too late Amanda," Peter said. He coughed and his face drained. "As a child I had a vivid dream of going through life on Earth all over again. School, homework, growing pains, life lessons… Very depressing." He tilted his head and gurgled. His words faded to a whisper. Amanda strained to listen. "So I decided to cheat destiny and achieve total control over my past, present, and future, but I messed up." Blood slid from his mouth.

"You found a way into the future?" Amanda asked.

Peter blinked. "I thought I did. If the past is stored within us, why not the future?"

"I know from my dreams it has to be," Amanda said, turning to Rotar. "The knowledge is in the silver book, right?"

Rotar frowned and nodded. "Somewhere."

"Can you help him?" she asked Rotar.

"I will try." He pointed his stick and said, *"He-li-um Back-to-tum-flee."*

Peter drew a deep breath. The cut in his shirt mended. The bleeding stopped.

"Now he must do the rest himself," Rotar said, handing the purple rock back to Peter. "It can give you strength my friend, if you ask it."

Peter grasped the rock with trembling hands.

Rotar explained, "Its codes can interpret human energy waves."

Peter whispered to Amanda, "We'll meet again, my sweet Amanda, out there somewhere amongst the stars."

Peter gazed at the sky beyond the window. "Take me to a healing place of peace," he asked the rock.

Sparkles of light surrounded him.

His face lifted in a bright smile. "I can see into the mirror… oh, my multiple miracle moons… I'm young again."

A sudden flash of light exploded and the two-tailed cat sprang from the rock, pouncing on Peter and disappearing inside him in a puff of lavender smoke.

A shriek cry shattered the silence when the swollen and disheveled cat leapt out of Peter and jumped back into the rock.

Peter's body vanished.

When the smoke cleared the rock crackled and pulsed on the floor.

"Where'd he go?" Amanda cried in horror.

"I do not know," said Rotar.

"Is he alive?!"

In an anxious tone Rotar said, "I do not know that either."

CHAPTER FIFTY-FIVE

Amanda found it difficult to breathe. She looked at the floor where Peter had disappeared and then at Rotar. He scooped up the rock but said nothing more.

Braun lay crippled on the floor gnashing his teeth, a hand over his bloody ear.

Howard turned to Braun in a rage, his sword pricking a vulnerable spot under his chin.

"Don't," Braun whimpered. "I'm just a government employee. My mother never understood me…"

Tony looked at him with disgust. "Stop blaming your behavior on your mother. You're a grown man."

"This is his first life here on earth," Rotar said. "He is a young, un-evolved soul."

"That is not an acceptable excuse," Howard raged. "My father, the hostages, Michelle and Elizabeth…" He glared at Braun.

"I'll cooperate if you give me the antidote," Braun said. "Make the exchange," he managed to say between sneezes.

Tony sniggered. "I don't know if there's enough to go around, Leo. You're last on the list."

Howard nudged his sword under Braun's chin. "You will clear Tony's name?"

Braun nodded. "I was only joking."

"Some joke," said Tony. "Tell your cohorts to assist us."

Rotar kept his musket trained on Jack and Ernie. Braun nodded to the two men. "Assist them—assist them—"

"Rotar, will you and Howard wait here while we make the exchange?" Tony asked.

They both bobbed heads.

"Do you think you can get the Russians out of that cage after we leave?"

Rotar slipped his gun into his belt. "I will try master."

Amanda nudged Tony's wing and said, "Why are we still in here?"

"We're leaving right now. Follow me." He gestured for Jack and Ernie to take the lead. Tony and Amanda floated behind them.

Outside, Gaspard got out of the S.U.V., eyes transfixed on the two angels.

Goldtooth jumped from the back of the truck and scowled. Jack and Ernie contained him after a brief scuffle.

Amanda floated on board, overjoyed to find Michelle and Lizzy unharmed. She hugged Michelle. Tony held Lizzy close and explained how they had also taken the potion. "I know our wings must seem strange but we'll soon be back to normal. Please wait here with Gaspard while we take care of a few last things. Then we'll all go back to the hotel."

Michelle nodded. "I could certainly avail myself of the Inn's water closet."

"And I shall do the same," added Lizzy.

Amanda fluttered her wings to leave. "Are you my flying mother now?" Michelle asked.

"Isn't it wonderful?" she answered with sparkling eyes.

Lizzy asked her father, "Are you an angel like Starbeam?"

Tony grinned. "I feel like one, but we'll have to give up our angel status very soon. Starbeam as well."

"Good," Elizabeth said. "I am anxious to return to the twenty-first century."

Tony sent Jack and Ernie back inside and asked Gaspard to watch the girls and the truck. Then he stopped by the other SUV to inform his security men that the Russian agents would be out to pick up Andersen and the bodyguard. Tony's two guards looked perplexed but remained silent. "Meet me later for a debriefing," Tony said to them. "The usual place. This is top secret."

The two American agents nodded.

Inside the museum Tony floated to Rotar and Howard. "The girls are okay, but I'm curious. You called me master a few minutes ago. Why?"

Rotar's eyes enlarged. "Because you are Teppen, Master of Androdon, where nature is your teacher. Many planets know of you. Your deeds are legendary throughout the universe. Your people are the final goal in our progression toward self-realization. Only the wisest with the purest hearts go on to Androdon."

"If that is so," Tony commented, "why am I here on Earth?"

Rotar chuckled. "You are an ambassador. You came here to help those in need. Think of yourself as a human angel. There are many like you, master."

Tony looked amused.

Rotar squeezed his eyes and smiled. "When you return to your human form you will not have wings, but you will be an angel nevertheless."

Braun sneezed and huffed. "He's no angel."

Tony ignored him. "What about Leo?"

"He is from Zotnar, the planet without a sun," Rotar said. "They use artificial light for their existence and hot houses to grow food. When someone dies, the funeral ceremony celebrates the soul's progression with large fires. They hope to be reborn on Earth to fulfill their greed, but they pay a heavy price for a self-indulgent existence by never knowing happiness. They live in fear and guilt all of their lives."

Tony looked bewildered. "How do you know all this?"

"It is documented in universal history and my people are the keepers of knowledge."

Braun laughed so loud that gray saliva dripped from his teeth. "I am Toller—ha, ha, ha," he roared again. Another sneezing frenzy squelched his voice. He sneezed so hard that black blood flowed from his nostrils. Amanda couldn't watch. Jack and Ernie seemed stupefied, gazing at his bloodied face.

"You're the wise one, Rotar," Tony said. "Not me."

Amanda floated toward Rotar and asked, "Why am I here?"

He smiled up at her. "On your planet you were the goddess of music and I am sure there are many good things ahead in your life."

"Have you any hint?"

Rotar shook his head. "You know I am not permitted to go into the future."

Tony interrupted. "I'm not sure that isn't a good thing—not knowing, I mean."

"Just one thing, please," Amanda urged. "Do they have choco-late on my planet? As good as here in Switzerland?"

Rotar snickered. "Something even better… The taste is so silky and euphoric that feelings of delight and happiness fall upon those who eat the natural sweets. And they will not make you gain weight. They grow on trees and are called merry-berries."

Merry-berries… she mused. "I think I remember them."

Tony took her hand. "The girls need the antidote. We have to go."

Howard said, "I will remain and guard Braun."

The Russians grew restless inside their prison. "Get us out of here at once," Thor demanded.

"Rotar will oblige as soon as we're gone," Tony said, and turned to Rotar. "Can you also clean up the mess in here?"

At Rotar's nod Tony said to Thor, "Instruct your driver to let me take the truck."

Thor gave a curt nod. "Send him here to me."

"And then you'll take Andersen back to Russia?"

He nodded eagerly, his eyes tinged with fear. "I have seen enough today."

"Rotar, after you're done here, Gaspard will bring you and Howard and Braun back to the hotel. I'll take Humfly in the truck. Starbeam takes up a lot of room but she'll fit."

Humfly whirred into action jerking up and down.

Rotar said, "She wants to go back to the other pigs."

"I heard her thoughts too, but stop the racket for a moment," Tony told the pig. Humfly shifted into neutral.

Tony addressed Jack and Ernie. "When you leave, speak to no one until you report to Sam Henry. Everything you've seen here today is classified. Understood, gentlemen?"

"Yes sir," they both said in unison. Ernie said, "We wouldn't be believed anyway. But what about Braun and this guy here with the missing tooth?"

"I'll take care of Braun," Tony said, "and you can leave Goldtooth with Andersen and his other goons. Thor will take them away." He nodded to Thor who nodded back. "The rest of us will meet in my hotel suite."

Tony floated closer to Braun. "Don't try anything stupid."

He sneezed. "Get me the antidote. My nose is raw."

The sound of a siren drew close. "If that's the police," Amanda said, "can you stall them, Rotar?"

He waddled to the window and aimed his stick at the approaching police car. The wind howled and forced the car to drive around in a continuous circle out front. Rotar laughed. The guard approached from a corner of the vestibule.

Amanda pointed. "He must have called them. Can you do something about him too?"

Rotar waved his stick and a funnel of wind pinned him against the wall. "When I leave I will see that he remembers nothing," Rotar said.

Jack and Ernie turned Goldtooth over to the men guarding Andersen, letting them know two Russians would be out shortly to collect them. Then they left in the van they had arrived in. Tony floated to the front of the truck and prepared to drive back to the hotel. Amanda held Michelle close in the back. Her daughter looked pale and weak. Elizabeth calmed the horse and watched the pig. Amanda would wait until later to tell Michelle about her father's disappearance. "I thought I'd lost you," Amanda said. "I missed you so much."

"I knew you would come," Michelle replied in a mature voice. "But you look so strange and feel like cotton. Is it not a wondrous thing?"

"Well yes, but it's frightening too," Amanda said. "I can fly, and I remember endless serenity on another planet. Right now I feel very special."

"I had a fine life in England," Michelle said. "I was a princess and lived in a castle. I think father's medicine is a miracle and I am not afraid anymore. I wish everyone in the world could experience this knowing from the past."

Amanda wondered what the world would be like if Michelle's wish came true and all humans could take a peek into their previous lives. But her only concern at the moment was to get the antidote and change everyone back to current Earth time. Otherwise they'd be hunted down like alien intruders.

CHAPTER FIFTY-SIX

They left the truck in front of the hotel with Starbeam and Humfly concealed inside. Tony had stopped at a costume shore where Lizzy purchased two capes for Amanda and Tony. Their wings still looked bulky under the covers but it was all they could do in the short time they had. Amanda slid across the floor of the lobby behind Tony, Michelle and Lizzy. She managed to keep her feet on the polished marble.

The manager approached. "What is this?" he shouted, his face red and angry.

Amanda cast an innocent smile. "We were at a costume party at the American Consulate last night. "We're guests here with some friends."

"No, no, no, you cannot come in here." He waved them away.

"We're going to our rooms," Tony stated. "I'm expecting business associates and we have to remove our make-up and costumes." He led them toward the elevator, ignoring the frustrated manager.

Amanda began to float.

Tony laid one arm over her shoulder and held her down, whispering. "Small steps, take slow small steps."

Michelle pulled her mother's hand to keep her feet grounded.

The manager scurried after them, checking Amanda's feet, then pointed to Michelle's gown. "That's no costume—that's a flimsy negligee."

"You're insulting my daughter," Amanda protested. "She's dressed as a princess."

"These all-night parties," Tony shrugged. "You missed a good one." He stepped into the elevator and the others followed. The doors closed.

Inside Tony's suite now, Amanda became worried when the courier from Verbier hadn't arrived. "When will he get here, Tony?"

"He'd better show up with the antidote soon," he said, "or that irritating manager will foul things up."

Amanda slid onto the couch allowing room for her wings and motioned Michelle to sit down next to her. "Having my princess back is a miracle," she said with a warm smile. Dressed in a filmy empire gown with silk ribbons braided in her long blonde hair, her daughter really did look like a princess. "How old are you, Michelle?"

"Sixteen, I believe."

Lizzy sat at the computer scrolling through e-mails. She dropped the lid. "I'm tired of this get-up." She grabbed her green velvet cape that covered a heavy gown and pulled it off. "It's warm and cumbersome. And I don't like the memories of my former life. Queen Victoria's court was not very interesting except for everyone trying to manipulate each other which reminded me of Mother. Plus they didn't have computers back then. The food was plain—no hamburgers or pizza or diet Coke." She screwed up her nose.

"And did I mention the smell of equestrian poop? Can you imagine Father, how much horse dung there was on the roads? And how cold the castles were?"

Before he could answer, she continued. "You have no idea how much protocol and formality we went through just to appear regal. We bowed and curtseyed and flittered over needlepoint—I can't wait to return to my life as a modern teenager. How did I ever survive back then?"

Tony laughed. "People survived because that was all they knew and I'm sure they found ways to enjoy themselves."

"Well I'm ready to be me again."

"We all are," he said.

Amanda began to rise off the couch. Michelle pulled her down and set a crystal ashtray on her lap for counterweight. "I'm so glad you're back precious," Amanda said. "You still my little pumpkin?"

Michelle straightened up and nodded. "But how did you find us?"

Amanda glanced at Tony. "We never stopped believing and you're safe now. That's all that matters."

Michelle looked pensive. "I had a dream Mother, the same dream twice. A real knight attempted to rescue me. He carried a broad sword. I ran and ran through the field, and he called to me but I was too far away. And there was a castle on top of the hill. It began to rain and I got wet and couldn't see him anymore. Then I woke up."

She stared at her daughter and glanced at Tony. "That's similar to Howard's story."

"What about Howard?" Michelle asked. "Where is he?"

Amanda said, "Howard's at the museum with Rotar wrapping things up. He was very brave and helped save you with his sword."

"But he is all right, is he not?"

"He'll be here soon, sweetie, with Gaspard and Rotar." Anxious for his return, she didn't want to show it.

"I can't wait to see him." Michelle stared into the fireplace. "I recall my life but it feels strange. I don't know who I am anymore."

"How far you regressed depends on how much of the potion you swallowed," Tony said.

"Just a small gulp. It tasted awful, but once I changed I wanted to learn even more."

Amanda added, "You're who you were in your last life, or perhaps several lives ago, but your father took too much."

"You were with Father?"

She stroked her daughter's long hair. "Yes."

"Where is he?"

Amanda caught Tony's look, nodding for her to go ahead. Realizing she was on her own, she said, "I don't know. He's gone again."

"Can we look for him?"

Amanda felt sad for her daughter and noticed Michelle's pooling eyes. "You okay sweetie?"

Michelle's mouth turned into a pout. "Why did Father leave us again?"

"Wherever he's gone to pumpkin, he's free. Hold that in your heart." A loud knock on the door gave her hope.

"Who's there?" Tony shouted and looked through the peephole.

"Kemper from Verbier."

"That's my man." Tony opened the door.

Seeing Tony the agent hesitated.

He motioned the man inside. "It's okay, I'm Tony Ramsey. I've taken the chemical. How was your trip?"

An African-American tall enough to be a basketball player, Kemper cast serious and fearful eyes. He handed the bag to Tony, glancing at Amanda's wings. "I brought it sir, but I had a devil of a time getting out of Verbier. The airport was guarded and the roads were blocked, and the train station was crawling with police and press spreading rumors of some flying creatures." He stared at Amanda's wings again.

Tony frowned. "When this hits the news Uncle Jacques will become involved. Alert Dr. Vidollet to confine himself to the house until the media finds something else exciting. We'll take the antidote while you make the call to Verbier."

"Yes sir," Kemper said, taking out his mobile. He hesitated and gawked. "My apologies but I've never seen an angel before."

Tony said, "And we've never had wings before. I can only hope you brought enough of this stuff—"

Removing the bottle cap Tony took a large swallow and winced at the taste. "It's supposed to neutralize the regressive chemical and detoxify us on a vibrational level. It should happen in a matter of minutes."

Kemper pushed buttons on his phone while staring at Tony.

"You've seen nothing here the past few days," Tony added. "National security, understand? In fact, this is classified as global security."

The agent said, "Yes sir." He moved to the door and stood guard, still punching buttons but watching Tony.

Michelle fiddled with a magazine on the table. Amanda worried. Could her daughter become a little girl again? Lizzy was more than ready to return.

They all watched Tony's gradual return to his former self. The wings shrank and disappeared, his face and body more recognizable again. He wore his modern clothes.

"What a transformation," Lizzy said. "You look like Father again."

"It would be hard to say good-bye to wings," said Michelle.

Amanda felt relieved that Tony was back. She pushed the crystal ashtray aside and floated off the couch.

Tony offered her the bottle. "Everyone take about the same amount you took of the original chemical," he said. "That's what Dr. Vidollet advised and it worked for me."

"Can't wait to stop floating," Amanda said. "Yet I feel so free and my insecurities have vanished. Hope I will remember when I'm back." She took a large swig.

"I'll remind you," Tony said.

The green smelly liquid cooled her at once. She handed the bottle to Michelle who said, "I'm not sure I want to change."

"Drink." Amanda told her. "You don't want to relive a life that's over. This one is still ahead of you, sweetie."

Michelle sipped.

Tony passed the antidote to Elizabeth.

"I'll be glad to change," Lizzy said, swallowing fast.

Amanda felt her change begin, her brain down-shifting into a lower gear while her insides expanded, intensifying the process. Millions of tiny prickles darted through her veins. It didn't hurt but made her edgy.

Another knock on the door. Kemper turned to look out the peephole.

"Who's there?" Tony demanded while checking his twenty-first century face in the mirror over the fireplace.

"Police," the manager's voice answered. "Open the door at once."

Tony shook his head in disgust and turned to the others. Amanda, Michelle and Lizzy were still transforming. "Hold on a moment," he yelled. "We have important papers spread out. It will only take us a minute to secure everything." He lowered his voice and mumbled to Kemper, "Block the door."

"Open it now or we're coming in," the manager yelled. The jingle of a key outside slid into the lock. Someone pushed from the other side but Kemper held firm.

Amanda had completed the transformation but the girls were still changing.

"They'll break in soon, give them a bit more," Tony whispered to her.

She gave her daughter another sip and one to Lizzy.

They both swallowed hard.

The transformations sped up.

The manager and police continued pounding and pushing the door. Tony and Kemper held on. When the door opened, it shoved Tony out of the way. Amanda scooted in front of the girls.

The manager pointed at them. "There they are—scantily dressed floating creatures," he accused, then his eyes bugged.

Two police officers gazed at Amanda who crossed her arms and glared at them in her understated DC clothing. The two girls moved out from behind her and stared back at the officers in their modern attire.

One officer with puffy cheeks and a handlebar mustache removed his hat, holding it in front of him. "I see nothing unusual here. These are the aliens you called us about?"

The manager huffed. "We are too late—they have changed."

"Perhaps the drama on the local news has affected people's imagination," Officer Mustache said to his partner. "Let us go back to our rounds."

The manager's face swelled with rage, but he followed the officers out, slamming the door behind him.

Tony chuckled.

Amanda and the girls giggled.

Kemper wiped his brow. "That was close sir."

Tony went to his bathroom and came back with some of the green mixture in a water glass. "I'll take this to Starbeam and Humfly."

"Make sure there's enough for the others," Amanda said.

He nodded and motioned for Kemper to follow him as they hurried out the door with the antidote.

Amanda hugged Michelle and Lizzy. The girls had dark circles under their eyes. "You're both too pale."

"I like pale," Lizzy said, returning to her computer.

Michelle crinkled her nose. "McBoring… All that little girl stuff again. I kind of miss my other self. I knew so many things in my dreams, and I was all grown up…"

"I miss my powers too," Amanda said. "I never got to really try out my wings to their full capacity. But we still have our dreams and you need to enjoy your childhood." She looked away, anxious for Howard to show up and return to his youth again as quickly as possible. And they had to have enough for Leo Braun, too. Otherwise the winds would never stop. Rotar had made it very clear that the wrath of Aeolius would not cease until everyone was human again.

CHAPTER FIFTY-SEVEN

Tony and Kemper used the emergency stairs to go out the rear of the hotel, entering the kitchen through the staff entrance. The cook shifted from one pot to another, leaning away from the steam that rose from the evening soup.

"Could I trouble you for a bowl of oats?" Tony asked him.

The cook stared at him, curious. "We do not serve oatmeal at this hour *monsieur*."

In a calm voice Tony said, "Raw oats. Uncooked in a big bowl, please."

The cook shrugged and did as Tony asked, handing it to him.

Both men hurried outside to the truck and rolled open its rear door. Barnyard odors overwhelmed them. In need of privacy they stepped inside, switched on a flashlight and rolled the door back down.

Tony mixed the antidote into the oats and offered it to the horse first. Starbeam snorted and pulled back. "You must eat this," Tony insisted. "It will help you."

Starbeam nibbled, and while chewing, blew air at the mixture. Tony held his nose. "He's blowing the smell my way."

Kemper shifted to another spot. "Mine too."

Humfly hummed and watched. "You're next," said Tony.

Starbeam began transforming while the pig grunted and ate. The smell didn't bother her. Kemper watched, bobbing his head at the pig as if to hurry the process.

The rear door squeaked and rolled up, catching Tony off guard. They'd forgotten to lock themselves in.

The manager pointed an accusing finger. "Ah ha!" he shouted, waving a clinking ring of master keys at Starbeam and Humfly.

"That is the horse in the newspaper and now it is here in front of my hotel!"

Starbeam snorted and sprayed gold dust on the keys. They disintegrated into small particles.

The manager's disbelieving eyes bulged. He ran back into the hotel shouting for the police.

Kemper chased after him.

Tony jerked the door down, but found nowhere to lock it. "Hurry," he told the two animals. "Change, you rascals, change…"

Both animals continued their metamorphosis. Starbeam's silver coat slowly disappeared, replaced by brown hair. His wings shrank away as though collapsing into his shoulders. Natural hooves appeared over the silver ones. Humfly's colorful adornments popped one-by-one and vanished. The helicopter horns and saddle shrank out of sight, returning the pig to its pink skin and curly tail.

Tony heard the manager arguing outside with Kemper. He waited.

When the horse finished its mutation, Starbeam showed gray hairs mixed in with the brown. Tony stroked its neck and turned to Humfly. "You seem a bit large, Humfly, and your belly's sagging. Did you eat too much?" He didn't expect an answer but Humfly looked happy.

Someone pounded on the back of the van. Tony sneezed. "I'm allergic again," he said to the horse and unlocked the door.

It rolled up and the manager leaned inside. "They've changed," he shrieked, pointing. "That horse destroyed my keys."

The same two policemen looked inside and surveyed the truck. The plain brown horse and pink pig stared back at them.

Kemper folded his arms. Tony waited.

"That's the flying horse," the manager bellowed. "And the helicopter pig the teenage girl described on television. I saw them before this man changed them back. Do something!" he told the officers.

When the manager turned away Tony pointed one finger to the side of his head and twirled it in the loose-screw sign. The officers saw it and nodded.

Humfly snorted and relieved herself. Yellow pig-urine crept across the floor toward the open door. The men stepped back and watched it dribble over the edge onto the street. The manager's face puffed red and his hands clenched.

"That pig will make a good ham one day," said the officer with the mustache

His partner added, "Perhaps if you drink a little less *monsieur?*" he said to the furious manager. A garbled voice came over his walkie-talkie in French. "We must go. There are outer-space Unicorns attacking alien pranksters in the park."

Both officers laughed.

"But I swear I saw it," the manager insisted. "I never drink before evening. I could not keep this job if I did. He's done something to the animals. They looked very different only a few minutes ago. They were alien creatures, I'm telling you."

Officer Mustache winked at Tony. "You mean our outer-space tourist clipped the wings of his space animals right here in the truck?"

"Yes. I mean no. He gave them something to eat—something from the kitchen. My cook gave it to him."

Officer Mustache climbed into the truck and looked around. "What did you give to the animals?"

Tony sneezed. "Oats. They were hungry so I got raw oats for them."

"Fine. Sorry to disturb you." In a lowered voice the officer said to the manager, "Maybe a long vacation and some rest would help. This is my recommendation." He climbed out of the truck.

"But it is the truth," the manager argued, his voice full of frustration.

"Even if it is, there is no law against feeding oats to a horse or a pig." He held up his palms. "We can do nothing."

The manager fumed. "Fine! Forget it. I will have a word with your superior."

"As you wish." The policemen tipped their hats and left. The manager stomped back into the hotel.

Kemper stood guard at the rear of the truck.

Tony noticed gold dust scattered on the street. Thankfully the manager had missed it. The pig urine had distracted him. He laughed. "Wait'll Rotar, Howard and Leo arrive. I'll have to warn them."

Kemper grunted. "The poor guy seems ready for a nervous breakdown."

"I don't like it either, but I had to discredit him. He could still ruin everything."

Tony patted the animals. "All we have left from you Starbeam, is some green space dung that will be sent to the US for analysis. And nothing from you Humfly except ordinary pig pee."

"I can't wait for this assignment to be over," Kemper said.

A moment later Gaspard pulled up behind them. Howard jumped out and clambered into the truck. "You have returned to yourself again, Tony. The horse and the pig as well. I was anxious that the animals might not survive."

"They're fine, and you'll be okay too," Tony said. "We have the antidote upstairs."

Howard looked concerned. "Are the others truly well again?"

Tony nodded.

"That is grand news, but I shall surely miss myself. It has been exceedingly pleasurable to live as a knight."

"You're a brave knight, Howard. I'm proud of you."

Howard beamed. "The Russians took Andersen and his men back to his laboratory."

"Good. I'll notify the Swiss authorities."

Braun got out of the SUV and hunched behind the truck, sneezing out of control. Gaspard kept a firm grip on him. Rotar joined them and waved to Tony. "Is my ancient book still safe, master?"

"Yes, but stop calling me master. I'm Tony now. But let's hurry upstairs." He turned to Kemper. "Will you guard Starbeam and Humfly while I oversee the antidote?

"My pleasure sir."

Tony said to Gaspard, "Your wife's waiting for you upstairs. I'll call you later. We'll be using the kitchen door and fire stairs. Otherwise the manager might have a heart attack."

Gaspard said, "Forget the manager. You are all guests here." He dashed into the hotel ahead of them.

With reluctance Tony led Howard, Braun and Rotar inside. Braun sneezed and growled, attracting attention in the lobby. The manager rushed up and stared wild-eyed at Braun and Howard, then backed away.

Tony said, "They're only in costume on their way to change."

"Never mind," said the manager. "I see nothing—you are not here." He scurried away muttering and slicking back his hair.

Tony felt bad for the man. "International protocol might not approve," he whispered to the others, "but when he realizes he's sane, he could stir up the media or post something on line." Tony worried also about the cell phone the manager always carried. Had he taken pictures? Dear god, he hoped not.

CHAPTER FIFTY-EIGHT

When Tony entered his suite with Howard, Braun and Rotar, Amanda rushed over to greet her son. Michelle joined her. "Mommy, Mommy, it's the man in my dream. He's here…"

"That's your brother, pumpkin."

Lizzy studied Howard, pinching her mouth to suppress a laugh. "You have a better chance as yourself, 'Howie'," she said. "With those funny leggings and that weird shirt… A real photo op."

Michelle moved closer to inspect him. "But he's the man in my dream who tried to help me in the field near the castle."

Howard smiled. "Yes, 'twas I." He pulled out his sword and waved it at Braun. "And this time I pinned down this evil demon with my sword so that Mother and Tony might have a chance to rescue you."

Michelle stepped back, shaken. "You don't look or sound like Howard…"

He knelt down on one knee and grasped his sister's shoulders with care. "I drank some of Father's potion and became a knight. I came here to lend aid to the others."

She blushed. "You did all that for me?"

"I had to, did I not? After all, you are my sister."

"For sure, Howie."

Amanda handed the antidote to Howard.

"Wait," he said, turning to Rotar. "If I returned to my world, would I be able to live there?"

Amanda gasped.

Rotar linked his hands behind his back and paced, staring at the floor. Then he stopped. "Yes, but the consequences could be severe. If you survive the journey they might consider you a warlock with the knowledge you would bring from the twenty-first century. And they might decide to kill you. If you take the antidote you will become Howard again. Think of it like a downstream being returning to current time. You do not belong there now and your knowledge would be alien and frightening to them. You could end up leading a solitary life and making many enemies."

Amanda pressed the bottle at Howard—there was nothing else to say.

He frowned and drank.

Then she passed the antidote to Tony. He poured some in a cup for Braun who guzzled the liquid between sneezes.

The others watched the two men mutate back to their bodies and modern clothes.

Howard stared down at his leg. "I'm crippled again," he complained.

After giving her son a comforting hug, Amanda turned to Rotar who looked upset. "What's wrong?" she asked him.

"You are all yourselves again, but I am still an alien."

"But you're our hero," she said. "Without your help we wouldn't have survived."

"But I am short and all of you are tall. Even Michelle will grow tall one day, but not me. I will always be an outcast here."

Amanda touched his cheek. "You're the tallest man I've ever known. Brave and fearless and wise. A champion." She looked to her children. "Would you like to invite Rotar to come with us to Washington?"

"Yes!" Michelle blurted.

"McNeato, Mom," said Howard. "Will you come home with us Rotar? I've got lots of cool stuff to show you."

Michelle ran and threw her arms around Rotar. "Puleeeze?"

Howard dragged his leg and shook Rotar's hand. Even Lizzy spoke up. "Awesome!"

"We could use your magic in America," said Amanda.

Rotar's eyes filled with dancing hearts. "Do you mean it?"

Amanda smiled and nodded. "Of course. Stay as long as you like."

Rotar's face brightened. "May I bring a few of my things?"

She hesitated. "What kind of things?"

"Just some books and my infinity candle."

"Infinity candle?"

"Yes, the children have seen it. And after I gather a few things I will seal my cave again so that no one can disturb it."

"What about your dingle dipper," Elizabeth hurried to say. "You can't leave *that* behind."

"Yeah," Michelle added with a grin.

"Mind telling me what that is?" Amanda asked.

"A cool ice cream maker from Rotarious," Howard said.

Amanda shrugged, "Is that all. Very well, bring that too."

"And don't forget your eternity eyes," Lizzy added.

"Dare I ask for an explanation?" Amanda asked.

All three kids shook their heads and laughed.

Braun sat by the window whimpering between sneezes. Dark stains covered his clothing and bandaged head. His arm was back in a sling.

"Leo," Tony said, "I've arranged transportation for you back to the US with agent Kemper."

Braun sneezed again and wiped his nose with his sleeve. "You can't do that."

"I already have."

"By what authority?"

"The *highest*."

Amanda looked at him. "I don't understand?"

Tony said, "He's my brother-in-law."

Her eyes widened. "That guy Sam is your brother-in-law?"

"No way," Braun said.

Tony laughed. "Not Sam Henry—the President."

"You're joking," Braun said.

Amanda stilled.

Tony shook his head. "No joke. My sister is our First Lady."

"Sam Henry never told me," Braun said, lifting his arm to sneeze into his elbow. He eyed Rotar with anger. "I was supposed to stop sneezing once I got myself back."

Rotar lifted his shoulders. "I told you nothing of the sort. That curse will be with you for five generations."

"Get me some handi-wipes, you wormy, squirmy, double-dealing shrimp," Braun whined.

"Enough," Tony said, tossing him a box of tissues. "Sam Henry never told you because he's dating my ex-wife. He does whatever she tells him."

"What?" Braun howled. "Sam's a puppet for your ex-wife? He can't do anything to squash you?"

"'Fraid not. My sister has more clout and it infuriates my ex—and Sam Henry, too."

Nestled between her children on the couch Amanda's mind raced so fast she forgot to breathe. How could he have kept that secret from her? Why didn't he tell her?

Tony continued, "So you're not the only one with important relatives, Leo."

Braun sneezed and glowered at Rotar. "You little devil."

Rotar smiled. "Talking like that will not endear you to the universal lords who can help."

"The who?"

"The lords of forgiveness. You must show them some gesture of forgiveness if you expect forgiveness for yourself."

Braun sneezed again. "I forgive. Now take away the curse and make me stop sneezing."

Rotar shook his head. "It does not work that way. The forgiveness must be real and must come from your heart. When it does, your curse will blow away with the wind."

He sneezed again. "I don't believe you."

Rotar shrugged.

Tony took Braun's arm. "He's going with Kemper now—I'll be right back."

Amanda gripped the edge of the seat cushion and inhaled hard. Had she known Tony's background and connections she might have gone home from London with her children and avoided all this crazy mess that they just barely got out of. Peter's discovery must have been so important that the most powerful leader in the world became involved.

She shivered, knowing her own lack of good sense had for a short time been known to the President of the United States.

And Tony still liked her.

That thought gave her chills. They shared a love of music but the rest of his world was on a different planet. Or was it? They had known each other on Androdon, if she could trust his recollection of their lives there…

And there it was again. Could she ever trust him now?

CHAPTER FIFTY-NINE

Amanda sat frozen on the couch with her arms wrapped around Michelle and Howard. It was hard to let go because then she would have to decide what to do next.

Tony returned and went to the window. "The wind has calmed. Want your book now, Rotar?"

He nodded.

Tony got it from the bedroom and handed it to him. Rotar clutched it to his chest. "Glad to see everything is back to normal," Tony added.

"I'm not normal," Howard said, scooting off the couch and smacking his braced leg with the palm of his hand.

Amanda didn't know how to comfort him.

Rotar stopped looking over Lizzy's shoulder at the laptop and turned. "You must exercise patience," he said to Howard.

"But I've been waiting twelve years," he argued.

"Time is of no consequence; you have many years to heal."

"I only have about sixty or seventy years left if I'm lucky. There's no time to waste."

Rotar sighed. "Time is an illusion Howard." He offered him the purple rock. "If you insist you may use this for healing, but you must know there could be a price to pay…"

Howard took it. "Are you sure the rock can heal me?"

Rotar nodded. "If you truly believe it can…"

Amanda felt anxious. If it didn't work, Howard would be devastated. If it did work, then what? Rotar mentioned consequences. She interrupted. "I'm not comfortable with this Rotar."

"It will be all right," Rotar told her

"Mom I want to try!" Howard shouted. He clutched the rock and closed his eyes. "Heal my leg please," he whispered. "I want that with all of my heart."

Amanda held back tears.

Tony clenched his jaw but said nothing.

Howard squeezed his eyes tighter. "Please heal me. Please."

A glow of light lit up in the rock. Tiny crystals sprang from it encircling Howard's left leg. "It feels warm," he said without opening his eyes.

He shook his leg. It straightened out.

His eyes popped open. He dropped the rock. "My leg!" he shouted almost ripping off the brace.

"Let me help you," Tony said. He pulled out a pocket knife with a screwdriver and dismantled the brace.

Howard flung it in the corner and scurried around the room. "It worked, I'm cured! I can play sports—I can do anything!" He rushed to Rotar and hugged him. "Thank you, thank you, again and again, forever." He continued to move about the room.

Rotar blushed in rainbow colors. "No gratitude is necessary. You and the rock did it Howard."

Amanda cried and hugged her son. Michelle jumped up and down in front of her brother. "You're healed," she squealed. She stopped jumping and picked up the rock. In a hushed tone she said, *"X-pro-zer-gun-to? Ma-shi-nee-wook…"*

Amanda stared at Michelle. "What did you say, sweetie?"

Michelle shrugged. "It was a man—sort of like Daddy."

"What?!" Amanda glanced in confusion at Rotar. "What's going on?"

He didn't answer.

"Michelle?"

"It's nothing Mommy," she chased after Howard.

After jumping all over the room Howard stopped to rest. "So if the rock can heal me, why can't you just use the rock to grow tall, Rotar?"

"It does not work for those of us from Rotarious—it only has powers here on Earth and works only on humans. I am not human."

"Have you tried?"

Rotar nodded. "I asked the moment the rock fell into my possession."

Michelle raised hopeful eyes. "But you can fix all the sick people on Earth with your rock, can't you?"

"I have pondered such things many times…but my master Aeolius forbids it. Humans are here to learn, and if life is too easy, what would become of research or advancement?"

Howard flexed and twisted his leg, glowing with excitement.

Rotar continued. "I made this small exception today because Howard has demonstrated bravery and loyalty as well as compassion and has earned it."

"We're all grateful for that," Amanda said. "But I can't help wondering why my daughter talks to a rock? She's done it before."

Rotar's reply was curt. "You asked her and she said it was nothing."

"I don't believe it." She turned to Michelle. "What were you saying?"

Michelle ran to Rotar and clung to him… "They told me not to tell anyone…"

"Who?!!!!" Amanda cried.

Rotar cleared his throat. "The child has not translated properly. They do not want to harm her."

"Who are 'they'?"

"We call them Inter-planetaries," Rotar said in a calm voice. "They originated at one time from a distant planet, but they are rogues now, like insects roaming the universe. They communicate through the rock. Michelle just happened to hear them, that is all."

"That's all?" Amanda's breathing escalated. "This is incredulous. How big are they? Can they reach her? Are they here on Earth?"

"Insects may not be the correct description. Perhaps space rodents? And as to their size, I do not know, and I have never heard of them coming here. It is too chaotic a place. But I beg you not to concern yourself. I will explore the matter further on my own."

Tony cleared his throat for attention. "Since Rotar has offered to investigate the mysterious voices, let's all go out together. I'll call Gaspard and Lotus for that tour and then we can go to dinner to celebrate Howard's new leg. The kids are starving. What do you say, Amanda?"

She drew a long, deep breath to un-stress. "I wholeheartedly agree."

"You're coming Rotar?" Tony asked him.

"If it is all right with Amanda."

"Of course, Rotar. You're half the reason we're celebrating. Howard and the girls are the other half. Please join us."

Tony said, "Good. After a scenic tour we can fortify ourselves at one of my favorite restaurants, the au Parc des Eaux-Vives. It's in an old mansion with a lakeside view and serves a terrific *racelette*. In the morning we can fly to Verbier and say good bye to Uncle Jacques and transport Dr. Vidollet back to Geneva. Is everyone okay with that?"

Cheers, claps and nods.

Amanda said, "But I'm not leaving this room until you tell us exactly what you do Tony. The faster you talk the sooner we'll eat."

He lifted his arms in appeal. "All in good time, Amanda. We have the entire evening before us."

She could see that it irritated him but didn't care. "Then now's the perfect time. Begin."

"Since you insist," Tony said with reluctance. "I'll just give Gaspard a quick call."

He hung up with Gaspard and leaned his elbow on the fireplace mantel. "Now then," he said, "I was on a special assignment by order from my brother-in-law, and given *carte blanche* to investigate Peter."

Amanda planted fists on her hips. "Who put you on Peter's trail in the first place?"

"Marta. She turned him in anonymously, concerned that his research had gone too far. Then you led me to her and to her lab."

Amanda relaxed. "So Marta has some redeeming qualities after all. And the rest?"

He squirmed. "Most of it is true. I'm still an amateur musical conductor on occasion but I gave up my law practice to work as a consultant for the Federal Air and Space Agency."

"Doing?"

"Investigating UFO sightings, crop markings, animal mutations, extraterrestrial biological entities, anything and everything that's alien or unexplainable in our world. Paranormal activities, psychic powers, you name it, I check it out."

"Keen!" Howard shouted.

"Wow!" Michelle added.

"Cool!" said Lizzy.

"And your seating arrangement on the flight to London?" asked Amanda.

"Arranged..."

Amanda grunted. "I knew it. And the gray car cruising my house?"

"We didn't know how far Peter had experimented or if he'd contact you...it was a matter of National..."

"Never mind," Amanda huffed.

"I knew you weren't just practicing law Dad," Lizzy said.

"When Elizabeth popped up in London, she was instructed not to mention our White House connection under any circumstances. She held her tongue but knew only that I worked abroad as an attorney."

"You both kept your secrets well," Amanda said. "I'm thankful my precious children are back to normal but I'm not sure I'll ever be." She took a breath before continuing. "So what's the Russian connection?"

"We work with them tracking UFO sightings. They have a vast storehouse of information from years of paranormal investigations and experiments. It's one of the few areas where we can work together. But Peter's discovery was up for grabs. The wrong people on both sides got involved."

Amanda put her hands to her head. "After all this can I ever live a routine life again?"

Tony smiled. "Life has a way of taking us along if we let it, but none of you will be able share this with anyone. Understand? If you need help to unscramble or store away what you've experienced, we have professional psychologists who can deal with that."

Could therapy heal the trauma they'd been through? She didn't know. "I might want to take advantage of your offer when we get home, Tony, but there's something that can't. Before this happened I believed there was only so much to learn and very little left to discover. Enough for a reasonable lifespan to contain. Now I see that my life is an eternity and this world is only a tiny part of a much fuller existence. I've even discovered a different color to my soul."

"What do you mean?" Tony asked.

"You'll think I'm crazy but I always thought souls were filmy white—like gauze. That's how it looks when we spread white light on things to create peace and harmony and love. There are groups of people who do that."

Tony nodded. "There are many who believe in that energy."

"Yes, well, the point I'm trying to make is that when I became Verilla, my soul was no longer white. I felt the color pink—a soft, misty pink. What does that mean?"

"I felt colors too, Mommy," Michelle blurted. "I was yellow like daffodils."

"I was soft green," Elizabeth said in a casual manner.

"Royal purple," Howard said. "My color was purple…"

Tony paced the room and paused. "Now that you've brought it up I felt a different color too but mine was sky blue and encompassed my entire being. The forest on Androdon was blue and pink, not green like forests here. It was just like the flashback I had on the flight when I first met you, Amanda."

"But I saw the blue and pink forests too," she said. "What do you suppose it means?"

"I don't know if it means anything," Tony said. "Those are the energy colors of Androdon. Perhaps in each life we pick up the energy of our surroundings and it coincides with our growth. It's a perplexing question and in my research I hope to find answers."

Tony clapped his hands. "Right, team. We can share our secrets with each other but not with anyone else unless you clear it first with me or Amanda, got it? Orders from the top."

The children and Rotar looked up and nodded.

And remember," he added, "this is real life, not a game. What you do can have serious consequences. Lives can be endangered including your own. We're a family now and need to protect one another. That's our safety net."

Lizzy said, "I'm not part of the family."

"Of course you are," Tony said. "You're my daughter."

"You don't care about me, Dad. I have to go back to Mom who I hate. You'll all have each other in DC but I'll have no one."

Tony blinked. "You won't be alone Elizabeth. I've got a proposal in mind to present to your mother and I think it'll work. But let's get ready now for our tour."

He turned to Rotar. "Now that you're joining Amanda and her family would you be interested in helping me with UFO research? You know more about outer space than I do."

"I would be honored." Rotar bowed, his smile exuberant. "But I must decide what to do with the Silver Book," he added.

"Perhaps I can help you with that, Rotar. I have a plan to discuss with you later."

"Very well."

"I can help you too, Dad," Lizzy said.

He smiled. "I'll have lots of research that you could assist with. You're on."

Gaspard and Lotus arrived. Tony greeted them. "Gaspard, will the two of you join us for a celebration dinner?"

"Of course," said Gaspard. He and Lotus looked pleased.

"Agent Kemper is returning the animals to the farm this afternoon," Tony told him. "Then we'll be returning to the US."

Gaspard nodded. "Perhaps one day Lotus and I will visit your country."

"You're invited any time. We owe you a great deal, Gaspard. It will be a pleasure to have you there. In the Spring perhaps? That's the most beautiful time."

"Thank you *Monsieur* Ramsey," Gaspard said. "We look forward to it."

The children moved about in excitement, anxious to leave.

"Do you want to say good-bye to the animals?" Tony asked them.

They nodded eagerly. Amanda noticed Howard slip the purple rock into his pocket just before they rushed out the door.

At the back of the truck the children petted and patted Starbeam and Humfly. Kemper had secured Braun in the front seat.

Amanda had an uneasy feeling about returning to Washington. She'd been so focused on their child-rescue mission that she wondered how she'd find the strength to deal with the divorce. She watched the children say good bye to the animals. A loud whine and then a scream pierced the air.

Howard grabbed the purple rock from his pocket. "It's vibrating again," he said. It glowed red in his hand.

He dropped it and the two-tailed cat sprang from its center, landing and falling over. It struggled to get up but its hind leg was crippled and shorter than the other legs. The cat wailed.

Howard pointed at it. "Mooooommmm?!"

Amanda gulped. "What's wrong with Dot Comet's leg?"

"*Ze-he-brak.*" Michelle yelled.

The cat shook its bad leg, attempting to straighten it.

Rotar swished his stick. "*Ter-ra-longia Mert-za,*" he commanded.

Dot Comet leapt forward but the bad leg dragged.

"This is what concerned me," Rotar said.

"What's happened?" Amanda cried.

"The rock healed Howard, but the cat..."

"Can you fix it?" she interrupted, not wanting to believe that Howard's victory had become the cat's misfortune...

"I shall try."

Howard looked at Rotar, devastated.

Rotar said, "I must seek the answer in the silver book."

CHAPTER SIXTY

Amanda woke to a sunny day in Geneva. The wind had calmed leaving the air clean and fresh. She attempted a deep breath but her head ached from too much wine the night before. She hugged her knees, trying to negate her thoughts of how close they'd all come to extinction.

At a tap on the door she whispered, "Who is it?" The soft words stabbed her head.

"It's me," Tony said. "I brought your breakfast. Come on out."

She got up and used the bathroom, wrapping herself in a fleecy robe. A breakfast tray adorned with a single red rose sat on the table in her small living room. "Good morning," Tony said in a cheerful tone. "The others are downstairs eating and I've brought good news."

She groaned, holding her forehead. "What? That none of this really happened and it was all a bad dream?" Right away she regretted her harsh reply.

"If it wasn't real Howard wouldn't be downstairs showing off his new leg. He's been skipping around the lobby all morning."

She managed to smile. "I'm glad, but he'll just create more suspicion. The hotel staff was aware of his limp."

"We can say he's recovered from an accident that required a temporary brace. The manager will refute their concerns anyway. I'm afraid we've turned him into a broken man."

She looked out the window. "Speaking of breaks, I can't seem to face the reality of going home without my husband."

"Do you still want him?"

"Of course not. But how can I get on with my life if I don't know whether he's dead or alive?"

"Give it time. As a lawyer I can help you with any legal details. And you never know, he might even show up. Would you like to hear the good news?"

She saw his eager smile. "Sure. And thanks for the rose. It's nature's perfection."

"Not even close to you. It amazes me how some people can look so beautiful even if they're exhausted or hung over."

"I don't feel beautiful."

"You will. Dr. Vidollet called—he's not coming back to Coppet."

"Why not?"

"He and Uncle Jacques hit it off. They want to collaborate on their research. A nice arrangement don't you think?"

She blinked. "That's wonderful news. I was worried about him now that the barn is gone. Will the neighbor continue caring for his sheep?"

Tony nodded. "Vidollet has arranged all that."

"This is a great turn of events. Now the two doctors will have each other's company and hopefully the 'La La' dog will get along with Fanny the goose." Her morning mood lifted by a smile, she said, "I still have to do something with Peter's farm, or what's left of it."

Tony poured himself a cup of coffee. "That property is extremely valuable with its lake-front view. I can help you arrange for a sale or rebuild or whatever you want later, but until Peter is found or declared legally dead, you won't be able to dispose of it."

Her face fell.

"There's more good news," he said in a teasing tone. "I have something for you." He pointed to a covered side plate on the breakfast tray. She lifted the small silver dome but instead of toast it held an envelope.

"I've been busy this morning," he said. "This might brighten your day."

She stared at the heavy vellum square envelope, her name written in blue ink. She pushed back her messy hair and felt awkward. "What's this?"

"Open it."

She read the handwritten invitation out loud. *"The President and First Lady have cordially invited you and your family for a celebratory dinner to honor your achievement in Switzerland."*

"What?" Stunned, she looked at Tony.

His face lit up. "Rotar's included and I'm available if you need an escort. I'm hoping we can continue seeing each other as ordinary citizens."

She waved the card. "This is far from ordinary."

"You must know that I like you Amanda."

Her intuition told her to give him a chance but her intuition had failed her with Peter. "And I like you Tony. Or is it Master Teppen?" She smiled. "And the children like…"

"Yes the children," he interrupted. "I've already started making arrangements for Elizabeth to live with me. She's ecstatic."

"Won't her mother object?"

He shook his head. "My ex was after me for a presidential appointment to the Embassy in Paris for her boyfriend Sam Henry. Now that Braun is out of the picture I offered him Braun's job in Geneva and they've accepted, but I also made a little side deal with the ex. In return for that favor I get custody of Lizzy."

The news lifted her mood like a sunny morning bloom. Elizabeth would be happy and Amanda had a White House visit to look forward to. She almost jumped up in excitement but remembered her headache just in time to avoid jarring it.

Tony's smile was understanding. "Are we ready to return to Washington?"

She nodded and hoped she wasn't trading one problem for another. But then again she hadn't committed herself to anything but a White House visit. And she was still married to Peter.

He caught her eyes. "How about a challenge for us both?"

"What?"

"If you give up chocolate, I'll quit smoking."

"You'll quit?"

"I'll try. I'm told it won't be easy."

She laughed. "Like this little adventure was easy? Quitting chocolates will be a breeze, especially now that I've gained weight from excessive consumption of it. Too much fat and sugar."

She thought of Hillary's Godiva chocolates. "But I'll miss the Godiva chocolates and the Swiss truffles and the Cadbury's," she said, casting a humorous look at him. "Kidding, but I haven't longed for any since yesterday. I might not need that anymore. Perhaps it was my security blanket like Peter always claimed, but now I feel like I can accomplish anything without them."

She saw that he was pleased. "Good for you," he said. "And your father? And your marriage?"

Her eyes drifted to the floor. Hesitant she said, "I've been thinking about that too and I know I have to forgive, forget and let go. I'm going to get some therapy when I get home."

"Glad to hear it. I went through weeks of divorce recovery and it helped me deal with the loss."

She snuffled. "Never thought I'd ever have to deal..." she looked up at him, "but back to the present, I still have to call Hillary and let her off the hook. Except for the flying insects in Verbier, which I really don't know anything about, I can honestly tell her there are no flying horses, no flying pigs and no extraterrestrial beings, and she can write her commentary about her own beliefs of what happened. And I need to update her on Peter: Location unknown or missing in action." She shook her head. "He's not in the military. Location unknown sounds best."

"Temporarily unknown," Tony said with a warm smile. "I'll leave you to finish breakfast and get your things together. Then we'll check out. I'll gather the troops."

Someone banged on Tony's door next door. Amanda gulped, reminded of the manager from the day before. "I'll see who that is," Tony said.

She followed him and listened from the connecting door.

"You want what?" she heard Tony say to someone.

"This is not a good time. You'll need to come back with a warrant," he added. The hall door banged shut.

She went into his living room. "Who was that?"

"The manager wanted to inspect the room. He had the hotel security officer with him this time."

Her mind whirled. The kids were downstairs. Frantic, she asked, "Who has the book?"

Tony wavered a moment. "Rotar took it but he's downstairs having breakfast. I saw it last night in your suite."

They hunted around in her living room. Tony found it under Rotar's blanket on the sofa bed and grabbed it.

"Thank God," Amanda said. "I figured it was here because the punishing winds haven't returned today either. I hope it lasts."

He didn't comment. "Hold on to this with your life," he said. "I'll round up the others and we'll be on our way. Now that Rotar has agreed to turn the book over to the US authorities we need to get it safely back to DC as fast as possible."

His words jolted her thoughts. Back to reality arriving with the speed of a bullet train. "Yes, well I'm anxious to get home anyway. I want to take some classes in Philosophy."

He looked at her, puzzled. "A bit far afield from music, isn't it?"

"Music is an expression of the soul. I grew up a Protestant and often wondered about life after death. What couldn't be explained tended to be dismissed. I have so many unanswered questions and want to learn more."

"Will you have time for all that?"

"I can take classes on-line. I've always put my personal needs on the back burner. I need to arrange some activities for myself."

He pondered a moment. "Sounds like you're making yourself very busy."

"Better than dealing with a missing husband, don't you think?"

He avoided the comment and said, "We'll be doing a lot of soul-searching after this experience. I think your plan is a good one."

She nodded with a look of confident resolve.

CHAPTER SIXTY-ONE

One week later, a white limousine approached the gates leading to the White House. Light snow signaled an early winter. Amanda watched out the limo windows along with Tony, Lizzy, Howard, Michelle and Rotar. She gazed at the large trees spreading frost-laden limbs across expansive lawns. The evening light of a full moon lit the area, melding with the glow of the White House decorations. The structure looked like a crystal ice palace with thousands of tiny lights flickering in the trees and outlining the windows.

"Will the President know who I am, Mommy?" Michelle asked.

"Yes, pumpkin." She winked at Tony.

"Do you think he'll like my new dress?"

"He'll love it. You look adorable in pink."

"Will he give Howard an award too for being so brave?"

"I don't know dearest."

"And what about Lizzy?" she asked with concern in her voice. Elizabeth wore a maroon velvet dress with matching coat and fur-trimmed hat. Amanda thought she looked regal.

"Wait and see sweetie."

"I'm glad you're getting one Mommy."

"Me, too," Tony added. "Perhaps we'll all receive a special commendation." He eyed Amanda. "How're you doing on your chocolate ban?"

"I fell off the wagon but at least I'm down to one a day—as needed. How's your withdrawal from nicotine?"

Tony sighed.

"He's been a grouchy bear," Lizzy said. "I caught him sneaking a few drags outside."

"I'm on meds now and they seem to help," he said.

"Looking forward to this Rotar?" Amanda asked, just to change the subject.

Michelle butted in. "I wanted to play my tambourine for the President," she whined.

"Yeah, and I've been practicing my guitar," Howard added.

"We're not ready," said Elizabeth. "We need to practice together as an ensemble. Anyway they didn't invite us to play music for them. They can get any professional musicians they want."

"I guessssss," Michelle said, pouting.

Rotar clutched the silver book tied together with a gold ribbon and squirmed on the seat. "This tuxedo is tight and makes me uncomfortable. I am not sure I like this award business, dressing up and facing a grandiose ceremony. I am not accustomed to such things. I am merely a solitary cave dweller, not a costumed monkey."

Howard snickered and pulled on the bowtie clamped to the collar of his white tuxedo shirt. "Maybe you were a monkey in one of your former lives."

"Careful or I will turn *you* into one," Rotar warned, but then he chuckled. "I was sent here to put this book into the right hands at the correct time in history. By passing it on to the proper authority, my master Aeolius is appeased. This time I hope I am giving it to the right person." He brushed his hand across the book. "But I am worried about Dot Comet. I have not yet found her a solution."

Tony said, "You'll still have access to the book, and turning it over for study is important to the world."

Rotar nodded.

The limo pulled up to the front door of the White House.

"Let's go meet the President," Amanda said, squeezing Tony's hand. "Howard, please leave your sword in the car. Rotar, would you leave your stick and rock also?"

"Must I?"

"Bring the book, but leave the magic. I'd appreciate it," she added. "We don't want any accidents."

Rotar pushed his stick under the seat but stared at the floor in concern. "I will leave my stick but I cannot leave the rock with Dot Comet inside. She is still injured."

Amanda frowned. "Very well but keep it hidden and let no one touch it." She noticed Howard turning away, his brows pinched in pain. She rubbed him between his shoulder blades and he relaxed, flashing a half smile. "Thanks Mom."

Michelle muttered, *"Ze-fren-to De-tong-lia?"*

"There she goes again, Mom," Howard complained.

Amanda puffed out air. "What did you say, Michelle?"

Grinning she said, "We're going on a long trip Mommy."

"We are? Will it be a good one?"

"I hope so." Michelle kicked the seat and grinned.

Rotar tapped the silver book. "We will need the book for our journey."

Amanda's desire to question Michelle further was halted when a man dressed in a black uniform jacket trimmed in gold braid and white pants opened the limousine door and helped them out of the car.

The team gathered in the First Couple's private living room where proper introductions were made. Tony had arranged for an informal viewing of the Hillary's special Thanksgiving report, and the TV was already tuned to the evening event. Amanda thought of her friend's call the day before, advising her that a group picture taken in Geneva showed Rotar's eyes with small gold stars in the centers. She had cringed at the news, but Hillary had agreed to keep the photograph to herself and not use it. Amanda was fully aware that they would have to protect Rotar from others like

Stefan Andersen and his goons. And she didn't know how long the authorities would contain Leo Braun, but at least they had him in custody. All of them had witnessed Rotar's unique powers.

When everyone settled into comfortable seating, Amanda turned her attention to the large television screen. The camera faded in on Hillary standing in front of the altar at the Washington Cathedral. A holiday cornucopia of food peaked behind her between large candles that brightened the dim lights in the massive nave. Ethnically diverse school children wearing native costumes of their heritage sat in a semi-circle on either side of her. Each held a candle. Hillary's blonde hair had been pulled into a short ponytail and her expression looked professional but somber. She raised her microphone and began.

"For the past few weeks the eyes of the world have been tuned to events in a small village in Switzerland to confirm or deny the existence of an extraterrestrial visitor from another planet. Rumors claimed an alien came here from Mars, the planet known in ancient times as the planet of war. Others say the visitor came from a star millions of light-years away. One report proposed that a scientist discovered a drug capable of regressing the human soul to former lives. The media has not confirmed or denied any of these suppositions.

"Eyewitnesses also reported that an outer-space rodent, a flying horse and a living mechanical pig, as well as giant flying insects invaded this peaceful region of Switzerland. But the only confirmed eye-witness was an intoxicated vagrant. There has been speculation that this was set up by a toy manufacturer as a marketing ploy that went bad." She stared into the camera with intense eyes.

"My message tonight is that the people of the world are not naïve, nor are they easy prey to political or commercial hoaxes. We may never know what actually occurred in Switzerland, but the study of the origin of mankind has been an age-old question that all manner of people have tried to answer throughout the ages." She took a deep breath and moved the microphone to her other hand.

"An American scientist spent a lifetime trying to prove that our soul never dies. His research may never be completed and his work has been classified top secret by the US government, but this American pioneer opened the hearts and minds of visionary people to the enormous possibilities of our lives. His research added a dimension to our past, present and future that stretches beyond governments, churches and even ourselves. It expands our minds and imaginations to beyond the moon, the sun, and the planets in our solar system to other galaxies and uncountable stars in the vast universe.

"If we believe that energy and intelligence are infinite, then anything can be possible. Each spirit might have the ability to create a destiny for every individual soul...souls with the ability to function at their finest through the power of love. Love that can draw us to miracles and achieve justice for all and give us hope." She took another deep breath. "And, of course, love that can unite us all in peace and harmony on this magnificent planet we call Earth." She opened her arms to the camera and let them fall to her side.

"A dear friend shared ideas that opened my mind to the possibilities of alternative realities in other dimensions. Whatever the answer is to the meaning of life, the questions are as varied as the mysteries of the universe.

"Thank you for listening. This has been a special commentary. I'm Hillary Windham bidding you a happy Thanksgiving and a blessed future. God bless you all and good night."

She set her microphone on the table and placed a red cap on her head. Sewn into the embroidered fabric were tiny mirrors that reflected bright flickers of light back at the camera. The spotlights overhead dimmed until all that remained was the glow of the cathedral's candles, the reflecting mirrors in the hat and the angelic children, their faces illuminated by their candles.

The camera faded to darkness.

Amanda couldn't suppress tears while the others clapped and cheered. When the reaction died away, she looked at the TV and whispered, "Thanks for wearing the hat I gave you, Hil', and thank you for honoring Peter's work."

Tony escorted her to stand with the President in front of the fireplace. A photographer raised his camera. The President, an imposing man with thick sandy hair, alert eyes and a friendly face, shook her hand. "Amanda Tregnier, I present to you this plaque bestowed by the President of the United States to honor your bravery and diligence in serving your country." He smiled at her.

The camera snapped.

She stepped away and Tony nudged Rotar into place. He stood up straight, arms to the side. The President leaned over. "Rotar, as the President of the United States, I present you with this plaque honoring you for bravery and citing you as the tallest man in the universe."

He gulped. "The tallest?"

The President nodded. "For fulfilling your duty and protecting the ancient book. And for entrusting it to us for safekeeping. It is a worthy title."

Rotar blushed and stood still while the camera flashed. Puzzled, the President stared at the rainbow colors rippling across his face.

Rotar handed the silver book to the President who gave it to a security guard. Then the entire group gathered in a semi-circle and the President gave Tony, Lizzy, Howard and Michelle similar plaques.

The camera popped again and again. The circle spread out and mingled.

The President turned to Rotar. "I understand you have agreed to work with my brother-in-law in our U.F.O. program?"

"Yes Mr. President, if you will have me."

He seemed amused. "I think I speak for every American and nearly every human being on the planet when I say we'd be proud to have you on our team."

Rotar beamed. "I am honored."

"Have you ever considered becoming an astronaut?" the President asked.

Rotar pointed at his own chest. *"Moi?"* he said, startled. "I mean, *me?*"

"With your help we could set up a space mission to venture out and look for your planet." The President gave a winning smile and nodded at Tony.

"My planet?" Rotar stammered. "Look for Rotarious? I have a rock that can guide us—I mean I can help." His face lit up like a beacon and he kangaroo-jumped into the air. "Whoopee…"

The President laughed. "Looks like it's settled then."

The President led the First Lady down a long hall to the dining room and the group followed. Amanda made her way ahead, nudging alongside the President. She stretched on tip-toe and whispered into his ear.

"What are you going to do with the secrets in the ancient book?"

He cocked his head and grinned. "Can you keep a secret?"

She nodded.

He leaned closer. "We have those crazy insects from the Verbier train station right here in Washington, but not a word."

A gust of wind blasted them both and swept down the hall. The President stopped. The others stopped. Amanda went rigid and looked around. The President eyed his security guards up ahead. They were perusing the walls and ceiling. Amanda said, "Thought I felt some wind in here but it's gone. False alarm."

The President frowned. "We'll check it out." He bored sincere eyes into hers. "But as I was saying, your husband's work will not be in vain. The book of knowledge will be secured and studied by the right people. We have his chemical drug and we have the formula for the antidote. I'm already establishing an elite committee of religious leaders, philosophers, scientists, doctors and lay people to collaborate in searching for the truth. By allowing all points of view to share and contest the issues, we might experience less resistance and more cooperation from the world community. Your journalist friend Hillary Windham has been invited to join the team. And of course we'll need Rotar's help to translate and interpret."

Amanda glowed. "Thank you for pursuing my husband's work and also for being so good to Rotar."

"Perhaps we can find a way to repay Rotar. Ever heard of growth hormones? Molecular biology?" He winked at her and smiled. "There's new research all the time and it might not be too late for someone like him."

"I hope you're right," she said before rejoining the others. With a confident smile, she took her daughter's hand as they headed for the dining room.

Rotar reached up and grasped Amanda's other hand. "Thank you for inviting me to join your family."

She smiled at him. "And thank you, Rotar for bringing us a little closer to touching the stars."

He beamed. His eyes filled with bursting stars. "Miles of smiles," he whispered.

The President turned down another hall. The dining room loomed ahead. A golden retriever bounded toward them wagging its tail.

Rotar's pocket bulged and started to vibrate.

The two-tailed cat jumped out shrieking in a terrific wail.

The First Lady screamed.

The dog halted and barked.

Dot Comet hissed and scrambled toward the dog while dragging her leg. Security guards rushed toward the President. The President grabbed his wife and pushed her behind him.

"Rotar!" Amanda shouted before remembering he'd left his stick in the limo.

The dog pounced on the cat but Dot Comet dove inside its body.

The dog froze.

A bark sounded from inside the dog's belly and Dot Comet sprang out, legs spread eagle with its hair raised like an electrocuted wet cat. She shook her hind leg and it straightened out. Without effort, Dot Comet sprang into the dining room and leapt like a powerful tiger onto the table covered with platters of food.

"*Ze-He-Brak!*" Dot Comet shrieked, heading straight for the chocolate cake displayed in the center.